DEAD AS A DODO

A HOMER KELLY MYSTERY

VIKING
Mystery
Suspense

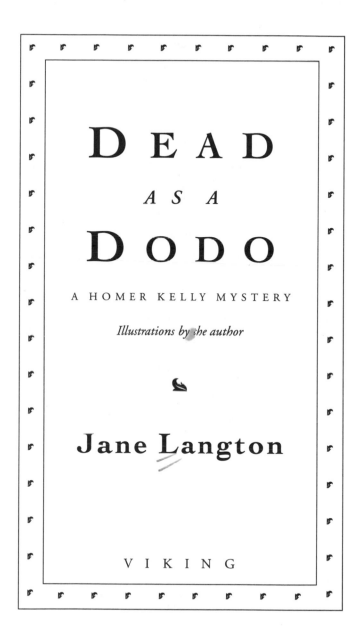

DEAD

A S A

DODO

A HOMER KELLY MYSTERY

Illustrations by the author

Jane Langton

VIKING

Toronto, Ontario, Canada M4V 3B2
Penguin Books (N.Z.) Ltd, 182–190 Wairau Road,
Auckland 10, New Zealand

Penguin Books Ltd, Registered Offices:
Harmondsworth, Middlesex, England

First published in 1996 by Viking Penguin,
a division of Penguin Books USA Inc.

1   3   5   7   9   10   8   6   4   2

PUBLISHER'S NOTE
This is a work of fiction. Names, characters, places, and incidents either are
the product of the author's imagination or are used fictitiously, and any resemblance to actual persons, living or dead, events, or locales is entirely
coincidental.

LIBRARY OF CONGRESS CATALOGING IN PUBLICATION DATA
Langton, Jane.
Dead as a dodo / Jane Langton : illustrations by the author.
p.   cm. — (Viking mystery suspense)
"A Homer Kelly mystery."
ISBN 0-670-86221-5
I. Title
PS3562.A515D43   1996
813'.54—dc20   96-6724

This book is printed on acid-free paper.

∞

Printed in the United States of America
Set in Adobe Garamond
Designed by Ann Gold

FOR JOHN AND JILL

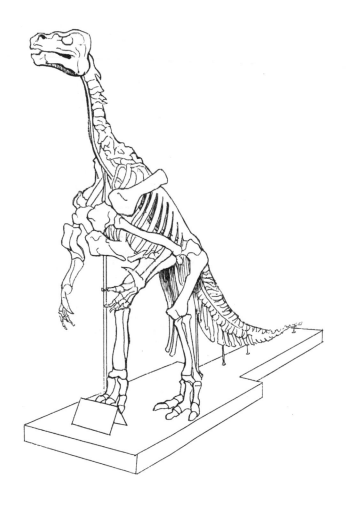

I am almost convinced . . . that species are not
(it is like confessing a murder) immutable.
Charles Darwin, letter to Joseph Hooker

DEAD AS A
DODO

A HOMER KELLY MYSTERY

CHAPTER 1

My Dear Hooker,
The hawks have behaved like gentlemen, and have cast up pellets
with lots of seeds in them; and I have just had a parcel of partridge's
feet well caked with mud!!! Adios,

Your insane and perverse friend,
C. Darwin
(1856)

W hen Homer and Mary Kelly came to Oxford that October, they were not the only new arrivals.

As their bus from the airport began nosing through the suburbs, a swarm of goldfinches landed on the oak trees in the Botanic Gardens, pausing on the way to their winter quarters in Cornwall. Chattering and calling, they rose from one tree, came down on another, and fluttered up again to change places.

On the Cherwell, beyond the University Parks, a flock of migrating swans settled on the water, remembering from last year the bridge where people threw down torn scraps of lettuce and kernels of cracked corn.

And beside the ditch next to the car-rental company on the Botley Road a small cluster of wigeon rested on their flight from the north. One of the females stood on the tangled bank and pecked furiously at the feathers on her back. Wading into the water, she loosened from her feet the mud of the River Spey. The mud settled at once to the bottom of the creek, but the seeds embedded in it rose to the surface and floated to the shore.

They were peculiar seeds, new to the county of Oxfordshire. They lay on the damp ground for only a few hours.

1

Then a succession of migrating mallards trampled them into the soil, and at once the foreign seeds made themselves at home.

Homer and Mary Kelly knew nothing about these arrivals. They saw only the other Americans on the bus from Gatwick. Most were reference librarians heading for a conference in the Oxford University Museum.

Mary introduced herself to the woman across the aisle. She was surprised to learn about the conference in the museum. "That's where my husband is going to be lecturing. What kind of conference is it?"

The librarian fished in her pocketbook and showed Mary a pamphlet, *New Directions in Information Storage.*

"Oh, then you won't be listening to Homer," said Mary. "He doesn't know anything about information storage. He'll be tutoring a few students, and he has to give a lot of lectures on American literature."

The librarian leaned across the aisle and stared past Mary at Homer, who was slumped against the window fast asleep. "You mean, you're Mr. and Mrs. Homer Kelly? Like your husband's a famous detective?"

"Oh, well, it's true he was a detective once, but not anymore. He's just a teacher now. I mean, we both teach. Homer has a lectureship for this term from one of the Oxford colleges. It's just Homer, unfortunately. They didn't offer one to me."

"How sexist!" said the librarian. "You two teach at Harvard, right? And now at Oxford? How distinguished!"

Mary smiled. If the librarian knew the truth about teaching at Harvard, she wouldn't be so impressed. It was like teaching anywhere. There were good students and bad students, academic rivalries, malicious gossip, the constant scrabbling up of the next day's lecture, the endless grading of papers and exams, and faculty meetings so boring they were like penances for abominable crimes.

"The golden towers of Oxford," said the librarian sentimentally, looking out the window as they crossed Magdalen Bridge. "The dreaming spires."

"Ah, yes," said Mary, gazing up at the tower of Magdalen, rising beside them on the right.

There were no dreaming spires at the Gloucester Green bus station, and no green. It was a busy square with buses pulling in and out and passengers getting on and off.

Homer roused himself sleepily and followed Mary and the librarians down off the bus. "What day is this anyway?" he said, smoothing down his wild hair. "Wednesday or Thursday?"

"Wednesday," said Mary cheerfully. "We're just in time for the reception."

"Reception? My God, what reception?"

"The reception at the museum. You remember, Homer, Dr. Jamison invited us."

"But everybody else will be bug experts and mineralogists, people of that ilk." Homer groaned. "All I want to do is go to bed. I didn't get a wink of sleep on that goddamned plane."

"Buck up, Homer." Mary prodded his arm. "Look, the taxis are right out of an old movie."

They dragged their baggage across the brick pavement, and Mary opened the back door of a neat black car with high rounded curves.

"Sorry, love," said the driver, "take the one up front."

"Ah," mumbled Homer, grinning. "British fair play. There's always a queue."

CHAPTER 2

"You are old, Father William," the young man said,
"And your hair has become very white;
And yet you incessantly stand on your head—
Do you think, at your age, it is right?"
Lewis Carroll, *Alice's Adventures in Wonderland*

M ark Soffit was a student of zoology, but he failed to notice the rare black squirrel dodging out of his way as he approached the Oxford University Museum. Nor did he look up to see the heavy flapping of a pair of gray lag geese racing over the roof on their way to the River Cherwell. His thoughts were fixed on the object of his journey from the United States.

The great William Dubchick would surely be present at this reception. Mark was eager to meet him. The whole thrust of his application for a Rhodes scholarship had centered on Dubchick. *The opportunity to study with the eminent Oxford zoologist William Dubchick will advance my investigation of the work of Charles Darwin.*

In his application he had not admitted that Dubchick had never heard of him. Nor did he explain that his concentration on Darwin would be an attack on that old nineteenth-century fossil. In any case, the application had worked, and here he was, a Rhodes scholar at the University of Oxford, about to meet the greatest naturalist in the world.

At the door to the museum Mark looked down at himself. Back in Arizona he had bought an expensive tweed jacket, assuming it was the right uniform for an Oxford man. The jacket was crisp and bristling with woolly fibers. But when he

4

opened the door and saw the crowd in the courtyard, there wasn't a tweed jacket in sight. Most of the younger people standing around with glasses in their hands were wearing jeans and T-shirts.

Blanching, Mark backed up, tore off his jacket, and dumped it over an umbrella stand. He wrestled with his tie, stuffed it in the pocket of the jacket, and undid the top button of his shirt.

Then, gazing at the men and women talking and laughing among the animal skeletons and glass cases, he started forward, wondering which was the great Dubchick.

God, who was this? An old man was walking toward him, smiling and extending his hand. He had a full white beard and a long fringe of untidy white hair. Mark placed him instantly as one of those embarrassing outcasts who hang around the edges of a party. Turning his back on the outstretched hand, he grinned at nobody, waved hugely, and walked into the courtyard.

And there his jittering self-doubt blinded him. He did not look up at the high pyramidal roof of glass, he did not see the towering cast-iron columns crowned with pond lilies and pineapples. He ignored the lofty grinning skeleton of the iguanodon, he missed the golden statues of scientists surrounding the courtyard, even though he ran smack into the pedestal of Roger Bacon. *Does it ever occur to you,* said Bacon, *that the mind is illuminated by divine truth?*

No such thought had ever occurred to Mark, who had barked his shin painfully. *Shit.*

He had to get *in* somehow. Mark studied the little groups of people standing among the bones and picked out a likely trio, a big sleepy-looking guy with frowsy hair, a clever-looking tall woman, and a plump balding man in a business suit.

"Hello," said the woman, moving aside to let him in. "I'm Mary Kelly. This is my husband, Homer. Do you know Dr. Jamison, the director of the museum?"

ROGER BACON

Suddenly the entire courtyard with all its bones and glass cases and stone statues and living people was transfigured by the sun. The lofty space was shot with arcs and shafts of light. There was a pervasive sound, too, as dazzling as the light, a murmuration of voices. Somehow it was more than the multiplication of the jabbering conviviality at the reception. The sum of all the talk and rustling movement was a pleasantly mysterious humming, not quite corporeal, not quite the simple product of sound waves ricocheting from stone and glass and bone.

Mark was not dazzled. He merely blinked in the blinding sunshine and raised his voice. Introducing himself, he explained hastily that he was a Rhodes scholar, here to study with William Dubchick. He looked around vacantly. "Can you tell me if Professor Dubchick is here?"

The tall sleepy-looking man looked around too. "I don't know what he looks like, but we've just met his daughter Freddy. There she is, over there beside the giraffe."

"Thanks," said Mark, turning away abruptly. Thrusting his

way past other clusters of people with wineglasses in their hands, he dodged carefully around the statuary pedestals. Aristotle glowered down at him and muttered something about *matter and essence,* but Mark paid no attention. His own matter and essence were bound up together in a gristly knot of anxiety. Where in the hell was Dubchick's daughter? She had vanished. She must be hiding behind another one of those damned statues.

Freddy Dubchick was not hiding behind a statue, she was lurking behind a construction of metal scaffolding in one of the shadowy arcades around the courtyard, trying to be alone with Oliver Clare. Oliver stooped over her. His clergyman's collar was modestly visible above his dark sweater. His hair was yellow, his eyes were blue. He was talking earnestly about her father.

There was a misunderstanding, Oliver said. Freddy just didn't understand how completely he agreed with her father. "I mean, I've been reading *The Origin of Species.* I've got a whole new understanding of creation."

"Oh, you mean you don't believe in God anymore?" Freddy grinned at him. She knew she shouldn't be teasing him about his faith, because it meant so much to him, but sometimes she couldn't help it. "I'm just joking."

But Oliver took it seriously. "Oh, of course I believe in God. Oh, not the God of Genesis. I know He didn't create the world in seven days. Of course not. I mean God as the designer of natural selection." Oliver's blue eyes looked away from Freddy, and he waved his hand at the courtyard, with all its bones and fossils and stuffed beasts. "All this. I mean God's plan is so much grander, when you look at it this way."

"Oh, so that's it," said someone, moving up beside them from the courtyard. "You mean it's God's fault? God is the villain? It's God who's responsible for carnivores, and all the disemboweling and bloodsucking? Well, I wondered who it was. Now I'll know whom to blame."

Freddy laughed. "No, no, I don't think that's what he means at all. Who are you?"

"My name is Shaw. Hal Shaw. I'm from Manhattan. Manhattan, Kansas, that is."

"Oh, of course," said Freddy, beaming at him. "I know who you are. You're working with my father."

Oliver Clare looked at Hal Shaw balefully. He was some sort of American barbarian, with his broad muscular body and violently red hair. Oliver appealed to Freddy, murmuring in her ear, "Freddy, I've got to talk to you."

But Freddy was interested in the barbarian from Kansas. She was interested too in his matching wife, who surged up beside him. The wife also had red hair, but it was a cosmetic purple-red, not the incendiary orange that had flamed up on her husband's skull the day he was born.

"You're Fredericka Dubchick?" said Margo Shaw. "Hal's going to be working with your father, and I've got a job in the museum too. I'll be topping up the spirit jars for a month or two. Isn't that exciting? What's Hal been telling you? That God is dead?" She had a brittle voice, a high-comic manner. Her husband stood silent while Margo waxed whimsical. "Isn't this place incredible? Do you suppose the skeletons talk to each other when we're not here? Perhaps they dance! Imagine the clatter!"

"Oh, I wonder if they do," said Freddy, enjoying the joke. "Can you imagine the elephant waltzing with the bison?"

Margo tittered. Oliver tried to laugh. Hal's face remained stony. He was trying to get used to the fact that his wife's vivacious chatter was a continuous repetition of a small set of playful remarks. She held only a single hand of conversational cards. In the Greek sculpture gallery of the Metropolitan she had said gaily, *Do you suppose they talk to each other when we're not here? Perhaps they dance!* And he had been charmed. But on the day before their wedding she had said the same thing to the best man about the stone dignitaries in the university chapel, *Do you suppose they dance when we're not here?*—and he had felt a pang of doubt. Since then, he had learned to his sorrow that his wife had conversational ploys filed away in the drawers of her mind, cross-indexed under appropriate cues. Whimsy was one of her stocks-in-trade, another was acid commentary. A third was an alarming aptitude for small wily plots.

"Freddy," urged Oliver Clare. He tugged at her arm, but at once someone else came pushing into the conversation, staring hungrily at Freddy.

It was Mark Soffit. At last he had found Dubchick's daughter. He introduced himself and explained hastily that he was a Rhodes scholar. "Can you tell me if your father is here?" *God, she was cute.*

Freddy Dubchick looked at him patiently. "Yes, of course. I'll take you to him."

Hal and Margo Shaw drifted away. The others made a small procession with Dubchick's daughter Freddy in the lead, the clergyman Oliver Clare next in line, and Mark excitedly bringing up the rear. Swiftly Freddy led them past the horny heads of the rhinoceroses in their glass case, past Isaac Newton gazing down at the apple between his shoes, and the tall melancholy figure of Charles Darwin. For once Mark glanced up and grinned. Darwin was the target of his dissertation. *Beware, old-timer.*

Then he paused in dismay. Freddy Dubchick was hurrying up to an elderly man, stopping beside him and kissing him. All Mark's anticipation collapsed at once in an awful sinking feeling. It wasn't, it couldn't be—?

It was. William Dubchick was the old man he had snubbed, the one who had stretched out a welcoming hand. "Father," said Freddy, "here's someone who would like to meet you." She turned to Mark. "I'm sorry, your name is—?"

Mark could hardly find his voice. He swallowed, tried to speak, failed, tried again. "Soffit," he croaked. "I'm a Rhodes scholar. You know, from the United States." He held out a trembling hand.

There was a slight hesitation before the old man took it and nodded at him soberly.

Blinking, blushing, Mark shook Professor Dubchick's hand fervently. He shook it and shook it. "I'm sorry, sir. I didn't recognize you at first."

As if that makes up for your rudeness. Dubchick smiled at his daughter and put his arm around her. He turned to the clergyman and included him in the smile. Then he glanced at his watch and said, "It's almost time for my talk." He nodded at Mark Soffit. "Excuse me. I'll just go upstairs for my notes."

"Oh, sir," said Mark. "I hope we can meet again. Like I'll make an appointment, okay?"

Professor Dubchick was heading for the stairs. Without turning around he waved his hand, as if to say, Do as you like. On the way up the broad stone staircase he reflected on the brutal way the young man had ignored him, and told himself sadly that it was his own fault. He had committed a sin. And with each passing year it was more sinful than before, more criminal.

He had been born so long ago, that was the crime. Every year it was worse than ever. The date of his birth was unspeakable. The evidence was visible in the mirror, that pop-up old gentleman who kept coming back, getting in the way of the reflected self he remembered. William was so old that he thought of his past life in epochs—the epoch of childhood, the years of schooling, the decade of zoological apprenticeship in Ecuador, the era of beach exploration and the study of crustaceans, the long season of teaching and research at Oxford, and at last the period of summing up in which he was now engaged.

Striding down the corridor of the gallery upstairs, he smiled grimly as he thought of the young upstart who had refused to shake his hand. In forty years that boy too would be an old has-been, and William would sit up in his grave and laugh.

CHAPTER 3

*I am the most miserable, bemuddled, stupid dog in all England, and
am ready to cry with vexation at my blindness and presumption.
Ever yours, most miserably,*
C. Darwin (letter to Joseph Hooker)

🐚

The golden statues were still looking down at the reception
in the courtyard of the University Museum. Watt fin-
gered his steam engine, William Harvey presented his model
of the human heart, Sir Humphry Davy dangled his lamp,
Newton gazed at his apple. The murmuration of combined
voices swelled to a roar.

From his office on the upper floor William Dubchick could
hear the noise of the party, but for the moment it could be ignored. The office was a refuge. He forgot the obscene statistics
of his age, said hello to his new assistant, Dr. Farfrae, and
rummaged among his papers for the outline of his talk.

The room was little changed from the 1860s, except that it
was now warmed by a radiator rather than by the defunct fireplace. For years it had been the Hope Entomology Room, but
the drawers full of insects had been moved to larger quarters.
It was now the Zoology Office. A long table ran down the
middle, and there were two desks between the pointed windows. On the mantelpiece, above the stone foliage with its
carvings of moths and stag beetles, lay the egg of an extinct
great auk in a glass case, looking ready to hatch. A large photograph of Charles Darwin hung on the wall above the mantel.
First editions of Darwin's works occupied a glass-fronted

14

HARVEY

bookcase behind William's desk—*The Voyage of the Beagle, The Formation of Vegetable Mould Through the Action of Worms, The Structure and Distribution of Coral Reefs, The Origin of Species, The Descent of Man, The Expression of the Emotions in Man and Animals.* Whenever William sat at his desk he was warmed by the thought of the drab bindings lined up behind him.

Dr. Farfrae was another comforting presence. She was not one of the robust young generation thrusting up around him, all so admirable, looking at him pityingly and speaking their own strange version of the English language. Sometimes it alarmed William to think of the thousands of clever babies who were being born every minute and surging into adulthood to challenge and overwhelm his own generation, like the young upstart downstairs just now. Dr. Farfrae was clever too, but fortunately she was nearly his own age.

Their relations were cordial and businesslike. She was a helpful and efficient colleague. This afternoon she sat at her desk under the window and did not at once turn to say hello.

"Oh, Dr. Farfrae," said William courteously, "why aren't you at the party? Listen, you can hear the noise from here."

There was a pause, while the reverberation of the voices swelled along the arcades around the courtyard, streamed past the columns of Aberdeen granite and Marychurch marble, and lost itself in the crevices of the foliated capitals. When Dr. Farfrae turned away from the pale screen of her computer, her eyes were cast down. "I just wanted to finish up a few things first."

She had been crying, William could see that. He felt an anguished sympathy. Dr. Farfrae's home life was reputed to be difficult. She never complained and William never inquired, but now he couldn't help asking, "Dr. Farfrae, is there anything—?"

He had overstepped. She stood up and grinned at him. "Guess what? The gecko laid a clutch of eggs. Look."

William laughed, and bent over the tank on the windowsill. "And we thought it was a male."

The noise from below was louder than ever. "Oh, dear," said William, "my talk. I've got some notes here somewhere."

"Here they are." Dr. Farfrae shifted the papers on the table and pulled out a sheet. "I'll be down shortly. I just have a few—"

"Oh, no, don't bother to hear me. It's just the same old stuff."

"But I'd like to."

William smiled politely at his colleague and departed with his notes.

Helen Farfrae took a mirror from her bag and looked at herself, then dabbed astringent around her eyes, still a little swollen from crying. She was a tall strong woman with plump cheeks and piercing hazel eyes and a nose with a bump in it halfway down. Her no-nonsense gray hair was clipped at ear level all the way around. Her only adornment was a pair of gold earrings, but she had paid for them with half a month's salary.

CHAPTER 4

The sound of laughter is produced by a deep inspiration followed by short, interrupted, spasmodic contractions of the chest.
Charles Darwin,
The Expression of the Emotions in Man and Animals

&

The glasses of Chardonnay had been filled and refilled. Homer Kelly's irrepressible euphoria was, as usual, exaggerated by wine. He woke from his jet lag and said loudly, "What's all this about a dodo?"

A goofy-looking young man was goggling up at him. They had apparently been in conversation for some time. "The dodo? You mean you don't know about the dodo?"

"It's extinct, that's all I know," chortled Homer. "It ain't no longer. It do not exist. It's a dead, dead duck. In fact"— Homer leaned drunkenly toward the goofy young man—"it's dead as a dodo, that's what it is, dead as a dodo."

"Well, hey," said the kid with the bulging eyes, "come on, I'll show you. It's like really famous. It's the most famous thing in the museum. Hey, my name's Stuart Grebe, and I know who you are. You're Dr. Kelly."

Stuart's accent was American. Homer had seen his name on the list of Rhodes scholars. The place was full of Americans. Homer beamed at him. "Happy to know you, Stuart."

"Well, thanks, but the truth is, Dr. Kelly"—Stuart looked at Homer apologetically—"I've been wondering if maybe you could give me some advice. Because I've got this problem."

"Well, I don't know. I'm a stranger here myself. But go ahead, what's your problem?"

"It's like this," said Stuart. "I'm a biochemist, and I'm messing around with molecular evolution. The trouble is, I want to do so much else—I mean, while I'm here."

It turned out that Stuart Grebe was a wild-eyed enthusiast who wanted to take advantage of everything at Oxford, to sip from every goblet. Surely at this ancient university a person should be allowed to wallow in Elizabethan Prose and Homeric Archaeology and Greek Epic Poetry, not to mention Nonlinear Systems and Parallel Algorithms and Cell Physiology and Excitable Tissues and—

Homer interrupted him with a glad cry. "Did you say excitable tissues? Hey, does the human body have excitable tissues? My God, that explains it. That's my whole problem. A diagnosis at last! Look here, Stuart, I don't know how to help you. Now that you mention it, I want to take all those things too."

Stuart laughed. It was a wild donkey's bray of a guffaw, and everyone turned to look. "Hey, like you're not much of an adviser, right?" He poked Homer in the chest. "Well, never mind. I'll do you a favor anyway. Come on." He led Homer past the stuffed ostrich and the golden figure of Aristotle and stopped in front of a display case on the west wall of the arcade surrounding the courtyard. Behind the glass were the remains of the dodo.

"Kind of pitiful, if you ask me," said Homer, staring at the skull and the single foot. "You mean, this is all that's left? Of all the dodos on earth?"

"Oh, there are a lot of other miscellaneous bones here and there, but nothing more complete than this." Stuart's eyes rolled upward. "Except for the portrait. See?"

Homer looked up at the comic bird in the big painting beside the display case. "Funny-looking critter. Looks familiar somehow."

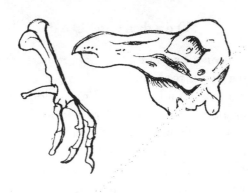

"Right, because of Alice in Wonderland," said Stuart excitedly. "Tenniel drew his picture from this one. Did you know Lewis Carroll taught math at Oxford? Well, he did, right there at my college, Christ Church, and then he came to the new museum and he was really crazy about the dodo, in fact he called *himself* the Dodo, because when he introduced himself as Charles Dodgson, he used to stutter and say *Do-Do-Dodgson.* That's the story, anyway."

"Well," said Homer, with morbid, intoxicated satisfaction, "Dodgson's dead too. They're all dead, all those people. Dead as dodos. Dead as a whole bunch of foolish-looking flightless extinct dodos."

"Well, I think it's a shame," said Freddy Dubchick.

Homer and Stuart Grebe turned around to find William Dubchick's daughter glaring at the remains of the dodo.

"Oh, hi, Freddy," said Stuart. "You mean they should have saved the whole dodo, and stuffed the whole thing? Well, they did, but it decayed, so they had to get rid of most of it. This is all that's left."

"No, no, I mean it shouldn't be here at all." Freddy's frown vanished. She beamed at Homer. "Hello again, Dr. Kelly."

Homer smiled back at her politely, but he was puzzled. "What do you mean, Ms. Dubchick, it shouldn't be here? Where should it be instead?"

Freddy's eyes were alight, but she only said mysteriously, "I can think of a place," and moved away with Stuart Grebe.

Homer shrugged and returned to the courtyard, where it dawned on him at once that the reception was like the Mad Tea-Party. Absurd groups of animals and humans were drinking together like Alice and the Mad Hatter and the March Hare. Before him in plain sight the Dormouse was stuffing itself headfirst into an enormous teapot. No, no, it was only a plump paleontologist bending over the giant sphere of an enormous brain coral.

"Oh, thanks," said Homer to a waiter, snatching up another glass of wine.

"Watch it, Homer," said his wife, putting a hand on his arm. Mary Kelly was a big-boned woman with a calm ruddy face and a clear eye. Most of the time she let Homer have his impulsive way, but when he became insufferable, she stepped in. Homer in his cups was horribly unpredictable.

"But it says *Drink me,* plain as day." Homer saluted her with his glass, then darted away and leaped up on the base of the towering iguanodon. "Beware the Jabberwock, my son!" cried Homer. "The jaws that bite, the claws that catch!"

The thousand bones of the giant reptile shivered and shook. There was laughter and applause.

"Homer!" Mary started after him, but thank God, someone was helping him down.

It was Hal Shaw, the redheaded scientist from the United States. "No, no, you've got it wrong," he said, grinning at Homer. "The iguanodon was a herbivore. It was perfectly harmless."

Mary abandoned her husband to Shaw's kindly care and went looking for Homer's sponsor, Dr. Jamison. Her move across the courtyard was part of a general shifting. Like the diners at the Mad Tea-Party, everyone changed places.

Homer tapped the redheaded zoologist on the front of his

shirt and explained his own, entirely new revelation. "Guess what?" he said. "Alice in Wonderland and Charles Darwin, they're the same."

"The same?"

"Right, right. The voyage of the Beagle and Alice in Wonderland! What is Alice but a mad tour of the natural world, with a dodo and a lobster and oysters, and a walrus and a rabbit and a jabberwock and a caterpillar and—and what else? All sorts of mammals and reptiles and birds and fishes and insects and crustaceans, right? I'll bet that's what Lewis Carroll was doing, he was making a sort of dreamlike voyage of the Beagle." Homer beamed at Hal Shaw, having made, he thought, the cleverest remark of his entire career.

"Well, maybe," said Hal cautiously. "I mean, it's an interesting idea."

🦢

"Freddy, Freddy." Oliver Clare found Freddy in the company of Stuart Grebe. Detaching her from Stuart, he hurried her back to the scaffolding in the south arcade. A blue tarpaulin had been draped over one of the metal bars, creating a corner of privacy.

But in spite of the scaffolding, Freddy's father caught a glimpse of them as he walked into the courtyard to give his talk. It was obvious to William that his daughter was making a mistake. Young Oliver was charming, no doubt, and honest and good-natured, but he was also a traditionalist, tied to a religion that no longer had any meaning for William. And the fact that Oliver had aristocratic connections seemed to have crystallized the blood in his veins. Worse yet, William suspected the boy was a little bit stupid.

But at this moment Oliver Clare was not a complete fool. He had discovered a marvelous change in Freddy, and he recognized it for what it was. To his delight she was warming toward him, leaning up against him, nuzzling her face against his shoulder. He murmured in her ear, "Oh, Freddy, Freddy, give me an answer."

"An answer?" Freddy pulled away and looked over the top of the scaffolding at the skeleton of the bottle-nosed dolphin suspended above the courtyard. Once upon a time the dolphin had been a happy omen to sailors on shipboard, leaping into the light, plunging down into the waves and splashing up again. Now the sunshine slanting through its ribs made slatted shadows on the floor. *No—yes—no—yes,* thought Freddy, and then, *no, no.* "I can't," she said, "not yet. Oh, Oliver, listen, my father's about to speak."

Disappointed, Oliver followed her out of the arcade into the sunlit courtyard.

The director of the museum, Joseph Jamison, stood on a box beside the stone figure of Albert, the Prince Consort. He cleared his throat and waited for the talk to die down, and then

began welcoming all the newcomers, the new lecturers, the new graduate students, the Rhodes scholars from across the sea.

"We particularly want to welcome my old friend Dr. Homer Kelly, from Cambridge, Massachusetts. Dr. Kelly will be lecturing on American literature this term under the sponsorship of Keble College. Oh, and of course we also welcome his wife, Mary Kelly." Dr. Jamison smiled at the two Kellys and clapped his hands, arousing polite applause from the men and women gathered around him, a miscellaneous collection of entomologists, zoologists, geologists, mineralogists and ornithologists, and a scattering of husbands and wives.

We also welcome his wife. Homer glanced at Mary and whispered, "Whoops." Perhaps the whole thing had been a mistake. Perhaps he shouldn't have accepted the invitation after all.

But as Jamison introduced Professor Dubchick, Mary seemed serene. "At last," she murmured, "the great man."

Margo Shaw was standing next to Mary. She giggled and made a joke. "Professor Metatarsal has found the missing link!"

There were scandalized whispers of *Sssh,* as the professor mounted the box and adjusted his glasses, which were held together on both sides by paper clips. His bald head was pink in the blazing light, and every strand of the white hair around his shining dome was picked out against the darkness of the arcaded corridor behind him. He cleared his throat and began to talk about Charles Darwin. "His earthshaking book, The Origin of Species, burst upon the world at the very time this museum was opening its doors."

He looks like Darwin, thought Homer Kelly with amusement. That bald head and white beard, that broad nose, those eyes shadowed under a pair of shaggy brows, they're just the same. Did hero worship do that to you? Did it turn you into the object of your admiration?

Mark Soffit was amused too. After his ghastly initial blunder in failing to take Dubchick's hand, he persuaded himself now that he didn't give a shit. He should have known Dubchick would be an old man. He must be at least sixty. And look at him! Early in Dubchick's life he had been this big expert on primates, and now, *God!* he looked just like one. Mark thought of the old caricatures portraying Darwin as an ape, because of his theory that humans were descended from the same ancestors as modern primates. What about a new species, *Gorilla dubchickea?* Mark laughed aloud. People turned to look at him, and he grinned, and wondered which of them he should attach himself to now. Again he wondered, *How am I going to get in? What's the hierarchy around here?*

Professor Dubchick picked up a cardboard box and lifted something out of it, a small drawer. "We are fortunate in this museum in having some of the specimens Darwin collected on his five-year voyage on the Beagle." Triumphantly William tilted the drawer to show the contents. It was full of mounted crabs.

Hal Shaw stood apart from his wife, staring at Dubchick. He too compared him with Darwin. Both Darwin and Dubchick had refused to specialize. They were grand general-izers, taking the entire natural world as their field of study. Darwin had wandered from beetles to coral reefs to pigeons to barnacles to orchids to earthworms. For Dubchick, too, noth-ing in all the kingdoms of life on earth—from one-celled or-ganisms to fungi, animals and plants—was beyond the range of his interest. Oh, there were occasional yelps of protest from a botanist here or a toadstool specialist there, but on the whole the name of Dubchick was sacred. Hal thought of him as a furry zoologist, one of the kind that went out into the jungle and lived with animals. In his youth he had climbed moun-tains in the Andes to study families of woolly monkeys.

These days, of course, most of the action was in molecular biology. Some of Hal's more radical colleagues were inventing fictitious creatures on the computer screen, setting them loose

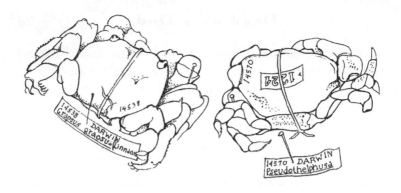

in time, throwing in random variation, and declaring them alive.

Hal watched as Professor Dubchick named the Darwin crabs one by one, and explained where they had come from. He was entranced. Like Dubchick he was filled with a sense of their preciousness. Perhaps there had been thousands of fresh-water crabs of the species *Dilocarcinus pagei cristatus* scuttling in the dry holes of the island in the River Paraná in Argentina when Darwin was there in 1833, but this was the one his hand had picked up, it was the one that had come home from his fabulous journey.

William put the drawer back in the cardboard box, then looked up in alarm at the sound of a crash. Heads turned. What was that?

The heads turned back again. It was just Dr. Farfrae's husband, tramping in late, knocking over a tray of wineglasses.

Hal Shaw glanced at the intruder, who was making a noisy business of cleaning up the mess, arguing with the porter and dabbing at the spilled wine with his wife's scarf—what a discourteous bastard. Then Hal looked back at Dubchick and forgot about Dr. Farfrae's husband. He began thinking instead about hero worship. Hal Shaw admired William Dubchick, Dubchick admired Darwin, Darwin had admired Humboldt, and probably Humboldt had modeled himself on some earlier explorer, like Captain Cook. Reverence had no end.

William was still warming to the subject of Darwin's crabs. He held up a sealed bottle. "Most of Darwin's specimens were sent home in jars of spirit like this one. Then they were dried out here in England. Unfortunately we have found only 110 lots of the 230 crabs he listed in his specimen book. Where are the rest? It is one of our mysteries."

William put down the jar and asked for questions. Hands were raised. He answered punctiliously, a little distracted by the muttering of John Farfrae in the background. The man was tugging at his wife's arm, and it was clear that she was resisting.

Poor Dr. Farfrae—she was obviously losing the argument. Her shoulders sagged. William kept his eye on her as she followed her husband into the arcaded corridor, then left the museum by way of the main door. Abruptly William called for an end to the questions and stepped down from the platform. Everyone clapped.

Hal Shaw applauded too, glancing aside at Professor Dubchick's daughter. Oh, God, she was pretty. Why didn't pretty girls wear veils like women in Muslim countries? They were attractive nuisances, like unfenced swimming pools. You could fall into that cheek, that throat, and drown. He watched her clergyman boyfriend bow over her and say goodbye. He didn't hear Oliver Clare say, "Please, Freddy, give me an answer soon."

The lecture was over. Homer Kelly's drowsiness had returned. He yawned and looked at his wife. "Thank God, Keble's right across the street. Let's go. I'm dead on my feet."

Mary yawned too. "It's nature's revenge because we went so far so fast. If we'd paddled a canoe across the Atlantic or flown in a hot-air balloon, she wouldn't exact this kind of punishment."

"She? Who's she?"

"Mother Nature, of course."

Homer wasn't listening. As they walked across the street, he made a confession. "Oh, God, Mary, something embarrassing happened in there just now."

Mary looked at him in surprise. "Surely you weren't embarrassed about shouting 'Jabberwocky' at all those distinguished strangers?"

"No, no, not that at all. It was something else. Do you know what I said to that fuzzy entomologist who was wearing two pairs of glasses? He said something polite about the pleasure of meeting newcomers from the United States, and I said—oh, I'm so ashamed—I said, *Ra-ther! Jolly good!* I did, I really did."

"Was it a joke? Surely you were joking?"

"No, no, it just welled up. I couldn't help myself. Oh, God, it's so humiliating."

Mary laughed, and pulled him back out of the way as a car plunged past them insanely on the left side of the street.

"It comes from reading all those English novels," said Homer. "People probably don't even say those things anymore—*rather* and *jolly good*." He looked up gloomily at the patterned bricks of Keble College, rising above them, tier upon tier. "The entomologist looked at me strangely, as if I were insulting him in some way. Of course I apologized at once."

CHAPTER 5

*I think it will be very interesting, but that I shall dislike it very
much as again putting God farther off.*

Emma Darwin

O liver Clare left the museum in an anguish of doubt and
confusion, thinking about Freddy. As he took a wrong
turn and walked slowly up Parks Road, the warm breeze tossing the leaves sounded confused too, as if the trees, like Oliver,
didn't know, they just didn't know. They too were waiting for
an answer.

With his eyes on his advancing feet, he paid no attention to
the colleges left and right—the great lawn of Trinity, the fan-
ciful view of Wadham, and all the concentrated architectural
wonders between the Broad and the High—the Clarendon,
the Sheldonian, the Bodleian, the Bridge of Sighs, All
Souls, the Radcliffe Camera and the University Church of
St. Mary the Virgin.

Oliver had long since given up hankering after the spires
and domes of Oxford. After failing to win a place, he had refused his parents' advice and chosen for himself a small theological college in London.

His mother regretted what he had missed. "If he'd gone to a
regular university, it would have given an edge to his piety,"
she told his father. "As it is, he's not been tried, not brought to
judgment."

END THE
MONARCHY

"Brought to judgment?"

"Oh, you know, he hasn't been given a real testing. The ridicule of his peers, their belligerent logic, their arguments from unbelief. If only he could have been knocked down and rolled over a few times by a bunch of skeptical fellow students, it would have toughened his faith."

"If it didn't destroy it altogether," said Oliver's father shrewdly.

This afternoon Oliver had been knocked down and rolled over by that redheaded American who had accused the Creator of cruelty. All that talk about disemboweling and—what was the other thing?—bloodsucking. That was what vampire bats did, they sucked blood.

Well, it wasn't new to Oliver Clare. He had wrestled with the sharp truths of science before. He thought he had made his peace. Oliver was an up-to-date Anglican priest, not one of your old mossbacks who relied on Scripture for every article of faith. Yesterday someone on the street had handed him a fundamentalist pamphlet, *The Truth and Authority of Scripture*, and he had tossed it away.

Oliver walked stiffly down the High Street and summoned up the evidence for his belief. It was all around him. Look at the roses still blooming in the Botanic Gardens, and the graceful willows swaying over the Cherwell, and—Oliver lifted his eyes to the tower of Magdalen—there was always some glorious work of man (that is, *man or woman*) to reverence as a gift from God.

His brain became more and more muddled as he thought about saintly deeds. Since all men were brothers (and *sisters too*, of course) under the fatherhood of God (well, the *motherhood too*, naturally), it was their belief in God that inspired concern for those less fortunate than themselves. Animals might be cruel and suck blood or whatever, but God had lifted humankind above all that. Men and women had been made in the image of God, and therefore the spirit of God was reflected in their souls.

Then Oliver woke up. What was he doing on the High? He hadn't been paying attention. Turning in his tracks, he made a rush for Cornmarket Street, feeling perked up. His arguments had convinced him all over again. Especially the fact of human goodness, the way people showed compassion instead of cruelty, the way they helped the poor and served those less fortunate than themselves.

Less fortunate than themselves? God help him! Oliver's spirits had risen, but now they plummeted as he thought about his own congregation. How on earth was he going to handle the eleven o'clock service next Sunday morning? The eleven o'clock called for a sermon, and last Sunday's had been a disaster, because the children had disrupted it so violently. There was no nursery care in Oliver's small parish, and the mothers had no way of leaving their kids at home. *Suffer the little children*, he told himself, but the experience of last Sunday had been terrible.

Wincing, he reminded himself that the poor souls you were trying to help didn't have to be good *themselves*. If they were good already, they wouldn't need *you*, would they?

With his mind in a tangle, Oliver turned into Cornmarket Street. At once his meditations on human goodness were cut short by the hiss of air brakes. There had been an accident. People were swarming across the street to see the poor woman who lay in front of the bus, and what was that thing rolling off to one side, landing in the gutter? Not an empty pushchair? Good God, it wasn't a dead woman and a dead baby lying there on the street? Not a dead baby too?

Oliver turned his back in horror, and ran all the way home.

The accident was bad enough, but as he panted up St. Barnabas Street and unlocked the front door of the house where he rented a room, another thought occurred to Oliver Clare. At once it struck cold into his lungs and sent a shaft through his stomach. On the steep carpeted stairs he had to stop and grasp the railing.

"Are you all right, dear?" said his landlady, looking up at him from her doorway.

"Oh, yes, thank you, Mrs. Jarvis," said Oliver, beginning to climb again. "I'm quite all right."

❧

Margo Shaw held the jar Professor Dubchick had used in his lecture to show Darwin's method of preserving specimens. "Am I supposed to return this damn thing? Look, I lugged it out at the professor's *magisterial* command." She thrust it at her husband. "You take it back."

Hal took the jar unwillingly. Margo had been hired to keep a sharp eye on the level of spirit in the jars of specimens in the two storage rooms, the Vertebrate Spirit Store and the Invertebrate Spirit Store. She was also blessed with the task of cleaning skeletons and fossil bones. As a woman with a degree in biology from Sweet Briar, she resented the lowly nature of her job.

"A dogsbody, that's all I am," she told Hal. Then, imitating the British accent of one of the women zoologists, she simpered, "Oh, Mrs. Shaw, would you be so *good* as to take this to the storeroom? Now, remember, Mrs. Shaw, *Invertebrate,* not *Vertebrate!*"

Hal winced, recognizing the voice of Helen Farfrae. His wife was wickedly clever at mimicry.

Margo fumed. "As if I didn't know a coelenterate from a reptile!"

"But it's important," said Hal, trying to keep his temper. "What you're doing, I mean. If the specimens dry out, they might be ruined."

"Well, they'll have to get along without me for a few days. You too. I promised your Aunt Peggy we'd visit her tomorrow."

"Oh, right." Hal cradled the jar in his arms and considered. "It's okay. I need to get some stuff from the house. Books I left there a long time ago. And it will be good to see the old dear again."

Margo's triangular face managed to look both inquisitive and acquisitive at the same time. "Someday it will be yours, all yours. And then we can sell it for heaps of money. So you've got to butter up the dear old thing. It's so funny, your uncle from Topeka marrying a rich Englishwoman. How old is she, anyway? God, she looks a hundred and two." Margo adopted a quavering voice diabolically like Aunt Peggy's. "Oh, *dawling* Hal, you're *too* sweet. And how *chawming* Margo looks in that *ravishing* gown!"

Sickened, Hal turned away and headed for the Invertebrate Spirit Store.

Instantly Mark Soffit was after him. After the reception Mark had lingered, hanging around in the courtyard while the caterers cleared away the serving tables and collected empty wineglasses from the pedestals of the stone scientists. One wag had balanced a glass on the hand of Galileo.

Mark was looking for a new sponsor. His hopes for the partisan interest of Professor Dubchick had vanished, and he told himself it didn't matter, because Dubchick was too old anyway—God, he was really out of it. He was supposed to be writing a book, but some mineralogist at the reception had passed along to Mark his doubts that it would ever be finished.

Professor Shaw, on the other hand, was still young, and it was obvious that he was moving in on Dubchick's territory, taking over. Mark took aim at Hal Shaw and fired the gun of his self-interest. "Oh, Professor Shaw, I was hoping to talk to you."

Agreeably Hal slowed his footsteps and invited Mark to accompany him to the Invertebrate Spirit Store. By the time they had negotiated a labyrinth of back halls and small stairways, Mark had explained that he was a Rhodes scholar, anxious to associate himself with the latest advances in evolutionary studies. He had hoped to be assigned to Professor Dubchick as a pupil, but that had fallen through. Perhaps Dr. Shaw could persuade Mark's college to assign him as Mark's tutor?

When Hal unlocked the door of the storeroom, Mark pushed in behind him, treading on his heels. Hal felt crowded in more ways than one. He told Mark he would look into it, and then he led him from one bank of shelves to another. After putting away the jar, he explained the precious nature of the other bottled specimens.

He picked up one and showed the label to Mark. "*Copepoda: Calanoida.* You see, it's a Darwin specimen." Hal stared at the crab in the jar and forgot about Mark Soffit as he imagined Charles Darwin on an island off the coast of Chile, lifting out a single crab from a great purple cloud of crustaceans, *infinite numbers pursued by flocks of Famine Petrels.*

"How the hell did all those specimens get lost?" said Mark.

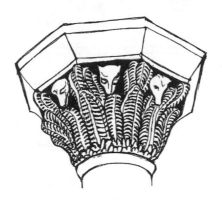

"The ones Dubchick was talking about. Was it carelessness on Darwin's part?"

"No, no, he was the soul of carefulness." Hal put the jar tenderly back on the shelf. "It was Bell's fault, I guess. Darwin gave all his crabs to Thomas Bell to identify, and then Bell never got around to it. He sold them to Professor Westwood, who gave them to the museum, and somehow during the transfers a bunch of them fell between the cracks."

"Well, then, maybe it was carelessness here in the museum," said Mark hopefully. "Maybe they're miscatalogued. Maybe they're in some drawer nobody's looked at in a hundred years. I mean, after all, this place is pretty musty."

"I've often wondered that myself," said Hal. "Ever since I came here last June, I've imagined opening up some old cabinet and coming upon a treasure trove. But things are too well cared for around here. It's not musty at all."

"No?" Mark didn't believe it. Inwardly he vowed to worm his way into every attic and closet and open every drawer. The place was a maze of little rooms and back halls. Anything could be hidden away and forgotten.

And in the process he would find out what everybody was up to, he'd learn who was really going places. Not like poor old Dubchick, who didn't know one end of an electron microscope from the other. It was rumored that the old man still liked to get out there in the jungle and look wild animals in the eye, and probably swing from tree to tree.

CHAPTER 6

Alice was not much surprised at this, she was getting so well used to queer things happening.

Lewis Carroll, *Alice's Adventures in Wonderland*

As a married couple, the Kellys should have been given a house for the Michaelmas term. But Homer's appointment had been made very late, in an enthusiastic burst of phone calls across the Atlantic. By that time all the faculty houses had been assigned to other people. So instead of a house they had been given a small set of rooms in the Besse Building, right in the middle of Keble College on Liddon Quad.

Mary busied herself with unpacking, whistling softly, while Homer collapsed on the bed in a stupor and fell asleep at once. He was promptly deep in Wonderland. And there was the dodo—not the extinct bird complete with feathers, like the one in Tenniel's picture, but the pitiful seventeenth-century remnant of one of the last living birds, the fragments from the glass case in the museum. The skull and bony foot floated above Homer's head in the branches of a tree.

"You're just like the Cheshire-Cat," said Homer politely, initiating a conversation. "I can only see part of you."

The dodo sighed, and stretched out its pathetic foot. "These pieces of me are all there is. I live in dread of disappearing altogether."

"Well, of course," said Homer, pointing out a painful truth, "you *are* extinct, after all."

"Oh, I know I'm extinct, I know, I know," whimpered the dodo. "But at least this much of me survives." Then to Homer's surprise it cried out in alarm, "Oh, oh, what's happening? I'm vanishing! Help, help!"

It was true, the dodo was fading, becoming fainter and fainter. Finally, with a pathetic cry, it vanished. There was nothing left but a tossing bundle of leaves.

Homer's dream went on and on after that, becoming more and more disconnected and absurd, but when he woke up an hour later, all he could remember was the fantastic exchange with the dodo.

Mary had finished her shower. Naked, she pranced around the room looking for her underwear. Homer sat up in bed and said anxiously, "What do you suppose they do for security in the museum? I wonder if all those exhibits are really safe."

Mary ransacked the drawers of the dresser. "Perhaps it doesn't really matter. Isn't it mostly a teaching museum? Not a collection of irreplaceable objects? If somebody stole the skeleton of the giraffe, they could probably find another one somewhere."

Homer was scandalized. "But what about the dodo? There aren't any more dodos! That dodo is *it*."

"Well, I don't know, Homer. I guess if it disappeared, it would be more extinct than ever." Mary hopped on one foot, pulling on her trousers. "I mean, not just a fond memory, but utterly and absolutely gone."

So from then on Homer felt a special protective concern for the welfare of the dodo belonging to the Oxford University Museum.

❧

While Oliver Clare ran home to his rented room on St. Barnabas Street and Homer Kelly lay dreaming about the dodo, William Dubchick and his daughter Freddy walked home from the museum to their house on Norham Road. They could have taken one of the little Park and Ride buses on the Banbury Road, but it was just as easy to walk.

Their house was a typical North Oxford brick Victorian. Comfortable and spacious, it was a mixture of homeliness and ostentation, with touches of Gothic grandeur. There were tall pointed windows and a few set pieces of stained glass. A carved armorial bearing rose above the mantel in the sitting room, honoring nobody in particular. William's wife had called it generic Arthurian. For the past hundred and fifty years this house and its neighbors had provided the security of varnished woodwork and a patriarchal hearth to a multitude of married dons. Now many of the larger houses had been broken up into flats or turned into schools.

There were few left of the army of servants who had once roosted in North Oxford attics and labored in its kitchens and pantries. After her mother's death, Freddy had been cared for by a succession of nannies, but in her own opinion she had brought herself up.

Her father wasn't so sure about that. William had done his best to be both mother and father to Freddy, but he knew how far he had fallen short. If his wife had lived, she would have provided an example, a pattern to follow. Without her, Freddy had been an adorable but headstrong little girl. Had he kept her at home too long? Perhaps she should have been sent away to the sort of public school where privileged young women were prepared for Oxford and Cambridge.

But Freddy had seemed too young to be sent away. William had enrolled her instead in the expensive high school around the corner. During all those years she had been a gawky young thing, skinny and childish long after her classmates had blossomed into hips and breasts.

Now Freddy was an Oxford student, an undergraduate at Christ Church, and to William's alarm her hormones were making up for lost time. She was suddenly far too pretty, a small delectable girl with deft hands and bitten fingernails.

William didn't know which was the stronger, his amused admiration of his daughter or his parental doubts and cautions. She was so eager and receptive, so dizzy with excitement, but at the same time so lacking in any protective coating of irony. Her mind was burgeoning, but it was only a ragbag of bright scraps—ends and swatches ripped from the things her tutors and fellow undergraduates knew. Freddy was a wild jumble. Lately she hadn't been able to finish anything. She would begin a project, then zigzag in another direction. There were no calm guidelines stretching before her, attached to sensible goals. Instead she was strapped to a pair of galloping horses, plunging blindly forward in no particular direction. Or perhaps the reins were only loose filaments dissolving in air like threads of spun sugar.

Now here she was, walking beside him, a quivering bundle of excitement, as though those jerking strings were tugging her forward from *now* to *now,* so that she strode forward too quickly along Bradmore Road.

William quickened his pace as Bradmore turned into

Norham. Should he now, too late, begin acting like a father? "Tell me about that young man," he said, trying to sound friendly and diffident. "Some sort of clergyman, is he?"

"Oh, yes! He was ordained last year. He's got his own church. He's the rector of his very own church."

"What church is it?"

"St. Mary's."

"St. Mary's?" In spite of himself William was impressed. "Do you mean the University Church of St. Mary the Virgin?"

But Freddy's little dog was barking, yipping behind the door as she ran up the walk. Freddy rushed up the steps, unlocked the door, snatched up the dog and hugged him, plucked his leash from the wall and raced after him down the path, while her father blundered into the darkness of the front hall. His glasses were askew. One of the temple pieces had lost its paper clip.

As a zoologist and a devout student of the work of Charles Darwin, William knew precisely what was afflicting his daughter. It was the basic animal urge to reproductive success, the pressure for sexual selection. She was responding to the urgent biological summons to reproduce the species *Homo sapiens,* to enrich the genus *Homo,* the family Hominoidea, the order Primates, the class Mammalia, the subphylum Vertebrata, the phylum Chordata, the kingdom Animalia. Like every barnacle in the sea and every creature on the land, like every other living thing, Freddy was responding to nature's call.

But it was too soon. There was plenty of time. Wait, Freddy dear, slow down!

William leaned out the door and called after her, "Freddy, I forgot to ask you. Tomorrow I'm driving down to Cornwall to close up the house for the winter. Do you want to come along?"

Freddy turned and walked backward, while the little dog

barked and tugged at the leash. "Oh, no, Father, I've got a date. Two, in fact. No, three."

DIARY OF FREDERICKA DUBCHICK

This is my new diary. I've thrown out the one from school because reading it makes me sick. There isn't a word of truth in it.

This time I'm going to be absolutely honest. I want to find out what I think, what I want, and what I don't want.

Resolution number one—no underlining.

Resolution number two—no exclamation marks.

I'll begin with how nice it feels to be looked at. How I love being looked at! This afternoon after Father's lecture in the museum, while everyone was applauding, I glanced around and that American was staring at me. I looked away again and went on clapping, but I knew his eyes were on the back of my head, and I could feel my hair because he was looking at it. I could feel my cells jiggling and all the spirals of my DNA molecules whirling dizzily around because his eyes were activating them, getting them all excited.

Important! *This diary is not concerned with guilt for disloyalty to anybody else. It's just the truth. That's all it is, the naked truth.*

CHAPTER 7

"What am I to do?" exclaimed Alice, looking about in great perplexity.

Lewis Carroll, *Alice's Adventures in Wonderland*

🖋

The visitor was at home in the house. He had explored every corner as a child. Even the rooms once occupied by servants were familiar territory.

But only once had he climbed up on the counter in the housekeeper's private kitchen. Only once had he opened all the doors of the cupboards that rose to the ceiling. The single occasion had left him with a frightening memory of standing on tiptoe on the counter and reaching up and opening the door of the highest cupboard and looking inside, and then slamming the door and jumping to the floor.

Now he dragged over a chair, climbed on it, and opened the selfsame door.

Yes, the shelf was still full. The same dusty jars of desiccated black stuff were still there, crowded together in untidy rows. Reaching up, he grasped one of them, stepped down carefully from the chair, and set the ugly jar on the counter. The label said *Chutney.*

But when he turned the jar and saw the dark spiny contents, it was hard to believe they could ever have been edible.

He climbed back up and extracted another jar. This time the label said *Jugged Hare.* But it couldn't possibly ever have been jugged hare, whatever that was. Once again the contents

43

were slumped at the bottom of the jar, broken objects with hooked projections on the corners.

He brought his gaze close to the glass, and saw a tinny-looking piece of punched metal, an identifying label.

Before the afternoon was out, he had brought down all the jars and lined them up in rows on the counter. They were *Griskin of Pork, Pressed Tongue, Haunch of Venison, Forcemeat, Peach Preserves, Calves Foot Jelly,* and a lot of other antique survivors from Mrs. Beeton's nineteenth-century cookbook.

Except that they were not. Every one of them contained something thoroughly inedible. Very carefully, he picked at one of the labels. It was dark and speckled with age. The spidery writing was nearly illegible. It refused to come loose easily. Someone had used good glue.

His heart quickened as he saw a second label under the first. He tore and scratched and scraped with his thumbnail, picking off the upper label at last.

The second was half destroyed but still readable. It showed only a handwritten number, 1347. When he climbed back up to fumble over his head for more jars—was there another, just out of reach?—he found something else, a book, an old journal. He blew the dust off the cover and opened it.

There were many closely written pages. The handwriting was difficult, and some of the passages had been written in code. For a moment he puzzled over the code, then smiled to himself. There was nothing to it.

Sitting down on the counter, he began to read.

CHAPTER 8

"The question is," said Humpty Dumpty, "which is to be master—that's all."

Lewis Carroll, *Through the Looking-Glass*

It was two days since Johnny Farfrae had forced Helen to leave the reception. Afterward she had refused to speak to him, and yesterday she had awakened early and fled to her job as to a haven of peace.

But coming home, she made up her mind to bring the warfare to an end. "Johnny dear," she said, hurrying into the house, "let's begin again. I can't bear going on like this."

It was no good. He started up out of his chair, glaring at her. "What do you mean, begin again? By God, if you want to begin again, you can get down on your knees and apologize."

So the battle went on all evening, sometimes in silence, sometimes in rage. Helen detested it, although she suspected that Johnny didn't. It was as though they were acting out the proper marriage roles for a husband and wife. Helen remembered Johnny's father, that domineering old bastard. She remembered too his timid mother, how cowed and stooped she had been, as though marriage had bent her back.

There was to be no submission for Helen. Once again this morning she had dodged out early, although Johnny hated to cook his own breakfast. He would have to cook his own dinner too. She couldn't face another night of confrontation. At six o'clock she called him. "I'll be late, Johnny. It's this grant application. The final draft is due tomorrow morning."

Johnny's response was a vicious explosion, but Helen endured it and stuck to her story, and then put the phone down gently. When it rang a moment later, she didn't answer. Would he come to the museum and drag her out? This time she would fight like a cat, because there would be no one there to see.

Helen's story about the grant application was a lie. The deadline was months away. Nevertheless, she turned on the computer and watched the code words race up the screen, then tapped a few keys to summon up her notes.

It was no use. The notes were meaningless. Helen was too miserable to focus her attention. She turned off the computer, then switched off the light over her desk so that no one on the upper levels of the Inorganic Chemistry building next door would see a middle-aged woman weeping in the Oxford University Museum. For a while she sat in the dark, sobbing. Then she stood up shakily and wandered out into the corridor.

There was scaffolding outside the office door. Bricklayers had been working all over the building for a month, pointing the walls. Other craftsmen were repairing the plaster. The dim lamps over the courtyard glowed softly. Helen walked slowly down the south staircase—the other set of stairs in the north tower was blocked with still more scaffolding. Downstairs she wandered aimlessly among the exhibits, her tears drying on her cheeks.

It calmed her to remember where she was. Her job as William Dubchick's assistant was new, but she was an old friend of the museum. She had been coming here all her life. Her childish collection of tadpoles in jars of murky pond water, her tank of swimming terrapins, her fossil ammonites from Lyme Regis—young Helen had collected them after pressing her nose against the glass cases in the Oxford University Museum, after beholding the dodo and gaping at the leg bones of *Cetiosaurus oxoniensis.* The tadpoles and the terrapins had led directly to the study of developmental biology, and eventually to a fellowship at her old Oxford college, St. Hilda's.

After twenty-seven years of teaching, Helen had retired gladly, but it had been a mistake. She should have foreseen it, that retirement wouldn't suit her. She should have guessed that from now on she would have no life outside her own unhappy home, and no self but as Mrs. Johnny Farfrae. One day she had heard of the job opportunity with Professor William Dubchick, the great authority on primates, on crustaceans, and in fact on the nature of all life on earth. She had applied for it eagerly, and to her joy she had been hired. And now here she was, a member of the museum staff. Helen told herself that her domestic troubles shouldn't matter anymore, not now, not here in this cherished place.

The corridors were dark. She walked along the north side, where the primate display cases stood against the wall. The illumination within the cases had been turned off, but the glass eyes of the tarsier shone with reflected light, and the skeletons of the bigger primates were white shapes in the gloom. Walking softly along the corridor, she caught up with *Homo sapiens,* who was marching jauntily away from the rest, heading east.

Then, turning back, she walked out into the courtyard. It was a great high volume of air, vanishing into darkness above the hanging lamps. The arcaded galleries rose above her like palaces in Venice, arch after pointed arch, announcing with their striped voussoirs, *John Ruskin was here.*

Helen was alone in the courtyard, but as usual she didn't feel alone. She was accompanied by the circle of stone scientists. In life, each one of them had grasped some new principle, each had forwarded human understanding of the workings of the world. In their solemn isolation and frozen gravity, they gave the courtyard an aura of distinction. The dim air was thick with history, knobbed with these pillars of earnest intellect. How many reasonable men did it take to ornament a public room? In one corner, Hippocrates lifted a stone finger, warning against the superstitious healing of the priests; in another, Leibnitz gazed upward at the admirable laws of the City of God; in a third, Joseph Priestley stepped nobly forward, displaying his apparatus for dephlogisticated air. Helen patted the bust of Dr. Acland, Regius Professor of Medicine, founder of the museum and friend of Ruskin's. She stroked the bony scapula of *Bison bison.* Then, wandering eastward, she edged around another set of display cases and found herself in a corner with Linnaeus, who was mildly consulting his notebook, recording a stand of Swedish sea holly or the habits of the ant lion.

Cornered with Linnaeus, she only faintly heard the opening of the main door of the museum and the sound of heavy footsteps on the south stairs. She knew who it was, Bobby Fenwick, making one of his random nighttime inspections of the museum. Bobby was the night watchman for all the science buildings in the neighborhood of Parks Road. Working late, Helen often exchanged a friendly word as Bobby moved along the gallery with his flashlight.

Tonight he wasn't making much of an inspection. He was clattering downstairs again in a hurry. Well, it didn't matter. She could have told him that the building was safe and sound. Helen stroked the stone cloak of Darwin and put her hand fondly on Newton's apple, then turned her head in surprise. The door was opening again, feet were climbing the stairs again. Bobby must have come back to do a more thoroughgoing job.

Again there was only a short pause before she heard him hurrying back along the upstairs gallery in the direction of the south stairs. Then suddenly he called out, "Hello, who's there?" Helen recognized Bobby's reverberating baritone, but it wasn't coming from upstairs. He was shouting from the di-

LINNAEUS

rection of the main entrance. He had just come in. The footsteps were someone else's, not Bobby's.

Listening, Helen heard the intruder stop, then start pounding along the south gallery and around the corner to the west. He was avoiding the south stairs because Bobby was climbing them, shouting, "Come on, now, who's there?" Did the stranger know the north staircase was blocked with scaffolding? She heard the footsteps stop, then start back the other way. But he was cut off. The gallery was like a game board with a single exit. Helen listened as the two playing pieces dodged around it, one fleeing, the other in pursuit. Bobby was shouting again. "Hey, stop. I said stop."

Anxiously Helen walked across the courtyard and hurried up the stairs. What if the stranger discovered the open door of the Zoology Office? The office was vulnerable. But when she stopped to listen, the footsteps faded. Bobby's voice was fainter too. The thumping of footsteps on stairs had started again, but it was dimmer, farther away.

Then Helen remembered another staircase, the stone spiral leading to the upper reaches of the tower. The two of them must be mounting the tower steps.

Helen found the door. It was standing open. There were shouts and halloos from above, the noise of running feet. Doubtfully, telling herself she was being foolish, Helen followed, feeling her way up the triangular steps in the dark. At the top of the stone spiral, breathing hard, she emerged into the archaeology storeroom. It was a high space with two magnificent windows, from which she had often stared out over Keble College and the church of St. Giles and the Radcliffe Observatory. Now the room was dark and empty, illuminated only by a soft glare from the lights of the city, spoiling the view of the stars.

Bobby was shouting again. Where was he?

From the archaeology storeroom two exits opened out. One was a blank, the iron staircase leading to the ventilators where the swifts nested. The other was a door looking out on the glass roof.

The door was open, showing a rectangle of night sky. Below the door a metal ladder ran down to the wooden walkway surrounding the glass peaks of the roof. Timidly, Helen stood in the doorway and looked out. At once she saw something amazing. Someone or something was bounding up the glassy slope. But the roof was too steep! No one could do that. Nothing human could do that. It wasn't Bobby. Where was Bobby?

Fear overcame her. Helen was afraid in the same way she had been afraid in the dark as a child, wondering if the blur in the corner of her bedroom was a lost soul trying to creep into her skin and push her out, so that Helen would no longer be Helen.

She fled, running carelessly down the winding stone steps and bursting out onto the floor of the west gallery.

Panting, she hurried into the office on the south side and felt around in the dark for her coat and bag. Then she stood for a moment, staring at the pale blob that was the telephone on her desk. Should she call the police? Of course she should call the police. But she didn't. What she had seen was too unearthly. She couldn't have seen what she thought she had seen. She was out of her mind. She was still too much afraid.

There were only two cars left in the parking spaces in front of the museum. Helen unlocked hers and drove to Kidlington, steeling herself for the tirade she would encounter at home.

But Johnny was not there. Had he slammed out of the house when she said she'd be working late? It didn't matter. It was a relief to be alone. Helen filled the electric kettle for a cup of tea, then dumped the water out and poured herself a whiskey.

Why didn't she call the police? Well, why didn't she? It was a question that tormented Helen Farfrae for the rest of her life.

CHAPTER 9

Humpty Dumpty sat on a wall:
Humpty Dumpty had a great fall.
        Lewis Carroll, *Through the Looking-Glass*

🖊

W hen the front door of the museum closed behind Helen Farfrae, the museum was still. For the rest of the night the solemn stone figures around the courtyard uttered no word. Aristotle did not turn on his pedestal and say a comforting word to Francis Bacon, *Though natural substance is corruptible, species is eternal.* Charles Darwin did not shake his head in sorrow at the tragedy taking place on the glass roof over his head, nor did the thousands of insects impaled on pins in the new Entomology Office buzz and flutter their wings in horror. In the display case near the front door the dodo might have cried, *Don't blame me, I'm extinct,* but it didn't. An occasional motorbike on Parks Road made a momentary whine, but otherwise there was no sound.

When the sun rose next morning, the museum was still silent, but across the street at Keble College there was stir and movement. Milk arrived by van. "Good morning, Arthur," said the head cook, accepting it, chunking the bottles into the refrigerator and pulling out six cartons of fresh eggs. In the cavernous dining hall, college servants laid the tables with cutlery and dishes and baskets of muffins. Along the nineteenth-century corridors and up and down the concrete staircases in Hayward, undergraduates dragged themselves out of bed.

Keble was not one of the Oxford colleges delicately spired with golden stone, nor was it rich in story. Erasmus had not visited Keble, Christopher Wren had not matriculated there, nor John Donne nor Lawrence of Arabia nor Evelyn Waugh. True, there had been a Pakistani cricketer named Imran Khan, but he was the only famous graduate so far.

The college had been founded in the eighteen-sixties for *gentlemen wishing to live economically,* young men who would be candidates for holy orders. Its founders had been Puseyites, conservative and high church in religion. Keble was *That new place near the Parks what's going to stop us all from saying*

"Damn!" Over the years its religious dogmatism had faded, but not the color of its brick, nor the giddy stripes and checkerboards of its architectural surfaces.

In the second-floor bedroom in the Besse Building, at the northwest corner of Liddon Quad, Homer sat up in bed with a book open on his knees. "Hey, Mary," he said, poking his sleeping wife, "listen to this."

"Oh, Homer, for heaven's sake."

"Look, my dear, we've got to start adjusting to British time sooner or later. And it's so clever, you see. He starts with a chapter on domestic selection, how farmers for thousands of years have selected the best cattle and sheep and horses, so why doesn't nature do the same thing?"

"What do you mean, he?" groaned Mary. "Who's he?"

"Darwin, of course. It's The Origin of Species. He asks this brilliant question, why doesn't nature do the same thing farmers do?"

There was a pause, while Mary thought it over. "Because nature doesn't wear overalls, that's why."

"What?"

"Nature isn't a farmer."

There was another pause while Homer digested the joke. "Oh, right, of course not, but the same thing happens by natural selection. The weakest are killed off, and don't live to reproduce, so only the strong survive. You see? It's natural selection instead of domestic selection, perfecting the animal in its own way."

Mary's voice was muffled under the sheet. "Horrible, it's absolutely horrible."

"Well, of course it's horrible. Darwin said so too. *What a book a devil's chaplain could write about the cruelty of nature.* That's what he said."

"Well, how could he stand it? *I* can't stand it."

"Because it's the truth. You've got to stand it. We've all got to stand it."

Mary threw back the covers and stretched her long legs over the side of the bed. "I could stand any amount of truth if I had a little breakfast."

By this, their fourth day in Oxford, they were accustomed to dining in the Common Room set aside for Keble's talkative dons. This morning Homer greedily loaded his plate with bacon, scrambled eggs, fried potatoes, blueberry muffins, slabs of butter and globs of marmalade.

Mary looked at his plate and raised her eyebrows. "My God, Homer."

He defended himself, leaning across the table to his friend Joe Jamison, who was joining them for breakfast in order to introduce them to the other Keble dons. "After all," said Homer, flourishing his fork, "gor-blimey, here we are. When will we ever get a chance like this again?" He stopped, and clapped his hand to his mouth. "Oh, excuse me, you people do say gor-blimey, don't you?

"Homer!" spluttered Mary, convulsed.

Joe laughed. "I haven't actually heard anyone say it, except perhaps in films."

Homer shook his head in embarrassment. "Oh, I'm sorry. I just can't seem to help myself. Every now and then some weird impossible British expression comes out of my mouth. Forgive me."

Joe forgave him, grinning. Then he interrupted a couple of mathematicians deep in a discussion of nonlinear systems to ask for the basket of muffins, and explained to Homer the arrangements for his lecture hall. "Normally it would be the Examination Schools in the High, but I've bent the rules a bit. I thought you'd rather be nearby in the museum. Friendlier, don't you see."

"Well, you're the boss there, aren't you?" said Homer. "You can do what you want."

After breakfast Mary went back to Liddon Quad to study the map of Oxford. She was plotting a campaign of exploration. What did it matter, after all, if Joe Jamison had not in-vited both of them to lecture on American Literature under the sponsorship of Keble College, the way they taught it to-gether at home? It didn't mean her time in England would be wasted. There were other things to do. She would see every-thing worth seeing—she would squeeze Oxford dry of aes-thetic wonders. After that she'd explore the countryside and perhaps go to London, and then to the Lake District and all the cathedral cities. There were maps to be studied and books to be read.

Homer wanted to see the lecture hall in the museum, the auditorium where he would be holding forth. He walked across the quad to the gatehouse, said good morning to the porter, and emerged on Parks Road.

There across the street rose the Oxford University Museum, flat-faced and sharp-edged in the morning light. It had a distinct character, like a person. All the Ruskinian didacticism that had gone into its design was visible at once, the absurdity of the notion that the only proper architecture for a science museum was medieval, the irrepressible playfulness of the sculptors, the founders' conceit that art and science should be united in order to inspire the young, because God himself was the master Artificer.

Somewhere a bell chimed eight o'clock. At once someone popped out of the front entrance like a cuckoo from a clock. It was Professor William Dubchick. Seeing Homer, he lifted one arm and called to him, "Oh, Dr. Kelly!"

He was obviously in distress. Homer ran across the lawn. "Are you all right, sir?"

"Yes, yes, of course. But something terrible has happened." William grasped Homer's arm. "Is it true, Dr. Kelly, that you were once some sort of detective in Massachusetts? It is? Well, then, good! Perhaps you can help us in our trouble now." He led the way indoors, then stopped in the corridor to explain. Homer stopped too, politely attentive, although he could see nothing of Professor Dubchick's face against the glare of the courtyard behind him, where the iguanodon stood bathed in morning light. "It's the night watchman, you see," said Dubchick. "I'm afraid he's dead."

"Good lord," said Homer. "What happened?"

"One moment." Professor Dubchick turned away as the porter burst out of his office.

"Sir, I reached the detective inspector. He's on his way."

"Thank you, Edward. When he arrives, would you bring him right up?"

Edward Pound was a solid man, big through the shoulders. He looked capable of handling any problem that might come up in the museum, from the whereabouts of the ladies' room to a matter of sudden death. "Yes, of course, sir."

"This way, Dr. Kelly. We're going all the way to the roof."

Homer followed obediently as Professor Dubchick led the way up the broad south staircase. On the gallery floor he strode along the west side, then stopped before a narrow door in the wall. It looked to Homer like the entrance to a dungeon keep. There would be a spiral staircase of stone, going down, down, down.

The staircase was there, but it went both down and up. At the top there would be a castellated rampart and armored defenders with cauldrons of boiling oil. William Dubchick led the way, running lightly, his feet slip-slapping on the triangular steps. Homer had to stop halfway to catch his breath.

At once his guide turned back. "Are you all right, Dr. Kelly?"

"Oh, certainly," choked Homer, wishing he too had as-

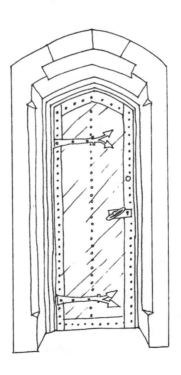

cended mountains in the Andes and climbed trees with the woolly monkeys of Ecuador. Heroically he flung himself at the stairs again, and reached the top in a single burst of effort.

They were high in the tower above the museum entrance. The room was a tall chamber crowded with boxes and files. Homer wanted to look at the view from the huge west windows, but Professor Dubchick was stooping through a small door and reaching one foot into the open air. "It's all downhill from here," he called to Homer, dropping out of sight.

Homer stuck his head out and watched Dubchick descend the steep metal ladder. Cautiously he followed, holding fast to the railings on either side. Before him as he descended rose the central peak of the roof, its glass panes overlapping like slates.

"Oof," said Homer with relief, stepping down from the bottom rung onto the wooden boardwalk.

"This way," said Dubchick, swinging around, hurrying to the right, then turning sharply left. At once he stopped, and Homer almost collided with his back.

At Dubchick's feet lay the body of a young man in uniform.

"Excuse me," murmured Homer. Professor Dubchick moved out of the way, and Homer knelt down to feel under the boy's sleeve for a pulse. He felt nothing. The brown eyes were open. The plump childish face was turned up to the sky. It was heavily scratched and lay at an odd angle to the shoulders. Homer said softly, "Broken neck."

William stooped and turned over one of the dead hands to see the scratched and bloody palm, then laid it down again. He looked up at the sheet of glass soaring above them to a distant horizontal ridge. "He must have fallen from up there."

"It looks like it," said Homer. "But what the hell was he doing? How could he climb so high? It's too steep, and there aren't any handholds. It's impossible."

There was a noisy clumping of heavy feet and a metallic shivering of the ladder. Edward Pound stepped off the bottom

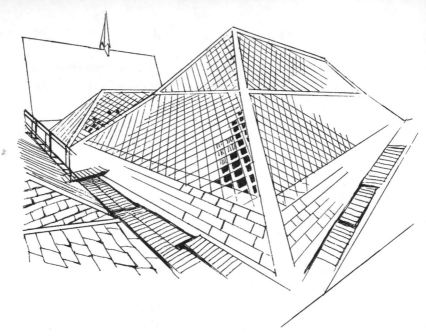

rung, with three men in his wake. In a moment the four of them were crowded together beside Homer and William Dubchick. The three police officers introduced themselves and shook hands over the body of the night watchman.

The good-looking dark-skinned man in the business suit was Detective Inspector Mukerji from the police station on St. Aldate's. The two younger men were Detective Constable Ives and Police Constable Gilly. The three officers leaned down to examine the body, while William explained how he had found it.

"I came in early and noticed that the door to the tower was open. I was concerned, because a lot of useful stuff is stored in the room above. So I went upstairs, and at once I felt a draft from the open door to the roof, so I came down the ladder to investigate." William stopped talking and looked down pityingly at the young man lying at their feet.

"What about you, sir?" said Mukerji, looking politely at Homer. Mukerji had a good-humored manner. His face was handsome with strongly marked features, a bold nose, a strong chin, arched brows and dark flashing eyes.

Homer hastened to explain that he was a visiting fellow at Keble College. Clumsily he reported his connection with the district attorney of Middlesex County in Cambridge, Massachusetts, but, humbly truthful for once, he admitted its antiquity. Then he stood back and watched the action of the British constabulary in the handling of a random unnatural death.

On the crowded boardwalk he had to edge back still farther as the detective inspector and the two constables were joined by a pathologist from the Radcliffe Infirmary. Now there were four officials huddled over the body.

Professor Dubchick looked at Homer and nodded, and touched Edward Pound's sleeve. The three of them made their way back to the ladder. Homer let the other two start up ahead of him, then put his hands on the shivering iron railings. With his foot on the bottom rung, he reached down and picked up a shiny object lying between two of the wooden slats of the boardwalk.

It was a small elliptical piece of stainless steel shaped into a pair of rings. He put it in his pocket.

❧

"What are these bloody boxes doing here?" said plasterer Daniel Tuck, speaking to himself indignantly. He had come to work early, meaning to busy himself with the vaulted ceiling of the south gallery, and here were these cardboard boxes in the middle of the floor. Some high and mighty scientist must have chucked them out, expecting somebody in the lower orders of the human race to carry them to the rubbish bin.

Not Daniel Tuck. Tuck was a professional, a bricklayer and plasterer. He was a craftsman, not a dustman. He stared at the boxes angrily. They were in his way. Impulsively he picked them up and tossed them over the railing.

One fell with a soft thunk on the top of a display case below. The other landed upside down on the stone head of

James Watt, hiding the anxious face of the father of the steam engine.

When Homer Kelly, Edward Pound and William Dubchick came hurrying along the gallery corridor, dodging around tarpaulins and scaffolding, Tuck was already at work on a long crack running up the wall above the door of the Zoology Office. He picked up his chisel as Edward Pound and Homer Kelly disappeared down the stairs. Professor Dubchick nodded at him solemnly and walked into the office. Tuck thrust his gouging tool deep into the crack.

CHAPTER 10

"In that case," said the Dodo solemnly, rising to its feet, "I move that the meeting adjourn, for the immediate adoption of more energetic remedies—"

Lewis Carroll, *Alice's Adventures in Wonderland*

"**G**ood lord, sir, it's gone."

"Gone?" said Homer. "What's gone?"

"The painting, the picture of the dodo." Edward Pound had stopped in his tracks at the bottom of the stairs. He was staring up at the blank wall beside the bony remains of the dodo.

Homer looked too. The wall was certainly empty. Only the label remained, *A Portrait of the Dodo by John Savery, 1651.* "Perhaps it was removed for cleaning?"

"Oh, no, Dr. Kelly. I would have known about it, and surely it would not have been removed for cleaning in the middle of the night." Pound hurried away to call Director Jamison with his two pieces of terrible news.

Homer gaped at the empty wall, told himself sorrowfully that his dream about the dodo was coming true, and headed for the door. At once it burst open in front of him, and an anxious-looking woman hurried in, tearing off her coat.

Homer didn't know her name, but he remembered standing next to her at the reception during Professor Dubchick's talk. There had been no chance to speak to her, because someone, probably her husband, had removed her. *Removed* was the right word. She had left under protest.

Helen breezed past him, then stopped and turned around. "Aren't you Dr. Kelly? I'm Dr. Farfrae. Helen Farfrae. I work with Professor Dubchick."

"Oh, good," said Homer. "Then perhaps you know what's happened to the picture of the dodo that was hanging here yesterday."

He led her to the empty wall, and Helen stared up at it. "Why, no. Nobody said anything to me about having it cleaned. It was here yesterday, wasn't it? Yes, it was, I remember seeing it yesterday afternoon. And last night—" Her expression changed. She looked at Homer fiercely. "Is it true, Dr. Kelly, that you've taken part in criminal investigations from time to time? Professor Dubchick thinks so. I wonder if you could—" Then Helen stopped and looked beyond Homer at the south stairway. Homer turned and looked too.

A mournful procession was descending. It was the official team from the police station on St. Aldate's, along with the pathologist from the Radcliffe Infirmary. The two constables carried a stretcher, holding it steady, setting their feet down carefully as they moved from step to step. A plastic sheet was draped over it, but the deadness of the human object under the sheet was plain.

Helen sucked in her breath. As the stretcher approached, she whispered to Homer, "Who is it?"

"The night watchman," said Homer gravely. "He fell from the glass roof. At least that's what we think. He was lying at the bottom with a broken neck. Professor Dubchick found him."

"Oh, poor Bobby." Helen sobbed once, then burst out at Homer, "Please, please, I've got to talk to you."

Homer was wary. He was enough of an old-fashioned male to think of women as the hysterical sex, while men were of course always perfectly reasonable. Homer cherished this opinion in spite of his own tendency to outbursts of emotion, forgetting also that his wife was far more sensible than he was.

Helen Farfrae's eyes were wet, but she smiled at him and pointed to the other side of the courtyard. "I like to sit over there sometimes. I pull up a chair between Darwin and Newton, and imagine them conversing about their health."

"Their health?" Amused, Homer followed her past the stuffed gray seal and the vast miscellaneous bones of *Cetiosaurus oxoniensis,* as the funeral procession vanished out the door.

Helen struggled to keep her tone jocular and light. "Oh, you must know about Darwin's continual gastric distress. He was troubled by it all his life. And Isaac Newton was obsessed with his own physical problems, like the incontinence of his bladder. I imagine some interesting exchanges."

Homer laughed, and pulled up a chair beside the pedestal of Newton. It was apparent that the nineteenth-century sculptor responsible for creating the likeness of the distinguished scientist, the author of *The Principia,* had been inadequate to his task. Newton looked small and childlike. He held a finger to his chin as if pondering some cloudy thought.

They sat down, and Helen got to the point at once, leaning forward, looking at Homer intently. "I know I should tell this to the police. In fact I should have called them last night. Would it have made a difference? Would Bobby still be alive?" Helen stared at Homer as if he knew the answer to the question, as if he could banish her tortured self-condemnation.

Homer tried to sound easygoing and comforting. "Look, why don't you just tell me what happened?"

Helen took a trembling breath. "I was working late in my office. It's the Zoology Office, right up there"—she pointed to the gallery above—"but then I . . . took a break, and went downstairs and walked around in the courtyard."

"You often stay late, Dr. Farfrae?"

"Yes, sometimes I stay late."

Homer looked at the fiberglass coelacanth in its glass case, and his mind wandered. How strange that the coelacanth's

fate was so different from that of the dodo! Everyone had
thought it was extinct, just like the dodo, but then it turned
up alive and well off the coast of Africa.

Abruptly he turned away from the coelacanth and probed a
little further. "Too much to accomplish during the day, Dr.
Farfrae?"

"Oh, that isn't it." Helen bit her lip, having said too much.
She hurried on. "Anyway, while I was walking about down

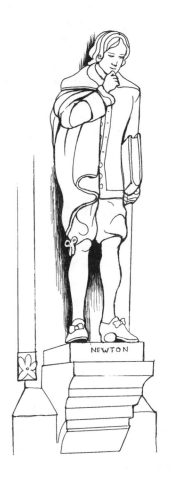

NEWTON

here, I heard someone come in." She went on to tell Homer about the footsteps on the stairs, the coming and going, the returning, the arrival of Bobby Fenwick, the chase up the stairs.

Homer interrupted her. "How did you know it was Fenwick?"

"By his voice. He shouted, and I recognized his voice. Everybody around here knows Bobby Fenwick. Of course he wasn't here every night. There isn't any night watchman just for the museum. Bobby took care of night security for this part of the university." Helen pointed this way and that. "Geology and Mineralogy, Atmospheric Physics, Biochemistry, Genetics—there must be twelve or fifteen science buildings around here. The night watchman goes from one to the other, looking in at random. I was often the only one in the building when Bobby came in."

"Did you see anything else, Dr. Farfrae? What happened after they went up into the tower?"

Helen put her head back and stared up at the glass roof. "The trouble is, you won't believe me." Homer opened his mouth to protest, but she hurried on. "I followed them up the tower stairs—oh, I know it was a stupid thing to do—and I looked out the door where the ladder goes down to the roof, and I saw—" Helen shook her head. "Wait."

On the other side of the courtyard, children were flowing into the museum. It was the first school visitation of the day. At once the murmuration of voices filled the courtyard, the corridor around it, the upstairs gallery and the peaked spaces under the glass roof. Helen's whisper blended with the murmur. "It was impossible. You won't believe it, and I don't believe it either."

"What was impossible? What did you see, Dr. Farfrae?"

"I saw someone on the glass tiles. He was bounding up that impossible slope. But I couldn't have seen it. How could anyone climb such a steep roof?"

"Nobody can. He fell and broke his neck. Did you see him fall?"

Helen shook her head and twisted her hands in her lap, while the children flooded out of the corridor into the courtyard and flopped down on the floor with their sketchbooks to draw the iguanodon.

"Did you see who it was?"

"No, I just saw it in silhouette."

"It? Did you say you saw *it?*"

"Well, yes, I did say that, didn't I? Because it wasn't a human thing to do—racing uphill like that, like a monkey in a tree, or a spider on a wall."

For a moment Homer was carried away by the fantastic imagery of her story, but then he chastised himself for imagining that some animal might really have been roving around the Oxford University Museum in the middle of the night. He wondered if Dr. Farfrae was a New Age believer in astrological influences, like some aging hippie in Cambridge, Massachusetts. But when she looked at him, her hazel eyes showed no wild glints, only flecks of the sunlight pouring down from above.

"Did you go down the ladder?"

"No. I didn't have the courage." Helen turned in her chair to look at the children sprawled on the floor around the iguanodon, as if to reassure herself that the world was still a place of lunchboxes and schoolrooms and children with dirty knees. "I was frightened. I went back downstairs and put on my coat and locked the office door and drove home."

"You did not call the police."

"No."

Homer could think of nothing more to ask. He stared at Isaac Newton's apple, which looked like a breakfast bun, and thought of Newton's law of gravitation. Beyond Newton stood the golden statue of Galileo, holding in his hands two objects, as though he were about to drop them from the

GALILEO

Leaning Tower to demonstrate his law of falling bodies. Poor Bobby Fenwick had obeyed both Newton and Galileo with absolute precision. He had slipped down the roof, the mass of his body attracted by gravity toward the center of the earth, accelerating in obedience to the law of inverse squares. His neck had broken at the bottom because of Newton's Third Law, *To every action there is an equal and opposite reaction. Snap!* How satisfying.

"Look," he said, "I'm pleased that you spoke to me, but I'm not the one you should be talking to. You've got to go to the police. Detective Inspector Mukerji, he'd be the one to see."

WATT

"Of course," said Helen, sounding desperate, "yes, yes, of course. But"—impulsively she stood up—"it's my husband. He'd be so upset. He wouldn't like it at all. He was—distressed already. I mean about my being here so late last night. I wish—"

It was obvious to Homer that *distressed* was a euphemism for *angry*. He stood up too. "I should think Mukerji would just want to hear what you have to say. I don't see why your husband should come into it at all."

"I see," said Helen humbly. "Thank you, Dr. Kelly."

Together they started back across the courtyard. But on the way to the corridor entrance between Aristotle and Roger Bacon, Helen stopped in surprise. "Good heavens, look at poor James Watt. Someone dropped a box over his head."

"Poor fella's in the dark." Homer reached up and removed the box, and they walked back across the courtyard with the schoolchildren flocking in front of them, crowding around the sales desk to spend their pocket money on plastic pterodactyls and butterfly coloring books and balloons in the shape of *Tyrannosaurus rex.*

CHAPTER 11

It is no doubt the chief work of my life.
Charles Darwin, *Autobiography*

🦢

It was a warm October. Some of the seeds that had been transported on the muddy feet of the wigeon from the north began germinating in the damp soil of the ditch beside the car-rental place on the Botley Road. Their pale stolons groped in all directions underground, sending eager stems into the air. Unfortunately, none of the Motorworld salesmen ever looked down at the ditch as they got in and out of the shiny cars in the parking lot. They never noticed the presence of the intruder, never cried, *Oh, my God,* never snatched up spades to dig it up. Unseen and unchecked, the new little shoots continued to thrive.

🦢

Homer Kelly was flabbergasted by *The Origin of Species.* Of course the state of being flabbergasted was normal for Homer. He had been an astonished baby and a dumbfounded child, and now he was a thunderstruck adult. He was always being wowed by one thing or another, and then something else would come along that out-wowed all the rest.

His conversation with Helen Farfrae yesterday had been staggering enough. This morning Homer supposed he should check up and make sure she had told her story to Mukerji. But overnight his confidence in her sanity had waned. He forgot her now, in his enthusiasm for Charles Darwin.

"Mary, listen to this," he said as they headed for the chapel. His head was down, his eyes were on the book. "He's talking about the Creator, but you know what he means by the Creator?"

"No, what?"

"Natural selection." Homer read a sentence aloud. *"There is a power, represented by natural selection or the survival of the fittest, always intently watching.* How do you like that! *Always intently watching!"*

"But he doesn't mean"—Mary took Homer's arm as he blundered onto the grass—"surely he doesn't mean some huge natural force, out there somewhere, looking on at everything?"

"No, no, but to him natural law was, well, it was godlike. He revered it with the same devotion his contemporaries felt for God. What he meant was—"

"Homer, take your nose out of that book. We have to climb these stairs."

Homer glanced at the broad stone stairs to the chapel and put one foot on the bottom step. "He meant that the natural selection of slight favorable variations was a precise instrument for improving any smallest part of an organism. As though it were being guided through a maze of choices."

"But that's like God."

"It's not like God, because the guiding happens by itself, and there isn't any goal. All those creatures weren't working their way toward *Homo sapiens.*"

"Well, I think it's depressing."

They entered the chapel. Homer closed *The Origin of Species* and looked around at the enormous space that had encouraged the piety of those nineteenth-century gentlemen wishing to live economically. It was fully supplied with all the elements of the Gothic revival—pointed arches and ribbed vaults, clustered piers and quatrefoils, colored glass and pat-

terned floors. Homer was comfortably reminded of Memorial Hall, back home in Cambridge. Once again he was surrounded by thick amber air embedded with splendid bugs from an earlier time. In this case the insects were Edward Pusey and John Keble, black-robed and red-robed like some of the glorious beetles in the museum across the street.

"Guano," muttered Homer, as they edged into a pew at the back.

"What?"

"Guano," he repeated loudly. "That's what built this place."

Homer's old friend and sponsor Joseph Jamison, the director of the museum, was there ahead of them, moving aside to make room. "That's right," he said excitedly. "Guano built this chapel. Indeed it did."

A string of undergraduates sidled along the pew in front of them. They stared at Joe and Homer as they sat down. Mary nodded and smiled at Joe. "What do you mean, guano built it?"

"The donor," said Joe, "was a devout importer of guano from the Pacific. All this"—he waved his hand at the lofty walls of brick, the elaborate fixtures behind the altar—"it comes from hawk droppings, mockingbird droppings, finch droppings, every kind of bird droppings. They shipped it here and there for fertilizer, made a fortune"—Joe quoted a famous verse—"*selling turds of foreign birds.*"

"This big British importer," Homer explained to Mary, "he just scooped it off the rocks of the Galápagos and shipped it home."

"Homer, for heaven's sake," said Mary, "you're insulting our kind hosts."

But one of the girls in front of them turned around and asked brightly, "What about cormorant shit? Did he scoop that up too?"

"Why, of course," said Homer.

"He wasn't particular," said Joe.

Homer turned to Mary, who was red-faced and grinning. "It's inspiring, really, when you think of it, because maybe he scooped up some of it while Charles Darwin was in the Galápagos, because they had a guano industry there at the same time, did you know that?" Homer nodded his head solemnly at the student in the front pew. "Inspiring, truly inspiring."

After the service they set off for a tour of the Bodleian Library, which was high on Mary's list of wonders.

It was a misty morning, with a barely perceptible rain.

Mary opened her umbrella as they ambled along Catte Street. "Homer, did you tell the police what Helen Farfrae told you yesterday? You did tell them, didn't you?"

"I told her to tell them. I don't know what the hell Mukerji will do with a simian creature dancing up the side of a glass pyramid. But it's up to them now. I'm not going to get into it."

The Bodleian Library was closed on Sunday, but they could see through the gate into the Old Schools Quad.

"Look, Homer," said Mary, pointing with her umbrella at one of the famous doors. There was a band of writing above it, SCHOLA METAPHYSICAE. Another door pronounced itself the entrance to the SCHOLA PHILOSOPHIA. They were two of the old schools, which had subdivided all learning among them.

Homer peered at them through the ironwork of the gate. Something ached inside him. He couldn't help thinking of his own pitiful education at the cheapest night school in Boston. Everything he knew about Philosophia and Metaphysica had been grubbed up afterward by himself out of books. Here the great harvest would simply pour over you its golden sheaves. Well, of course that probably wasn't really true. But here in the Old Schools Quad it looked as though all you had to do was turn the key and walk into one of these ancient doors, and be blessed with learning forever.

Homer found himself wondering about Helen Farfrae. She was a graduate of Oxford, she had told him so. She had a doctor's degree from St. Hilda's. Presumably she had been handed a great basket of these golden sheaves. How strange that a woman so blessed, so liberated by learning, should become a submissive wife. Homer had thought marriages like that were extinct, as dead as the dodo in the glass case. But here they were, Mr. and Mrs. Farfrae, alive and well like the coelacanth, right here in the city of Oxford. Perhaps they should be stuffed and exhibited as natural wonders in the Oxford University Museum.

CHAPTER 12

"Have you guessed the riddle yet?" the Hatter said, turning to Alice again.
"No, I give it up," Alice replied. "What's the answer?"
"I haven't the slightest idea," said the Hatter.
Lewis Carroll, *Alice's Adventures in Wonderland*

On Monday morning Homer had a summons from Detective Inspector Gopal Mukerji.

Edward Pound beckoned to him as he entered the museum. He was holding a telephone.

"For me?" said Homer, pointing at his chest in surprise.

He picked up the phone and said hello.

"Good morning, Dr. Kelly." Mukerji's speech had the crisp syllabic distinctness of a highly educated Bengali Brahmin. "I wonder if by any chance you are free to come to the station right now?"

For an instant Homer felt puffed up. Obviously Detective Inspector Mukerji remembered his standing as an ex–lieutenant detective. He was calling on him to act as a colleague. "Well!" said Homer, beaming. "Certainly, Inspector. How can I help you?"

"I have tried to reach Dr. Jamison, but Mr. Pound informs me he is in London. Mr. Pound himself cannot leave his post as porter. No other responsible person seems to be around. We need someone to identify a picture. We've just had a call from a postgraduate at Christ Church informing us that a painting has turned up in their Graduate Common Room. We assume it is the museum's missing picture."

"Oho, is it a dodo?"

"I have not seen it myself." Mukerji's chuckle was a high cackle. "But the postgrad referred to it as a dodo. Perhaps if you were to take a look?"

Homer sighed. He was not, after all, a famous investigator from the United States, he was merely a random bystander. "Where shall I meet you, Inspector? Christ Church is one of the colleges, isn't it?"

"Yes, of course. I'll wait for you in the porter's lodge in Tom Tower. It's just up the street from my office. Could you be there by eleven o'clock? Do you know the way?"

"I have a map."

Homer hung up and stared blankly at Edward Pound.

"Have you seen this, Dr. Kelly?" Pound had a copy of the *Oxford Mail.* "It's full of Bobby Fenwick's death and the theft of the dodo painting and Dr. Farfrae's story about the intruder. They happened the same night, and the paper's keen on the idea that they're all related."

"Dr. Farfrae's story? Oh, God, she'll be unhappy about that. I told her it wouldn't come out. Her husband—well, never mind." Homer went back to Keble for his map, then set off for Christ Church.

It was in a part of Oxford he had not yet explored. Mary had marched up Cornmarket Street to St. Aldate's, changing traveler's checks at Lloyd's and buying stamps at the post office, but to Homer it was unfamiliar territory. He had expected a charming old lane with red-cheeked farmers in Wellington boots selling fruits and vegetables from the backs of wagons. It was not. The closer he came to Cornmarket along Broad Street, the thicker were the crowds. The crossing was a locked grid—little Park and Ride buses running north and south, massive long-distance buses, and a double-decker bus with a tour guide shouting through a megaphone, "THREE TOWERS DOMINATE THIS STREET, THE CHURCH OF ST. MICHAEL AT THE NORTH GATE IMMEDIATELY TO YOUR LEFT, CARFAX

TOWER TO THE RIGHT AT THE NEXT CORNER, AND TOM TOWER, WHICH YOU WILL SEE IN THE DISTANCE, THE WORK OF— MADAM, WOULD YOU KINDLY RESTRAIN YOUR CHILD?"

This was town, not gown. Thick streams of local folk clotted the streets and sidewalks. Mothers pushed babies in strollers, grandmothers hurried along the sidewalks with a rocking British gait, their arms sagging with plastic bags from Marks and Spencer. There were long lines at the bus stops. People flooded in and out of Pizza Hut and McDonald's, boys on skateboards rattled past the stalled buses and leaped around in hundred-and-eighty-degree turns. Crowds of teenagers leaned against the windows of the Jean Factory, spread themselves over the sidewalk, smoked, guffawed. They were dressed to appall. *Hate us. Go ahead, hate us.*

It was easy to oblige. Homer avoided bunches of them by dodging left and right and moving out into the street. He looked anxiously at his watch. He was going to be late. But at last the pedestrian traffic thinned, and there were no more shops. As the bell in Tom Tower sounded eleven, Homer hurried across the street and walked into the arched entrance. At once a tall porter in a bowler hat came forward and asked a courteous, "May I help you, sir?" It was a kindly warning that admission was limited to members of the college.

But Mukerji was already there. He bustled forward, and spoke up for Homer. "It's all right, Mr. Aubrey, Professor Kelly is with me." Grinning, he led the way into a spacious quadrangle.

It looked familiar to Homer. Surely he had seen it in guidebooks. Yes, there in the middle was the famous Mercury fountain. To Homer's uneducated eyes the place looked bare. There were no clipped hedges or spreading trees like those on an American college green. He felt like Alice, going through the looking-glass. British cars drove on the wrong side of the street, British cyclists wore ordinary clothes instead of helmets and tight-fitting spandex, the British language was quaintly eccentric, and this college quadrangle was unadorned with pom-

poms of shrubbery. It was the differences that made everything so interesting.

As they crossed the quad and headed through a passage at one side, Mukerji expounded on the history of the college and named some of its celebrated graduates—John Wesley, Charles Dodgson, W. H. Auden. "And me, of course," he said, chuckling. "I graduated one day, and next day I walked around the corner and became a police officer. I confess," he said, astonishing Homer with his frankness, "that it was not my college degree that mattered, so much as the influence of my uncle in military intelligence. Come, Dr. Kelly. The Graduate Common Room is up these stairs."

"Tell me, Inspector," said Homer, "what's a common room anyway? A dining hall, is that it?"

"No, no. It's like a club. It includes everyone at the same level in the college. Only senior members use the Senior Common Room, and I suppose only postgrads use this one." Mukerji cackled again. "I don't know why the hell the undergraduates bother with the Junior Common Room. Myself, I preferred the local pubs."

Mukerji's mild profanity, spoken in his perfect diction, amused Homer as he puffed after him up the stairs. "Tell me, Inspector, did Dr. Farfrae tell you what she saw on the roof of the University Museum? You know, when the night watchman fell to his death? I told her to call you."

Mukerji stopped at the top of the stairs and rolled his eyes dramatically at Homer. "Oh, yes, she called it a creature. What a strange lady. Why did she not report it at once?"

Homer reached the top step and gasped for breath. "I think she has a rather odd marriage. Her husband is easily"—Homer groped for a word, then picked the one Helen had used herself—"upset. I think she hoped to stay out of it altogether."

"Inspector, will you come this way?" It was a genial servant of the college. He led them down a corridor, unlocked a door and gestured them inside.

Once again Homer had a feeling of recognition. Surely he had seen this room in a picture somewhere, this layout, these windows, this door at one side of the hearth? But no, it couldn't be. How many rooms in Oxford had windows on the wall to the left of the fireplace, and a door on the right? There must be hundreds of them, thousands. He banished the eerie sense that he had seen the room before, and burst out laughing.

There between the windows was the portrait of the dodo, taking up most of the wall between the long red draperies. It looked huger and more ridiculous than ever.

Mukerji laughed too. "Is that it? That thing is a dodo?"

"It's the dodo, all right. I must say, it looks perfectly at home. How on earth did it get here?"

The answer came from an unexpected source. A key turned

in the door and two people walked in. One was Stuart Grebe,
the goggle-eyed Rhodes scholar who had introduced Homer
to the dodo at last Wednesday's reception. The other was
Freddy Dubchick.

"It was my idea," said Stuart.

"We stole it together," said Freddy.

CHAPTER 13

"But I don't want to go among mad people," Alice remarked.
"Oh, you can't help that," said the Cat: "we're all mad here."
Lewis Carroll, *Alice's Adventures in Wonderland*

🐦

After the tragedy of Bobby Fenwick's death, the theft of the dodo painting seemed to Homer like a comic turn. But everyone in the museum was alarmed about it, he knew that. They wanted their painting back, undamaged by thieving vandals.

And here were the vandals in person. As thieves, Freddy Dubchick and Stuart Grebe were an unlikely pair, but Homer could see that they were dangerous. Freddy was young and suggestible, and Stuart was brash and clever, with funny ideas rattling around in his head like marbles in a pinball machine.

"But why?" said Homer, looking at Stuart. "Why did you steal it? What was the point?"

"Because it belongs here, that's why." Stuart's eyes popped affectionately at the dodo.

"That's right," said Freddy stoutly. "And it must stay here forever."

They were obviously deranged. Homer opened his mouth to ask *Why?* once again, but Detective Inspector Mukerji forestalled him. He raised one finger, and said, "Aha! I know. It is because Lewis Carroll once occupied these rooms, is that it? And he put the dodo in Alice in Wonderland?"

Stuart and Freddy spoke as one: "Of course."

Homer nodded his head vigorously, understanding at last why the room had looked so familiar. He had seen it in a photograph, *Charles Dodgson's sitting room.* "I remember now. He taught mathematics at Christ Church most of his life, isn't that right? So you people just decided, all on your own, that the painting of the dodo belonged here, is that it?"

Freddy nodded, her face radiant. Stuart beamed with pride.

"Do I understand," said Mukerji, his jovial face now grave, "that you both freely admit having stolen this valuable painting from the University Museum? Do you realize that, among other things, you will both be sent down?"

Stuart's face fell. "Sent down? You mean, expelled?"

"I don't care," said Freddy, defiant.

Mukerji made them sit down side by side on the enormous red sofa that occupied the center of the room. He sat opposite, leaning forward in an armchair. Homer pulled up a straight chair and disposed himself to watch the interviewing technique of this distinguished representative of British law enforcement.

The detective inspector looked at Stuart and began strangely. *"Come to us, youth, tell us truly why there is madness in your eyes?"*

"What?" said Stuart, dumbfounded.

Mukerji chuckled. "Forgive me, Mr. Grebe. I couldn't resist. I am quoting from the Bengali poet Tagore. Tell me, what time did you remove the picture from the museum? And how did you get in?"

"Midnight," said Stuart promptly. "Freddy had a key."

Freddy laughed. "We sort of enjoyed the idea of meeting at midnight to rescue the dodo. And I used my father's key. I mean I just sort of borrowed it."

"What about a key to this room?" said Mukerji. "Ah, I know. You are a Rhodes scholar here at Christ Church, Mr. Grebe? You borrowed a key to the Graduate Common Room from a friendly postgrad?" Stuart grinned. Mukerji nodded wisely, then fixed his dark shining eyes on Freddy's face. "Have either of you been reading the newspaper? Or listening to the news? Do you know what else was going on in the museum on Friday night?"

Freddy and Stuart looked at each other, their faces blank. "No," said Stuart. "No," said Freddy.

"You mean to say you unlocked the front door of the museum at midnight, lifted the picture off the wall and went away with it? You did nothing else? You never left the ground floor?"

"That's right," said Freddy. "It couldn't have taken us more than five minutes. We popped the picture into the back seat of Stuart's car and drove away."

"You have a car?" Homer had not meant to interrupt, but he couldn't help it. Stuart Grebe didn't look like the kind of American kid who could afford to own a car in a foreign country. His gawky wrists hung out below a ragged shirt, and his torn jeans had not been deliberately ripped by Ralph Lauren.

"It's a borrowed car. My roommate, he's from Rhode Island. He bought this old Rover."

Mukerji's brilliant eyes bored into Stuart, then looked back at Freddy. "During this five minutes in the museum, did you hear anything? Anything at all?"

Freddy and Stuart looked at each other again. "Well, there was this guy sort of yelling, upstairs somewhere," said Stuart.

"So we hurried," said Freddy. "We were afraid he might come down."

"Then the yelling stopped," said Stuart. "Everything was quiet when we left."

&

Afterward Mukerji left them in no doubt as to the seriousness of their offense. "I will not report this to the college authorities, at least not yet, although it may be necessary to do so in the weeks to come." He wagged a warning finger. "But the picture is to be restored to the museum at once. Professor Kelly, will you supervise its return?"

"Of course," said Homer.

They stood up. The interview was over. Mukerji's round cheeks shone, his eyes sparkled, his black brows were more commanding than ever. He shook hands all around and darted away, leaving the rest of them to cope with the return of the painting.

The aged Rover was in a minimal state of repair. The enormous picture barely fitted in the back. A chip fell off the gold frame as Stuart wedged it into the back seat.

"Tell me, Stuart," said Homer nervously, climbing in beside it, "do you know how to drive in this country?"

"Oh, sort of," said Stuart. "Don't worry. I pick things up fast."

It was a wild ride. The car shivered and shook. "Left, left," shouted Homer, as Stuart wobbled into the crossing at Carfax. There was a moment of frightening confusion at the Martyrs' Memorial as he yawed left and right, trying to head into the Banbury Road, and another as he made the right turn onto Keble, with Freddy shrieking in warning.

In front of the museum, Stuart and Freddy emerged from the car cheerful and unshaken. Homer was trembling, having escaped death by the narrowest of margins.

CHAPTER 14

The female . . . with the rarest exceptions, is less eager than the male . . . she is coy, and may often be seen endeavouring for a long time to escape.

Charles Darwin, *The Descent of Man*

🦢

DIARY OF FREDERICKA DUBCHICK
Oliver is having dinner with us tomorrow.

Solemn note: I know what he wants. I'm supposed to give him my answer. Oh, the question is so boring. I wish he'd stop tormenting me. I wish—

What shall I make for lunch? Lentil soup, salad, stewed pears? I've got a new French cookbook, but I think I'll save it for a really royal occasion.

Important announcement: this entry is to be a further dissertation

ON BEING LOOKED AT—

a subject of IMMENSE interest.

Item 1) My tutor, Dr. Swann, doesn't look at me at all. I don't know how he knows it's me, and not somebody else. His eyes skitter around the room and land on the windowsill or the rug or the lampshade. Yesterday he actually looked at my shoelaces. Maybe he'll work his way up to my knees and eventually to my face, then rear back and say, Good heavens, I thought you were Miss Smith!

Item 2) My dog Fluffy looks at me with worshipful yearning, his brown eyes misty with love.

Item 3) Oliver looks at me the same way!

Item 4) The American looked at me again last Wednesday in the Examination Schools.

It was a lecture by Professor Heddlestone, who has just won the Nobel Prize for something or other. I took a lot of notes, but when I glanced at them afterward they were meaningless. At one point I dropped my pen, and when I reached down for it, I saw that he was sitting right behind me, and he reached for it too, and for a minute our hands were touching, in fact his kept missing the pen and running into my hand, and it was like—oh, God, it was like being kissed, it really was. Afterward we walked out together and he looked at the cupola of Queen's and said it reminded him of a pet albino spider he had kept as a boy. He didn't look at me while we were talking, but he knew it was me, all right, not Miss Smith!

Item 5) Oh, brrrr, this is a different kind of being looked at. On Cornmarket Street yesterday I saw a horrible old woman shuffling along, stopping to reach into one of the litter containers. She had long dragging hair and grim yellow eyes and an immense posterior, and for a minute we looked at each other, and she didn't say anything, but a message came out of her eyes, and I could understand it as plainly as if she had said it out loud—

> As I am now you too shall be,
> Prepare for death and follow me.

It's what they used to write on gravestones. And it was true! Right away I could feel my head wedged down into my shoulders and my big bottom cantilevered out behind me. It was a foretaste of my own old age.

Item 6) The way Father looked at me when I told him about my scrape with the police!

Homer Kelly made me tell him. After we brought the dodo picture back to the museum, Homer scolded me. He *said I was lucky not to be thrown out, and Stuart was lucky too, and I should confess everything to my father. So I ran upstairs to Father's office and burst in without knocking, and found him trying to fix his glasses with a couple of safety pins. I told him about the Great Dodo Caper, and then I laughed as though it had all been such fun. "It's all right, Father," I said. "Dr. Kelly has hushed it up."*

It was a horrible mistake. Father looked at me in this terribly GRAVE way, and said that I was "fortunate indeed." It was worse, oh, much worse than the ghastly stare of that fearsome old woman on Cornmarket Street!

CHAPTER 15

"Make a remark," said the Red Queen: *"it's ridiculous to leave all the conversation to the pudding!"*

Lewis Carroll, *Through the Looking-Glass*

Oliver Clare was making a painful effort to seem relaxed, but things started off badly. When Freddy opened the door her dog Fluffy yipped wildly at him as though he were about to make off with the family silver.

Oliver was not a physical coward, but he was afraid of Fluffy. "Hello, there, boy!" he said heartily, stretching out his hand. At once Fluffy jumped up and bit it.

There followed a scene of apologies by Freddy and protestations by Oliver that it was nothing, really nothing, followed by antiseptic, bandages and adhesive tape.

Freddy's father, Professor Dubchick, smoothed the situation by showing the scar on his finger and talking about the monkey that had bitten him in Ecuador. Freddy displayed the scars on her knees, achieved by falling off her bicycle. Oliver reached out a tender hand to touch them, then pulled it back.

The next awkwardness was the Episode of the Decanter, as Freddy described it afterward in her diary. In his nervousness Oliver managed to knock over the crystal decanter from which Professor Dubchick had been pouring sherry. The old family heirloom flooded his trousers, then smashed on the floor. Again there was a scene of yelped apologies, this time by Oliver, and protestations by Freddy and her father that it was nothing, really nothing, followed by sponges, wet towels and grovelings under the table, as Oliver tried to find all the broken pieces.

Afterward he stayed an hour longer than he should have, trying to glue the decanter back together. He was hoping for a chance to ask Freddy his enormously important question. Instead he conversed uncomfortably with her father. His voice sounded pompous in his own ears, but he couldn't stop talking like a clergyman of the Church of England.

He did his best to go halfway. "I wonder, sir," he said, as Freddy vanished to dish up the stewed pears, "if it's possible to reconcile contemporary evolutionary theory with the views of the enlightened Christian church?"

William maintained a polite face, but he was bored with this question, tired of this young man, fatigued by his earnestness. If only Oliver had hurled the decanter at the wall, he might be someone you could take an interest in. "Well, plenty of people have tried," he said mildly.

"I mean," said Oliver, pressing two pieces of crystal together with his thumbs while the glue took hold, "wouldn't it be true to say that natural law in all its complexity is the work of God?"

William tried to forgive this naive remark. Patiently he gave his usual answer. "To attribute everything to the intervention of God is simply to beg the question. But if it makes you happy to overarch the natural world in all its splendor and terror with a being of great magical power, so be it. Darwin would say you were merely restating the problem in dignified language. He found grandeur enough in the variety of species and in the natural laws governing their growth and change."

Poor Oliver tried to cobble up a response, but his mind was a blank, and then the two pieces of crystal shot out of his hands and disappeared under the table. When Freddy hurried in with her tray of stewed pears he was once again down on all fours.

"Oh, Oliver," she said, laughing at the sight of his black-trousered bottom, "you look as if you're praying. Forget about the decanter. We'll throw it away."

They ate their pears and sipped their coffee, retreating to the safe subject of ancestors.

Here Oliver was more confident. He smiled modestly and mentioned a pair of eighteenth-century admirals, a nineteenth-century Bishop of Warwick, and another eminent fore-bear, Sir Wilfred Clare, who had been admitted by Queen Victoria to the Most Noble Order of the Garter. "My family once owned land in the neighborhood of Burford, but of course it's all gone now." Oliver rose to go, still reeking of sherry. "I'm afraid the end of the story is rather sad. Now it's just my mother and father and me. My illustrious family has dwindled down to this poor vicar of the Church of England."

"Honor enough, surely," said William politely. He watched through the curtains, as Freddy escorted Oliver down the front walk. Oliver was doing all the talking. At the end of the walk Freddy stood head down, staring at her shoes.

William smiled grimly. He knew that stubborn look. Oliver was asking something of her, and she was refusing, shaking her head violently.

Poor old Oliver! William watched him turn away, looking heartsick, and walk in the direction of the Banbury Road.

Freddy wasn't heartsick. William grinned as he heard the scramble in the hall. She was chirping at Fluffy, fastening the leash to his collar. The door slammed, *bang,* and they were off, dog barking, Freddy whistling, trotting away from the house, away from Oliver Clare, away from William Dubchick, away, away!

CHAPTER 16

The rattlesnake has a poison-fang for its own defense, and for the destruction of its prey.

Charles Darwin, *The Origin of Species*

❦

M argo Shaw was carrying out her job in the museum, in the two spirit storerooms, Vertebrate and Invertebrate, unsealing the jars with their human embryos and coiled snakes and mollusks, filling them to the brim with alcohol, then sealing them up again.

This morning, in the Invertebrate Spirit Store, she was disgruntled. She had won an argument with Hal, but it had been nasty and uncomfortable. Hal had given up at last and fallen silent, and then he had left the house without a word. Just because she didn't want to spend another couple of days at Aunt Peggy's! And miss the party in the master's lodge at Balliol, after wangling an invitation! It was so important to be seen at functions like that. It was what Oxford was all about. Margo had heard of another affair at Oriel, coming up in November. Taking another jar down from the shelf, she paused with her hand on the lid. Whom did she know at Oriel?

Corystes cassivelaunus, said the label on the jar, *Mr. C. Darwin.* Margo wrenched it open. Oh, God, couldn't Hal see how dull it was for her at Aunt Peggy's? Last time he had insisted on exploring the *entire* house, every *hideous* room. And then he had sat down beside Aunt Peggy on the *flatulent* sofa, looking at *hecatombs* of snapshots of the happy summers he had spent there as a child while his divorcing parents *sued* each other back in Kansas. And then he had jammed the car so full of boxes of books and papers, there was hardly room for Margo. She couldn't face another visit.

Margo poured alcohol into the jar from her container, readjusted the lid, and looked at the rows of shelves. Would she ever be done? Sometimes when a snake seemed to look up at her, or a fetus bobbed its tiny head, she shuddered, and thought of finding other employment. This sort of thing was pure routine. Any housewife could do it, any old-fashioned homebody with experience in preserving garden produce. Margo had heard about another museum job, and she coveted it. A new woman had been hired to repack the egg collection in acid-free tissue paper and mount new specimens of lepidoptera. It sounded a lot more pleasant. Maybe she could pry that woman out and wangle herself in. And there was an even better job she could try for. That slot too was filled, but perhaps by the most *delicate* maneuvering she could dislodge the current occupant and *slither* into her place.

Margo unsealed a jar of centipedes, her mind floating free. She had found a way of amusing herself on the job by thinking up cameo studies of her new British acquaintances. It had become a hobby, inventing vicious little thumbnail portraits to be recited to her friends later on. It didn't disturb Margo that the same friends were all included in her character studies. She would tell Friend A about Friend B, then take B aside and skewer Friend A.

The next jar was Number 12998, a container of Darwin myriapods. Languidly Margo removed the lid, inventing at the same time a mental sketch of William Dubchick. Her husband admired him so much, but why?

WILLIAM DUBCHICK: Bald head, whiskers like Father Time, nose like a turnip, bristling hairy eyebrows nourished by Oxford dews and damps. They're something like the

*fancy feathers with which male birds attract females, al-
though he's far too old to attract anybody. Imagine being
embraced by Dubchick, engulfed in that forest of whisker!*

Margo topped up Jar 12998 and pressed the top back on.
*As for his zoological expertise, I understand it's pretty much
passé. I'm told he spent the last eight years studying crabs.
Now, that's what I call pedestrian. He's supposed to be writing
a book, but people doubt it will ever be done. And as for his
daughter—*

Margo moved on to a jar of squid, and recoiled at the long
tentacles bundled together in the narrow container, their suck-
ing disks clearly visible through the glass. Bravely she removed
the top and put her mind on the problem of Fredericka
Dubchick. *The girl is cunning to look at, one has to admit, but
what else is there to recommend her? She's an undergraduate at
a prestigious Oxford college, but surely that's due to her father's
influence. Freddy Dubchick is a classic example of a spoiled
child, and she's also the kind of pretty girl who throws herself
at anything in trousers. I'll bet she's sleeping with that good-
looking kid who calls himself a clergyman. She's even started
to work her charms on Hal, and the poor fool is just a little bit
bewitched.*

Margo put back the top on the jar of squid and sealed it
with a brush dipped in grease, making an inner vow to keep an
eye on Freddy Dubchick and report her findings to Hal. She'd
see to it that he was unbewitched in a hurry.

She was tired of the Invertebrate Spirit Store. Margo turned
off the lights, locked the door, and made her way back to the
courtyard. This time she paid no attention to the stone scientists standing among the display cases and the fossil bones. She
did not even imagine them dancing when no one was there.
When Roger Bacon held up for her admiration his model of
the heavens, and cautioned her that *true philosophers could not
conceive the causes of things unless their souls were free from sin,*

Margo tossed her head and turned away to mount the south staircase.

It was almost impossible to reach the top, there was so much in the way. The repair of the museum was going forward, but it was far from finished. The north stairwell had been completed, along with the plaster walls and vaulting of the gallery arcade, and now the bricklayers were erecting metal scaffolding over the south stairwell.

Margo worked her way up the steps, dodging past the workmen, who politely moved aside. There were more of them in the corridor above, busily taking scaffolding apart. As she picked her way past them, two men gathered up the ends of the plastic tarpaulin that had been protecting the railings and the floor from driblets of plaster. They were holding it like a sheet, folding it over and walking together to join the two ends—when there was a crash of breaking glass.

Margo skipped to one side. "What was that?" she said sharply, as one of the men stepped back.

"Bloody hell," he said, "I didn't know there was bottles under there. Jesus."

His colleague lifted the blue tarp out of the way, and together they surveyed the damage. Dozens of jars were lined up on the floor. Some were rolling, colliding, knocking down others. One jar lay in a smash of broken glass, its clotted contents leaking out in a dark puddle.

"God!" said Margo, recoiling.

The workman who had kicked the broken jar appealed to her: "I didn't know they was here, honest. There wasn't any here, I swear, when I put down the tarps. No way they could have been here. I'm sorry I busted one, but how was I to know?"

"Don't look at me," said Margo, shuddering, staring at the dark jars. They were like the grisly bottles in the Invertebrate Spirit Store, the bottled squid and the jars of embryos, and she wanted nothing to do with them at all.

CHAPTER 17

We will now turn to the characteristic symptoms of Rage. Under this powerful emotion the . . . face reddens, or it becomes purple from the impeded return of the blood, or may turn deadly pale.
Charles Darwin,
The Expression of the Emotions in Man and Animals

❧

Mark Soffit existed in a globe of rage.

For one thing, he was disappointed in his Oxford living quarters. Back in the United States he had imagined elegant rooms off a private staircase in some medieval tower. But when he arrived in the city and took a cab to Wolfson, he was chagrined to discover that it was not one of the ancient colleges clustered around the Broad and the High. Unlike Balliol, Magdalen, and Christ Church, it had not nurtured famous men of British history. In fact it had been founded only thirty years ago, and it was in North Oxford, way the hell and gone out of the center of town. It was a graduate college with an emphasis on the natural sciences, which explained why the fools had put him there.

Mark's room was not on a private stair. It was a narrow cubicle on a long corridor. Most of the other members of the college were clever Hindus or sober Chinese or dark-skinned Africans from Senegal. The only other white man on his corridor was Arnie Cohen, another American, your archetypical nerd, a skinny Jew from New York City with a buckled briefcase. And Christ, he was another Rhodes scholar!

Cohen had tried to cozy up to Mark, but Mark had cut him off, nipping an embarrassing friendship in the bud (along with

99

the opportunity to know a future Chief Justice of the Supreme Court).

Now Mark entered the museum for a conference with his tutor, Hal Shaw. He supposed he should be grateful to Dr. Shaw for taking him on, but his failure to become the pupil of William Dubchick still rankled. Mark did not say to himself that he had soured his own chances. His memory had a way of developing blisters over pricks to his vanity.

The core of his problem was his inability to lose himself in anything. His selfhood clung to his consciousness with sharp claws. *Here I am, Mark Soffit, Rhodes scholar, walking down the High Street. This is me, Mark Soffit, Rhodes scholar, entering the Oxford University Museum.*

Below lay a wincing misery. *They don't know me. They don't like me. I've got to show them.*

Gloomily now he climbed the south stairs, edging angrily past the scaffolding, failing to notice the active beehive in the window, although it was one of the museum's most interesting exhibits, ignoring the display of beetles at the top of the stairs.

He also failed to notice the jars on the floor of the corridor, although in striding past them he crunched a piece of broken glass under his foot. *God, you couldn't even walk around this place in safety.*

&

Homer's first lecture was scheduled for the afternoon, but he dropped into the museum in the morning in a state of nervous anticipation. What if it was a flop? What if everybody coughed and walked out in the middle? The Oxford career of Homer Noodlehead Kelly would be a failure. People back home would hear about it and sneer at the colleague who muffed his chance abroad.

A flood of children poured into the courtyard. The soft roar of their voices ricocheted from every surface. Homer looked at them, relieved to get his mind off himself. They were dark-skinned children, eager and energetic. A couple of mothers were with them, and a tall blond man in a clerical collar. Homer recognized Freddy Dubchick's clergyman boyfriend.

He watched as the young man tried to get the children's attention. They were making too much noise. The hum of their voices obliterated everything but an occasional phrase—*God's world—this proof of His creative power.* Well, good for Freddy's boyfriend. Somehow he was managing to unite science and theology, and that was no easy task, as Homer knew to his sorrow. He had spent a lifetime trying to blend into a single whole the same gigantic incommensurate things.

Soon another group of children thronged into the courtyard. Now the two sets of overlapping voices mounted until they were a vast soft echoing, as though the building were a cave. The children swarmed past the fossil bones to gaze at the gray seal and the horny heads of the rhinoceroses and the gigantic spider crab. Would they notice the stone scientists on their pedestals?

They did not. If the golden statues had been placed there by the founders of the museum as an inspiration to the young, the spell wasn't working, at least not on these children.

It worked on Homer. He liked the stony presences. He especially liked the brooding figure of Charles Darwin, looking down in melancholy wonder at the coelacanth below him in its glass case. The carved stone image might have been the living man himself, the author of the books Homer was reading with such awe. The struggle for existence was occupying the two of them now, Charles Darwin and Homer Kelly—the flies in Paraguay that laid their eggs in the navels of cattle, which checked the cattle's increase, which protected the vegetation from overgrazing, which led to the increase of insects, and therefore to more insectivorous birds, which protected the cattle in their turn. It was battle within battle, horrifying and majestic. It was the truth in all its fierce beauty.

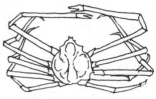

"Oh, there you are, Dr. Kelly." Hal Shaw emerged from an aisle between two rows of display cases, accompanied by a sullen-looking student. Homer remembered the student from the reception. He was the Rhodes scholar who had been so eager to find Professor Dubchick.

Hal was glad to interrupt his tutorial session with Mark Soffit. He had brought him down to the exhibits in the courtyard to point out some really basic things about which the guy seemed oddly ignorant. "The legs of the isopods, you see, are less specialized. Look at the decapods. Do you see the difference?"

"Tell me about it," said Mark, gruffly sarcastic.

$\mathbf{\backslash}$

William Dubchick left his office and groped his way into the hall. His glasses were askew on his nose, and he couldn't see a thing. He had made another attempt at fixing them with tape, but the temple pieces became unhinged at once. Everything was out of focus. He was barely conscious of dark objects on the floor of the corridor, but he managed to stumble around them and squeeze past the scaffolding on the stairs.

On the ground floor, peering into the brilliant sunlight, William made out a group of people at the other end of the courtyard. One of them was Homer Kelly.

He was anxious to speak to Kelly, to thank him, to apologize for his daughter, and he called out, "Oh, Dr. Kelly," and started blindly forward, stepping carefully over an obstacle that reared up in his way.

But the obstacle was only the shadow of the collection box. He did not see the box itself. Stumbling into it, he lost his balance and hit the floor very hard.

Homer Kelly, Mark Soffit and Hal Shaw saw his strange high step, and then his fall. All three ran across the courtyard to help the old man get to his feet.

As they ran, Mark murmured to Hal, "Did you see that? He's going senile."

"No, no," said Hal, hoping with all his heart that it wasn't true.

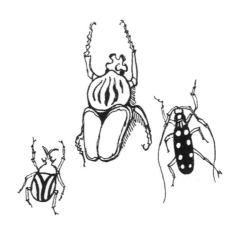

CHAPTER 18

I mark this day with a white stone.

Charles Dodgson

So it was Helen Farfrae rather than William Dubchick who noticed the significance of the jars on the floor of the corridor outside the Zoology Office. She came in late and rushed upstairs, scrambling past the scaffolding, saying a breathless good morning to the men mortaring bricks high above her on the wooden platform. Then she stopped short in the gallery corridor and stared at the jars. One of the workmen was sweeping the mess of glass and blackened contents to one side.

Helen was instantly alert. "What happened? Where did all these jars come from?"

"I'm sorry, missus. It was my fault it broke, I didn't know there was anything under the tarp."

"Under the tarp! You mean all these jars were under the tarpaulin?"

"They weren't here when I put the tarp down. This very same tarp."

"But who—?" Helen stared at the jars, then reached down slowly to pick one up by the edge of its sealed lid. She read the label aloud, "Griskin of Pork."

"Right," said the workman. "It's a lot of preserves. My grandmother, she used to put things up. But this stuff, it's pressed tongue and stuffed pheasant, weird stuff like that.

DEVONIAN LIMESTONE
MARYCHURCH

DEVONIAN LIMESTONE

Somebody's idea of a joke, dumping them here. Don't worry, we'll have them out of your way in a jiffy. Frank'll be up with a bunch of boxes."

"It sounds like an old cookery book." Helen took the jar to the railing and held it to the light. Turning it carefully to examine the dim contents, she shook her head. "This isn't griskin of pork."

At that moment Frank appeared, carrying a couple of cardboard cartons. "It's okay, love," he said to Helen. "We'll pack these right up and get 'em out of your way."

Helen looked at Frank with flashing eyes. "No, no, I don't want them out of my way. For God's sake, don't throw them away. Here, I'll tell you what to do. Pack them in the boxes very carefully. Hold the jars by the edges, like this, do you see? And bring them into my office, this office right here." Swiftly she unlocked the office door, then turned back and said eagerly, "Oh, and don't throw away the broken one. Wait, I'll get you a container to put it in. Save all the pieces. Save the contents too, if you can, that black stuff in the corner."

&

Homer Kelly was dithering with stage fright. He whined aloud as he dressed for his first lecture. "The idea of somebody from a barbaric provincial institution trying to enlighten a bunch of highly educated British undergraduates, my God, how did I get myself into this?"

Mary looked up from the Oxford map she had bought at Blackwell's. "A barbaric provincial institution—you mean Harvard University?"

"Certainly."

"Oh, Homer, for heaven's sake, you've got an inferiority complex about your own country. That's ridiculous."

"No, it's not. Americans are a bunch of callow, sentimental, gushy, undereducated louts, and I'm the worst of the lot."

"And your average British kid is all-wise and all-wonderful, is that it?"

Homer fumbled with his tie. "That's it. That's precisely it."

"What about Stuart Grebe? He's an American. He's supposed to be really clever."

"Oh, God, don't talk to me about Stuart. I spent the morning getting him out of trouble. He's like some wacky computer hacker at home. He's been blundering around in the private computer files of a couple of biochemists and a very important geneticist. They caught him at it, and they're mad as hell. No, Mary dear, Stuart Grebe will not do as a model of American brilliance. And neither will I."

"Now look here, Homer, don't you think Dr. Jamison had a reason for inviting you here to lecture?"

"Oh, God, I don't know. The point is, I'm scared out of my wits."

Homer's fear increased as he crossed Parks Road. He felt like a fool. Who was he, the son of a traffic cop, educated in a Boston night school, to think he had anything worthwhile to say to Oxford undergraduates? Homer thought of institutions of higher learning all over the place, Ivy League universities back home, homely little schools in Zaire, or Kenya, or Malaya, and glassy new colleges in Third World capitals around the world. Some of them might be good, just as good as this place, or better—who could tell? But Oxford had the most glitter in the air around its name, it had the most lions and unicorns and heraldic bearings, it was the most revered educational institution in the world.

He was an hour early in the museum. Homer went to the lecture hall and tested the equipment, switching on the speaker's lamp and switching it off again, muttering into the microphone, *It was a dark and stormy night*. He tried out the podium, leaning on it this way, then that way, then stood back ostentatiously with his hands in his pockets. He looked at his watch. He still had fifty-five minutes to go.

At loose ends, he wandered out into the gallery. His alarm was mounting. Then to his relief he saw something going on across the courtyard. Helen Farfrae was laughing and carrying a box into the Zoology Office. Homer loped around the gallery to see what was happening.

"Oh, Dr. Kelly, come in," said Helen. "See what we've found."

Homer beamed, his fear giving way to curiosity. "Please call me Homer, Dr. Farfrae."

"Oh, good, Homer, but only if you'll call me Helen. Now look, just look at these things." She spread her hands over the boxes on the table. "I think this is why that intruder was here on Friday night. He was putting all these jars on the floor outside the office door, hiding them under the tarpaulin. Did you see one out there in the corridor? Remember, I told you I heard him come in and go out again a couple of times? Obviously he couldn't bring all of them in at once. Next morning one of the workmen found a couple of empty boxes on the floor of the corridor, and he tossed them over the railing." Helen's voice rose in excitement. "Remember, Homer, we saw that box on the head of James Watt? They must have been *his* boxes. He brought them up here one at a time, full of jars, and shoved the jars under the tarpaulin. Then he heard Bobby Fenwick coming after him, so he left the boxes on the floor and took off."

Homer was delighted. "It was a reverse burglary, bringing stuff in instead of taking stuff out. What did the guy think he was doing? What *is* all this stuff anyway?"

Helen held up one of the jars. "You see, it says 'Potted Beef' on the label, but look at it—that's not potted beef. And a lot of the labels don't make sense. You wouldn't put haunch of venison in a jar. It's some kind of marine animal. A lot of little crayfish, I think." She returned the jar tenderly to the box. "They're in terrible shape."

"But what the hell for? I mean, why on earth did someone

bring all this old stuff here in the middle of the night? Why didn't he want to be seen doing it? And why did he put it outside your door?" Homer held up his hand and counted fingers. "So there were three things going on in the museum that night. What have they got to do with one another? Someone was dumping all these mysterious jars outside this office, the night watchman fell to his death from the roof—a roof it's impossible to climb—and a couple of crazy kids stole the picture of the dodo. Did you hear about that?"

"Make way there," said Hal Shaw dramatically, coming into the office with William Dubchick on his arm.

"Oh, Professor Dubchick," said Helen eagerly, "look what we've found." Then she stopped, shocked to see him hobbling to his desk. "Oh, sir, are you all right?"

"It was just a little spill," said William.

"No sign of a fracture on the X ray," said Hal. "They told us he has the bones of a young man."

That's what comes of climbing trees in Ecuador, thought

Homer enviously, feeling his own bones go soft. He said nothing, and watched as Helen explained the jars on the table.

She was glowing with excitement. She lifted one bottle out, and then another. "Whoever made these cookery labels didn't know anything about preserving food. And of course they're not preserves at all. They're marine animals, all of them, I'm sure they are."

William and Hal caught the infection at once. They bent over the jars and picked up samples and held them to the light.

"This one's a Grapsus of some kind," said Hal. "And this one—wouldn't you say it's some sort of Porcellana, Professor Dubchick?" He looked up at William, then glanced eagerly at Helen.

Homer stared at the three of them. They were grinning at one another. "Oh, I get it," he said, as the light dawned. "You think they might be Darwin's missing crabs, is that it?"

Hal shook his head doubtfully. "Of course the jars aren't right. Darwin didn't use this kind of jar. Neither did Thomas Bell, who got the crabs from Darwin."

"What about the labels?" said Helen. "Look, one of them shows under the cookery label. It's got a number."

"Good, good," said William, rubbing his hands gleefully, "then we can compare them." He turned to Helen. "Haven't we got all the old Bell Collection labels filed away somewhere?"

"Of course. They're in the file downstairs." Helen disappeared with a flick of skirt and a swirl of short gray hair. In a moment she was back with a manila folder. "Here we are." Delicately she extracted a sheet covered with small strips of paper, and read the heading aloud. *"Labels removed from jars of crustaceans in the Thomas Bell Collection."*

Homer peered at them over her shoulder. "Uh-oh, the handwriting's different."

William's face fell. "Oh, too bad."

"What about the numbers?" said Hal quickly. "If the numbers are the same, the handwriting doesn't matter."

They looked at each other blankly.

"Well?" said Homer. "How about it? You can tear off the cookbook labels, can't you? I mean, they're not important, are they?"

"It isn't that," said William. "It's just that the numbers and descriptions of the missing crabs aren't in this museum. They're at Down House, Darwin's house in Kent."

"Ah," said Helen, nodding wisely, "we need the red notebooks."

Homer burst out laughing. "The red notebooks! The sacred books of the holy shrine! What's the matter? Are they kept in a tabernacle and brought out once a year to perform miracles of healing? What's the trouble?"

Hal's homely face lit up. "There's no trouble. It means somebody has to go there, that's all. I hereby volunteer."

"May I go with you?" said Homer impulsively.

"Of course."

William laughed. "Excellent."

"I'll give you a list of all the Darwin crabs in the museum," said Helen eagerly. "Then when you find a crab in the red notebooks that isn't on the list, you'll know it's one of the missing ones, and we can see if it's in one of these jars."

"Can you go this afternoon?" said Hal to Homer. "There's a train to London at three o'clock."

"London? Is Down House in London?"

"No, but you have to go to London first, then take a train to Kent. It will take the rest of the day and half the night to get there and come back."

"Well, I just have to deliver my lecture"—Homer glanced at his watch and yelped—"my God, in five minutes! But then I'll be free, so that's fine. Righteo." Then he gulped. "Oh, sorry. Do you people say righteo? You don't? Oh, I say, I'm sorry. Whoops, there I go again. You do say, *Oh, I say,* don't you?"

Helen laughed. "Just in old films. Don't worry, Homer, your Briticisms are so out of date, they sound like Americanisms to me."

Homer said goodbye and galloped down the corridor in the direction of the lecture hall, dodging past another bunch of workmen putting up scaffolding in a new place.

"Sorry," said one of them, moving a bucket of mortar out of Homer's way.

"Oh, it's *quite* all right," said Homer, falling into old British film language once again.

Hal Shaw was also in a rush. He hurried in the direction of the north staircase and the Vertebrate Spirit Store to tell his wife he'd be away until midnight. But as he ran he glanced down into the courtyard and saw Freddy Dubchick looking at the elephant skeletons, then moving on disconsolately to stare up at the stone figure of the Prince Consort.

Margo had been telling him about Freddy. She was a spoiled child, Margo said, immature and ignorant, wild for sex. Hal kept his mouth shut, a response learned by hard experience. At home in their rented flat on Walton Street he shuffled from room to room like one of Darwin's giant Galápagos tortoises, grunting noncommittal replies to his wife's sharp interrogations. His marriage was a mistake, but he was doing his damnedest not to let it ruin his life.

He wondered if Freddy was really wild for sex. She might be immature, but she certainly wasn't ignorant. Talking to her he felt nimble and intelligent, like the gray seal in the museum courtyard, *Halichoerus grypus,* diving and plunging around her, bobbing to the surface, offering conversational fishes plucked from the depths of the sea. And Freddy too sported and splashed, her round eyes bright. He went to her at once.

Helen Farfrae looked down at them from the gallery above. Hal Shaw and Freddy Dubchick were laughing together, talking, gazing at each other. *She's a silly girl, of course,* thought Helen enviously, *so young and pretty, so lucky. No, no, she's not silly, she's just young. How wonderful to be able to laugh like that!*

"What are you laughing at?" said Hal, grinning at Freddy. "What did I say that's so funny?"

"It's not that," said Freddy impulsively. "It's your feathers. They're so—" She burst out laughing again.

"My *feathers?*"

Freddy tried to control herself. "It's nothing. Never mind." She couldn't possibly explain her Darwinian revelation, that Hal Shaw's peacock tail was even more splendid than Oliver Clare's, even though Hal wasn't nearly as good-looking. His sharp mind and cleverness were his peacock tail, and they were iridescent, the feathers were radiant, green and gold and blue. But how could she tell him that? Oh, she shouldn't have laughed.

Hal looked at his watch. "I've got to go," he said brusquely, and tore himself away.

His feelings are hurt, thought Freddy regretfully. *He thinks I'm laughing at him, when really the truth is, I'm falling in love with him.*

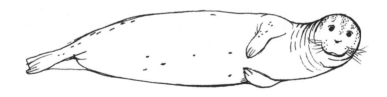

CHAPTER 19

I this day paid horse-hire for thirty-one leagues.
Charles Darwin, *The Voyage of the Beagle*

It was phenomenal, the speed with which the wild new canes established themselves beside the ditch on the Botley Road. Up they sprang, their thick stems fleshy and splotched with red. The rain came down and the warm sun of autumn shone. Cars moved in and out of the parking lot, but none were rented to botanists, who might have looked down into the ditch and taken quick action.

Homer's lecture passed muster. He began with an arrogant roar from Walt Whitman, *Come, muse, migrate from Greece and Ionia!* and went on to picture her tossing on the Atlantic in her frail bark, leaving the European poets gasping on the shore, while the lusty young Americans held out welcoming hands. Homer's audience tittered politely. They seemed accustomed to insults.

"As soon as I got a look at them," said Homer as he boarded the London train with Hal Shaw, "I forgot to be scared. They looked just like kids at home, scruffy and healthy and young, very young. I threw in a couple of my best jokes, and they seemed to like that." They sat down in the half-filled car. "Stuart Grebe was there, unfortunately. He asked some really

115

sharp questions, damn him, and I had a hell of a time invent-ing plausible answers."

"Stuart Grebe?" said Hal. "What's Stuart doing at one of your lectures? He's a biochemist."

"Pure hoggishness. Stuart's a megalomaniac. He wants to gobble up everything in the university, swallow it whole. The trouble is, he's also a dangerous criminal."

"A criminal?" said Hal, startled. "You don't mean it?"

"Well, no, not really. It's just that he has too many strokes of genius for his own good." Homer looked around as the train silked forward on its way to Paddington. "I must say, I'm disappointed. Where are all the compartments? I thought British trains had lots of little doors and charming compart-ments full of mysterious-looking occupants, some of them in disguise."

Hal laughed, and picked up a newspaper someone had left on the seat. "Sorry, Homer."

He was unable to read a word. Homer kept him talking about *The Origin of Species*. "Tell me about the eye. It was a ghastly problem for Darwin, wasn't it? People said it couldn't have evolved little by little because it wouldn't do any good until it was all there—lens, cornea, retina, iris, everything."

"Chapter Six," said Hal patiently. "You'll get to it. The point is, there were a lot of small steps that were useful, like gelatinous spots on starfish that helped them tell light from dark. Things like that. The eye developed gradually, just like everything else."

"Oh, I see," said Homer humbly. "But what about—?"

Only in the London underground did he quiet down, be-cause of the racketing roar. He kept his mouth shut too in the passageways between platforms, where they were carried along in thick floods of Londoners all pouring in the same direction.

"My God, Hal," puffed Homer, "how does a guy from Kansas know his way around so well?"

"My mother's British. She got rid of me every summer by sending me to my Aunt Peggy in Nottingham."

Hal kept talking as he dodged into another passage. Homer struggled to keep up. He sprinted forward, edging around a throng of elderly women upholstered with shopping bags. "What did you say?"

"I said things were pretty bad at home. Aunt Peggy saved my life. She took me to the Natural History Museum in London."

"The Natural History Museum, I see. That's how you started being interested in zoology? Well, listen, what about—?" As they boarded the train to Bromley South they were deep in blind moles and eyeless animals in caves. Even on the bus from Bromley South, Homer didn't stop asking questions. He was still babbling as they walked along the country road from the village of Downe. Only at the door of Down House did his interrogation break off at last.

Here they were greeted by an excited old gentleman. "Come in, come in, Dr. Shaw. And this is Dr. Kelly? Oh, do come in. My name is Frolic. Yes, yes, the notebooks are here. You are in luck. They were loaned to Cambridge years ago, but they have recently been returned. So fortunate. Come right this way. Have you seen Mr. Darwin's study? No? This is your first visit? Oh, you must see it, you must see it! Come right this way!"

They followed Mr. Frolic into the study, and admired the rolling stool and the round table with its mineral specimens. Homer imagined the Darwin children popping in to borrow the foot rule. Was this the sofa where he lay groaning while Emma read aloud? The room looked like a place where work had been going on until only recently.

"I wonder if these are really his books," said Hal. "Homer, do you know what he did with a heavy book? Too big to hold? He tore it in half."

"How sensible," said Homer.

"How dreadful!" said Mr. Frolic, who had been rising and falling on his toes. "Now, if you're *quite* finished, I'll show you the Beagle memorabilia. This way, if you please."

The object of their journey was in the next room. There they were, many small notebooks, lying side by side in a large display case, along with tools and instruments carried by *El Naturalista Don Carlos* in Brazil and Argentina and Tierra del Fuego—collecting boxes, folding compasses, a spyglass, a pistol.

"Imagine fitting yourself out for a voyage that would last for years," said Homer. "How could he possibly know all he would need?"

Mr. Frolic jingled his keys. "If you're *quite* ready?" he said, dancing forward.

"We'd better get to work," murmured Hal.

At once the impetuous Mr. Frolic opened the case and ex-

tracted three of the little red books. Each bore a pasted label, *Catalogue for Animals in Spirits of Wine*.

Homer took them reverently. Mr. Frolic waved his arm at a table, swooped out a pair of chairs and bowed in invitation.

They settled down. "We don't have to copy everything," Hal said to Homer. "Just the entries labeled C for Crustacean. And then only the ones that aren't on the museum list. Be sure to write down Darwin's numbers, so we can compare them with the numbers on those mysterious jars. You got it?"

"Got it," said Homer, opening the first of the small books. At once he began copying entries.

1832 PORTO PRAYA
41 C Two upper Crustacea from Praya.—
others taken at sea between this & Canary.—

1832 BAIA BLANCA
404 C Crust: Isopod: body very flat crawling on sand
bank at lowest ebb.

Susceptible as he was, it was impossible for Homer to be unmoved. In this pleasant room in the English countryside he felt the heat of tropical latitudes, the winds of the Atlantic, and the rocking of the ship that had kept its naturalist seasick all the way around the world. He imagined Darwin going ashore whenever the Beagle dropped anchor, eating roast armadillo in the Argentine, buying cigars in Buenos Aires and biting his matches alight, looking eagerly at every organic or inorganic thing, collecting every kind of mineral, insect, butterfly, and mammal, reaching into tide pools along a rocky shore. Back on shipboard, as the Beagle sailed by the light of an erupting volcano, he would pick up one of these little books and jot down every creature—*taken by one of the sailors out of a large fish; water but slightly salt.*

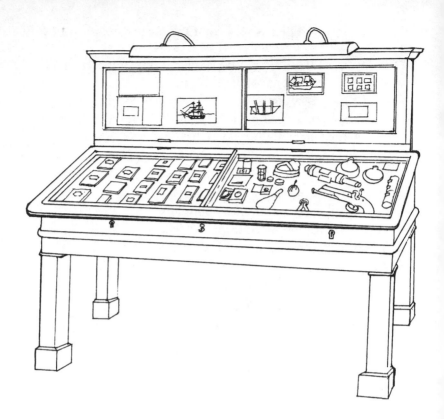

"How're you doing?" said Hal, reaching for another book.

"Whoops, sorry. I'm way behind. Daydreaming. Won't happen again."

Within the hour they were finished. They had a list of entries—crabs that were not on the museum list, that were not to be found in the museum, either in the drawers of Beagle specimens or in the rows of jars in the Invertebrate Spirit Store. Mission accomplished.

It was a long way back. Homer dozed. Hal flipped through the new lists, reading the entries over and over, memorizing the numbers. Sometimes Freddy Dubchick's fresh face obtruded itself, and his thoughts were violently diverted. *Her face is round like a smooth stone. Margo's is triangular like—what is it like?—oh, God, I know, the head of a praying mantis.*

Then Hal's mind would jump back to Bahía Blanca and the centipedes with long blue legs. What was their number? Thirty-five. *Centipedes at Bahía Blanca, thirty-five.*

Back in Oxford at last, climbing into a cab in the dark, Homer was sleepy and starving, Hal was merciless.

"Parks Road," he said to the driver, "the University Museum. We've got to find out," he said to Homer. "We've got to see if the numbers match."

"Oh, right," said Homer drowsily, thinking of the contents of the little rented refrigerator in the improvised kitchen in the Besse Building. "Big excitement if they do match, right? Big discovery? Headline news?"

"Well, it will certainly be a big satisfaction," admitted Hal, trying to suppress his excitement.

In the museum a sawhorse blocked the south staircase. Hal and Homer skirted it and climbed the stairs, sidling past the scaffolding. The dim lamps over the courtyard barely lit the shadowy gallery, but Hal in his eagerness could have found his way in pitch darkness. Unlocking the door of the Zoology Office, he plunged in, snatching the Down House lists from his pocket.

Homer switched on the lights and watched him kneel beside the table to study the labels on the jars, which no longer said Jugged Hare or Boiled Brisket. Helen Farfrae had soaked off the cookbook labels. Hal kept looking down at the list in his hand and up again at the jars, then down again, shaking his head.

"What's the matter?" said Homer sleepily. "Don't they match?"

"No, goddamn it," said Hal, getting up off his knees. "They don't match at all." He looked angrily at Homer. "The numbers on the jars don't make sense. They're completely random. This one's numbered seventeen, and here's a *three thousand* seventeen. And there are only about eighty jars all together."

Homer had a bright thought. "How many things did Darwin collect? Wouldn't the numbers be sort of miscellaneous, scattered among all the other kinds of things? Guanacos and tortoises and beetles and whatnot?"

"Oh, sure, but his numbers only go up to fifteen hundred or so. This is some miserable collection gathered a long time ago by some nut or other, and totally neglected. I'm afraid it doesn't have anything to do with Charles Darwin at all."

"But why," said Homer, "did somebody dump it in the museum?"

"Damned if I know." Hal turned out the lights, and they started gloomily down the south staircase, dodging once again around the sawhorse that acted as a barrier. "Careful," said Hal. "You can't tell the stairs from the boards they've laid over the scaffolding. Watch out."

They parted company in the driveway. But as Homer slogged across the lawn, Hal called after him, "Of course there's still one more thing we can do, although it's a hell of a job."

"What's that?" said Homer, his mind's eye fixed on a bottle of cold beer.

"We can look at the contents of the damn jars. Maybe they'll match the list of missing crustaceans, even if the labels aren't right."

And cheese! There was a big smelly cheese in there somewhere.

"Is it possible to figure out what they are? I mean when they're in such bad shape?"

"Oh, probably. At least some of them. I'll put that Rhodes scholar kid onto it. What's his name? Soffit, Mark Soffit. Test him out. See if he knows one crustacean from another."

CHAPTER 20

*I am out of patience with the Zoologists . . . for their mean
quarrelsome spirit.*

Charles Darwin, letter to J. S. Henslow

M ark Soffit was determined to find the missing Darwin crabs. He was convinced that they were lost in the museum somewhere. He had no keys to locked offices, but there was nothing to stop him from knocking on doors.

He began with a room where a geology technician was using a pressurized drill to free the bones of a pliosaur from its stony matrix. "Hi, there," he said, speaking up over the noise of the drill. "My name's Mark Soffit. I'm a Rhodes scholar. I'm interested in what's going on around here."

The technician nodded, then bent over the pliosaur again with his back to Mark. His drill whined. Mark explored the room, softly opening cupboards and drawers.

In the new Entomology Room, where two other technicians were setting up an exhibit about the habits of locusts, he found an interesting closet, but it yielded nothing, only a couple of discarded displays on anthophorine bees in Israel and a box labeled DUNG BEETLES, TANZANIA.

In the Mineralogy Office two graduate students were cataloguing new donations. "Look at this bottinoite," said one of the mineralogists. "See the label? It's from Ysbyty Ystwyth in Wales. My sister goes out with a guy from Ysbyty Ystwyth. It's a small world." He looked up at Mark. "Well, hello there, you want something?"

"I'm a Rhodes scholar," recited Mark. "My name's Mark Soffit, and I'm interested in what's going on around here."

"Oh, well, we're pretty busy right now," said one of the mineralogists, dismissing him.

His partner winked at him. "Why don't you give him your paper on compreignacite from Cornwall? That would be a start."

"No, thanks," said Mark, refusing to be put off. "I'll just take a look around." The mineralogists stared at him suspiciously as he opened a closet door.

It was no good. Mark gave up and went back to the Zoology Office. Surely there were nooks and crannies in this ancient office that hadn't been examined in years.

But Hal Shaw was in the Zoology Office, and at once he wanted to put Mark to work. "Look, how'd you like to try your hand at identifying these things? We were hoping they'd match the list of missing Darwin crabs, but the numbers don't fit."

Mark looked with distaste at the wizened contents of the jars on the table. "Identify them? But there's nothing to identify. They're half-rotten."

"Just see what you can do."

Mark felt put-upon. It was an insult. They were palming off on him the dirtiest job, the most unrewarding. This wasn't legitimate research. Dr. Shaw himself said they weren't really the missing crabs.

Hal left him to it. Mark stared at the ugly jars. He was filled with resentment. If Hal Shaw thought a Rhodes scholar like himself was going to spend his valuable time in Oxford sorting decomposing trash, he had another think coming.

When Professor Dubchick came in a moment later with an armful of books, Mark went over Hal's head at once, and complained about the assignment. "Professor Dubchick, I wonder if I could read with another tutor? Like yourself, for instance? I mean, Dr. Shaw wants me to identify all this putrefying stuff on the table here." Mark waved his hand contemptuously at the jars of desiccated crabs. "I feel I should have a more worthwhile assignment. I mean, as a Rhodes scholar I didn't cross the ocean in order to—"

Professor Dubchick interrupted him sharply. "Why *did* you cross the ocean, Mr. Soffit?"

"Well," blustered Mark, "I thought you people were at the cutting edge around here. I thought—"

"Perhaps this putrefying stuff *is* the cutting edge," said William. Without another word he put the books down softly on his desk and left the room.

Mark's face turned purple with mortification. Picking up one of the jars, he stared at the clotted fragments inside it, then slammed it back down and went in search of Hal Shaw.

He found him in the lecture hall, battering at the blackboard with a piece of chalk. Swiftly Mark made it clear that he wasn't about to work on those crummy mildewed jars.

"Well, then," said Hal, his voice cool, "perhaps I'd better find someone else to do them."

"Perhaps you'd better." Mark smiled, having won this encounter. He wasn't about to allow a guy only a few years older than himself to put one over on him.

ے

Margo Shaw, too, was unimpressed with the jars of desiccated crabs. She stared at Hal, disbelieving. "You mean you want me to top up all this trash?"

"Well, yes, I do." Hal was irritated. "They've got to be rehydrated with a special formula. Here, I've mixed up some to start with, a three percent solution of Decon 90 in de-ionized water. They're in desperate need of care. Look at them, they've been neglected for years."

"I am looking at them. What the hell are they doing here?

They're disgusting. Who says they're Darwin's? You said the numbers don't match. Why don't you throw them out?"

"Because Professor Dubchick is curious about them," said Hal defensively. "And so am I."

"Oh, it's Dubchick's idea, is it?" Margo looked sly. "Look, Hal, why don't you grow up? The old guy is past it. He's doddering. You're wasting your time. Dubchick's a has-been, and his daughter is a tramp. Listen, let me tell you what else I found out about her."

BACON

Hal blew up. Margo gushed a stream of poison, and stalked out of the office. Hal calmed his rioting nerves and went looking for Professor Dubchick.

He found him in the courtyard, leaning against a stone pedestal, jotting a note to himself. Above Dubchick's head Francis Bacon looked down at the two of them shrewdly, and warned, *There is no other course but to begin the work anew.*

It was precisely what Hal had in mind. Trembling with anger, he told Professor Dubchick he would work on the crabs himself. It would, he said, be an honor.

William smiled at him and put away his notes. "No, no, you've got your own important work to do. Tell you what, my book can wait. I'll do the jars myself. Dr. Farfrae and I, we'll do them together."

And they did. They spent a couple of days carrying out the process of rehydration, then got to work. After removing the contents of the first jar to a sterilized saucer, William probed carefully, and examined minute slices under Helen's powerful microscope. "I think this is a species of Cancroid," he said, peering into the eyepiece. He stood up. "What do you think?"

It was pleasant work, if a little foul-smelling. "It's going to take weeks," said William, as Helen sat down. "Can you take so much time?"

"Of course I can, if you can. Whenever you're ready with your last chapters, I'll get back to checking references. In the meantime—" Helen lowered her head and stared into the microscope. "It certainly does look like a Cancer. *Cancer gracilis,* perhaps?" She looked up at William and asked the nagging question that had been troubling them from the beginning. "But why? Why did someone leave them there, hidden under that cloth, and say nothing? Who was it? And where have all these jars been for the last century and a half?"

"Oh, Dr. Farfrae, you're assuming they're the missing Darwin crabs." William shook his head. "Don't forget, they may not be."

"But look, there's a Cancer on the list." Helen snatched up one of the typed pages she had copied from the Down House list. "*Number 311, July 1832, picked up in Monte Video.* This may be the very same one."

"But Cancer is a very common crab. I had one for lunch the other day." William bent over the microscope again. "All we can do is carry on, and see how many matches we can get, if any."

"I hope," said Helen dreamily, watching him make delicate focusing adjustments, "Detective Inspector Mukerji is working on it."

"You told him about the jars?" murmured William, staring at the translucent fragment of a maxilla.

"Oh, yes. He seemed most interested. I told him we'd tried to be careful about fingerprints, and he said he was grateful. He sent over a detective constable named Ives to take prints from the jars, and he was very thorough."

William looked up. "Did he find anything?"

"Our prints, of course. Yours and mine. We've been a little careless. Nothing else. All of them showed the imprint of leather gloves." Helen moved away from the table and looked out the window at the building next door. "How strange to be working on something that came to us so mysteriously, like a gift from—" She paused, afraid of being melodramatic.

"From the unknown," said William, sounding melodramatic himself.

"From the dark, I was going to say," said Helen. "A gift from the dark."

❧

The truth was that Gopal Mukerji was in the dark himself. He too was bewildered by the mysterious things that had happened in the Oxford University Museum during the night of October fourth and the early morning of the fifth.

In the first place, he took with a grain of salt Dr. Farfrae's story about the person she called "the creature," the one she had seen climbing the museum roof. In Mukerji's opinion, Farfrae was an odd woman. Strange, the way she had wandered around the courtyard in the middle of the night. It was not what you would call normal behavior. And it was rumored that her family life was troubled. Just for the hell of it Detective Inspector Mukerji sat down in front of his office computer and tapped out her husband's name.

There he was, *John Farfrae, Woodstock Road, Kidlington.* Drunk and disorderly, two convictions. Disturbing the peace, complaint by a neighbor, raised voices, family fight, another conviction.

Family fight? How strange that the dignified woman with the gray hair and the D.Phil. degree from Oxford University should be raising her voice in a domestic battle with her husband in the town of Kidlington! Mukerji wondered if another dispute had followed the publication in the newspaper of the story she had told him. She had been so anxious to keep it from her husband, but of course it had leaked out.

And then there was the doubtful prank of the two young people from Christ Church, their so-called rescue of the painting of the extinct bird. Was it too much of a coincidence that they should have been there in the museum at precisely the moment when the young night watchman was falling to his death? Surely the statistical chances were small.

The final perplexities were two. Was the thing Dr. Farfrae had seen on the roof of the museum the night watchman, or someone else? If not Bobby Fenwick, then who was it? And what had become of him? At the moment, the whole thing was beyond Mukerji's understanding, and he threw up his hands.

CHAPTER 21

Many cock birds do not so much pursue the hen, as display their plumage, perform strange antics, and pour forth their song in her presence.

Charles Darwin, *The Descent of Man*

DIARY OF FREDERICKA DUBCHICK

Americans are so interesting. I've always liked them, but I used to lump them all together. I thought

1) they were loud and vulgar,

2) they talked through their noses,

3) they said anything that came into their heads, without British restraint and reserve and all that bilgewater.

Now I can see that they're all different. I mean they're just as different from one another as we are. Look at Homer Kelly, for instance. He doesn't talk funny, and neither does his wife Mary. Homer talks fast and is so amusing and excited, and he uses good grammar. Sometimes he sounds like a phony Englishman, but then he hits his head and apologizes and tries to stop. He has a big nose, but he doesn't talk through it.

His wife talks like a New Englander, that's what Stuart Grebe tells me. And, oh, Stuart is so funny! He speaks like somebody in an old gangster film. Then there's Mark Soffit. I can't figure him out at all. Father doesn't like him. He hasn't said so, but I can tell. Mark doesn't say much, he just stares.

Hal and Margo Shaw came to dinner the other day, and I made something from my new French cookbook, Filets de Poisson Gratinés à la Parisienne—in other words, fish poached in white wine. The sauce was supposed to be like velvet, but instead it was lumpy. The whole thing was an awful flop, but Father laughed, and Hal had three helpings (so kindly, because it really was the most terrible failure), and then he insisted on helping with the dishes, while Father talked to Margo in the sitting room, and we had such a good time in the kitchen. Hal juggled the salt and pepper pots and the knives and forks.

I challenged him to try our best teacups, but he refused. He knows all there is to know about crustaceans, and he's found new sorts of fossils in the Swiss Alps on remote mountain peaks. Father likes him.

So do I!!!!!!!!!!!!!!!!!!!!!!

Margo Shaw left most of her dinner on her plate!

I've promised to go to Burford with Oliver. It's the home of his sacred ancestors, all those bishops and archbishops and Knights of the Garter. At first I said I was too busy, but he said it would just be two or three hours because it's only eighteen miles away, so I said all right, but the truth is I don't want to go! A POX ON BISHOPS AND KNIGHTS OF THE GARTER! (Putting a pox on things is my favorite new curse, it sounds so eighteenth-century, like Henry Fielding or Samuel Johnson.)

C H A P T E R   2 2

"I have answered three questions, and that is enough,"
Said his father. "Don't give yourself airs!
Do you think I can listen all day to such stuff?
Be off, or I'll kick you down-stairs!"
    Lewis Carroll, *Alice's Adventures in Wonderland*

M argo Shaw cornered Professor Dubchick in the south
gallery as he approached the Zoology Office. "Oh, Professor Dubchick, I've been wanting to speak to you."

William paused and looked at her soberly. At last week's
dinner party he had taken a dislike to the woman. She had
questioned him eagerly about his years in Ecuador, but she
had really been boasting at the same time, showing herself an
old hand at primate physiology. Glibly she had touched on the
digestive systems of proboscis monkeys and the grooming
habits of baboons. William had responded politely as she
skipped from primate to primate, while her flattery ran off
him and puddled on the floor. Her understanding was shallow. He guessed she had been reading some sort of popular
book, *Our Cousins of the Jungle.*

Now she slipped an envelope into his hand. "I hope you
will look favorably on my little plea," she said, simpering.
Margo was the possessor of one dimple. Turning her head
slightly, she gave it full play.

"Certainly," murmured William. Turning away abruptly,
he thrust the envelope into his coat.

In the office he read Margo's letter with mounting anger.

Dear Professor Dubchick (William, if I may presume!),

As you know I have been engaged in topping up the containers in the museum's vertebrate and invertebrate spirit stores. While this is not an onerous duty, it makes little use of my education and experience.

I have an undergraduate degree in biology from Sweet Briar, summa cum laude. My master's thesis at the University of Virginia was a study of malocostracans in Chesapeake Bay. (Hal and I met beside a rock pool, each with our collecting nets!) And to cap it all, I am au courant with computers and all current office software. In other words, I feel highly qualified to act as your assistant, particularly in the preparation of the book on which, I understand, you have been working for the last decade. Perhaps my strictly technical help would hurry it along a trifle?

Yours most sincerely,
Margo Shaw

William glanced up from the letter and looked at Helen Farfrae. She was sitting calmly in front of the computer, running patiently through the entries for his index, cross-referencing, expanding, adding the common names for species as well as their Latin names—*dingo* for *Canis dingo, seahorses* for *Syngnathidae.*

His anger increased. He was surprised at the ferocity of his feeling. Furiously he crumpled Margo's letter and uttered an obscenity.

Helen looked up. "Is something the matter?"

"No," said William. "Nothing is the matter. Nothing at all. Everything is perfect, absolutely perfect." Going to her he put his hand on the back of her chair and looked at the screen. "Oh, good," he said, "pygmy hog. How stupid of me to think I could get away with *Sus salvanius.*"

CHAPTER 23

"She's in that state of mind," said the White Queen, "that she wants to deny something—only she doesn't know what to deny!"
Lewis Carroll, *Through the Looking-Glass*

&

DIARY OF FREDERICKA DUBCHICK

I'm quite sure Father's forgiven me for stealing the picture of the dodo. He seems happier with those dried-up old crabs than he's been for years. Maybe it's because his book is almost done. I hope he'll be satisfied with what people say about it. Margo Shaw says it might be embarrassing. Did Hal tell her that? I can't believe it!

I think Oliver senses something new about me, that I've changed again (he calls me capricious, and maybe I am).

Yesterday he took me to Burford, to visit the stately home of his ancestors. It's called Windrush Hall, because it's right beside the Windrush River. It's a hideous nineteenth-century pile with enormous rooms full of ghastly furniture. Even the guidebook has nothing good to say about it except "Notable for early plumbing, a patent toilet and a monumental bathtub."

It doesn't belong to Oliver's family anymore, because it had to be given to the Crown or the National Trust or something when his grandparents died, in order to avoid death duties. Oliver was five years old at the time, and he's never forgotten the shock of moving out with his mother and father. He told me his parents pretend they don't mind, but he thinks they must.

Oliver certainly does. He preens himself on his connection with that heap of spoiled marble and all those gigantic bedsteads and glowering portraits and thick carpets. He had a secret place to show me, he said, and he was as proud and excited as a little boy, but it was really pitiful. It's a couple of little rooms he rents from the trustees, so that he can sleep there sometimes. How pathetic!

Then it was on, on! to the local church to see the tombs of his ancestors. It was so important for me to understand the glorious nature of his forebears (Father Bear, Mother Bear, Baby Bear, and Itty-Bitty Bear).

Oh, God, how I detest inscriptions clotted with lichen! But then we went inside the church, and I found a stone that was extremely interesting.

Oh, not the heraldic shields and elegant inscriptions all over the wall, memorials to ladies Gifted in Arts and gentlemen Virtuous and Holy. And certainly not the grandiose tablet describing the glorious qualities of His Grace, the Bishop of Warwick, 1800–1863. Oliver made me stand in front of it while he talked about the bishop's important tracts and his friendship with other princes of the church, like Pusey and Keble and Samuel Wilberforce, Bishop of Oxford.

Oliver's face simply glowed. He wants to walk in his ancestor's footsteps, he said, and start a new movement of reform, just the way the bishop did, with a revival of High Church principles and a loftier standard of Christian life in the British Isles. Oh, dear! I thought the bishop sounded terribly stuffy, but I didn't say so.

The only interesting thing about him was his early demise. According to the inscription, he was "SNATCHED BY UNTIMELY DEATH." Oliver doesn't know what happened to him. Lots of people died young in those days.

So I was only half listening when I discovered a funny little inscription crowded into a dark corner, way down near the floor. I had to get on hands and knees to read it, and then I gasped. It was a memorial to another Oliver Clare!

So of course I jumped up and asked Oliver about it, and he looked shocked, in fact he turned pale, like a Victorian lady about to swoon, and said he didn't know anything about it, but I think he did. (He does have the most beautiful pink-and-white complexion, with the rosy color coming and going.)

The dates of the first Oliver Clare were 1810 to 1863. There was only one other word on the stone:

FORGIVE!

I almost forgot the duck. Someone had scratched a crude drawing of a duck beside his name. What does it mean?

CHAPTER 24

*If you knew some of the experiments . . . which I am trying, you
would have a good right to sneer, for they are so absurd even in my
opinion that I dare not tell you.*

Charles Darwin, letter to Joseph Hooker

They were having lunch with Helen Farfrae. "I'm sorry,
Helen," said Mary. "This place is Homer's choice."

It was a tiny café on St. Giles, serving cheap greasy
food. There were small plastic tables, each with its own
ketchup, mustard, soy sauce, ashtray and paper-napkin holder.
The menu on the wall listed GAMMON STEAK & CHIPS, COR-
NISH PASTY & CHIPS, SAUSAGE EGG & CHIPS, and BEANS ON
TOAST. The tables were crowded. Amplified music boomed
above the sizzle of frying sausages.

"Number twelve!" shouted the woman behind the counter.

"That's us." Homer squeezed past a crowd of teenage girls
in heavy boots, took a handful of change out of his pocket,
looked at it with baffled concentration, and paid for his
order.

The woman picked up the coins, slapped them back
down, and gave him a drop-dead look. "I said pounds, not
pence."

"Whoops, sorry." Homer groped in his billfold and produced a ten-pound note.

She snatched it, dropped the change in his hand, and
roared, *"Thirteen!"*

Homer took the tray of beans and sausages, fried eggs and
chips, to the corner where Mary and Helen were deep in

shouted conversation. He sat down, struggling to fit his legs under the table, and said, "Humbling educational experience, living in a foreign country."

"Homer," said Mary, "Helen's wondering if the police have learned anything more about who could have dumped those jars outside her office."

Homer dug his fork into a sausage. "I talked to Mukerji this morning. He thinks Dr. Helen Farfrae is either slightly insane or else she's some kind of holy woman with second sight. I think he was joking, but I'm not sure."

Helen leaned forward and stared at Homer keenly as he opened his mouth for a forkful of sausage. "But haven't they found any sort of clue? I should think a self-respecting criminal would have the decency to drop an initialed handkerchief or a monogrammed button or something."

"Not this criminal, I'm afraid." Then Homer remembered something. He patted his jacket pockets. The left one was lumpy. He pulled out three wadded tissues, a Park and Ride ticket stub, and a small oval of stainless steel rings. Homer stuffed everything else back in his pocket and held up the object for inspection.

"What is it?" said Mary.

"I don't know. I found it at the foot of the ladder on the roof. It might have been there for ages."

"Let me see." Helen reached for it, turned it over in her hand, then gave it to Mary.

"Helen, tell me," said Homer, "why did you use the word *creature* when you talked to Mukerji about the person you saw on the roof? What did you mean, *creature?*"

Helen put down her fork and clasped her hands in her lap. "It was so extraordinary, the way it ran up the side of the glass roof. Not the way a person would try to climb it, leaning on the glass and holding on with his fingernails. It was almost *running* up that steep slope. Like—it was like—"

"Like a monkey, that's what you said."

Helen's lips tightened, and she nodded. "Yes, exactly like a monkey."

"Wow," said Mary. "Did you tell Inspector Mukerji it looked like a monkey?"

"Oh, yes. He was very polite. He wrote it down."

Homer dabbled another forkful of sausage in a pool of ketchup, and changed the subject to the scientific methods of Charles Darwin. "There was something he called fool's experiments. Did you know about that?"

"Yes, of course," said Helen eagerly. "Fool's experiments. He asked his son to play his bassoon beside a sensitive plant to see if it was affected by the music. Things like that."

"Right. He was so imaginative and clever, he tried all sorts of simple things, so simple a child could have invented them, or a fool. Only nobody did. It took someone as brilliant as Darwin to think them up." Once again Homer's conversation took a crazy zigzag. "Helen, tell me, isn't there a zoo in London somewhere?"

"Of course, in Regent's Park."

"A zoo!" said Mary. "Oh, Homer, what do you want with a zoo?"

"I want to play my bassoon, that's what, like Darwin's son."

"Your bassoon?" Helen laughed. "Oh, I see. You mean metaphorically speaking. You want to conduct a fool's experiment, like Darwin."

"Oh, good," said Mary. "I love zoos. May I come along?"

"Certainly. We'll take the 7:52 to Paddington tomorrow morning. How about it, Helen, do you want to join us?"

"I'd love to, but I can't."

A trio of large boys surged up beside them, cutting off air and light. The table was in demand. "Let's go," said Homer, standing up. "Come on, you lot." On the way out he apologized loudly, "Oh, God, I've done it again. I said 'you lot.' I can't help it. I'm really sorry."

❧

Fool's experiments—Homer tried one that afternoon. He stood in the north aisle of the museum for half an hour, looking at the display of stuffed primates, from the tiny painted tree shrew and the long-haired spider monkey to the indri and the pigtailed macaque. They clung to their short pieces of branch against the blank wall of the display case, looking homesick for the jungles of Sarawak, Brazil, Madagascar, and Java.

Then Homer moved on to the primate skeletons in the same case farther to the east—the orangutan, the gibbon, the chimpazee, the gorilla and, as a glorious final ornament to the family of anthropoid apes, a human skeleton in all its bony glory.

God, they looked alike! Well, for that matter Homer had been stunned from the beginning by his own resemblance to the iguanodon, that long-extinct dinosaur. Most of its bones were repeated in his own wincing physique.

It was even more so with the primates. Everything was the same, just warped a little out of shape. Their arms, look at the way they dangled almost to the ground! The chimpanzee was doing its best to stand upright, and the gorilla was hunched only a little forward, staring through its huge eye sockets at the backbone of *Homo sapiens*, who was marching along so arrogantly in front of the rest of them on his way to cash a check in Barclay's Bank. The orangutan brought up the rear. It didn't look so cousinly, bowed down behind the others, its fingers brushing the bottom of the display case.

Even so, it aroused twinges of recognition in Homer's bones. On the whole he recoiled from the anthropoid apes. They were too close for comfort.

But the question was, could a creature like one of these have prowled around the museum one night in October? *Exactly like a monkey,* Helen said. It wasn't hard to picture the chimpanzee, for instance, scuttling up the side of the glass roof, but of course it was impossible to imagine it with armfuls of jars containing antique crabs.

As a mental exercise, the examination of the primates in the north aisle of the museum was a perfect example of a fool's experiment. *You're a fool, all right,* Homer told himself.

But they went to the zoo anyway. It was easy to get there, once the train pulled into Paddington. You took the underground to Baker Street, then walked across Regent's Park.

"Oh, Homer, look!" said Mary. "Look at the penguins."

"You look at the penguins." Homer barreled ahead, ignoring the penguins and the grazing antelopes. In the primate house he sped past the cages of lemurs and twittering marmosets.

"Homer, wait," shouted Mary, "you've got to see the squirrel monkeys. Come back."

"No, no, they're too small." Homer emerged into the sunlight and looked around. "Ah, there we are." He bounded forward and stopped in front of the gorilla's cage. "This is more like it."

"Oh, isn't he handsome," gasped Mary, catching up. They stood silently looking at the gorilla, which was sitting calmly against a tree trunk, sorting a heap of fruit. The gorilla looked up at them briefly with its great flat face, its eyes projecting from a mass of wrinkles. They were world-weary eyes, glowing with intelligence and contempt. Delicately it plucked at a bunch of grapes.

Homer had read a book by Darwin's friend Huxley. Mary listened patiently while he explained. "He said the gorilla is more like us than any of the other apes. I don't know what people think now. I guess these days it's a matter of similarities in tooth enamel and nucleotide sequences, stuff like that, and nobody agrees with anybody else."

"Well, I don't care whether he's related to me or not," said Mary. "I like him."

Homer was mesmerized by the gorilla's great sad face. "Come on, friend," he muttered, "why don't you climb that tree?"

The gorilla showed no interest in climbing the tree. It just sat there. While they watched, it skinned a banana and ate it neatly, showing its white teeth.

They moved to the next enclosure, where four or five orangutans were swinging back and forth on ropes. "Hey, look at that," said Homer.

The orangutans were huge and red, with heavy fat bodies and long hairy arms. Their expressions were impassive, their eyes small and beady. One of the females swung her rope in the direction of a distant branch. Grasping it, she heaved herself up and sat on it solemnly, disregarding the applause of a family of children crowded at the railing.

"Hey," said Homer, "wasn't that neat? Really neat."

The children ran away to look at the chimpanzees, but Homer and Mary went on watching the grave acrobatics of the orangutans. Back and forth they swung their heavy bodies from rope to rope, from branch to branch. There was no sense of playfulness in their swinging. It was simply what orangutans did all day.

Homer was charmed. Surely an orangutan could do all sorts of things normal humans couldn't do? It might even be able to swing to the top of a glass pyramid, for instance.

His fool's experiments, he decided, were not altogether wasted.

CHAPTER 25

In all cases, in order that the males should seek efficiently, it would
be necessary that they should be endowed with strong passions.
                              Charles Darwin, *The Descent of Man*

≤

DIARY OF FREDERICKA DUBCHICK

Diary, I raise my right hand to swear to the truth. Hal
Shaw has stopped making jokes and kidding in a friendly
way and looking at me when he thinks I don't know it. He's
not just flirting anymore. For the last two weeks it's been re-
ally heavy breathing. He turns fiery red when he tries to talk
to me, only he can't talk because his voice is knotted up in
his throat. (How I love it! How I love every embarrassed
blotch on his face! every choked remark about the weather!)

But he's married! Oh, a pox on Margo Shaw! Mostly I
don't think about her at all. I just enjoy prancing along this
high wire between Hal and Oliver, twirling my parasol,
teetering one way, then the other. It's so exciting!

Oliver was shocked when I told him I'd never been to a
service in Christ Church Cathedral, even though it's the seat
of the Bishop of Oxford, and the cathedral is right there in
Tom Quad. Now I know why I'm always running into
him—it's not just me he's come for, it's the cathedral, and
the bishop, and the glory of finding himself among all the
top clerics of Oxfordshire. He's terribly fond of bishops. I
think he yearns to be one himself.

But it does seem strange, the way he hangs around the

cathedral when he's got a perfectly good church of his own.
He's even changed the hours for services in his parish so that
he won't miss anything in the cathedral.

This afternoon he made me go with him to vespers. And
of course the choir looked charming, marching in procession
up the nave, their robes swaying, their mouths opening and
shutting in that miraculous way, and all those harmonious
noises coming out. I confess I get a little tired of the same
chants repeated over and over. Of course it's dreadful of me
to say a thing like that, because Evensong is sacrosanct. The
tourists come in droves and sit there reverently, then fly
home and roll their eyes in rapture and tell all their friends
they heard Evensong in Oxford Cathedral, and their friends

swoon with envy. *The spiritual experience of a lifetime!* (But I'll bet even the tourists, if you could plumb the very depths of their hearts, get a little tired of all those musical repetitions of God the Father, God the Son, God the Holy Ghost.)

Afterwards Oliver introduced me to the bishop, who happened to be there that day, sitting on his throne near the communion table, demonstrating his majestic rule over the diocese of Oxford. Oliver worships the bishop. He's trying to persuade him to make him a canon in the cathedral, or a verger or a sacristan or an acolyte or something, only the bishop always says no. Today I thought His Grace seemed a little absentminded. He hurried off rather fast, and then we were all alone in the sanctuary, and Oliver showed me the throne. He couldn't take his eyes off it. He stroked the arms and patted the cushion, and for a minute I thought he was going to sit down on it, but of course that would have been <u>blasphemy</u>.

Then we had coffee and some really delicious cinnamon buns at a place across the street, and Oliver was radiant, and he told me about his hopes of becoming a more significant person in the church. He wants to be like his ancestor, the Bishop of Warwick (the one Snatched by Untimely Death). He wants to start a movement of revitalization and fill all the churches in England with overflowing congregations, because now it's mostly a few little old ladies in sweaters and thick stockings.

Well, I admit I was charmed by his earnestness, but I had to speak to him frankly and ask him why he didn't fall in love with someone more pious and devout, not the daughter of a scientist.

"Oh," said Oliver, gulping his coffee, "but you don't understand! This is a modern movement. We're eager to recognize the achievements of science and incorporate its discoveries into our concept of the divine."

"I see," I said, taking a big bite of my cinnamon bun, which was choked with raisins and oozing with frosting. But I didn't see.

I do wonder a little at the way Oliver hangs around the cathedral. He's never taken me to his own church. I've never even seen it!

I wonder why?

CHAPTER 26

Thus, from the war of nature, from famine and death . . . the production of the higher animals . . . directly follows. There is grandeur in this view of life.

Charles Darwin, *The Origin of Species*

On the roof of the Ashmolean Museum:
"Hand me the broomstick."

"My God, Stuart, people can see us from the street. I'll lose my job if they find out I let you in."

"Now for the string. Good. And the umbrella."

"Christ, Stuart, it looks *fabulous.*"

In the Kellys' sitting room in the Besse Building:
Homer got up and blundered around the bedroom, getting dressed, trying to read from the *Origin* at the same time, muttering to himself, wondering why one species didn't completely annihilate all the rest, like an army of ants pouring across a forest floor, destroying everything in its path, or a kudzu vine blanketing a county. He was distracted by the thought that the real army was death itself, advancing over the face of the earth, annihilating everything without mercy. Creatures might run from its approaching regiments, and turn and twist, only to find another battalion cutting them off at the pass.

"Death and extinction," he said aloud, summing up everything neatly, "that's what drives evolutionary change, not life." He dropped the book, picked it up again, and riffled the pages. "Look here. Just look at this chart."

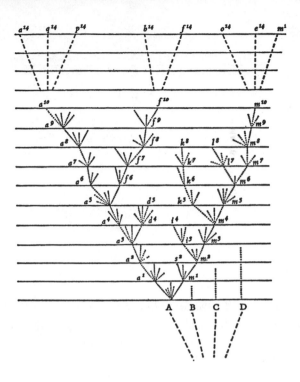

Mary was in a hurry. "Oh, Homer, never mind. I'll read the book myself. You don't have to keep telling me about it. It's like hearing the plot of a film I haven't seen."

"Oh, sorry, but you've got to see this diagram. It makes everything so clear." Homer pushed the book under his wife's nose. "Do you see all these horizontal lines?"

"Yes, of course I see those horizontal lines."

"Well, they're a thousand generations apart. You see? The whole diagram covers fourteen thousand generations. It shows the process of variation and change and the extinction of most species and the survival of a few through time, do you see? Dead ends, most of them are dead ends. They last only a thousand generations or so, and then they perish like the dodo."

"It makes a sort of tree, doesn't it?" said Mary, doing her best to share Homer's enthusiasm.

"Oh, right, right! That's what he said!" Homer flipped the

pages, wrenching his disintegrating paperback this way and that. "Where is it? Is this it? No, that's not it. Oh, here it is. Listen to this." Homer grasped Mary's arm, because she was reaching for her coat. "*So it has been with the great tree of life, which fills with its dead and broken branches the crust of the earth, and covers the surface with its ever-branching and beautiful ramifications.* Beautiful, isn't that beautiful?"

"Yes, Homer dear, I'm sure it is beautiful, but I've got to leave. I have an appointment with Helen Farfrae. We're planning a picnic at Hampton Court. I told her I hadn't ever been to London, and she said why didn't we make a lot of little journeys here and there, and I think that's wonderful, don't you?"

"Of course some people say," said Homer, brandishing the book at her, "that the tree image is all wrong, that it's more like a bush." Half the pages of Homer's copy of *The Origin* fell out on the floor, and at once he got down on his knees to pick them up, still raving. "Because it isn't just a matter of one more perfect species emerging from another. But Darwin doesn't say that anyway, as this diagram makes perfectly clear. Did you see it? Did you really see it?"

Mary flung open the door and ran down the stairs.

❧

On Saturday they went to Hampton Court. It turned out that a lot of people in the Zoology Department had never been to Hampton Court, even though it was a popular tourist attraction, and some of them agreed to come along. Margo and Hal Shaw were coming, and so was William Dubchick, along with his daughter Freddy and her clergyman boyfriend Oliver Clare. Even the Rhodes scholars were coming, Mark Soffit and Stuart Grebe.

Helen made dozens of sandwiches. Mary used the hot plate in the small sitting room at Keble to hardboil two dozen eggs.

William brought up a basketful of wine from the basement of the house on Norham Road. Freddy made a cake. Nothing was forgotten—the bottle opener, the salt, the plastic glasses, the paper plates and napkins, the knives and forks. And the day was fine, sunny and warm for October.

Stuart Grebe was one of the drivers. Once again he had borrowed his roommate's old Rover. "You want to come with me?" he said, grinning at Homer.

"Oh, no thank you, Stuart." Homer looked around for an escape. "I think we're going with somebody else."

"Oh, too bad," said Stuart. "I was hoping to tell you about a little problem I'm having with the proctors."

"Oh, no, Stuart, not again. What is it this time?"

"Oh, it's nothing. Like, a couple of us got up on the roof of the Ashmolean and put an open umbrella in Apollo's hand. You know that statue up there on top? I mean, he really needed something. His arm just sticks up there and looks really stupid, so we gave him the umbrella, and then he looked absolutely terrific, you know, sort of predestined, as though the sculptor's inspiration fizzled out before he was really finished. I mean, the idea of the umbrella was probably right there on the edge of his mind, only he couldn't quite focus it, he was seeking and seeking, trying this and trying that, so then he put down his hammer and burst into tears, which is sad, because he would have been so proud if he could have seen the triumphant completion of his original concept. You should have seen it, Dr. Kelly. I mean, everybody laughed like anything, only then we got caught."

"Oh, my God, Stuart, what do you want me to do?"

"Well, I sort of thought you could, like, talk to them or something."

Homer groaned. "I'll see what I can do."

When the drivers and passengers were sorted out, Homer and Mary Kelly and the Shaws managed to go with Helen Farfrae, Freddy and Oliver were driven by Freddy's father, and

Mark Soffit reeled down the road with Stuart Grebe in the borrowed Rover, shouting at Stuart and clutching the dashboard.

At Hampton Court they drifted apart. Some took the stately-home tour, and some visited the great conservatory with its ancient grapevine. Homer and Mary Kelly were attracted to the maze.

Mary was soon lost. She wandered here and there, not caring. Homer discovered at once that he had an unfair advantage. Standing six-feet-six, he could see over the tops of the hedges. By concentrated inattention, he managed to avoid doing so. Meandering freely, choosing pathways at random, he became more and more excited—because the maze was just like Darwin's chart. The dead ends were extinctions. The right way through was like the long-term survival of Darwin's species A, which lasted through fourteen thousand generations, while B, C, and D died out along the way. "Uh-oh," Homer said to himself, as he was blocked once more, "another extinction."

He could hear someone in the next aisle sounding puzzled. Looking over the top of the hedge, he saw Freddy Dubchick at a fork in the maze, wondering which way to go.

"I'm lost," she said, laughing up at him. "But don't tell me. I'll find my own way." Gamely she set off to the right.

"You're heading for extinction," warned Homer, but Freddy hurried on.

She turned left, then right, then backed up and tried the other way. At the next bend she ran into Hal Shaw. He turned and saw her, and then, impulsively, he held out his arms. Freddy flew into them. Stupefied with joy, he pulled her closer and closer, and they melted rapturously together.

At the next dead end, Homer looked over the hedge and saw Margo Shaw and Mark Soffit. They were arguing. "This way, I think," said Margo, pointing grandly to the left.

"I just came from there," said Mark. "It must be this way," and he pointed to the right.

Homer left them to find the way out. At once, without cheating by looking over the hedge, he saw the final opening in the labyrinth, and grinned in triumph. He was not extinct, he was Species A, surviving into the present day. Then, turning the last corner, he stopped short and backed up.

Freddy Dubchick and Hal Shaw were in each other's arms, passionately kissing and kissing, and murmuring *I love you,* and kissing again.

Sticky wicket, thought Homer, plucking a cricket expression from the pages of British literary history. He backed up around the corner again, and at once collided with Oliver Clare. "Wait a second," he said to Oliver, holding out a warning hand, "this is the wrong way."

Oliver looked at him gloomily, and pushed past him. There was a pause, during which Homer could hear only the voices of Hal and Freddy, repeating in their mutual gladness, "Oh, Hal, my darling, my darling," "Oh, Freddy, Freddy."

He could hardly bear to look at Oliver's grim face when he came back around the corner. Avoiding Homer's eye, Oliver stumbled away in the direction of the labyrinthine center of the maze.

Homer stayed put, waiting for the lovers to finish their embraces. He wanted to leave by the proper exit, not become extinct and give up his survival status as a member of the fourteen thousandth generation. But, oh God, they were still billing and cooing. When would they be done?

At last the loving murmurs stopped. Homer peered around the corner. Hal and Freddy were walking through the opening in the hedge a few feet apart, heading for the conservatory.

They too were survivors unto the fourteen thousandth generation. They had climbed to the top of the branching tree. Not that it was likely they would survive together. The fact that Shaw was firmly attached to his wife would surely mean an extinction of the Hal–Freddy connection, but who could tell? A change in the climate, some vast movement of populations from one side of the mountain to the other, the retreat of a glacier—in other words a tidy little divorce—might advance their joint survival.

Homer looked over the tops of the hedges once again as he left the maze. He could see Mary plodding doggedly in the right direction and Oliver Clare becoming extinct in a particularly tricky dead end.

CHAPTER 27

After describing a set of forms as distinct species, tearing up my MS.,
and making them one species, tearing that up and making them
separate, and then making them one again . . . I have gnashed my
teeth, cursed species, and asked what sin I had committed to be so
punished.

Charles Darwin, letter to Joseph Hooker

It was Monday morning. In the courtyard of the museum it
was too early for squads of schoolchildren to flock around
the bones of the iguanodon and the bison and the two little
elephants. The exhibits in the glass cases waited to be looked
at. The anglerfish gazed at his little joke, the mock lure at the
end of his bristling fishline, the quetzal displayed the long blue
feathers of his tail, the penguin stared blankly at the giant
brain coral across the way.

Around them the stone scientists stood silent, lost in
reverie, having nothing to say to one another. If Leibnitz and
Newton had struck up a conversation, it would have been a
wretched argument, *The calculus is mine, not yours!* But neither
said a word. Newton was mesmerized by his apple, Leibnitz
stared skyward at the City of God, that perfect commonwealth
of minds.

Upstairs in the Zoology Office, Helen Farfrae dropped new
metal labels into the mysterious specimen jars:

Freshwater crab, Cambaridae?
(10 genera, 264 species)
Possibly Darwin 239
Rio de Janeiro, May, 1832.

Some kind of Grapsus?
(40 genera, 340 species)
Is this Darwin 326?
Bot Island, Monte Video,
July, 1832.

She was waiting for Mary Kelly. They were setting out on another excursion, going by themselves instead of organizing an expedition. Mary was glad to have a knowledgeable guide, Helen was grateful for a new friend. When she heard a knock at the office door, Helen called out, "Come in," and stood up, reaching for her coat.

The door opened slowly, and Oliver Clare stood gloomily in the corridor, looking at her. "Oh," said Helen in surprise, plopping back down in her chair, "hello, Oliver."

"I'm looking for Freddy. Have you seen her?"

His voice was hollow. His shoulders sagged. His beauty was as amazing as ever. Helen looked at him and counted up his separate splendors, his golden curls, his perfect features, his tall well-shaped frame. Oliver was rumored to come from a distinguished family. They weren't peers of the realm exactly, but their bloodline was supposed to be exalted. Were aristocrats more beautiful than ordinary mortals? Probably they had their pick of mates, and therefore natural selection would tend to produce offspring who were progressively more gorgeous—baronets handsomer than earls, dukes more good-looking than baronets, kings and queens so dazzling they would knock your eye out. But of course they weren't, and they didn't. It was a nice theory, but obviously false. Except in Oliver's case.

These Darwinian thoughts shot through Helen's mind in a fraction of a second. "No," she said, "I haven't seen her. Did you try her college? She lives at home with her father on weekends, I think."

But of course Oliver knew that. Helen felt intensely sorry

for him. It was painfully obvious that he was being abandoned by cruel, adorable young Freddy Dubchick. It was common knowledge that Freddy was experimenting dangerously with someone else's husband.

"Yes, I've already tried those places." Oliver seemed to be struggling to find something else to say. Helen wondered why he didn't leave, and she cast about for a friendly remark. But he dredged up something on his own. "I read about you in the paper."

"No, surely not."

"A while ago, after the night watchman fell. You know."

"Oh, that." Helen remembered her despair when Johnny thrust the *Oxford Mail* under her nose and shook it and shouted at her, *This is what comes of staying out all night.* She had almost made up her mind, right there and then, she had almost decided—but she had lost her nerve. "That was weeks ago."

"I know, but Freddy showed it to me yesterday." Oliver looked at her sadly. "I don't often read the paper."

Helen made a feeble joke. "Of course not. The daily news doesn't matter to a clergyman." Her laugh was hollow. "You live in eternity, after all."

"What?"

Helen waved her hand, dismissing her own silliness.

"You heard someone," said Oliver. "It was in the paper."

"Heard someone? Oh, you mean— Why, yes, it was very strange. And then I saw him on the roof, the glass roof. He was climbing like a monkey. Or like one of those mountain climbers who go up the sheer faces of cliffs."

Oliver looked at her in surprise. "But that wasn't in the paper."

Helen shrugged her shoulders, and he drifted out of the office, wrapped in melancholy.

🦢

So far, Helen and Mary had seen the manuscript poems of Shelley in the Bodleian Library and the Alfred Jewel in the Ashmolean Museum. They had walked to a famous inn at Godstow, the Trout. From now on, Helen said, she would use her university status to show Mary the scholarly privacies of the most beautiful of the colleges. This morning they started with the fabulous beasts in the Great Quad at Magdalen.

Mary gasped. There they were, crowning the buttresses between the arched windows of the cloister, monsters with heads sprouting from their bellies, strange mixtures of man and reptile, beast and bird.

"I think of them as weird predecessors," said Helen, "failed organisms that didn't make it in the struggle for life. Nature tried creatures with two heads, but it didn't work. The heads were always arguing with each other, so in a crisis they couldn't make up their minds."

Mary laughed. "So they became extinct." She pointed to the molding below the crenellated edge of the roof. "There's an angel. What about angels? Are they extinct too?"

"No." Helen looked at the angel and figured it out. "They must be a future stage of improved adaptation, one we haven't reached yet."

"I see," said Mary. "Maybe the human race will start growing wings. You know, a little bit at a time. There'll be a child with extra-large shoulder blades, and it will jump higher than the other kids, and then some of its children will jump still higher, and eventually—"

"But will they take a kindly interest in the rest of us, the way angels do?" said Helen. "I doubt it."

They left Magdalen and took Rose Lane to the Broad Walk and the wide path to the Thames. There were shaggy long-horned cattle in Christ Church Meadow. From the riverbank they watched crews of girls in racing shells. A coach was teaching them to execute turns. *"Slow—slow! Now then, five, make sure your blade is square."*

Mary turned to Helen. "But you must be tired of all this. You've seen it so often."

"Not at all. It's like reading a favorite book to children. You're eager to introduce them to something you love, and so pleased when they like it."

"Do you have children?" said Mary inquisitively, wondering if this was a violation of British reserve.

"No, I don't," said Helen shortly.

There was an awkward silence, until Mary suggested going back to Keble for lunch.

The truth was that Helen was on the verge of telling Mary a thousand things. She wanted to tell her, she was dying to tell her. Only a kind of perverse loyalty kept her silent. Loyalty to what? The institution of marriage? Hardly. But whatever it was, it was the very thing that had kept her attached to Johnny Farfrae all these years, in spite of the absurdity of their differences. She told herself that it was not altogether his fault she was so unhappy. It was class snobbery on her part, and she refused to give in to it.

She knew what her friends were saying, *She should never have married him in the first place. How can she endure it?*

But it was easy to understand why she had married him. What a blithe boy he had been! They had met on a Saturday night in a village pub in West Yorkshire, where Johnny was the performing folksinger, the best for miles around. Helen had been captivated by his light tenor voice and his merry air of authority. Like any young fool, she had been swept off her feet.

The singing was over now, along with the merriment. *How does she stand it?* Helen stood it because Johnny aroused her pity as well as her contempt. Oh, it didn't matter that he was only a postal clerk, while she had a couple of university degrees. That didn't matter a bit. All of those class barriers were gone now, weren't they? That kind of ranking by speech, by accident of birth? Well, good riddance to it.

What Helen failed to consider was that Johnny couldn't get rid of it. He punished her for being different, for her *poshness*, as he called it. *Oh, aren't we la-di-da today.* If she brought home a woman friend and the afternoon sparkled with laughter and talk, he would glower and rattle his paper and turn his back.

And, oh, God, the drunken brawls on the street, and the fights at home—

Sometimes Helen imagined herself giving in and giving up. One day she would curl up in bed and pull the covers over her head. They would take her away and put her in a narrow room in an institution, and she would crouch in the corner, her hair long and straggling, her mouth hanging open. She would lose the power of speech.

This pathetic woman accompanied Helen every day. She was a cautionary presence, and yet in some way, when things were really bad, Helen almost welcomed her. She could imagine being drawn in by that skinny arm. It could happen, it could happen to anyone. Any healthy person on the street might give up and say, it's too hard, oh, it's too hard.

Well, so far she had fought back. She had turned away from pathos. She had tried passionately to reject class warfare. Helen's idealism was inherited from her socialist parents and her Fabian grandparents, but so was her poshness, and it continued to burst out. She couldn't control it. She admitted to herself that she hated the people on Cornmarket Street, the young kids in their burly jackets, the crude giggling girls. *I hate the babies, too,* she thought ruefully. *I hate the very babies in their pushchairs.* And that was wrong, surely it was wrong. As for her husband, she never formed the words in her head, but the unshaped meaning was there, racking her body with self-knowledge—*I hate him, too. I hate Johnny Farfrae, too.*

Unformed words fester in the throat, they lie coiled in some wet, red compartment of the body, they are fed by the events of every day and grow fat.

❧

Stuart Grebe found the door to the Zoology Office ajar. It was Wednesday afternoon. The museum was open, families and students were milling around the exhibits, but the office was empty.

He was disappointed to find nobody there. He had come in a spirit of sociability, his gregarious nature having made him a disciple of William Dubchick's, an admirer of Helen Farfrae's, an enthusiastic pupil of Hal Shaw's, and the friend of everyone else in the department.

But the office itself was interesting. Stuart brought his near-sighted eyes close to the jars on the table and peered inside. He admired the photograph of Charles Darwin over the fireplace. He inspected the egg of the great auk and ran his finger over the carved leaves and insects along the mantel.

Then he caught sight of the computer. It drew him across the room. Stuart had been a computer freak from infancy, and he longed to test this one out. It was British, but surely not very different from the one he used at home.

He stood in front of it and struck a key. And of course the differences soon vanished. Before long he had called up the list of directories.

One was entitled *Dubchick.* Could it be the long-awaited book?

It was. Stuart punched up *Chap1,* ran down the pages and read them at a glance. Then he called up *Chap2.*

No one interrupted him. No one entered the office. Stuart Grebe helped himself to a blank floppy disk, sat down at Helen Farfrae's computer, and had his way with it for the next quarter of an hour.

CHAPTER 28

She never finished the sentence, for at this moment a heavy crash shook the forest from end to end.

Lewis Carroll, *Through the Looking-Glass*

T here was a new security officer roaming among the science buildings at night, dropping into the museum, shining his flashlight along halls and corridors. No one but Helen Farfrae missed the old night watchman, Bobby Fenwick. She was still deeply troubled about his death. Detective Inspector Mukerji had scolded her for her delay in calling 999, but he had assured her that she could not have saved young Bobby by calling earlier. His fall had killed him instantly, Mukerji said. Then he had looked at her with his shining dark eyes and asked why had she waited so long, and she had been unable to answer.

It was one of his weirder problems. In his office in the St. Aldate's police headquarters, Gopal Mukerji kept running its strange facets over in his mind—Dr. Farfrae's insistence that she had heard an intruder, her visionary account of an impossible ascent up the side of the glass roof, Fenwick's fatal fall, the ridiculous burglary of the dodo and the equally absurd *reverse* burglary, the return of the antique crabs. Well, *perhaps* it was a return. Professor Dubchick was not at all sure about the provenance of the battered fragments in the jars.

At the inquest, the whole thing had sounded ridiculous. Mukerji felt like a fool. Usually his eccentric cases were more intriguing than the ordinary violent crimes that came his way, but not this time. It wasn't the solemn nagging of his superiors that bothered him, it was the phone calls from Mrs. Fenwick, asking tearfully if he had made any progress in his investigation of her husband's death. Inspector Mukerji could not refuse to talk to the poor widow, but it was always painful, and he had little to say to her. Oh, he could quote from Tagore, *The frail flowers die for nothing, and the wise man warns me that life is but a dewdrop on the lotus leaf,* but what good would that do?

By the time of Homer's third lecture, his panic was over. In a crowd of Keble undergraduates he walked serenely across Parks Road. Some of them were his students, and they grinned at him and said hello.

But Homer was anxious enough to be an hour early. There was time to kill. He dawdled on the lawn in front of the museum, and looked up at its long flat front.

Even from the outside it had an aura of metaphysical authority. Its history had become the stuff of legend, because the University Museum was coeval with *The Origin of Species.* They had emerged into the world at the same time: the mountain of brick and stone, glass and iron, the building that was meant to be a glorification of life on earth, a celebration of the Creator's power—and the book promoting a monumental idea that was about to shake that mountain to its foundations. No sooner was the last glass slate attached to the roof than the glorification of the Creator's power and the defiance of that glory were embattled in the museum, in a famous debate between the Bishop of Oxford and the supporters of Charles Darwin.

Local history had long since awarded the prize to Hooker and Huxley rather than to Bishop Wilberforce, and since then the Oxford University Museum had been a temple to death as well as to life, the ceaseless murder of one creature by another, the multitude of clawings, rippings, gobblings and swallowings that had gone on every day in every jungle, forest, and field and in all the oceans of the world from the beginning of time. And all the polite gentleman scholars—Ruskin, the Slade Professor of Fine Arts, Acland with his gentlemanly sideburns, and Dodgson with his clever stories, as well as the current crop of researchers with their learned papers—they were all accessories after the fact, whether they wanted to be or not.

Homer walked into the museum and stopped in front of the glass case displaying the skull of the dodo. Extinction was omnipresent among the exhibits. Oh, it wasn't just the dodo, it was *Iguanodon bernissartensis* and *Megalosaurus bucklandi* and *Cetiosaurus oxoniensis* and all the rest. "Pax vobiscum, you guys," said Homer, turning around and wandering dreamily in the direction of the south staircase.

"No, sir, better go the other way."

Homer stopped short. "What?"

A workman was dragging a sawhorse to the foot of the staircase, setting it squarely in Homer's way. "The other stairway's open," he said. "You'll have to go up that way."

"Oh, sorry, I forgot." Homer stood in the ground-floor corridor and looked up at the fabric of metal pipes and wooden planks blocking the way to the gallery floor. But instead of turning and making for the stairway at the other end, he continued to stand there, looking up.

The workman, whose name was Ben Cobble, found him dense. He pointed down the hall. "The other staircase, you see, sir."

"Of course. I just wondered, you're revamping the whole museum, is that it?"

"Oh, no, just bits and pieces here and there." Ben's mind was on the work he was about to do, but this bloke was still standing there, staring at him. "Well, we made some repairs to the vaulting in the gallery."

"Oh, right, I remember. You finished that last week."

"And now there's this, and then there's the public toilets downstairs."

"Oh, I see. And that's all you're doing, I mean, in the whole museum?"

Ben looked at him, trying to keep his temper. "Well, before I come along, they was doing some kind of work on the glass. I dunno. Me, I'm a bricklayer."

"The glass? You mean the glass roof over the courtyard?"

Ben picked up his mortaring tool and waved it toward the heavens. "Right, that's right."

"Well, what were they doing up there?"

The bricklayer started back up the stairs, squeezing past the scaffolding. Homer guessed he was sick of answering the questions of an inquisitive American. But Ben was yelling Homer's question to someone in the upper gallery. "Hey, Tuck, what was that bloke doing up there on the roof last month?"

The answer came floating down. Tuck had a ringing tenor voice. Homer could imagine him singing in church, the darling of the choir director. "The slates flew off the tower in a high wind. There was that storm last summer, remember? They were replacing the slates."

Homer yelled another question to the invisible Tuck. "Oh, so it was just the tower, is that all?"

"No, worse luck," caroled the celestial Tuck. "The slates hit the glass roof, cracked the glass tiles, hell of a job repairing the tiles. They're laminated and pinned and stuck on with mastic, and I don't know what else." Tuck leaned over the stair railing and looked down kindly at Homer. "Chewing gum? Library paste?"

Homer was surprised to see that the choirboy looked like a chimpanzee, or perhaps an amiable baboon—but then Homer had primates on his mind. "How did they climb the roof? What did they have, scaffolding like this?"

"No, no, nothing like this. It was all ropes and pulleys, you know, like window cleaners use."

"Ropes and pulleys? No kidding!" Homer leaned over the sawhorse barrier and beamed up at Tuck. "Tell me, when did he finish up there? When did he call it quits and take away all his equipment?"

"Oh, Christ, I dunno." Tuck screwed up his chimpanzee face and tried to remember. "Do you know, Ben?"

Ben shook his head. *He* didn't know.

Tuck began counting off days under his breath. "I remember the day Charley come down, he was draped all over with ropes, and he said, 'Thank God, that bloody job's done.' It must've been— Wait, I know." Tuck laughed, and it was like the ringing of heavenly bells. "It was the day there was this big party in the museum. They told us we had to get the hell out, leave everything all neat and nice. So I put down me bucket of mortar, and then along comes Charley with his blasted rope and drags it over the bucket and tips it over. So I says, Clean it up, you fool, and he says— Well, never mind what he says. It was October second. The day of the party, October second."

Homer was disappointed. October second was two days before the dark night when Helen Farfrae had seen something on the roof of the museum, someone or something bounding up the glass. The repairman's rope had been taken away too soon. Homer's precious fool's experiment, the visit to the zoo, his delight in the way the orangutans had swung back and forth so easily on their ropes, had been a waste of time.

❧

That afternoon Johnny Farfrae had a fight with his district supervisor. The supervisor dropped in without warning and found him opening mail. Not sorting it, opening it. There was a hell of a row.

"Inadequate addresses," claimed Johnny. "Christ, I was just trying to find information inside, so we could—"

"Hand them over."

The addresses were clear and complete. The envelopes contained benefit checks.

There had been episodes like this before. "Get out," said the supervisor. "You're lucky I don't turn you in. Rifling the Royal Mail is a criminal offense."

"Well, fuck you," said Johnny. He went for the supervisor's throat, and there was a wild scramble. Johnny's fellow clerks came running.

Within the hour he was out on the street. Seething with rage and despair, he took the bus back to Kidlington, but he didn't go home. He spent the rest of the day in his favorite pub. By the time he stumbled out at last, he was roaring drunk. The inside of his brain was hot and red and his clenched fists trembled, as though they remembered long-ago Saturday nights when his father had come home sloshed and knocked his mother around just to clear the air. And then from his own room Johnny would hear them going to bed, his father purged of his anger and his mother weeping. From behind their bedroom door her sobs would go on, changed and muffled but still audible.

Now Johnny knew what had been going on behind that bedroom door, and his blood rose with anger at the way Helen had been shutting him out. He stormed up to the house to find it dark. Her car was not in the garage.

He knew where she was, all right, and his rage increased. With boozy extravagance he called a cab.

🦢

William Dubchick and Helen Farfrae were totally absorbed in the mysterious jars of crabs. Helen had begun staying late, just to do one more, or two or three. Steadily she moved from jar to jar, dumping the contents into the porcelain dishes, looking at them with the high-tech microscope. The crabs were plumper now, less wretched-looking after their rehydration.

William often joined her in the evening, coming in after eating a hasty supper and walking Freddy's dog. Tonight he came in early. At ten o'clock they were still hard at work.

"You know," said William, looking up from a shriveled carapace and a mess of jointed legs, "it's true that we've matched a lot of these with crabs in the Down House catalogue, but there's still a problem."

"The matching is so rough," said Helen.

"Yes, because Charles Darwin didn't know enough about the individual crustaceans to give them specific names. Well, for heaven's sake, how could he? When there are so many species in every genus."

"And he was still so young."

William smiled at his colleague. Dr. Farfrae always jumped to his thought. It was a pleasure to work with her on something as important as this. "Dr. Farfrae," he said impulsively, "do you think you could call me William from now on? I'd be very much relieved if you would."

There was only one answer to this morsel of a question. Helen tried to sound matter-of-fact. "Only if you call me Helen."

"Her name is Mrs.—John—Farfrae."

They looked up in surprise, and then Helen turned her head away in outraged embarrassment. How grotesque! Her husband was standing angrily in the doorway. "I wonder, Mrs. Farfrae," he said sarcastically, "if you are ever planning to come home?"

"That reminds me," said William gracefully, "that I meant to leave some time ago." Taking his coat from the back of a chair, he said, "Good night, Dr. Farfrae." Nodding amiably at Helen's abominable husband, he walked out into the corridor, turned sharply to the left, and was gone.

For a moment Helen sat with folded arms, staring at the

photograph of Darwin, her pulse racing. Her husband too was silent, breathing heavily, listening as William's footsteps pattered down the north stairwell and faded out of hearing.

Then Helen turned around savagely. "How could you, how *could* you?"

Johnny blustered back at her, "What do you mean, how could I? What the hell do you think you're doing, spending every night with Dubchick?"

Livid with anger, Helen stood up. "How could you embarrass me like that, how could you embarrass Professor Dubchick? It was so vulgar, so cheap. I'm so ashamed."

"Oh, you're ashamed, are you?" ranted Johnny. It was obvious to Helen that he was in over his head. "The *professor* might be embarrassed, what a pity! You don't give a shit for your husband, a mere post office clerk, going without his tea!"

The trick had always worked before. Johnny had only to mention his lowly position to force his wife into an apology. But not this time. "Well?" said Johnny. His voice shook as he struggled to control his shame. "Are you coming home with me or not?"

"No," she said coldly. "I'm going to stay right here and work a little longer."

"Well, goddamn you." Nearly demented with self-loathing, Johnny waved his hand at everything in the room, the picture of Darwin, the bookshelves of Darwin editions, the jars of crabs, the books and papers, the computer, the typewriter, the copy machine, the gecko in its tank. "Shit," he said in a delirium of bitterness and envy, "all this stuff, it's just a pile of shit."

He whirled around and blundered out into the corridor, running away from his wife. In his wretchedness he didn't care where he was going. The place was black as pitch. In total darkness, head down, tears running down his cheeks, gasping and sobbing, he stumbled in the direction of the stairs.

Blindly, carelessly, he ran out on the planking that had been laid over the scaffolding, although it shivered and echoed under his feet.

Helen sank back into her chair and listened to his pounding footsteps, her eyes closed in torment. Tears brimmed under her eyelids. Even in her fury she felt a wincing sympathy for Johnny's misery, for his virulent jealousy of her Oxford degrees, for his refusal to take pride in his own perfectly good grammar school education. What did they matter, all the spidery filaments of her specialized knowledge? Not a damn, they didn't matter a damn. Why didn't he know that?

There was an appalling, shattering noise. She sprang to her feet.

CHAPTER 29

A strong desire to touch the beloved person is commonly felt. . . .
Hence we long to clasp in our arms those whom we tenderly love.
                    Charles Darwin,
                    The Expression of the Emotions in Man and Animals

🦢

By some miracle Hal Shaw and Freddy Dubchick found themselves alone together in the Oxford Playhouse. Alone, that is, except for two hundred fifty-seven strangers who had also bought tickets to *As You Like It*. Their aloneness consisted in the absence of Oliver Clare and Margo Shaw.

Their seats were far apart, but Hal recognized Freddy's small neat head from the back, and at intermission he pushed through fifty people moving up the aisle to intercept her. She saw him coming, and thrust through half a dozen bodies, her face glowing.

"I intend to kiss you," he said, leaning over her, "sometime in the next thirty seconds. I mean, life is short, and we've got to get in as many kisses as possible."

"Not here," said Freddy, laughing. "Not in front of all these people."

"I'll tell you what we need," said Hal impulsively. "You know that thing they have on the streets of Paris called a *pissoir*, so that men can relieve themselves in the open air? Well, what we need right now is a *kissoir*. It's the same sort of thing, but for people in love. Oh, God, Freddy, I love you so."

In the lobby of the theater people were buying drinks,

175

standing in clots and clusters, talking cheerfully. Hal touched Freddy's face and kissed her.

"Are you really eager to see the rest of the play?" breathed Freddy.

"No, no, I hate Shakespeare." Hal put his arm around her and they went outside.

Beaumont Street was the usual Oxford mixture of seediness and grandeur. Across the street the Ashmolean stretched left and right. On the crest of the roof the white figure of Apollo was half-submerged in a low-hanging mist. Rain had been threatening all day. Trucks rumbled past. Hal remembered to look to his right before hurrying Freddy across.

They walked all the way to Norham Road. On the way it began to mizzle with rain, and Freddy popped up her umbrella. "Our kissoir," she said, and under its skimpy protection they clung together and walked and kissed. They didn't say anything. There was nothing that needed to be said. Somewhere in the world there were a couple of enormous obstacles in the shape of Margo Shaw and Oliver Clare, but right now under this amorous umbrella they were totally irrelevant. It would be vulgar to mention them.

There were lighted windows in Freddy's house. "Oh, dear," she said, "my father's home. I thought he was working late." She steered Hal into the side garden, and they sat down on a damp wooden bench. Hal held the umbrella.

Indoors, Freddy's dog jumped up on a windowsill and whimpered. William rose from his chair and looked out. He could see the two figures on the bench, and in spite of the umbrella he recognized the young man who was embracing his daughter so passionately. He didn't know whether to be glad or sorry.

CHAPTER 30

What a trifling difference must determine which shall survive and which perish!

Charles Darwin, letter to Asa Gray

John Farfrae lay at the bottom of the south staircase for six hours after his wife rose from beside him and moved away. In the first hour the blood drained from the right side of his body, which was lying uppermost, and pooled in the vessels of the left, which lay below. While Helen sat brooding on a chair beside the stone image of Isaac Newton, her husband's body heat seeped through his skin and mingled with the surrounding air. By the fourth hour, the muscles of his face began to stiffen. In the fifth and sixth, his arms and fingers locked in rigor mortis.

In death John Farfrae's sprawling posture was exactly like that of Bobby Fenwick. His head was skewed sideways at the same impossible angle.

"You're joking," said Homer to Edward Pound. "It's not another broken neck?"

"I'm afraid so. Mr. Farfrae seems to have lost his way in the dark, and somehow he got out on the boards they laid over the stairs and he fell from the end."

"My God." Stricken, Homer stared at Pound, who responded with a sorrowful shake of the head.

"Dr. Kelly?" Someone was calling from the end of the arcaded corridor. It was Detective Inspector Mukerji, examining the scaffolding on the south staircase.

Homer went to him at once, and for a doleful moment they looked at each other and said nothing. Then Homer glanced up at the wooden planks that had provided a platform for the workmen, Ben Cobble and Dan Tuck. "He fell from up there?"

Mukerji shrugged. "One assumes so. They have taken him to the Radcliffe, but he is very, very dead."

"Well, Christ, how did it happen? Couldn't he see where he was going? What about the sawhorses that were here yesterday?"

"Sawhorses?" Mukerji looked puzzled. "Ah, I see," he said, making a sawing gesture with his arm, "it is an American expression. You mean the trestles. Yes, the men who were working here insist they left one at the top and one at the bottom."

"Then someone must have removed them." Homer looked up at the landing. Within the glass-enclosed hive attached to the high south window he could see the bees moving around slowly. "You don't suppose the bees were after him? I remember a case—"

"No, no, the bees cannot get into the museum. They can only go out." Mukerji grinned at Homer. "I confess, I asked the same stupid question."

"Well, forgive me for putting in my two cents," said Homer, "but it strikes me that if these two deaths were deliberate homicides, they were the work of an amateur. A professional killer would have used a gun, or a knife, or—oh, I don't know—poison or something. An amateur, on the other hand—well, take me, for instance—if I wanted to kill somebody, I'd take him to the edge of a cliff and give him a little push. Easy as pie. No weapons lying around, no sticky jars of cyanide to be found later in a drawer."

Mukerji had a dazzling smile. His cheeks were ripe pieces of fruit. "You are a man after my own heart, Dr. Kelly. I would do precisely the same. In fact, I sometimes imagine inviting a certain superior officer to a picnic on some rocky promontory above the sea. Quite often I imagine it." Mukerji stopped smiling, and turned solemn. "So if we take the classic triad of weapon, motive and opportunity, we can in this case eliminate the weapon. But we must still consider the motive. *We seek to know the meaning as the moon would fathom the sea.* Forgive me, I cannot help myself, it is the poet Tagore. Do you know, Dr. Kelly, why anyone would want to kill Mr. John Farfrae?"

"Homer, please call me Homer."

Mukerji shook his head, bemused. "Americans, they are so informal. What would my constables think if they heard me addressed as Gopal? They would lose all respect." He threw back his handsome head and laughed. "Soon they would be slapping me on the back and sending me out for coffee." He sobered once again and shook Homer's hand. "We will chance it. Thank you, Homer. Call me Gopal. My question remains. Why would anyone want to kill this man Farfrae?"

"All I know about him," said Homer, "is that he browbeat his wife. Have you talked to her? Have you spoken to Dr. Farfrae?"

"Oh, yes. It was she who found him. She called us, although she waited for several hours before doing so. She was very frank. She said she and her husband had been quarreling in her office on the upper floor, and then in a fit of anger he slammed out of the room and hurried away while she remained in the office. The next thing she heard was the crash. She ran to him at once, feeling her way down the stairs past the scaffolding, and found him lying dead at the bottom." Mukerji shrugged. "Perhaps the reason she did not call us immediately was that he was not yet quite dead. She delayed, thus preventing any lifesaving care. Who knows?" Mukerji looked keenly at Homer. "You will remember that it was Dr. Farfrae who saw a miraculous vision on the roof when the night watchman fell to his death."

"Yes, of course."

"It is a very strange story. And on that occasion also she did not inform us right away."

They climbed the stairs in single file, edging past the scaffolding. At the top they found one of Mukerji's detective constables interviewing Daniel Tuck.

Tuck turned at once to Homer in appeal. "I'll swear on oath, we left them barriers all the way across, top and bottom, *top and bottom,* right, Professor? You saw them, remember?"

Once again he sounded like a choir of angels and looked remarkably like—which one would it be? This time Homer settled on the colobus monkey he had seen in the zoo, a little primate with a wild spray of hair sprouting from its forehead. "Of course I remember."

"And anyway, why couldn't he see where he was going? They leave the lights on, don't they? Every night they leave them on, so how the bloody hell?"

William Dubchick appeared beside them, walking down the gallery corridor from the Zoology Office. "No," he said solemnly, "the lights were not on. It was completely dark. I was here with Dr. Farfrae last night. When I left, I used the other staircase, but I had to grope for the railing to keep from missing my footing."

"Ah," said Mukerji, "Professor Dubchick! Is it not unusual, Professor, for the lights to be turned off at night?"

"Indeed it is. I don't remember ever seeing them turned off before. In fact I have never seen the museum so black. It was a rainy night, which increased the darkness."

Homer watched as the polite exchange continued. Detective Constable Ives flipped a page in his notebook and scribbled furiously. Daniel Tuck picked up his trowel with a conspicuous gesture of getting back to work.

"You were here last night, then, Professor," said Mukerji, "in the company of Mr. Farfrae and his wife?"

"Yes, I was. When I left at about nine o'clock, Dr. Farfrae and her husband were still in the office. I don't know how much later it was that he fell."

"Were they arguing, husband and wife, when you left?"

William paused before saying, "I suppose you could call it that. Mr. Farfrae seemed—not altogether himself."

"And Mrs. Farfrae?"

"*Dr.* Farfrae. I don't know. I left only a moment after he came in."

Detective Inspector Mukerji was serenely relentless. "Did you remove the barrier in front of this staircase, Professor Dubchick?"

"No," said William quietly. "I knew this stairway was blocked, so I went on around the gallery to the stairs on the other side."

"In the dark?"

"Yes, in the dark."

"It was not you who turned off the lights in the courtyard?"

"No. My key will open the porter's door—that's where the switches are—but I didn't use it. I went straight home."

"Can anyone corroborate your presence at home? Your time of arrival?"

"I doubt that anyone noticed when I got home. But my daughter—" William stopped. Freddy must have known he was at home, or she wouldn't have sat outdoors in the rain to make love to Hal Shaw. But that was Freddy's business. He would not get her into it.

"Your daughter was in the house, was she?"

William spoke carefully. "No, she was not in the house. She came in a good while later, about midnight." It was almost the truth. Freddy had been *at* home, but not *in* it.

Homer wondered how Mukerji was going to bring up with William the question of a motive for the murder of John Farfrae. Would he suggest that William might have killed Farfrae in order to free Helen from her abusive spouse? But to Homer's surprise, the questioning was over.

William walked heavily back to his office. Mukerji excused himself and led Detective Constable Ives down the stairs, keeping to the left to avoid the scaffolding. Homer walked around the east side of the gallery and entered the lecture hall, mulling the problem over in his mind. Perhaps it had never occurred to Mukerji that anyone as old as William could commit a crime of passion. Nor that Helen Farfrae, a woman in her fifties, was worth killing for. Mukerji himself must be no older than thirty. Homer, who was considerably older than that, saw things differently. He found Helen a very attractive woman.

❧

"It's about time you showed up," said Tuck. "Where you been?"

"It's not my fault," said Charley Firkin, heaving himself over the sawhorse at the bottom of the stairs. "I been tracking down my rope."

"Your rope? What rope?"

"Oh, aye, what rope? The rope you stole, that's what rope. Listen, mate, what I want to know is, who the bloody hell stole my best rope?"

Tuck exploded. "Oh, right. First they accuse us of manslaughter, and now it's robbery. God damn you, I didn't steal your bleeding rope."

"I came down here," explained Charley Firkin, who was a professional window cleaner and steeplejack, "with some of my stuff. You know, after I finished risking life and limb on that bloody roof. Only I left some of it behind. God, I was worn out, bloody exhausted. Came back to get it, few days later, fucking thing's been stolen. The whole bloody thing, rope and pulleys. Bloody rope cost a fortune. Best on the market. How much you think it cost me? Go ahead, guess. Well, fuck you, I'll tell you how much it cost me. A hundred quid, that's what it cost me. So where the hell is it?"

"Well, my God, man," said Tuck angrily, "I haven't got your bloody rope. What would I do with a rope?"

"You'd sell it, stands to reason. I wouldn't put it past you."

"Get stuffed."

The argument died out as Director Jamison came along the corridor. He too wanted to know how anyone could have blundered out onto the scaffolding. "How did it happen that the lights were out? The porter assures me he left them on at closing time."

"Don't look at me," said Ben Cobble.

"I been sick," said Charley Firkin. "I only just come back to work."

"Well, for Christ's sake," said Tuck. He picked up the barrier blocking the top of the stairs and held it off the floor with a massive show of strength. "I put this here trestle right on this spot last night before I left. Me personally. I personally placed this trestle right here to block the stairs, and then I personally put another one at the bottom." Tuck lifted the trestle higher, and dropped it with a mighty slam.

CHAPTER 31

Alas! a scientific man ought to have no wishes, no affections—a mere heart of stone.

Charles Darwin, letter to T. H. Huxley

It had been a terrible night. But one thing was more dreadful to Helen than all the rest. Not Johnny's death, although that should have been the worst. Poor Johnny, poor unhappy Johnny! She kept remembering him as he had been at first, the Johnny Farfrae who had sung so sweetly, who had danced with her so gaily, who had one day jumped over a fence to come to her. Last night, kneeling beside his body on the stairs, she had seen him floating above the fence rail, poised in air. If only she could forget everything else!

No, his death was not the worst thing. And to Helen it did not seem terrible that she had wandered around the museum in the pitch dark for hours, feeling her way past the leg bones of the giraffe, sliding a groping hand along the frames of the display cases, while the rain drummed on the glass panes of the roof over her head. Nor had it been painful to climb back to the office and telephone the St. Aldate's police station, nor to open the museum door when they came, nor to see them setting up their bright staring lights over Johnny's broken body, nor even to answer the gently probing questions of Detective Inspector Mukerji in the gray light of dawn.

No, the most terrible thing had been her instantaneous reaction when she guessed that Johnny was dead, the relief that had slipped in ahead of the sorrow.

&

Mary Kelly went looking for Helen Farfrae.

"Have you seen her?" she asked William Dubchick in the Zoology Office.

He looked at her gravely and shook his head. "She doesn't answer her telephone. No one seems to know where she is."

But then Mary found her at once, in the basement ladies' room. From one of the compartments came a strangled sob.

"Helen, is that you?"

There was a pause, and then Helen emerged and put her arms around Mary. She sobbed once or twice, then stood back and said, "I'm all right, really."

"Well, I'm not," said Mary. "I'm starving. Come and have lunch. Do you mind going out? I mean, where people are? There's a place I want to try."

It was a pub called the Eagle and Child on St. Giles, not far from the greasy spoon café where they had eaten before. Mary led Helen to a far corner in the farthest of the small crowded rooms.

Helen looked around furtively, but the other people jammed together at the tiny tables looked like students. All were strangers except for Mark Soffit, who was sitting by himself two rooms away, eating his lunch and writing postcards:

I'm writing this from C. S. Lewis's favorite pub. He's quite a legend around here, but as you can imagine famous people are a dime a dozen. Heard Dubchick the other day, no big deal. I know his daughter. I'm writing a paper or two, punting on the Cherwell, crewing on the Isis, working in the Bodleian. How are things at Podunk U?

Most of this was lies, but Mark copied it over three times on postcards to other Americans. Staring at his pen, he didn't see the cynical glances directed at his scarf. It was a brand-new crew scarf, bought at a shop on the Broad, a tourist place specializing in Oxford sweatshirts, Oxford T-shirts and Oxford teddy bears. It had been hard to decide which of the college scarves to choose, because they were all elegantly striped and all expensive, and some were adorned with college crests. The scarf for Christ Church was the one he picked, because the *House* (that was what people called it) was the most prestigious of the colleges—a far cry from poor old Wolfson. Mark never mentioned Wolfson on his postcards. He used a box number as a return address.

Mary Kelly, carrying two pints of bitter from the front of

the pub to the back, caught a glimpse of another familiar face in the Eagle and Child. Stuart Grebe was there, jabbering with the people at the next table, and they were jabbering back. Stuart made friends wherever he went, overcoming the effect of his foolish face with jokes and cheerful enthusiasm. He had not fallen prey to the Oxford scarf shop. Such fripperies were beyond his means. And anyway it turned out that his baggy sweater, his mother's despair, was right in style.

"Here we are," said Mary, setting down Helen's mug with a thump. "Do you know why I like British beer? Because it doesn't bloat your insides. It doesn't swell you up and make you belch." She took a swig and grinned at Helen. "A refined note from across the Atlantic."

Helen laughed. It was a wholesome laugh, and she felt better for it. And then she began to talk.

Mary sat calmly, eating her thick sandwich, drinking her glass of bitter, and listening. Sometimes she wondered if she physically resembled a tall curtained closet, people seemed so eager to lean toward her and whisper their troubles in her ear. She had always been a target for confessions.

At the end she asked if it would be okay to tell Helen's story to Homer. "I promise he won't pass it on to Detective Inspector Mukerji."

"Yes, of course," said Helen.

🦢

"For years!" said Mary. "All that stuff has been bottled up inside her for years."

"Well," said Homer, "that husband of hers must have been the stopper in the bottle. A really rancid character, I gather, John Farfrae. Marriage, my God, the ghastly choices people make, the ways they can go wrong. Some sweet little teenage morsel turns into an alcoholic, or she's like your friend Marcia and never stops talking, or she's extravagant and lazy like Minnie, or terminally messy like Joan, or maybe she takes up causes like your friend Louisa and torments her family and friends—"

"Or *he* doesn't get up in the night with the baby or clean up after the dog, and maybe he runs after women"—Mary thought of all the rotten marriages she had run into—"or he weighs three hundred pounds, or he's a hypochondriac, or too nutty to hang on to a job."

Homer spread Roquefort cheese on his slab of bread. "I've always been amazed by what it takes to be just an ordinary everyday wife. You, for instance. What if you couldn't face it? All those things you have to do, from getting thousands of edible meals and scrubbing the crud out of ten thousand pots and pans—oh, I know I don't help the way I should—to exterminating plagues of ants and dismembering chickens and sending Christmas cards to all my relatives. Not to mention writing books and teaching legions of college kids. There must be plenty of women who can't handle it, who just can't get up in the morning." He pulled his wife to him, and murmured, "Lucky, I'm so lucky."

"Oh, Homer, we both are. But next Christmas, you know what? You're taking over the Christmas cards. I am not writing any more hollow greetings to your Aunt Milly and your cousin Jack." Mary pulled away and grinned at him. "Make me a sandwich too, heavy on the cheese."

Homer reached for another loaf of bread. "Tell me, who do you think was meant to fall from that scaffolding in the dark?"

Mary thought about it. "Well, I doubt it was Johnny Farfrae. Helen didn't know he was coming. Probably nobody else did either."

"Oh, but after he got there, William Dubchick knew. When he left the office he could have gone straight to the south stairway and removed the barriers. And then he could have gone down the north stairway and turned off the lights."

"But why?" said Mary. "Oh, well, perhaps he did have

a motive. He'd be doing a work of charity, relieving Helen of her frightful spouse. And perhaps"—Mary grinned at Homer—"perhaps he wanted Helen for himself. After all, my darling, you and I know that the fires don't burn out, just because we're no longer young."

"Oh, we do, do we?" Homer put down the loaf of bread and took his wife's hand. Crowded together into one of the twin beds, they made comfortable old married love.

Afterward Mary said, "Was this a proof of something?"

"Certainly," said Homer. "We're proving William Dubchick had cause to kill John Farfrae. Quod erat demonstrandum."

Mary laughed and got out of bed. "Would it stand up in a court of law?"

"No, because the fact is, it couldn't have been William who moved those sawhorses and turned off the lights, hoping to lure John Farfrae to his death. When William left the office, he couldn't guess that Farfrae would leave first, and plunge down that stairwell all by himself. Surely he'd think the man would tyrannize his wife into coming with him."

"Of course," Mary thought about it. "So if it wasn't William, it was someone else who knew Helen often worked late, who thought she'd be there alone. My God, Homer, you know what I think?"

"I think so too. Someone was trying to kill her. But why? Why in hell would anybody want to kill Helen Farfrae?"

"I don't know why. I do know she mustn't work late anymore."

CHAPTER 32

*In these still solitudes, Death, instead of Life, seemed the
predominant spirit.*

Charles Darwin, *The Voyage of the Beagle*

ohn Farfrae died on Tuesday night. On Saturday morning Mrs. Dorothy Jarvis found Oliver Clare lying flat on
his back on the floor of his rented room with his throat cut.

Mrs. Jarvis's yellow brick house was one of several on the
west side of St. Barnabas Street. All of them backed up to the
Oxford Canal. Mrs. Jarvis lived downstairs. The house was
also in the neighborhood of the gardens of Worcester College
and the golden stone buildings of the Oxford University Press,
and not far from a lovely stretch of the Thames and the Rainbow Bridge to Port Meadow and the Holy Well of St.
Frideswide. But closer to Oliver's house were the tracks of
British Rail and the public allotment gardens. The Oxford
Canal itself was no longer a bustling artery for commercial
narrowboats. Behind the church of St. Barnabas, its banks
were lined with brushy tangles and a littered parking lot.

Like the rest of the city, the neighborhood was a mixture of
the sublime and the tawdry. The short public ways off Walton
Street were a kind of downmarket North Oxford. The blocks
of modest houses had once been occupied by the servants of
North Oxford dons. Now they were rooming houses, bed-
and-breakfast places, lodgings for working people and visiting

scholars. Babies blossomed on Walton Street. Young mothers heaved strollers over the humps of the pavement, and undergraduates from Somerville College were thick on the street. Graduate students from every college in the university lived in nearby digs. They strode along the narrow sidewalks, dodging the bicycles chained to the railings, heading for the corner where Little Clarendon Street led to the Woodstock and Banbury Roads and the few acres of Oxford where the most ancient of the colleges were huddled together.

Dorothy Jarvis was a sensible and levelheaded woman. On the discovery of the body, she did things in the right order. First she went straight to the loo to be sick, and then she called the St. Aldate's police station.

Homer Kelly would not have known about Oliver's death until the evening news on television if Detective Inspector Mukerji had not taken the trouble to track down his phone number at Keble. "I believe this young man was more or less engaged to the daughter of Professor Dubchick. Could there be a connection of some sort with the events in the museum? I suppose not. It is a wild thought. But then I am given to wild thoughts. After all, my Hindu holy books are wilder than your Old Testament. You have a creator in the shape of a man. Ours is a snake." Mukerji chuckled and hung up, good-humored in the face of calamity.

Homer snatched up his map of Oxford, scribbled a note to Mary, plunged down the stairs, and half-ran, half-walked, in the direction of St. Barnabas Street.

It was straight west for a mile and a half, and Homer was tired when he rounded the massive apse of the church of St. Barnabas. From inside he could hear the plangent voice of the priest blessing the wine. Holy Communion was being cele-brated at the moment, although some of the parishioners had forgone the sacrament in order to stand outside and watch what was going on next door.

There was no mistaking the house. Police cars were every-where, tilted up on the sidewalk, blocking the street. An am-bulance was on its way, its siren audible from a distance. Here it came, reeling around the curve of St. Barnabas, the siren winding down.

Now for the first time Homer was overcome by the misery of the young clergyman's death. The dreariness of the neigh-borhood made it poignantly real. A bicycle leaning against the front of the house summed it up. Its wheels were crazy ellipses, as though they had been ridden over by some heavy vehicle. Bad luck. Homer suspected it was Oliver's bicycle, and that misfortune had dogged him all his life.

Some people were born that way, thought Homer sadly. As one of the lucky ones himself, he often grieved at the brutal destiny afflicting some of his friends. Their bread fell butter-side-down, they were dogged by tragedy. Their children were born with cerebral palsy, their wives fell victim to multiple sclerosis, they died young themselves from some torturing kind of cancer. Well, all right, one shouldn't expect life to be fair, but it shouldn't be so cruelly unfair either.

Police Constable Gilly guarded the door. "Good morning, sir. My boss said to let you in." Gilly held open the door and murmured in Homer's ear, "It's pretty bad."

Homer winced, and climbed the stairs. At the top stood a majestic woman, gazing calmly at Detective Constable Ives, who was holding an open notebook. His pencil was poised over a blank page.

"It just seems to me," said the woman, "that the police are not protecting the citizens of this city." Her words were petulant, but her manner was transcendent, like God chastising Ives from a burning bush.

The detective constable nodded at Homer, rolled his eyes, put his pencil in his teeth, opened the door of Oliver's room, stuck his head in, removed the pencil, and murmured, "Dr. Kelly is here."

"Come in, Homer," called Gopal Mukerji. "Be careful, there isn't much room."

Homer sidled in. At first he couldn't see the body on the floor, there were so many people in the way. Then someone moved aside, and he had a clear view of the white face and the shirt soaked in blood. The yellow curls were unspotted. Homer tried to appear unmoved, but nausea heaved inside him.

Mukerji drew close and spoke to him softly. "Well, you can see it for yourself, the jackknife in his right hand."

"Suicide?"

"Or an attempt by someone to make it look that way. I don't suppose you know whether or not Oliver Clare was right-handed?"

"Sorry, no."

"And then there's that." Mukerji pointed to a strip of paper taped clumsily to the wall above Oliver's bed. Words were scrawled on it in capital letters. They could be read across the room:

THE ANSWER IS NO.

At once Homer was struck with a fit of shivering. It was all so eerie and terrible—the message on the wall, the bloody body on the floor, the scantily furnished room crowded with too many people, the absence of anything personal to the dead boy except the crucifix over his bed. At this hour not a single ray fell through the window from the October sun that was bathing all outdoors with cheerful light, brightening the roofs and chimneys of the houses on St. Barnabas Street, glittering on the red paint of the narrowboats in the canal, shining on the river as it moved serenely to the sea, its surface scattered with leaves from the trees along Fiddler's Island and soda cans dropped from the Rainbow Bridge.

Homer nodded at the strip of paper on the wall. "What does it mean, *The answer is no?* The answer to what question?"

"That's just it." Mukerji gave him a look, while a couple of policewomen dismantled the lighting equipment. "To what question would you yourself answer no?"

Homer could think of several. *Should there be so many violent deaths in the city of Oxford? Should clergymen die young? Should* Homo sapiens *have evolved into this dangerous and bloodthirsty subspecies?*

But there was one painfully obvious question to which the answer had surely been no: *Freddy Dubchick, will you marry me?* It was a trite and sentimental solution to Mukerji's problem, but it was probably correct.

"Might it have been a question put to someone else?" said Homer cautiously. "A woman, for instance? I gather that Oliver's affair with Professor Dubchick's daughter was on the rocks."

"Oh, is that so?" Mukerji's clever face brightened. Homer was reminded of the pictures in Darwin's book on facial expression—chimpanzees pouting, babies crying, little girls beaming. Mukerji's face would fit right in.

Homer wanted to get out. The room was too full of people, the air too sickening with the smell of blood, too heavy with a gruesome combination of tragedy and businesslike action. The medical examiner pushed past Homer and joined the detective sergeants, who were stepping cautiously around Oliver's body as though it were a pit into which they might fall.

Mukerji nodded as Homer gripped his arm and said goodbye. Stepping out into the hall, Homer at once caught sight of a commotion at the foot of the stairs, a woman sobbing, Police Constable Gilly shouting, "No, no, miss."

It was Freddy Dubchick, making a rush at the stairs. Mrs. Jarvis reached out to stop her. Detective Constable Ives put his body in the way, but she squeezed past both of them. Homer too tried to hold her, but Freddy had become immensely strong. She thrust past him and burst into Oliver's room.

P.C. Gilly charged up the stairs and followed her in, breathlessly apologizing. "I'm sorry, sir," he said to Mukerji. "She got away from me. Now, miss, please come downstairs."

But Freddy moaned, "No, no, I didn't say that," and fell to her knees. Homer caught her as she went down.

"Here," said Mukerji quickly, "put her on the bed."

Homer lifted her by the shoulders and Gilly took her ankles, still apologizing. "Oh, God, sir, I'm sorry, I'm really sorry." Together they laid her on the bed.

Again Homer slipped out of the room. At the foot of the stairs he nodded grimly to Detective Constable Ives, who had taken Gilly's place at the door. On the way home he told himself that he had expected a different sort of university city. People would be civilized and subtle here at Oxford, inhabiting a realm of sophistication in which he would feel like a small child, a raw and clumsy American. But instead—look at them! Brutal husbands tormenting their wives, fainting women, rejected suitors killing themselves for love—it was like a music-hall melodrama from the nineteenth century, not part of the splendid heritage of eight hundred years of learning.

Had Oliver Clare really killed himself for love? Had Freddy Dubchick answered no to that all-important question? Or was she denying it when she said, "No, no, I didn't say that"? Did she mean she had not really turned him down? But the fact was, she didn't have to say it in so many words—"No, Oliver, I will not marry you." She had made it perfectly clear at Hampton Court. Homer saw again the stricken face of Oliver Clare as he walked away from the sight of Freddy in the arms of Hal Shaw, the redheaded zoologist from Kansas.

Another surprise was waiting for Homer, back at Keble. He found Mary watching television in the sitting room. Before he could say hello, before he could tell her what he had witnessed, she held up her hand and whispered, "Homer, sssh."

He was offended. He was also exhausted and starving. But at once he forgot his hurt feelings and his tiredness and hunger. There on the screen was the house on St. Barnabas Street. Beside the ruined bicycle stood a famous BBC correspondent, reporting from the scene of the tragedy. His vowels were plummy, his voice deep and rich. "Here in Oxford this morning the descendant of a famous Oxfordshire family was found dead with his throat cut. The body of Oliver Clare, who was ordained last year as an Anglican priest, was discovered in this house on St. Barnabas Street in the area of Oxford known as Jericho. If his death was by suicide, the motive has not been determined. His grief-stricken parents had nothing to say to our London correspondent as they emerged from their house on Pont Street."

At once Oliver's rooming house vanished, replaced by a glimpse of a London street and a dignified-looking elderly couple hurrying into a car. As the car door slammed, the London correspondent whispered into her microphone, "Robert Clare, originally the squire of Windrush Hall in Burford, is now a retired solicitor."

The car on Pont Street zoomed away. At once the scene shifted and the troubles of the royal family blossomed on the screen. Another correspondent piped up, her voice tuned to a note of mocking insinuation.

CHAPTER 33

My theology is a simple muddle.
Charles Darwin, letter to Joseph Hooker

It was Sunday again. Homer lay flat on his back in bed while Mary bumped around the room, getting dressed. "Mukerji's awfully smart," he said, gazing at the ceiling. "You have to admit that. I wonder if he's dogged at the same time."

"Dogged!"

"Like Darwin."

"Oh, Darwin!" Mary discovered a run in her stockings, and cursed.

"He didn't think he was very intelligent. You know, not a genius like his friend Huxley. He thought it was his dogged-ness that made the difference. *It's dogged that does it,* that's what he said. So he studied barnacles for eight years before he wrote *The Origin of Species*. And he spent his last years investigating—guess what?"

"I can't. Damn and blast."

"Earthworms. He did a lot of nice little dogged experiments on earthworms."

Mary pulled bureau drawers open and slammed them shut. "Oh, Homer, my God, it's half-past. I'll be late for church." She threw open the closet door and tumbled the shoes this way and that.

198

Homer leaned up on one elbow and looked fondly at his wife. "I like the way you're doggedly working your way through the churches of Oxford. Which one is it this Sunday?"

"The University Church of St. Mary the Virgin. You know, that big one on the High Street."

"Hey, no kidding." Homer sprang out of bed. "Hold it, wait for me. Wasn't that Oliver Clare's church? The one where he was rector? That's what Professor Dubchick told me. St. Mary's, he said. I want to see what it's like."

"Well, all right, but for heaven's sake, hurry up."

They rode their rented bikes, pedaling straight up Parks Road and Catte Street and bumping uncomfortably over the cobblestones of Radcliffe Square. Dismounting, they locked their bicycles to the railing around the Radcliffe Camera in a tangle of undergraduate wheels and handlebars. Walking along the passage to the High, they peered into a college entry where a sign said

BRASENOSE COLLEGE

CLOSED TO VISITORS

and approached the church by the front door.

The entrance on the High was one of Oxford's marvels. Its two fantastic columns reminded Homer of rubber bands in windup airplanes. Someone had twisted the two columns of golden stone, the left one clockwise, the right counterclockwise, until they writhed upward, charged with potential energy, ready to take off. Above them rose an architectural confection of curling volutes and statuary.

"You know what I like about Oxford?" said Mary. "They went whole hog. The architects, I mean. They didn't give a damn about restraint and functional form. It was excess all the way."

"Oh, right," said Homer as they made their way inside. "If

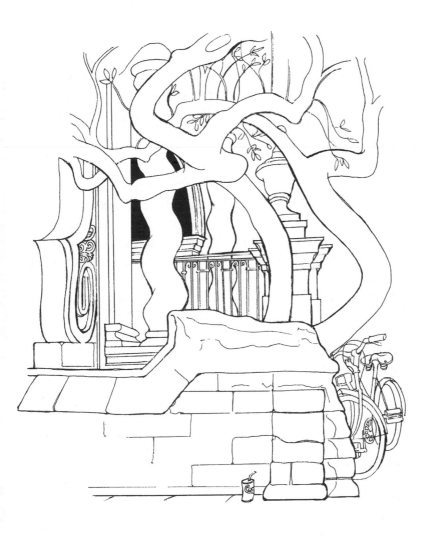

you wanted a useful building, you stuck a tower on top, and then you stroked your chin because you weren't quite satisfied, it wasn't enough, it needed a little more somehow, so you stuck pinnacles all over the tower, and then you pasted on ten thousand crockets. Whole hog, that's right, that's Oxford. They went whole hog."

"Homer, sssh."

Softly they pushed open a glass door and made their way to one of the pews at the rear, as the broad high spaces of the church opened around them. The congregation was standing, singing a hymn. A layman in a dark suit brought them two orders of service and a fat green hymnal opened to the right page.

Mary didn't need it. The hymn was familiar, "The Spacious Firmament on High." She sang it lustily, thumping out the repetitive undergirding F-naturals in the alto line, showing off a little, giving hearty tongue to Joseph Addison's recitation of the wonders of the heavens and the rejoicing in reason's ear and the spreading of the truth from pole to pole, the truth that the entire creation was the work of an almighty hand. Then, bang! Mary closed the book with a tidy slam, nudged Homer, and whispered, "Okay, Charles Darwin, deny that if you can."

Homer grinned and sat down. He could imagine Darwin sitting on his revolving chair at Down House, explaining courteously to Mary Kelly that Addison had used the word God to personify natural law. *It is Newton's gravitational law that rules the planets, Mrs. Kelly, not some almighty hand with nice clean fingernails.*

Mary enjoyed church services, even when reason's ear gently shucked off most of what she heard. This church was very grand. Tall piers soared around her, the shadows of birds darted across the wall, the organ made a massive articulated noise, and the vicar was a handsome old man with a magnificent accent. His sermon was intelligent, mildly addressing the ear of reason.

It was time for the Nicene creed. "All stand," said the vicar. Homer stood silent while the congregation murmured the words,

We believe in one God, the Father, the almighty, maker of heaven and earth, of all that is, seen and unseen.

The collective soft humming reminded Homer of the murmuration in the museum, somehow representing more than the sum of the voices actually speaking. It was entire populations whispering and talking. In the museum it was all the creatures of the earth softly barking or growling, it was the reverberating fall of trees in the forest. Here it was the faithful, it was bishops and archbishops, worshiping a great invisible personage who had made them, who had created the universe and miraculously fathered a son whose death would save all of them into eternal life, all of these young churchgoing undergraduates and their elders, every single human being sitting around Homer in these noble pews.

We look for the resurrection of the dead, and the life of the world to come. Amen.

Now for the prayer of intercession. Mary and Homer bowed their heads and leaned forward, while kneeling stools were pulled out all around them, scraping the floor, and bodies were lowered with a slithering of coats. At home in Concord, Massachusetts, the Kellys were not members of any of the local churches, although they occasionally visited the First Parish Church on Lexington Road. The First Parish was Unitarian, with a freethinking congregation for whom kneeling would have been a strange and unfamiliar act.

Homer stared at the knees of his trousers, which were so politely refusing to lower themselves. He did not expect to be resurrected. Someday his body would be buried or cremated and that would be it. His bones would never spring together on some final day of judgment, some moment of the universal clattering enhingement of all the buried bones in the world. Nor would his dead muscles be reborn, to clap themselves once again to his bones. His blood would never pour into his body from some giant overarching pitcher. It was too bad, but Homer could not force himself to believe otherwise.

Mary sat quietly during the communion part of the service, coming to a conclusion. It was slowly dawning on her that this was the wrong church. Young Oliver Clare couldn't possibly have been the rector of the University Church of St. Mary the Virgin. Homer must have been mistaken. Surely Oliver had been too young and naive to stand before this congregation and preach with authority. It must have been some other St. Mary's entirely.

CHAPTER 34

The more one thinks the more one feels the hopeless immensity of man's ignorance.

Charles Darwin, letter to Lord Farrer

After the service there was a jolly reception in the church hall. Mary and Homer accepted cups of coffee, and Mary introduced herself to the undergraduate who had assisted the rector in serving communion. "My husband and I are wondering what church Oliver Clare was connected with, the young man who—"

"—who died yesterday," supplied the undergraduate, whose name was Matthew Friendly. "I saw it on the telly. Too bad. No, sorry, I don't know where he worked."

"We assumed it was a local Anglican church, because he lived—"

"—in Oxford, yes, I saw that too. Well, all I can suggest is that you ask the rector." Matthew Friendly nodded amiably in the direction of the priest who had led the service.

Mary thanked him, then lowered her voice, "Tell me, how does one address a rector? I don't know the British forms of—"

"—of address, I see, of course not, naturally not." Friendly had a disagreeable habit of finishing one's sentences. "It's just 'Mr.' You just say 'Mr. Gideon.' There's no other—"

"—form of address," said Mary, teaching him a lesson, but she doubted he noticed.

Mr. Gideon, too, was ignorant of Oliver's church connection. He had never heard of Oliver Clare.

Homer and Mary left the reception and returned to their bicycles.

"Freddy Dubchick would know about Oliver's church," said Mary, settling herself on the tall seat and wobbling forward. "Do you think you could ask her?"

"Poor kid. I should have stuck around to hear what she said when she woke up from her fainting spell. When we get back, I'll call Mukerji."

But Gopal Mukerji was in a querulous mood. "Never," he told Homer on the telephone, "be a gentleman. I didn't keep the girl for questioning. I told her I would speak with her in the afternoon, and then I sent her home with Police Constable Henrietta Lark. P.C. Lark drove Ms. Dubchick to her house on Norham Road and handed her over to her father." Mukerji uttered an unfamiliar word. Homer guessed it was a Bengali curse. "In the afternoon Ms. Dubchick could not be reached. Her father could not be reached. They have fled."

"Oh, not fled," said Homer. "Surely not fled." He said goodbye to Detective Inspector Mukerji, then turned to his wife. "They've gone. William took Freddy away. Why don't I call Helen Farfrae? She might know where they are."

"No, wait, Homer. It's too soon. Too much has happened. She's still working only part-time. Let her alone."

"But she's your devoted pal and confidante. You could call her."

"No, no. She's withdrawn from me a little. I think she regrets pouring out all the violence of her feelings the day after her husband's death. And now there's this horrible thing about poor Oliver, which involves Freddy Dubchick, the daughter of Helen's boss. I don't want us to play big investigators, not now, not at a time like this."

In the end they agreed that Homer would make a simple businesslike call and ask a single straightforward question.

Mary stood listening uneasily while he called Helen's number in Kidlington.

She answered warily. Then she sounded relieved. "Oh, Homer, hello."

At once he abandoned his businesslike plan. "Helen, are you all right? Are you safe there, all alone?"

For a moment Helen said nothing, afraid to betray the pleasure she felt in her newfound solitude. Her tumultuous feelings were beginning to settle down. Guilt and sorrow had convulsed her, and the news of the violent end of Oliver Clare had shocked her, but no grief could match the sordid misery of her married life. "Yes," she said at last, "I'm fine."

Mary was making faces at Homer. He asked his question. "Inspector Mukerji tells me Professor Dubchick and his daughter have run away. Do you know if it's true?"

"Well, it's true that they're gone," said Helen, "but they weren't running away. William called to say he was taking Freddy away for a while. That was all. He said she'd had an awful blow."

"I see. Did he say where they were going?"

"No, he didn't. Perhaps to Cornwall. They have a house there, and Professor Dubchick's sister lives nearby. I don't know where it is in Cornwall."

"Well, perhaps you can tell me what I wanted to learn from Freddy. We're trying to find the church where Oliver Clare was rector. It was called St. Mary's, but it wasn't St. Mary the Virgin. Do you know of any other St. Mary's?"

"What about St. Mary Mag?"

"St. Mary Mag?"

"St. Mary Magdalen. You remember, it's the church at the triangle between St. Giles and Broad Street, near the Martyrs' Memorial, right across from Balliol."

Homer did not remember. There were too many splendid colleges on the Broad and the High for one more medieval-looking building to register on his memory. But he saw the

church at once as he emerged from the Lamb and Flag Passage and ambled past Balliol, where another army of bicycles cluttered the wall. As he crossed the street, a dozen kids romped up the steep encircling steps of the Martyrs' Memorial. Above them Ridley and Latimer gestured mournfully, reminding all and sundry of their sad burnings at the stake. The children paid no attention. The two martyrs might have been catapulted into space, for all they cared.

The church occupied an island between the two streets. There was a sign on the iron fence around it, proclaiming it to be the Parish Church of St. Mary Magdalen. The sign listed the hours of Sunday and weekday services, but it did not give the name of the rector. Homer found his way in, and spoke to a woman who was setting out pamphlets on a table in the entry.

"Excuse me, my name is Homer Kelly. I'm a visiting lecturer at Keble College. Can you tell me if a priest named Oliver Clare was the vicar here?"

The woman had a handsome presence. She was obviously one of the pillars holding up the church. "You mean the young man who died yesterday?" She shook her head sadly. "No, I'm afraid I never even heard his name before I read about him in the *Times*."

"But I understand he was vicar of a church called St. Mary's."

"Oh, there are lots of St. Marys in Oxfordshire. I don't know which is which. Try the phone book. There's one in my office. Come in."

"Thank you," said Homer humbly. He sat down with the phone book, made a list of churches called St. Mary, and thanked the pillar of the church. Then he made his way to the Eagle and Child, where he was meeting his wife for lunch.

Mary had commandeered a tiny table and ordered two tall glasses of beer. "Maybe it's just Americans who order pints of

bitter in British pubs," she said to Homer, as he lifted his glass. "I don't care."

Homer looked around the narrow room, which was crowded with people making loud conversation. "Isn't this C. S. Lewis's old pub? Where he met those other guys of similar literary and theological persuasion?"

"That's what it says on the wall," said Mary. "It's too bad I'm not the sweet innocent young girl I was before I met you. I was a big Lewis fan once."

Homer was charmed to learn something new about the wife of his bosom. "You were? You mean you changed your mind?"

"Well, of course I admit he's charming, and he can certainly spin a story. But I think his logical proofs for the existence of

God and the lessons of the Bible are just clever ways of playing with words. It's all from Cloud-Cuckoo Land, that's what I think."

Homer took a swig from his pint. "It always seemed to me that he didn't start far enough back. He takes the doctrines of the Anglican church as already granted, as though everybody agreed they were the ground of all being, then goes on from there. I always get grumpy at about page twenty-five. Look." He hauled his scribbled list out of his pocket. "I'm still not getting anywhere in trying to find the church where Oliver Clare was the pastor. It wasn't Mary Magdalen. But look, there are all these other places called St. Mary's."

Mary pulled her chair closer and together they consulted the list. There was a St. Mary & All Saints in Beaconfield, a St. Mary the Virgin in Charlbury, a St. Mary's in Cogges, and a St. Mary the Beneficent in a council estate called Nightingale Court. There were also St. Mary's Centres in Banbury, Haddenham and Wendover.

"I'll call them," promised Mary. "I'll go home and call them all."

CHAPTER 35

We have lost the joy of the household, and the solace of our old age.
Charles Darwin, on the death of his daughter Annie

🐦

"I t's St. Mary the Beneficent on the Abingdon Road," said Mary, coming into the sitting room where Homer was working at a table littered with papers and books. "Oliver was the rector there. It's in a council estate called Nightingale Court. They're planning a memorial service for him a week from today. The woman on the phone sounded all broken up. Well, of course they would be."

"We'll be there," said Homer, slamming one book shut and picking up another. "Memorial services are always brimming over with fact and fiction about the dear departed."

The next Sunday afternoon they walked to Cornmarket Street and waited for a bus. The sidewalk was thronged with children heading for a Disney film. When the Abingdon bus wheezed to a stop and unfolded its door, Mary looked up at the driver and asked, "Is this the right bus for Nightingale Court?"

He glanced at her as though surprised. "That's right. That'll be eighty pence."

They climbed on, paid their fare, and sat down. The other seats were filled with people of all races—Indian, African, Chinese, Japanese, Caribbean. An elderly couple in the seat behind them conversed in German. The bus chugged along

212

Cornmarket to the High, then slowed down behind a double-decker tour bus and stopped cold at the tortured crossing of Carfax, where Roman legions had once, perhaps, herded oxen to the ford across the river.

"Oh, look, Homer," said Mary, "something's happening." She pointed at the Carfax tower, and Homer leaned across her to take a look. Everyone on the street was gazing up at a man standing on the parapet at the top. He was wearing a crash helmet and fiddling with a rope.

"My God," said Homer, "what's he going to do?"

"It's a charity of some sort," said a learned-looking Indian gentleman, turning around in the seat in front of them. "He'll be coming down the side pretty soon. They're raising money for something."

"Do you think," said Mary doubtfully, "he really knows what he's doing?"

"Oh, I suppose so," said Homer. "He's probably a rock climber in his spare time. They're insane, those people, but they're pretty careful."

The bus was stuck in gridlock with three small Park and Ride buses, an Oxford Citylink bus, and half a dozen cars. Pedestrians streamed in all directions, further scrambling the tangle.

The bus passengers had an unobstructed view of the action at the top of the tower. Homer and Mary watched as the man in the crash helmet climbed over the parapet and began rappelling down the stony vertical wall with the rope hooked to his belt. Another rope was paid out by a colleague at the top. Halfway down, the climber took courage and made a brave jump, flinging himself away from the wall and bouncing back. By the time the bus began moving forward into St. Aldate's, he was at the bottom of the tower, standing upright on the pavement, unhooking the rope while the onlookers clapped.

It was not a long ride to Nightingale Court, but there were a number of stops. One by one the white people on the bus got off, until only people of color remained. At last the bus driver called out, "Nightingale," and stepped down for a smoke. It was the last stop.

"There's the church," said Mary. "See? It says St. Mary the Beneficent."

It was a small modern building, its triangular lines recalling the architectural stereotypes of the nineteen-fifties. Behind it rose the towers of the council estate. Nightingale Court was a city unto itself at the end of the bus line. Mary thought of communities like this at home, Columbia Point in Boston, Cabrini Green in Chicago. In the United States they were warehouses for the poor, and as communities they were not very successful. Was this one any better? And how on earth had Oliver Clare fitted in, that blond and blue-eyed scion of the upper class? His fair-skinned beauty could not have been what was needed, and his inexperience must have been a joke.

The entrance to the church was draped in black. Mary and Homer followed the Indian professor across the street. While they waited in the crowd gathered around the door, a car pulled up at the curb. "Homer, look," murmured Mary, "Oliver's mother and father."

"How do you know it's Oliver's mother and father?"

"We saw them on television, remember?"

"Oh, of course."

They tried not to stare. The tragedy was beyond expression. The faces of Oliver's parents were drawn and pale. As they walked to the door, stumbling a little, someone came out to greet them, a burly black man in a dark suit. He murmured a welcome, they murmured in reply, and he ushered them into the church ahead of everyone else.

Solemnly Homer and Mary shuffled in after them. The interior of the church was like the outside, dramatic and trapezoidal, with a ceiling swooping from low to high. Families occupied the pews. Children sat beside their parents, swinging their feet, bobbing up and down. Maternal hands cautioned them, pulled at skirts, adjusted neckties, arranged hair ribbons. Homer and Mary sat down beside a black woman nearly as tall as Homer. As everyone rose to sing she smiled at them and proffered her hymnbook. Children squealed, a baby cried. Nobody seemed to mind. With a pang, Homer remembered seeing Oliver in the courtyard of the museum with a band of little dark-skinned children. It should have dawned on him at once that they belonged to his own parish.

The eulogist was kind. Oliver's memory was well served by the big black man who had welcomed Oliver's parents. "His faith was a beacon to those of us in doubt, his youth was a blessing to the elders within our congregation, his athletic program was an inspiration to the young. We trust in the mercy of God, in the resurrection of the dead, in the glory of heaven for our brother, the Reverend Oliver Clare, so tragically taken from his loving mother and father and from his parish. Let us pray."

Mary couldn't help watching Mr. and Mrs. Clare as they knelt together, conspicuous in the front row. Their heads were bowed. Mrs. Clare's plump shoulders shook. Her husband put his arm around her, and the shaking stopped.

After the service there was a reception in the parish hall. Children ran around among the folding chairs. Teenagers passed trays of cakes. Oliver's mother and father stood bravely beside the man who had conducted the service and shook hands and nodded gratefully as their son's parishioners came forward to say how sorry they were. Tears flowed.

When their turn came, Homer and Mary murmured their sympathy, and explained that they were friends of William Dubchick and his daughter Freddy.

Mrs. Clare looked vaguely around the room. "Where *is* Freddy? I expected to see her here. Why didn't she come?"

"I think her father took her away," explained Mary uncomfortably. "She was terribly upset."

"I see," said Mrs. Clare, tight-lipped.

Someone else pressed forward to say polite things to the bereaved parents. Mary and Homer moved aside, and were promptly offered cups of coffee by the tall woman who had sat next to them during the service. They introduced themselves, and Mary said the first thing that came into her head. "He was so young."

"It was what we loved about him," said the woman, whose name was Mrs. Marilyn Kinshi. Her skin was very dark, her hair a work of art, braided in a thousand strands and threaded with beads. Her speech had the precise articulation of East Africa. "It is true that he could not spend much time with us, we are so far out of the city, and of course he had many duties in the cathedral, but he did his best. He was very good with the children."

"The cathedral?"

"Don't you know the cathedral?" Mrs. Kinshi laughed, delighted to educate these poor outsiders from the United States. "The Oxford Cathedral is for everyone, it is where the bishop belongs, the Bishop of Oxford. It is also the chapel of the college of Christ Church. You see how learned I am! Our Oliver was very important in the cathedral. Oftentimes he had duties there that kept him away." Mrs. Kinshi leaned forward and lowered her voice. "The cathedral! You know, there has been something of a scandal about the cathedral."

"A scandal?" said Mary.

Mrs. Kinshi nodded in the direction of the man who had read the eulogy. "Mr. Benshara was convinced that Oliver would have preferred the cathedral. You know, with the bishop presiding and all the music? But when he inquired, the bishop refused! He was very stuffy!" Mrs. Kinshi threw back her head and laughed. Then she grew solemn again. "And anyway, Oliver's parents insisted that the service should take place in his own parish. Wasn't that good of them? We are so happy!"

"Tell me, Mrs. Kinshi," said Homer boldly, "was Oliver a good preacher?"

Again Mrs. Kinshi laughed heartily. "No, no, he was a terrible preacher. But he was a nice boy. All the women felt like his auntie. It is dreadful that anyone should kill such a nice boy."

Homer turned confidential, following Mrs. Kinshi's example. "Do you think he might have killed himself, Mrs. Kinshi?"

"I am not sure what I think." Mrs. Kinshi's good humor turned sober. "He suffered from self-doubt, I know that. He worried about his preaching, because he knew it was not good. And his girlfriend, we heard that she—" Mrs. Kinshi's hand spread wide. "Where is she? We have not met her. She is not here."

Once again there was no good answer to the question. Impulsively, Mary asked, "Do you think he believed in God?" Homer looked at his wife, amazed.

Mrs. Kinshi didn't seem to find it strange. "Oh, yes! He was a believer. He gave a sermon about God. When was it? Oh, my Lord"—a tear ran down her cheek—"it was just two weeks ago. It was really a very good sermon." She mopped at her face with a tissue.

They thanked her, and smiled at the children, and shook the hand of Mr. Benshara, and said goodbye.

Outdoors they crossed the street to the bus stop, where the Oxford bus was about to pull out. It was full of passengers. The door was shut. Homer knocked on it, and the door unfolded. He climbed in and put coins in the driver's tray. But then Mary said, "Oh, Homer, wait a sec," and raced back across the street to the straggling lawn in front of the church.

"Mary," shouted Homer, jumping down from the bus, "hurry up, what's the matter with you?"

She gave him an odd look as she crossed the street again, walking slowly. The bus driver stared at her, his hand on the brake release.

Homer urged her up the step in front of him, and they reeled down the aisle as the bus whirled around in a U-turn. "What were you doing?" said Homer. "I thought he wasn't going to wait."

Mary looked at him. "I was reading the notice board. Oliver's last sermon was still posted, although it was two weeks ago. Do you know what it was called, the sermon about God that Mrs. Kinshi was talking about?"

"I can't guess."

" 'The Answer Is Yes.' "

"What? You don't mean it! 'The Answer Is—' "

"*Yes.* That's what Oliver called it—'The Answer Is Yes.' "

CHAPTER 36

"What do you know about this business?" the King said to Alice.
"Nothing," said Alice.
"Nothing whatever?" persisted the King.
"Nothing whatever," said Alice.
"That's very important," the King said.

Lewis Carroll, *Alice's Adventures in Wonderland*

Next day Homer went to the St. Aldate's police station to tell Gopal Mukerji about the service for Oliver Clare in the church of St. Mary the Beneficent. He also described the strange tension between the message on the wall of Oliver's room and the title of his sermon on the notice board in front of his church.

"Ah," said Mukerji, "that is interesting. Optimism—*The answer is yes.* Followed by pessimism—*The answer is no.* What does it mean?"

"Perhaps," said Homer, "it means that his death had less to do with his sexual frustration over Professor Dubchick's daughter than we thought. I understand the sermon was about God."

"God!" Mukerji laughed, and shrugged his shoulders. "Well, naturally, what else would an Anglican clergyman preach about? Although what you Christians think about God is to me a mystery. I am a Hindu. To me your God is an underprivileged second cousin of my God. He is deprived of divine company. He is without avatars for all human and earthly qualities."

"But I'm not exactly a Christian either," protested Homer. "Not anymore. I'm a transcendentalist. Did you know that Henry Thoreau had a great interest in the Hindu sacred books?"

Mukerji raised his eyebrows to show his ignorance. "Who is Henry Thoreau?" Then he got back to brass tacks. "Look here, we know all about Oliver Clare's church. We were out there this morning. It is a high-crime area. Most of the residents are good folk, really, but there are also a lot of young thugs whose weapon of choice is a knife. There was a murder in Nightingale Court only a month ago. Someone else got his throat cut. We've been looking into it. And this morning a computer was stolen from the church office."

Homer gasped. "Did you say another murder? You mean there was another murder with a knife?"

"Part of a burglary, probably. A stereo was taken, and a handful of lottery tickets. We're wondering if the clergyman's death was also part of a botched burglary. The woman downstairs, Mrs. Jarvis, she said Oliver Clare's telly was stolen last week. Someone broke through a window when the house was empty. She was angry because she had to pay for the repair. She shook her finger at me and wanted to know why the police didn't do a better job." Mukerji laughed. "I was frightened. She is a formidable lady."

Homer was curious. "What about the rest of his stuff? What happened to the things in his room?"

"There wasn't much. His personal possessions, we took them away. We will keep them for a while. Do you want to see them? There was a lot of stuff in his wardrobe, sort of thrown in higgledy-piggledy."

Higgledy-piggledy—the expression struck a familiar chord in Homer's memory. It was what Sir John Herschel had said about Darwin's theory, *It is the law of higgledy-piggledy.* For some reason the two higgledy-piggledys jiggled and giggled together. "Yes, of course I'd like to see them."

Mukerji dispatched Detective Constable Ives, who returned a moment later with a box of Oliver Clare's belongings, grinned at Homer, and went away again.

"You didn't want to see the bloody shirt, did you?" said Mukerji. "We've got the jackknife and the clothes he was wearing in a separate collection. And that strip of paper on the wall. You know, the one that said—" Mukerji shook his head fiercely from side to side. "*The answer is no*—not on your life, nothing doing. If you want to see those, I'll—"

"No, no," said Homer, staring into the box of Oliver's possessions, "this is fine. Is it okay if I just reach in and take a look?"

"Certainly. We have done whatever analysis was possible. We found only two things of interest. One, this little penknife. As you can see it is quite sharp, but too small and feeble for the cutting of a throat. And two, these ropes." Mukerji leaned over the box and pulled out a lumpy plastic bag.

"Telephone, sir." It was Detective Constable Ives, holding up a phone.

Mukerji dumped the bundle on the desk. "Excuse me, Homer."

Left to himself, Homer pulled out the contents of the plastic bag, two coils of yellow rope. At once he remembered the kid who had been rappelling down the side of the old tower at Carfax, raising money for charity. Hadn't his rope been yellow like this one? The wall had been vertical, but he had come down it like a fly.

Like a fly! If you had a rope you wouldn't have to be an anthropoid ape in order to climb the side of a wall. You wouldn't even have to be an orangutan like the ones in the London Zoo. You could be an ordinary member of the human race and haul yourself up with a yellow cord.

Homer examined the coils of rope. They were tightly woven, but they looked too narrow to bear much weight. He stuffed them back into the bag and groped around in the box, fishing up a black sweater, a pair of gray pants, and a black woolen jacket, the kind of inconspicuous clothing a pious young clergyman might wear. There were boxer shorts, two pairs of skimpy dark socks, and a couple of priestly collars in a plastic container.

At the bottom of the box Homer struck gold. He found a lumpy sack full of small steel objects and an aluminum pulley. It was obvious that they went with the rope. Reaching into the inside pocket of his jacket, Homer took out the small metal oval he had picked up on the roof of the museum on the morning after Bobby Fenwick's death. The sack contained two others just like it.

Delighted, Homer held the three of them side by side. They were a perfect match. What did it mean? Was Oliver Clare the *creature* Helen Farfrae had seen climbing the glass roof? Had he been using this very rope, belaying it with the pulley and the small steel gadgets, in order to do the impossible?

"Homer," said Detective Inspector Mukerji, bursting in the

door, "it's one damn thing after another. That was the proprietor of the little post office store on Walton Street. She says Mrs. Jarvis told her somebody came to see Oliver Clare on the night he died."

Homer stared at him. "Mrs. Jarvis told a storekeeper something she didn't tell you? While she was buying a stamp?"

"I called her at once." Mukerji heaved a sigh. "She says she didn't tell us because we didn't ask her. Myself, I think it is some neighborhood mystique. *Don't tell the police anything. What have they ever done for you?*"

Homer could think of another reason. He too had met Mrs. Jarvis. She struck him as a woman of godlike whim. Sometimes she raised her hand to bless, sometimes to curse, sometimes she neither blessed nor cursed. "Well, who was it? Did she know who the person was?"

"Only that his name was Hal. He was wearing a heavy parka with a hood. Oliver came downstairs and said, 'Come in, Hal.' Then both of them climbed the stairs and Oliver's door closed behind them."

"Hal! Could it have been Hal Shaw?"

"Who is Hal Shaw?"

Homer bit his tongue. Should he get poor Hal in trouble? Should he tell Mukerji that Hal Shaw was a married man who happened to be emotionally entangled with Freddy Dubchick, although Freddy had loved Oliver Clare only a few weeks before? Should he tell him what Oliver had seen at Hampton Court? "Did she hear this person leave?"

"She did. But first she was gone for a couple of hours at her book club. They were reading"—Mukerji consulted his notes—"*Sexuality and Health*, by Lady Clarissa Montagu. The storekeeper is a member of the same book club, and she told me all about it." Mukerji looked slyly at Homer. "I now know everything there is to know about women's intimate affairs. Yes, Mrs. Jarvis heard him leave. She was just coming home from her book club, just approaching the house as he walked out. She claimed he did not see her."

"Good lord."

"So there could have been a fight, a life-and-death struggle, but she wasn't there to hear it. Hal Shaw could have cut Oliver's throat and seen him fall, then wiped his fingerprints off the knife and put it in Oliver's hand, and pressed Oliver's fingers into the blood. And then he could have cleaned himself up at Oliver's sink and pulled on his parka and left Oliver's room. And then he could have gone home and sudsed his clothes up and down to remove all traces of blood, and then I suppose he went to bed and woke up all sunny and smiling next morning." Gopal Mukerji glowered at Homer. "Tell me about this man Hal Shaw."

Reluctantly Homer began to tell what he knew about the zoologist from Kansas, without mentioning Hal's infatuation with Freddy Dubchick. Before he was done, there was a scuffling in the hall.

"Sorry, sir," gasped Detective Constable Ives, glancing in the door, disappearing again. His arms and legs were obviously in violent motion.

Mukerji was amused. "What have you got there, Ives? Bring it in."

The scuffling stopped. "Well, go ahead then," said Ives angrily.

At once someone catapulted into the room, a slight wiry man, looking disgruntled. "All I want to do is report a stolen object. You'd think I wanted to blow the place up."

Mukerji lost his good humor. "Ives," he said testily, "can't you handle this?"

"No, he cannot," insisted the wiry man. "What do you want me to do? Tell him my name's Charley Firkin? Describe the stolen object? What bloody good does that do? He writes it down, stuffs it in a drawer! Do I get my rope back? I do not!

I told my wife, I said, I'm going straight to the top, and she said, Charley, don't be a fool. I mean, my wife and me, we don't get along."

"Rope?" said Homer. "Did you say rope?"

"What rope?" said Mukerji.

"My rope, that's what rope. A hundred quid the bloody thing cost. On a place like that, you bloody well better have the best, that's what I told my wife when she complained. She wanted a washing-up machine instead, she said. I was selfish, she said. I told you, we don't get along."

"What place?" said Homer eagerly, hardly daring to hope. "Where did you use the rope, Mr. Firkin?"

"Goddamn roof, that's where. Glass whatchamacallit, pyramid. I spent two weeks up there in all weathers repairing the bloody glass. Had to use a blowtorch, melt the mastic, peel off the laminate, take out the broken pieces, nearly cut off my thumb, replace 'em, stick 'em on again, laminate 'em. Christ, I thought I'd never be done."

Homer tried to keep his voice from shaking. "You don't mean the Oxford Museum by any chance, do you, Mr. Firkin?"

"I don't know what the hell it's called. Parks Road. You know. Dinosaurs, ek cetera."

Firkin was one of those people who think every image in their minds is clearly visible to everyone else. Homer glanced at Gopal Mukerji, who pushed Firkin a little further. "The rope," he reminded him. "What's this about your rope?"

"Well, how the hell you think I got up there? I got these ropes, I got this belt, I got these pulleys. Steeplejack, church steeples. I get up there, repair the flashing. Nearer to God, my wife says. Bloody fool."

"Are you saying," said Mukerji patiently, "you were employed to repair the glass roof of the Oxford University Museum, using a rope?"

"Well, Jesus, haven't you been listening? And then some thief stole my best rope. I cleaned up everything, gathered up all my stuff, scrapers, laminating fluid—horrible smell it's got, toxic, I bet, and they don't give you no insurance, only for falls—blowtorch, ladders, so on and so forth. Left my best rope there coupla days. And when I come back, it's gone." Charley Firkin glowered balefully at Detective Inspector Mukerji. "I know who took it too, kid working on the gallery. I'm gonna bring charges, see if I don't."

He was talking about Daniel Tuck, guessed Homer, the workman with the golden voice. "Mr. Firkin, can you tell us when you found it missing?"

"Jesus, how would I know? You think a person remembers one day from another without they take notes?"

"Well, could you describe the rope to us, Mr. Firkin?" said Mukerji.

At once Firkin was specific and businesslike. "Special first-grade eleven-millimeter Dacron. Best there is. You think I'd trust my life to anything less, you got another think coming."

"What—uh—color was the rope, Mr. Firkin?" said Homer.

"What color?" Firkin narrowed his eyes, instantly suspicious. "Why, you got my rope? You trying to trip me up? What color rope you *got*? I'll tell you if it's my rope or not."

Mukerji glared at him. "Mr. Firkin, what—color—was—your—rope?"

Firkin turned sulky. "Well, jeez, it was yellow, wasn't it? Special first-class eleven-millimeter Dacron, best there is, and if you've got it, I want it back."

Mukerji sighed and nodded at Homer, who picked the bundle of rope out of the box of Oliver Clare's possessions.

Firkin reached for it. "You're damn right, that's my rope. My God, it's been here all this time? It's me daily bread, this here rope. You've purloined property essential to my livelihood. And, Christ, what's this? It's been cut!" Wrathfully

Firkin held out a slashed end. "Bloody hell! You'll pay for this."

"I assure you, Mr. Firkin, we didn't touch your damn rope," said Mukerji.

"Oh, sure, a likely story. It's your goddamned fault. You owe me a hundred quid."

CHAPTER 37

One, two! One, two! And through and through
The vorpal blade went snicker-snack!
Lewis Carroll, *Through the Looking-Glass*

❧

On the first wintry night of the Michaelmas term the growing canes on the edge of the narrow ditch beside Motorworld were frozen out, along with the water plantain and the alders hedging the little stream. By morning the banks of the creek had lost every trace of green. Dead leaves hung from gray twigs. Every one of the new seedlings was cut down by frost.

But during their few weeks of life the stolons under the burgeoning plants had spread in all directions. The new arrivals from the north were merely hunkering down.

❧

Hal Shaw was asked to appear at the St. Aldate's police station in order to be fingerprinted. When he approached the front desk, Police Constable Gilly conducted him through the gate and into an office in the rear.

"You have a right to refuse," said Gilly, looking at him questioningly, "unless you are charged with an offense."

"Why should I refuse?" said Hal, his heart sinking. He held out his right hand.

"All right then." Gilly took it and rolled his fingers on the ink pad one by one. "Now the left."

228

Hal smiled wryly. He felt like someone in an old American film. The process seemed primitive and old-fashioned, as though police technicians had learned nothing new in thirty years.

He soon learned that they had. His fingerprints went by overnight dispatch to the main office at Kidlington, where they were compared electronically with those taken from the knife that had slit the throat of Oliver Clare.

Next morning Police Constable Gilly found Hal in the Zoology Office, where he was examining one of the mysterious jars of crabs in the company of William Dubchick.

"It's obviously a decapod," Hal said, following Gilly to the door, "possibly from the Beagle Channel," and then he was gone. William was deeply distressed.

Once again Hal found himself at the St. Aldate's police station. This time he faced Detective Inspector Mukerji. Wordlessly Mukerji held up the printout from Kidlington, so that Hal could see the patterns of lines, ovals and curlicues of two thumbprints side by side. One was smudged, but it was obviously identical to the other.

Still silent, Mukerji held up something else, an evidence bag. Through the clear plastic Hal could see a jackknife. "Well, yes, it looks just like mine," said Hal. "Oh, God, it's not the one—"

"I'm afraid it is the one," said Mukerji, looking at him gravely. "This knife was found in the hand of Oliver Clare. It is certainly the knife that cut his throat. Underneath Clare's fingerprints are many overlaid prints from the hand of someone else. As you can see, our computer identifies them as yours."

Instinctively Hal looked at his right hand. "Of course. It's my knife. I use it all the time. I'm a practicing zoologist."

"Practicing?"

"I mean I'm out in the field. You know, poking at things, prying things apart, cutting up worms, fish, insects, inspecting the stomach contents of raptors. I wondered what I'd done with it." Hal flushed. "No, of course that's not true. I knew at once where I'd left it. I should have come forward."

"Indeed you should have." Mukerji's eloquent eyes drove into Hal's, piercing the pupils, illuminating every corner of his brain. "As has been said by the great Bengali poet Tagore, *Do not keep to yourself the secret of your heart, my friend.* What," he went on softly, "was your knife doing in the hand of the dead man?"

Hal looked troubled. "I will explain."

"Please do so. Sit down, Mr. Shaw."

Hal looked unhappily at the chair, and sat. "I'm afraid it was carelessness on my part. I left it on the table by mistake."

"By mistake. Please explain your mistake."

Hal sighed. "You won't believe me." He reached into one of his trousers pockets, brought out a miniature plastic box, and dumped the contents on Mukerji's desk.

It was a small spider. At once it began walking delicately toward Mukerji. "There, look," said Hal, "did you see it hop? It's a jumping spider." He scooped it up and held it in his hand, and produced from the same pocket a folding lens. Reaching spider and lens to Mukerji, he said, "Here, take a look."

Gamely Mukerji took the lens and inspected the spider on the palm of Hal's hand. Its two principal eyes looked back at him hugely. Mukerji shuddered, and gave back the lens. "I suppose it pounces on its prey?"

"Of course. That's why it has those big eyes. Web spiders don't have eyes like that. Their vision is poor because they don't really need to see well. They can feel the threads vibrate when something lands on the web, and then they just home in on it."

Mukerji shook his head. "I still don't see—"

"You will," said Hal patiently. "I showed the spider to

Oliver. He was going on and on about God's plan and the perfect balance of nature, and he even brought up the rattlesnake."

"The rattlesnake!"

"How its rattle is meant to warn its prey before it strikes, as though God were insisting on fair play."

"And you debunked this sentimental idea, I suppose?"

"Of course. People are always bringing up the rattlesnake. Darwin disposed of it in his book. He said it rattles to alarm its enemies, not to warn them. He said his theory would be destroyed if any part of one species was there only for the good of another. So I told Oliver about that, and then I showed him my jumping spider."

"Whatever for?"

"Well, isn't it obvious? As an example of the way the world really works. Its eyes are big to identify its prey. It jumps to capture it, then inserts its toxin to dissolve the contents of the body." Hal looked anxious as he dropped the spider back in its box. "Under the circumstances perhaps I shouldn't have shown it to him."

Mukerji's patience was running out. Exasperated, he said, "Mr. Shaw, you still have not explained the knife."

"I'm getting to that. I took everything out of my pants pocket, trying to find this little folding lens—my change, my knife, my billfold. I set everything down on the table. Then later, when I put everything back, I forgot the knife."

"Aaah, you forgot the knife." Mukerji sounded intensely skeptical.

🖋

Afterward, discharged by Mukerji, at least for the moment, Hal went back to the museum and waited for Homer Kelly, buttonholing him as he came out of the lecture hall. Together they walked downstairs and drifted into the courtyard. They were alone on the floor. The soft echoing of the building was at its lowest level—it was only the basic underlying hum of the terrestrial wheels.

Homer went right to the point. "What in the *hell* were you doing on St. Barnabas Street in the middle of the night?"

Hal stared at *Ichthyosaurus communis* Conybeare, a swimming reptile flattened by some convulsion of the earth sixty-five million years back in time, when all of southern England had been covered by water. He nodded at the exhibit, which was a squashed mass of vertebrae and skewed ribs with a long reptilian skull at one end and a tail at the other. "Oliver wanted to talk about this."

Homer's mouth opened in surprise. *"This?"*

"Not just this. Evolution, natural selection, Darwin, cuckoos and cowbirds—"

Homer was bewildered. It was an Alice in Wonderland conversation. "Cowbirds?"

"Oh, you know. They lay their eggs in the nests of other birds, and then the big babies crowd out the smaller hatchlings. It's an ugly story. Nobody likes cowbirds."

"Oliver wanted to talk to you about that? He called you?"

"Yes. He asked me if I'd come to his place, and of course I said yes. I thought"—Hal hesitated—"I thought he wanted to talk about something else."

"About Freddy Dubchick," said Homer quietly. It wasn't a question, it was a statement of fact.

"Yes. I thought he'd talk like a clergyman and lecture me about a husband's sacred duty to his wife, and then he'd quote the Bible about looking at a woman to lust after her. I dreaded it, but I went. And then it wasn't like that at all. He wanted to talk about God."

"God!" Homer was flabbergasted. God again! Oliver Clare's final sermon had been about God. "Why did he want to talk to *you* about God?"

"He wanted to discuss with a scientist his idea that God had set evolution in motion. In his opinion, the transmutation of species went forward through the ages under God's direction to an eventual culmination in *us, Homo sapiens.* Everything was providential, he said, even mass extinctions. Well, of course he didn't invent the idea. It goes back way before Darwin. It's called natural theology." Hal looked at Homer and shook his head. "It's the classic theologian's way of trying to adapt his faith to modern science. You'd think all those ecclesiastics would come up with something new."

"So what did you say in answer to that?"

"Well, I'm afraid I brought up some ugly facts about competing species—the nasty habits of langur monkeys and certain kinds of wasps." Hal took his jumping spider out of his pocket and lifted the lid of its box. "Spiders jumping on their prey, owls disemboweling baby rabbits. That kind of thing."

"Oh, God, baby rabbits." Homer looked at the spider and flinched. He had a particular nightmare about rabbits. Once as a child he had heard a rabbit scream in the night, and the scream had pursued him all his life. The rabbit was screaming still. "So how did Oliver take it, your rebuttal?"

"Well, it bothered him, I could see that. I guess he'd been mulling it over all this time, and he'd reached some sort of crisis. He kept trying to bring God into it, and I kept pushing God out of it. We didn't see eye to eye at all."

Homer opened his mouth to say that in Oliver's fragile state of mind, Hal might have had the sense to moderate the scariness of his universe. Then he thought better of it. Perhaps Hal was in a shaky condition himself.

A crowd of children thronged into the courtyard and gathered around the iguanodon. Their voices beat against the sculptured capitals and the polished columns and the walls of newly pointed brick, they surged against the glass roof above and the glass cases below, and ricocheted from the stony figures of Linnaeus and Hippocrates, Darwin and Watt. Hal had to speak up over the general roar.

"After a while he stopped responding to what I said, so I got up to go. And then, just before I left he said something very odd—I mean it was odd for him. He was barely whispering. I thought he was talking to himself, so I put on my coat and said goodbye."

"What? What did he say?"

Hal closed his eyes, remembering. "Natural selection is no more godlike than gravitation. Let the strongest live and the weakest die."

"Let the weakest die!"

"Afterward those words kept going through my head, because they rang a bell somehow. I knew I'd read them somewhere, and of course I had, in *The Origin*."

"Darwin's *Origin of—*"

"Yes, of course. He must have been reading it. At home I picked up my copy and leafed through it, and pretty soon I found the passages he was quoting. He didn't have them exactly right, but they were near enough. I give him credit for plowing through the whole volume. It must have taken a long time. It's not an easy read."

Homer remembered the two books beside Oliver's bed in his small quarters in Windrush Hall. Charles Darwin must have won out over C. S. Lewis at last.

The flood of children divided into rivers and streams. One tributary flowed into the aisle where Homer and Hal stood beside the ichthyosaur. They were small boys in rumpled gray uniforms. At one glance they absorbed the lesson of the imprisoned fossil from ages past—"Look, a shark!"—then poured across the courtyard to stare at the giant crab.

"Tell me," said Homer, "do you think you convinced him? I mean, did you persuade him to your point of view?"

Hal looked at him uneasily. "You know, Homer, usually that sort of disagreement doesn't get you anywhere. Neither side will budge from its own preconceptions. But this time—well, I don't know. Afterward I was sorry I'd been so dogmatic."

"Do you think you joggled his faith?"

"I don't know. He looked so melancholy, so sort of—"

"Bleak?" supplied Homer.

"That's right. Bleak. He looked very bleak indeed."

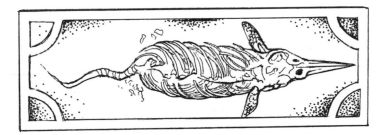

CHAPTER 38

The Red Queen shook her head. "You may call it 'nonsense' if you like," she said, "but I've heard nonsense, compared with which that would be as sensible as a dictionary!"

Lewis Carroll, *Through the Looking-Glass*

T o Mary Kelly's delight, Helen Farfrae called her to suggest another tour of Oxford's wonders. She sounded relaxed and normal.

"Oh, yes," said Mary. "That would be wonderful."

Therefore, while Homer Kelly and Hal Shaw stood talking in front of *Ichthyosaurus communis* in the Oxford University Museum, Helen and Mary made their way along Walton Street, heading for the Radcliffe Observatory. But as they crossed Little Clarendon, Mary took Helen's arm. "That woman across the street, coming out of that bed-and-breakfast place, isn't that Mrs. Jarvis? Oliver Clare's landlady? I saw her on television. The whole country saw her on television."

They stopped and watched Mrs. Jarvis stride majestically away in the direction of St. Barnabas Street. Mary grinned at Helen. "I'm going to poke and pry. We're looking for a room, aren't we? Two visiting scholars."

"Fine with me," said Helen gamely.

Mary rang the bell of the door from which Mrs. Jarvis had just emerged.

There was a long pause, until at last a portly woman opened the door a few inches and put her head out. "Looking for a room, are you? Sorry, we're full up."

"Oh, not for now," said Mary quickly. "Two months from now."

"Oh, well then, come in." The door was opened wide. "I'm Mrs. Lucky. And you're? Very good, come in, Ms. Kelly, Ms. Farfrae. As I was just saying to my friend Mrs. Jarvis, I said to her, we'll be full up until the New Year, and then things will fall off, but well now, look at this." Mrs. Lucky swept open her guest book. "I'm getting quite a houseful for January."

"Did you say Mrs. Jarvis?" said Mary boldly. "Is that the Mrs. Jarvis we saw on television? The one who owns the house where—"

"Where that awful murder took place? It is indeed." Mrs. Lucky led the way down the narrow hall, her wide hips nearly brushing the walls. "Now, this room here is a nice one. View of the garden."

"Where's the loo?" said Helen, wise in the ways of finding accommodations for visiting zoologists.

"Just up the landing." Mrs. Lucky wallowed ahead of them up the stairs, and displayed the bathroom. "Oh, wasn't it dreadful. It made my friend Mrs. Jarvis quite sick, all that blood everywhere."

Mary sensed that she was eager to tell all, to partake of the glamour surrounding her friend, the television star. "She told you all about it, I suppose? We're so interested. I mean, we read all about it in the paper, but it didn't say much."

"Oh, that's right," said Helen. "Was it suicide, do you think?"

Mrs. Lucky led them to the top of the stairs and said dramatically, "As to that, Mrs. Jarvis has her own opinions." She opened another door. "Now, this is one of my nicest rooms. Single bed, with a view of the street." She sat down comfortably on the bed, with a sighing of the mattress and a creak from the springs. "Well, of course, I can tell you all about it."

Mary was delighted. It must have been like this in the time of the Odyssey. *Sing in me, Muse, and through me tell the story.*

The room was very small with Mrs. Lucky in it. Mary found a plastic chair, and Helen sat down beside Mrs. Lucky on the bed.

"Because she told me," went on Mrs. Lucky, "she said there was a *couple* of people who could have cut that young man's throat, that poor young clergyman! Imagine that! What's the world coming to, when a man of God isn't safe from being cut down in his prime? She told me, she said, 'Isabel, I hope never to see such a sight again in my whole entire life.' She said—"

"Wait," said Mary, "did you say *two* people might have killed Oliver Clare?"

She glanced meaningfully at Helen, who loyally chimed in, "But the paper only mentioned one, Mrs. Lucky, somebody called Hal."

"Oh, the paper." Mrs. Lucky threw up one arm in rejection of the *Oxford Mail*, bouncing Helen up and down on the bed. "My friend Mrs. Jarvis doesn't tell *them* everything." *I, however, am her intimate friend. She tells me all.*

Mary leaned forward in her plastic chair. "But who was the other one? Can you tell us, Mrs. Lucky? Because we're just *so* interested in this case."

"Oh, yes, we are," breathed Helen, rising and falling on the bed.

Mrs. Lucky laughed with satisfaction. Glorying in her role, she too leaned forward until her enormous bosom lay in her lap. Lowering her voice to a whisper, she said, "The other one was a young thing, cute as a button. She came late, it must have been two in the morning, long after Dorothy returned from her book club, but Dorothy sleeps light as a cat, and she heard her unlock the door—the girl had a key of her own!" Mrs. Lucky widened her eyes. "You know what *that* means. And a clergyman, too, with his collar turned round. Can you imagine, a pretty young girl in the street in the middle of the night? But Dorothy could tell by the way the girl talked that she was *uppah clawss.*" Mrs. Lucky made a funny face and tossed her hand with a silly flourish. "Well, I don't know, do you? Society is as society does, that's what I think."

Mary said softly, "What did she look like, did Mrs. Jarvis say?"

Mrs. Lucky bounced up and down in her excitement. "Dark hair, cut short all round, trim little figure. Dorothy got a good look at her. She was like this, Dorothy said." Mrs. Lucky's vast amiable face drooped in a facsimile of Mrs. Jarvis's imitation of Freddy Dubchick's melancholy expression.

Helen was seasick. Gripping the edge of the bed, she said, "Could Mrs. Jarvis hear them talking?"

"Oh, no, I mean she couldn't make out what they were saying, just their voices going on and on."

"You're sure of that, Mrs. Lucky?" said Mary. "This was the middle of the night, *after* the man called Hal came and went away again?"

Mrs. Lucky nodded wisely. "Oh, yes, he'd been gone for two hours when the girl came."

Mary was bewildered. "But Mrs. Jarvis never told all this to the police, did she?"

"Oh, Mrs. Jarvis keeps her own counsel," said Mrs. Lucky, shaking her head in admiration of the shrewd wisdom of her friend.

"What about afterwards?" said Helen. "Could she hear anything after this girl left? To show that Oliver Clare was still alive?"

"Not a whisper, not a sound." The tale was ended, the story was complete. *Call off this battle now, or Zeus who views the wide world may be angry.*

Recollecting that she was the proprietor of a commercial establishment, Mrs. Lucky heaved herself off the bed, bounced Helen to her feet, and got back to business. "Now, this room here is ten pounds a day, with breakfast in the dining room. Would you like to see the room opposite?"

"Oh, no, Mrs. Lucky," said Mary. "We've seen enough. As soon as we know the exact date of our stay, we'll call and let you know."

CHAPTER 39

"Who are you?" said the Caterpillar.
. . . Alice replied, rather shyly, "I—I hardly know. Sir, just at
present—at least I know who I was when I got up this morning,
but I think I must have changed several times since then."
Lewis Carroll, *Alice's Adventures in Wonderland*

F reddy Dubchick was back. She and her father had been staying with his sister in Cornwall, in St. Ives, in a house overlooking the ocean.

William had used the time profitably, wandering along the shore looking for crustaceans. One never knew when something interesting might wash up with the tide. The mid-November days were cool but pleasant. The water lapping over his bare feet was not too cold.

As for Freddy, she had been coddled by her Aunt Augusta. She had slept late every morning and spent every afternoon trying to catch up on the reading assigned by her tutor. She had tried not to think about Oliver Clare lying on the floor with his throat cut, but the image kept rising up through the page at which she was staring, beginning as a small stain in the middle of a paragraph, then wicking out and blotting the whole page. She would close the book and cry, and Aunt Augusta would hurry in with comforting endearments and a cup of chocolate.

Freddy was better now. She opened the door of the house on Norham Road and smiled wanly at Mary Kelly.

"I was hoping to find you at home," said Mary. "May I talk to you? I've been speaking with a friend of Oliver's landlady, Mrs. Jarvis, just this morning, and I'd like to ask you—"

"Of course, Mrs. Kelly. Come in." To Freddy, Mary Kelly looked like another Aunt Augusta. "I was afraid you were that policeman, but I suppose he doesn't know we're back. I'm really glad to see you."

She brought Mary into the sitting room, with its high carved mantel and family photographs, its worn oriental rugs and sagging upholstered chairs.

"I just wondered—" said Mary, plunging in at once without preamble, fearing to come up against a polite barrier of resistance.

But Freddy was eager to talk. "Mrs. Jarvis saw me, didn't she? I saw her, of course, looking up at me from the bottom of the stairs."

"Nosy landlady," suggested Mary.

"Well, it's her own house."

"It was awfully late, wasn't it? Can you tell me why you were there?"

Freddy hesitated, then looked bravely at Mary and said, "It was Hal. He called me. It was really late, and I was sound asleep. I could tell he was calling from a pay phone, because somebody broke in to ask for another ten p. He said Oliver was in a bad way, and perhaps I should do something to cheer him up."

"Hal! Hal Shaw? Did he tell you he had just been there?"

"No. I didn't ask him. He just said he thought I'd better talk to Oliver." Freddy's eyes brimmed. "It was sweet of him, really, because Oliver was—" Freddy couldn't finish, but Mary knew what she meant: *Oliver was his rival. They both loved me.* Freddy pulled herself together and went on. "When he hung up, I decided I should talk to Oliver in person instead of just calling him. So I got up very quietly and crept out of the house so as not to wake my father, and biked over to St. Barnabas Street."

"In the middle of the night? It's a long way," murmured Mary.

"Not if you know Oxford as well as I do. After all, I've lived here all my life. It was more or less a straight line. I mean, I'd done it before. Oliver gave me a key, so I could get in without—um—disturbing Mrs. Jarvis."

Mary smiled. "What did you find when you got there? Was he despondent?"

Freddy shook her head. "Not despondent exactly. It was so strange. For weeks he had been pressuring me, begging me to give him my answer. You know, about whether I would marry him or not. He couldn't seem to understand that I just wasn't ready to say yes or no. So this time I told him I was just too mixed up. I was in love with two people at once." Freddy paused, looking thoughtful. "The funny thing was, he didn't seem to care. It occurred to me that he hadn't asked me for my answer for some time. And there's something else." Freddy leaned forward eagerly, her small face tense. "Something very strange. I haven't told anybody about it, not even my father. It was in the cathedral, one day that last week."

"Which week?"

"The week before Oliver died, I forget which day it was. A couple of paleontologists were visiting the museum, and Father asked me to show them around Oxford. So there we were in the cathedral, and I saw—"

"The cathedral?"

"At my college, Christ Church Cathedral. It's where the bishop is. It's the cathedral for the diocese of Oxford. Well, of course, first I showed them the St. Frideswide window in the Latin Chapel, and then we walked down the north aisle on our way out and stood for a minute looking back. And then I saw someone approaching the sanctuary, far away at the east end. It was Oliver." Freddy stared at the carved heraldic shield over the mantel, but she was obviously seeing something else.

"I remember now," said Mary. "One of his parishioners told us he was an important person in the cathedral."

"Oh, no, he wasn't important," said Freddy, shaking her

head. "He *wanted* to be important, he wanted the bishop to notice him. But I don't think the bishop paid much attention. Anyway"—Freddy sat up straighter in her chair and looked at Mary—"we saw him there, and I wasn't surprised, knowing how much he loved the cathedral. And I wasn't surprised when he fell on his knees in front of the bishop's throne."

"The bishop's throne?"

"The bishop sits on this big throne near the communion table. And then, do you know what Oliver did? He gave a sort of muffled cry, and then he stood up and tried to push it over."

Mary gasped. "He tried to push over the bishop's throne?"

Freddy threw out her arms, outlining a huge object in the air. "It must weigh tons, but he shoved it and dragged it, and of course we were watching from the other end of the nave, and I was horrified to see him so desperate. Finally he managed to tip it sideways, but it was too heavy, and it rocked back and came down with a crash, and then Oliver ran into the chapel that's there at one side, and I didn't know what to do, but I had these friends of Father's to take care of, so we went away."

Mary stared at her, astonished. "Did you ask him about it afterward?"

"I didn't see him again until—until the night of his death. And then I didn't have the courage to tell him I'd seen him in the cathedral. And I didn't ask why he tried to knock over the bishop's throne. Oh, of course I talked and talked, mostly about myself and my feelings, but Oliver didn't seem to be listening. He kept looking out of the window, only there was nothing to see out there but the moon. Excuse me, I'll make coffee."

Freddy jumped out of her chair and disappeared. Mary wondered if she had innocently spun this version of events out of nothing, this impression that Oliver had been indifferent,

that he hadn't cared what her answer was going to be. Perhaps her story was an unconscious protective device, avoiding responsibility for his death.

Mary stood up and walked across the room to look at the pictures on the mantelpiece. There was a black-and-white studio portrait of a pretty woman in a dress from the nineteen-seventies, probably Freddy's mother. Beside it stood a silver-framed color photograph of little Freddy in her father's lap. William's whiskers were yellow as straw. And here was an older Freddy dressed as Nanki-poo in a class play. At the end of the row was a snapshot of William sitting on the branch of a tree with a tiny primate in his arms, grinning down at the photographer. Mary thought again of the strange climber on the glass roof of the museum. She tried to imagine

William scrambling up the steep slope in the dark, and couldn't do it.

Freddy came hurrying in again. "I'm afraid we don't have anything yummy to go with the coffee," she said, setting down the tray. "Just dry biscuits. You call them something else. I forget."

"Crackers. They're fine."

Sitting down again, Freddy needed no encouragement to carry on. "So after a while, I saw that he wasn't paying much attention to me and I was in the way. I thought he probably just wanted to go back to bed. So I left. And you know, it's terrible to say this, but I felt better. Because if it wasn't me he was grieving for, I didn't need to feel so guilty."

Wordless, afraid to interrupt, Mary sipped her coffee.

"Of course when I heard next morning that he was dead, everything changed. I saw that I had failed him, that I had left him just when he needed a friend more than anything. I couldn't bear it. I went running back. Oh!" Freddy's composure vanished. Tears ran down her face. She mopped at her cheeks with her napkin.

"Who told you what had happened?"

"It was on the morning news," said Freddy, sobbing.

"So it was." Mary waited, wanting to put her arms around her, deciding against it.

Freddy recovered. "I'm sorry."

Then Mary thought of a way to comfort her. "What you've just said about Hal should get him out of trouble. It's been touch and go. Detective Inspector Mukerji found his fingerprints on the knife that killed Oliver."

"Oh!" said Freddy, her eyes round and frightened.

"But you saw Oliver *after* Hal left him. And he was alive and well."

"Oh, yes, he was," exclaimed Freddy. "That is, he was alive. I don't know about well."

Mary leaned forward and looked at her earnestly. "Tell me, Freddy, do you think Oliver could have killed himself?"

"What else can I think? He was so odd with me. He seemed almost unaware that I was there at all. He seemed so hopeless." Freddy sought for the right word. "So *bleak*. He kept looking out of the *window*."

"Bleak?" repeated Mary softly. According to Homer, Hal had used the same word. Surely it was grammatically wrong. Situations were bleak, landscapes were bleak, but people were something else—wretched? gloomy? depressed?

But *bleak* was the word Freddy wanted. "That's right. He was just so bleak."

Mary changed the subject to something more comfortable. "How did you two meet, you and Oliver?"

Freddy's taut face softened. "Oh, it was last winter in Switzerland, at Zermatt. There was this whole group of people, and one of them was Oliver. He told me he lived in Oxford. And he sort of took me under his wing and taught me the ropes."

"And he was smitten, is that it?" Freddy made a face, and Mary chastised herself for American vulgarity.

"Well, we both were, I suppose." Freddy struggled with herself, remembering her vow to be truthful. "But before long there were some rough edges. Differences."

"Differences? Between you and Oliver?"

"He wanted me to know all about his family background. He was so proud of his genealogical heritage, bishops and so on. I forget all the others, except there was a Knight of the Garter." Freddy was talking in a rush. "He loved to tell me about them, and he took me to see his stately home, only it isn't really his anymore. His parents had to give it to the National Trust to avoid taxes. You know, so that they wouldn't die possessing it." Freddy hunched her shoulders in distaste. "It meant so much to him, all that lost grandeur."

"Where is it, the stately home?"

"Not far, really. It's near Burford. It's called Windrush Hall because it's on the Windrush River. It's where Oliver was born." Freddy stifled a laugh. "Oh, it's so horribly ugly. Architecturally it's famous for a very early bathroom with a patent toilet, but not for anything else. And there are a lot of tablets on the wall of the Burford church. Bishops and so on. We had to look at them too."

"And you weren't impressed?"

"No, I wasn't. And I didn't like the way it meant so much to Oliver. He used to go to Windrush Hall as a tourist, and dream about the glory of it all. In fact," said Freddy impulsively, "he persuaded the proprietors to rent him a little corner of it, the old housekeeper's quarters. He took me there once, thinking I'd be so excited. But it was pitiful. There was hardly room enough for a cot. Somehow he got a tremendous lift out of taking on the mantle of his ancestry, even if all he had was a coal cellar. You know."

"Is that all it was, a coal cellar?"

"No, no, but you see what I mean."

Mary put down her coffee cup, groped for her handbag, and stood up. "So you weren't sympathetic? Ancestor worship doesn't appeal to you?"

Freddy stood up too. "Not at all. Oh, I didn't mind his having elegant ancestors, but it bothered me that he was so fixated on it. He was so—so"—Freddy pounded the arm of her chair with her fist—"*stuffy*. He kept talking about his heritage, this wonderful thing he was going to share with me. He just couldn't understand why I wasn't honored and thrilled."

At the door Mary thanked her and started down the steps. Then she turned and looked up at Freddy. "What if Homer and I were to rent a car one day and take you to Windrush Hall? Do you think we could see the room he rented?"

Freddy brightened. "Oh, yes, I'd like that. I'm sure we

could get in. I know the curator there. I'll write to her. Oh, Mrs. Kelly, isn't your husband some sort of policeman?"

Mary waved her hand and pretended not to hear. How could she say yes or no? Homer's status as a criminal investigator was far too fishy to be explained.

&

After Mary left, Freddy ran upstairs. It had been weeks since she had written in her diary. She was anxious to start again.

Last time I wrote in this book, it was about being looked at. I'm so ashamed. Last time Oliver wasn't dead, and I was driving him crazy and falling in love with somebody else. It was all so Darwinian. I was the female of the species choosing between two competing males, and one of them had more spectacular tail feathers than the other—as though that made it all right to torment Oliver the way I did. And now Hal may be in awful trouble.

I've got to stop and read Aristotle. <u>Intellect alone is divine</u>, that's what he said. Intellect! Mine is smashed to pieces. There's nothing left but feelings, and they're all so miserable.

CHAPTER 40

*The struggle very often falls on the . . . young; but fall it must . . .
with extreme severity.*

Charles Darwin

Mary told Homer as much as she could remember about
her visit with Freddy. "Bleak, Freddy said. She said
Oliver didn't seem interested in her at all. He kept looking out
the window, but there wasn't anything out there, just the
moon. He just seemed so *bleak.*"

"Bleak," echoed Homer. "Well, everybody feels that way
sometimes. You get up in the morning and it's raining, and
everything you cared about has turned to ashes, and then you
get a disappointing letter in the mail. That's the word for it—
bleak." Homer blundered around the small sitting room, picking up books and setting them down again. "Mukerji thinks
Hal Shaw murdered Oliver. His fingerprints are all over that
jackknife. Of course Oliver's are on top, but Gopal thinks that
after killing Oliver, he put the knife neatly into Oliver's dead
hand."

"Oh, but I didn't tell you. Freddy says she was there *after*
Hal went away. And Oliver was alive and well when she came
along. And why on earth would Hal kill Oliver Clare? It's absurd." Mary stopped and thought about it. "Well, maybe it's
true that he had a crude sort of motive—killing off Freddy's
boyfriend because he loved her too. But it's impossible. It
wasn't that heavy an affair."

"Well, I don't know." Homer remembered the passionate embraces he had witnessed in the maze at Hampton Court. "Suppose Hal and Freddy are in cahoots, and they figured out this story together."

"Oh, Homer, I don't think so. She wasn't lying to me. When she said Oliver was staring out the window at the moon instead of listening to her, it was the truth. She couldn't have made up anything like that."

"Or suppose," said Homer remorselessly, "that Hal hung around on the street until after Freddy left, then went back and did the deed."

"But wouldn't Mrs. Jarvis have heard him? She heard everything else."

"The woman has to sleep sometime," said Homer lamely.

"Homer, I'm convinced Oliver killed himself."

"Well, prove it. That's the question, all right. Did he or didn't he?"

"Wait," said Mary, struck by an idea, "I know what I'll do. I'll go to the Samaritans. Remember the Samaritans, Homer? When you feel so bleak you want to do away with yourself, you call up the Samaritans. They've got a branch in Oxford. I'll find out if they ever encountered Oliver Clare."

"The Samaritans? Oh, of course, the suicide people. Right, good idea. If Oliver was really feeling suicidal, he might have talked to them. If he did, we'd know he was at least thinking about it, which reduces the possibility that he was killed by somebody else. Good for you."

Mary started with the yellow pages. At first she tried SUICIDE PREVENTION, but there was no such heading, only STUD FARM PROPRIETORS and SUN TAN CENTRES. Next she looked under THERAPISTS, but they were either transcendental meditators or holistic massagers or acupuncturists. Then she was distracted by the entries under THATCHING—*Freeman & Son, Wheat Reed, Water Reed, Long Straw, Established five generations.* "Oh, Homer, listen to this."

But Homer was at the window, looking out. "Nothing out there but the moon, she said, isn't that right? But the moon isn't nothing. The moon is something. I mean, it's really *something*."

"Homer, what are you talking about?"

"Nothing, but I've just thought of a little research project of my own. Just me and the moon."

❧

Mary finally found the Samaritans in the regular phone book under their own name. But when she presented herself at the door of Number 123 Iffley Road, the response to her question about Oliver Clare was noncommittal.

"I'm sorry," said the soft-spoken gray-haired man, leading her into the sitting room, "that's not the way we work."

The room was bland and nondescript. The posters on the wall were unprovocative—the Alfred Jewel, Van Gogh's irisis. A box of tissues on the table was the only thing suggesting the possibility that emotions might sometimes run high. Mary sat on the sofa, the Samaritan sat down in a straight-backed chair. "We never," he said politely, "give out the names of the people who come to us."

"Oh, but—" said Mary.

He would answer only general questions.

Mary tried to think of one. "The people who come here, you try to talk them out of killing themselves, is that it?"

"No. Lots of people think that's what we do, but it's not true. We never try to talk anyone out of it."

"But what do you do then? What are you for?"

The man smiled gently. "We let them talk. Sometimes that's all they want, a chance to talk."

Mary was nonplussed. "So you won't tell me whether or not Oliver Clare ever came here?"

He shook his head. "Our interviews are confidential. We never give names."

"Even to the police?"

"Not even to the police."

"But don't they—?" Mary had been going to say something dramatic: *Don't they arrest you? Don't they threaten to close you down?* Thinking better of it, she got up to go, and tried one more question. "Do clergymen ever come to you, you know, troubled about their faith or something like that?"

There was a flicker on the Samaritan's serene face, as though Mary's question had struck home. "Perhaps sometimes," he said.

Mary went home and told Homer about it. "Oliver went there," she said. "I swear he did. I can't prove it. I just know he did."

CHAPTER 41

I am a bold man to lay myself open
to being thought a complete fool.
Charles Darwin, letter to L. Jenyns

🖋

It was another fool's experiment. Homer was too embarrassed to tell his wife the exact nature of the expedition. Getting up at one o'clock in the morning to set out for St. Barnabas Street, he nudged Mary awake and told her where he was going, but not why.

"Oh, Homer," she said drowsily, heaving herself to a sitting position, "it was a month ago. They will have cleaned everything up. You won't find any threads on the floor or anything like that. Does Mrs. Jarvis know you're coming?"

Homer groped for his pants in the dark. "Yes, it's all right. She's expecting me."

"Funny woman. Maybe she'll tell you another juicy piece of information she's been withholding from the police."

Mrs. Jarvis was indeed voluble. Early as it was—two o'clock in the morning—she was there to answer Homer's knock, fully dressed. She was a tall powerful woman in a flowered wrapper. Her laced-up shoes were masterful, dominating. Her inquisitiveness about her deceased lodger and his guests was not the prying curiosity of a landlady, it was more like the interest taken by a goddess of ancient Greece in all of humankind.

"Go right up, Mr. Kelly. I've left the door open. It's all

cleaned up now. Those police constables, poor things, they did the best they could, but their mothers didn't teach them right. I scrubbed the floor for an hour, and it came out spotless. Fantastik, it's called. They advertise it on TV." From some hole in the air Mrs. Jarvis summoned a plastic bottle with a nozzle. "Fantastik really does the job."

It was a television commercial by the Queen of England. "I'll tell my wife," promised Homer, as he stumbled upstairs, realizing at once that it wasn't the sort of thing you told Mary Kelly.

"Just give my door a tap when you come down."

She had turned on the overhead light in Oliver's room. The place was sparkling clean, the floor scrubbed and bare, the bed neatly made. The crucifix was gone. There was nothing to remind Homer of the unhappy young man whose throat had been cut. Nothing but the southwest window overlooking the Oxford Canal.

Homer switched off the light and went to the window. Yes, there was the moon.

The astronomy of it was simple. According to Freddy Dubchick the full moon had been shining over the Oxford Canal on the night she visited Oliver Clare. She had stayed about an hour, she said, between two and three in the morning. Tonight on the twenty-fourth of November it was a full lunar cycle later, with another full moon. Would the view from the window be the same?

Homer stood for a long time looking out the window, seeing what Oliver saw. At last he turned away, closed the door behind him, descended the stairs, tapped on Mrs. Jarvis's door, and left the house on St. Barnabas Street.

Perhaps his fool's experiment was a success. Then again, perhaps it wasn't, and he was a fool for sure.

CHAPTER 42

How nice it would be if we could only get through into Looking-
Glass House!

Lewis Carroll, *Through the Looking-Glass*

🕊

Burford was eighteen miles to the northwest. Mary and
Homer took a bus to Motorworld on the Botley Road to
hire a car for the day. As the salesman led them out into the
parking lot, the new weed in the neighboring ditch was not
something anyone would notice. It was only a few dry stalks
puncturing the brittle patches of ice along the narrow stream.

"Do you want to drive?" said Mary, offering Homer the
key.

"Me?" Homer waved it away. "No, thank you. No killer
roundabouts for me. It's all yours."

"Oh, why is it," said Mary, getting in timidly on the wrong
side of the car, "that two friendly countries like the United
States and Great Britain insist on driving on different sides of
the road?"

As it turned out, she had no trouble keeping to the left. The
problem was how to avoid the curb on that side. At home
the bulk of a car was on the right, here it was on the left, and
she kept getting too close to the edge of the road. Homer kept
shouting, "Right, keep right! No, not that far right, just—
There, that's better. No, no! there you go again, keep right!"

By the time they picked up Freddy Dubchick at her house
on Norham Road, Mary wasn't speaking to Homer. As he

held open the left front door for Freddy, he suggested brightly, "Perhaps Freddy could do the driving?"

"Of course," said Freddy. "I'd be glad to."

It was an insult. "No," said Mary, "I've got to learn."

Fortunately by this time she had caught the trick. It was only at the roundabout where the Woodstock Road joined the A40 that she was in trouble. "Homer, don't say a word," she said between clenched teeth, as other drivers blatted their horns.

Homer closed his mouth, Freddy murmured, "Here, move to the left, this is where we get off," and the crisis was past. They could stop leaning forward, bodies tense and eyes straining. The car sailed forward in the direction of Burford. Homer relaxed in the rear seat, and Freddy looked back at him anxiously. "The police," she said, "have they found out anything? They don't really think it was Hal, do they? Not anymore?"

Homer glanced uneasily out the window at a field of sheep. "I don't think Mukerji has made up his mind." The field of sheep was succeeded by another field of sheep. "Of course there's the possibility of suicide, but the pathologist isn't sure." Homer wished he could forget the medical examiner's gesture, the slashing stroke from left to right. "He said either one was possible."

"I see," said Freddy in a small voice.

The village of Burford was a pleasant little resort town with a main street running up the hill. "The church," said Freddy impulsively. "Let's stop here first. I'll show you the family memorials."

Mary found a parking place in front of a Laura Ashley shop, and Freddy led them across the street and into the church. "The chapel's this way," she said, hurrying ahead.

On the walls of the chapel were the tablets to the memory of many a departed Clare. "There's the bishop," said Freddy, pointing to a grand inscription with pediment and garlands. "Oliver was very proud of him."

Homer was interested in the last line. "I see he was *Snatched by untimely death.* I wonder what happened to him?"

"Probably blood poisoning or typhoid or something," said Mary. "They had no protection against those things. Look at this, a brother and sister carried off in their teens. You know, I've always wanted to spend a couple of weeks in the middle of the last century, but only if I could bring antibiotics with me, as if I were traveling deep in the jungle in some foreign country."

"The past *is* a foreign country," murmured Homer, reciting a famous phrase. He looked at Freddy, who was kneeling in a corner, reading an inscription next to the floor.

"This is the one I like," she said. "You see? It's another Oliver Clare, but all it says is *Forgive.* What do you suppose he needed forgiveness for?"

Mary and Homer stopped to look. "How strange," said Mary. "Look, someone's scratched a picture on it, some sort of duck. It's very crude. Insulting, too, I should think, defacing a tombstone like that."

"Oliver told me he didn't know anything about this one," said Freddy, "but I think he did. There must have been something shameful about it, and he didn't want to tell me."

They went back to the car and Freddy directed the way to Windrush Hall, which overlooked the river a mile or so to the north of town.

"Good God," said Homer, staring at the great heap of stone, "is that it?"

"I'm afraid so," said Freddy.

Homer's anarchist sympathies flared up. "My God, did any of those people deserve it?"

Freddy gave him a bright flash of a look. "Exactly, that's exactly what I said. Nobody should own so much. Oliver was shocked when I said that. He couldn't understand why I wasn't impressed. He thought I must be kidding."

"Well," said Homer sarcastically, "I suppose a place like this gives employment to an army of servants. That's always the excuse for any ghastly enterprise."

Mary pulled into a field where a sign said PARKING. "Back in Massachusetts this would be a nursing home," she said, getting out of the car, "or an institution for the criminally insane. Does anyone live here now? Or is it just a big museum?"

"A monument," snarled Homer, "to the subjugation of the poor."

Freddy laughed. "That's more or less what I told Oliver. But he said, oh, no, the family was always so *kind* to the staff, and they felt such a *responsibility* to the village and everybody working on the land. Anyway, nobody lives here now except the guides who show visitors around. They open it every afternoon from two to five, so tourists can gawk at the portraits and the Venetian chandeliers. Come on, we go in this way."

Freddy walked past the massive entrance, with its great staircase and gesturing statuary, and rang a bell beside a door at one side. They were admitted by a woman wearing a badge on her large bosom.

"Oh, hello, Miss Dubchick. Yes, yes, I've been expecting you. Come in. Your friends are—? Oh, how do you do. My name is Ophelia Flatt. Follow me."

She led them down a narrow hall odorous with the smell of soup, noisy with the clash of cutlery. "The staff kitchen," explained Ophelia Flatt. "They're clearing away lunch."

They followed her down intersecting passages, all painted a gloomy brown. Homer trailed after Freddy and Mary, who followed close on the heels of Ophelia Flatt, who kept up a mournful eulogy on the virtues of Oliver Clare. "So sad. Such a charming young man. A member of the Family." She led them briskly through an enormous old-fashioned kitchen, part of the public tour, and stopped at a narrow door on the other side. They stood back while she opened it with a key, jerked a light string, and took her leave.

It was the old quarters of the housekeeper—a high narrow

kitchen-pantry, a small bed-sitting room, and a miniature old-fashioned bathroom. "It's so pathetic," whispered Freddy as they stood crowded together in the bed-sitting room.

It was empty, except for an uncomfortable-looking cot and a bedside table with a lamp and a few books. Homer glanced at the books—a Bible, Darwin's *Origin of Species,* and one of C. S. Lewis's religious books, *The Case for Christianity.* Homer wondered if Oliver had been examining the two sides of an old-fashioned argument. Well, actually, he reminded himself, it wasn't so very old-fashioned. It was still a mighty question that rattled around the world. This very day it overarched the city of Oxford like a canopy stretched from the tower of the University Museum to the spire of St. Mary the Virgin, and the canopy still trembled and jerked and swayed from side to side.

There was nothing else to look at. Homer felt like a fool. Well, it was another fool's experiment, a flop from the beginning.

They moved into the narrow pantry. Dark varnished cupboards rose to the ceiling on three sides of the room. There was a small sink in the middle of the wooden counter. A window on the fourth side admitted no light at all. The tiny lavatory was little more than a closet.

"Isn't it sad?" said Freddy dolefully.

"I've seen enough," said Homer. "Let's go." Rebellious hairs were rising on the back of his neck. His Irish ancestors had been in service in Cambridge, Massachusetts, and on their behalf he felt uncomfortable. He wanted to get out.

"No, no," said Mary. "Not yet. How about it, Freddy, do you think we could look in the cupboards?"

"Of course." At once the two of them began opening doors.

One of the lower cupboards revealed Oliver's supplies—half a loaf of moldy bread, a large cheese, a jar of instant coffee, another of sugar, three cans of soup, and a few plates, mugs and utensils. On the counter a kettle sat on a hotplate.

"Well, all right," said Homer testily, "I can see it was possible to live in this mouse hole. Let's go home."

"Wait, Homer," protested Freddy, flinging open more doors and shutting them again.

"I'll bet I can reach the high ones," said Mary. To Homer's alarm she climbed on the counter and stood up carefully. Tall as she was, her head was still far from the ceiling. Reaching high, she tugged at the remotest of the cupboard doors. "This one's empty." *Bang.* "This one, too, and this one." *Bang, bang.* "And this one. No, wait, I think there's something in here." Standing on tiptoe, Mary stared into the fourth cavernous cupboard.

"Well, what do you see?" said Homer.

Instead of answering, Mary reached up and brought something out into the open air. It was a jar. "The label says pickled peaches. But wait, there's something else."

Freddy took the jar, and Mary groped in the darkness. Then she said, "Oh."

"Oh, what?" said Homer.

"Oh, Homer!"

"You can't just say, oh," said Homer indignantly. "What is it?"

"A book."

"Well, bring it down."

Tenderly Mary brought the book into the light. "It's got a leather binding, but I don't see any title or name or anything."

She climbed back down and put it on the counter beside the dusty jar.

For a moment Homer ignored the book. He was staring at the jar. "That's not pickled peaches. It's another one of those damned dried-up old crabs."

Freddy was excited. "It's just like the jars in my father's office. It must have been Oliver who found them here, all of them." Then Freddy's face changed. She looked at Homer, startled. "But that means—"

"It means he was the one who brought them into the museum," said Homer, pouncing. "He found them here and packed them in a couple of cardboard boxes and drove to the museum and dumped them outside the Zoology Office and covered them with that tarpaulin."

"Only he missed one," said Mary.

"But what the hell were they doing *here* in the first place?" said Homer.

"Maybe the book will tell us that." Mary held it under the light. "How odd—look, it isn't dusty. Not like the jar."

Homer ran his finger over the leather cover. "Maybe Oliver took it down and read it, then put it back. Well, go ahead, open it. Let's see what it is." Eagerly Homer and Freddy looked over Mary's shoulder as she turned back the cover and smoothed the first page.

The title was handwritten in a difficult angular script, but Mary deciphered it quickly and read it aloud, *"Oliver Clare, His Journal, 1839."*

"Oh," gasped Freddy, staring at the page, "is that really what it says, Oliver Clare?"

"I think so." Mary looked at Freddy. "But surely that's the same—"

"Yes, yes, that's right." Freddy heard herself babbling, but she couldn't stop. "It's the same name as the one on that little tombstone in the church, the one that says *Forgive*."

"Perhaps this will tell us what there was to forgive." Mary turned the pages carefully. "Oh, no. Look at this. We may never find out. Some of it's in code."

Homer and Freddy looked on as she flipped gently through the book. It was true. The black ink was crisp and clear, but many of the paragraphs were in a strange language.

Then Freddy said impulsively, "Oh, wait, I can read it. There's nothing to it. It's really so silly." She took the book from Mary and ran her finger along a line. "Crabs—small—and—large—"

"Oh, of course." Mary read on, delighted. "Worms—with—legs—"

Homer bent over their shoulders and took up the decodification. "Worms—without—legs—"

They looked at each other and laughed.

"Have you ever kept a diary?" said Freddy. "I do, but I'm so afraid somebody will read it, I use mirror writing. It's easy, once you're used to it. It's like Leonardo's notebooks, only I never think of Leonardo, I think of Alice going through the looking-glass."

"I could transcribe it," said Mary. She looked at Freddy. "Do you think we could borrow it?"

"Well, technically, I suppose, it belongs to the National Trust. Does all the National Trust property belong to the Crown? Perhaps not."

"We'll just borrow it from the National Trust for a few days," said Homer grandly, reaching for the book. "The Crown won't mind. Those Royals have plenty of other things to read, like the headlines in the gutter press. They won't miss the journal of Oliver Clare."

CHAPTER 43

*The spikes stand in such a position that, when the lobes close,
they inter-lock like the teeth of a rat-trap.*
                                    Charles Darwin, *Insectivorous Plants*

🖋

Margo Shaw had struck up a friendship with Mark Soffit.
It wasn't a man-woman relationship at all, but on the
other hand it wasn't platonic either, because they were both
more concerned with the nature of the bad rather than the
good.

Mark, detecting a tiny crack in the Shaw union, inserted a
prying wedge. "Too bad about Hal. I hear he's in trouble with
the law."

"Oh, isn't it frightful! I must say, when he came courting I
never expected to find myself in this humiliating position, the
wife of a *felon*."

"They say," said Mark, dropping his voice, "that the trouble
began with a woman."

"I know," whispered Margo. "Professor Dubchick's little
strumpet of a daughter. I knew from the beginning she was up
to no good. And Hal is so simpleminded. I mean, I'll be honest with you, compared with Hal, I know so much more about
life. The poor dear doesn't have a clue."

Rejoicing, Mark passed along the latest rumor. "I hear he
may be indicted for murder. I mean, that's what people say."

Margo had heard the rumor, too, and she had already decided what to do. Now her resolve stiffened.

Next morning at breakfast she came straight to the point. "You see, Hal dear, I'll be perfectly honest. This is straight from the shoulder. It would be so foolish to carry on as if everything were just the same."

Hal looked at her dumbly. What goofy thing was she going to say now?

"The fact is, you're still so immature. And I no longer have confidence in your prospects. You've attached yourself to the wrong man. Dubchick isn't going anywhere. He's finished." This conviction had soothed Margo's damaged amour propre, after Dubchick had denied her offer to become his assistant. "Everybody says so."

Hal's face remained expressionless. "Everybody?"

"Mark Soffit, for one. I mean, he seems to know all about these things. You know, the inside scoop about the pecking order. He says Dubchick is out. He's too old-fashioned. He's still making field studies of animals, when that's not where it's at. All those years with monkeys, and now eight whole years on crabs! The cutting edge right now is in biochemistry. Dubchick doesn't know DNA from RNA, that's what Mark says."

"Mark is wrong," said Hal shortly.

"Oh, of course you defend Dubchick because your future is tied to him. You'll go down with him, Hal! And I'm not going down with you. And then there's all this appalling nastiness about a probable indictment. I couldn't bear it. Dear, I'm leaving. I'm moving in with Dolores. We'll make business arrangements later, you and I. Of course when Aunt Peggy kicks the bucket, I'll expect a substantial increment. Get a lawyer. You see, I'm being absolutely practical. I want us to part friends."

"Oh, certainly," said Hal.

"I don't know if I'll marry again," said Margo dreamily. "Who knows? Marriage is such a gamble."

But Margo had already bought her outfit for the chase. And

that afternoon she wore it to the long-awaited cocktail party in the provost's lodge at Oriel. The dress was emerald green to go with her eyes. With her triangular face she looked more than ever like a praying mantis, sending out pheromones to attract the male she would consume in the act of mating.

The provost's lodge was rich in portraits of Oriel worthies. Margo wandered past them, gazing up reverently. By increasing her speed she caught up with another art lover, an *extremely* attractive man in evening dress, probably an Oriel don. Margo stood close to him, staring up at the muttonchop whiskers of the elderly gentleman in the portrait.

"Do you ever wonder," she said, "if they talk to each other when we're not here? Imagine what they must say about us! Terrible things, I'm sure."

"I don't know, madam. Excuse me." The attractive man picked up a tray of wineglasses and hurried off.

Strike one. But Margo had stick-to-it-iveness, and after a couple more failures she was happy to find her old friend Mark Soffit standing in a corner by himself. He too had finagled an invitation. Quickly they entered on the character assassination that was so comfortable a bond between them.

"Poor Dubchick," said Margo, "I hear his new book is nearly done. Can you imagine what it will be like? He's such a dinosaur. He's extinct!"

"Wait till the peer reviews come in," said Mark, his dim eyes brightening. "They'll tear him apart."

"On the contrary," said someone sharply, joining them. "If you're talking about Professor Dubchick's new book, you're completely wrong. It's a masterpiece."

Mark's face turned an ugly red. Margo said tartly, "And who, may I ask, are you?"

"It doesn't matter," said the newcomer coldly. "But believe me, you are misinformed."

He walked away. Margo was shaken. "Who in the hell was *that?*"

Mark spluttered. He could hardly speak. "I'm afraid it was—oh, Christ, it was Jeremiah Heddlestone."

"Jeremiah *Heddlestone!*" Even Margo knew the august name. "You mean, the insect man? The Nobel Prize winner? Oh, my *God.*"

" The Bridge of Sighs "

CHAPTER 44

On these grounds I drop my anchor . . .
                    Charles Darwin, letter to Asa Gray

In the Zoology Office, Helen Farfrae was listening to Christmas music on Radio Three. A boys' choir in some college chapel sang about the e'er-blooming rose. The office radio was turned way down. It was eight o'clock in the morning.

Helen was only barely conscious of the music as she watched William's paragraphs dance up the computer screen. It was the final chapter of his book. There were new entries to be made, new conclusions to be drawn from some of the crabs that had turned up in the jars they had been examining, crabs belonging to species that were now extinct.

> *. . . Of Jesse's lineage coming*
> *As men of old have sung.*

Helen's attention was diverted by the thought of the genetic inheritance of Jesus Christ. If you thought of him as the son of Joseph, some of his genes would have come from David, and before David, from Jesse. And there were a whole lot of other ancestors mentioned in the Bible, going all the way back to Abraham. What sorts of characteristics would have come down from all those people? Intelligence, certainly, and pugnacity. But suppose Mary had really been impregnated by the

268

Holy Spirit, what sort of stunning inheritance was that? All those celestial combinations of deified guanine, adenine, thymine and cytosine, combined, of course, with the human material supplied by Mary?

> *It came, a floweret bright,*
> *Amid the cold of winter,*
> *When half spent was the night.*

Across the street in the Besse Building at Keble, Homer Kelly was obsessed with the discovery about Oliver Clare and the jars of crabs. He hauled on his parka, snatched up the jar from Windrush Hall and his lecture notes, strode around the quad, and crossed Parks Road.

Today the museum looked different. Its long flat front was hidden under scaffolding. The complex structure of socketed pipes had been taken down from the inside of the building and reerected on the outside. Homer recognized Daniel Tuck sitting high above the ground, eating his lunch, and he waved to him, and said, "Don't fall off."

Tuck waved his sandwich and promised not to, his tenor vowels as melodious as ever.

Homer found Helen Farfrae in the Zoology Office. "Here's another one for you," he said, presenting her with the jar.

"Oh, Homer," cried Helen, "how wonderful. Where on earth did it come from?"

"Well, it's a long story."

Homer sat down and told it, interrupted by gasps and exclamations from Helen. "Oliver! Oliver Clare! You mean it was Oliver who brought the crab jars to the museum? Do you suppose he was the one I saw on the roof?"

"That's what we suppose. Tell me, do you think he discovered afterward that you were here that night?"

"Why, yes, I do." Helen remembered the morning when

Oliver had come looking for Freddy. "Well, of course, part of it was in the *Oxford Mail,* the fact that I heard someone come in and go out and come in again. The paper didn't say anything about my going up into the tower and looking out. But Oliver came in here one day and asked me point-blank, was I here that night, and I said yes. And I told him I'd seen the person on the roof, how he had climbed up the glass like a monkey climbing a tree, or like one of those rock climbers going up a vertical precipice."

"A rock climber!" Homer thought of the yellow rope left on the roof by Charley Firkin, the same rope that had turned up in Oliver's room after his death, the very same rope with which an experienced person might have climbed that impossible mountain of glass. Had Oliver been an experienced person? Homer stared at Helen, and saw her plainly. He saw her keen hazel eyes and her big glasses and every strand of her short gray hair. "That's why, then. That's why he tried to kill you. You had *seen* him. He didn't know that before."

Helen was shocked. "Oliver didn't try to kill me."

"What day did he talk to you? What day did he find out about you?"

Helen thought back. Then she nodded sadly. "It was the same day. The morning of the day my husband fell from the scaffolding. You mean someone moved those trestles, hoping *I'd* be the one to fall? You mean Oliver was trying to get rid of me? Because he thought I'd recognized him up there on the roof? But I hadn't." Helen shook her head in disbelief.

"But he thought you had. And he figured out this nice easy way of getting rid of you. You often worked late, so all he had to do was move the barrier away from the staircase and turn out the lights. It was so simple, nothing murderous about it at all."

Helen tore off her glasses and protested. "But you're forgetting. William was there too, and so was my husband. No,

Homer. Oliver couldn't have guessed which of us would fall from the scaffolding."

For a moment Homer was stopped cold, and then he understood. "Oh, wait, I see what happened. He set things up to catch you, and then he left, assuming you'd be alone all evening. The bounder, he didn't know the others were coming. Whoops, sorry about *bounder*." Homer smiled forlornly. "It's all those old black-and-white British movies—I can't seem to get rid of them."

"It's all right, Homer." Helen stood up from her chair in front of the computer and went to the table where the jars of crustaceans stood in their long rows. Half of them were newly labeled, half still awaited inspection. "But why were these jars hidden away in his family place in Burford? And why did he bring them here so secretly? Why did he have to be so furtive? Why was it so terrible that I might have guessed he brought them into the museum?"

"Ah," said Homer mysteriously, "wait and see. Mary's about to work on it. We may have an answer from ages past."

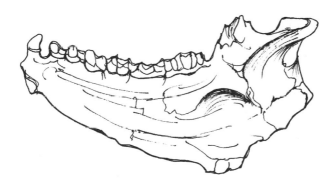

CHAPTER 45

I'll tell you all my ideas about Looking-Glass House. . . .
Well then, the books are something like our books,
only the words go the wrong way.
                    Lewis Carroll, *Through the Looking-Glass*

🦢

M ary removed the brushes and combs from the top of
the dresser. She pulled up a chair in front of the mirror
and sat down. She was not interested in her own reflection.
Opening the book in the middle, she held it up to the glass. At
once the backwards language of the journal of Oliver Clare became plain English.

She turned the pages back to the beginning. Here there was
no need for a mirror. The entries began sensibly enough. The
writing was slanted and difficult, but the words went forward
rather than backward.

I make my first entry on this day, July 17, in the Year 1839.

*It is a day of CELEBRATION at Windrush Hall. Even His
Grace, my brother the Bishop, has condescended to approve
my friendship with Mr. Bell. "Well, little brother," said he,
looking down his nose, "it seems your malodorous preoccupation with slimy things has been noticed in high places."
And then he departed to meet with the Archbishop of York
on the question of the Bishops' Pension Bill, shortly to come
before the House of Lords. Bishops and archbishops are my*

*brother's preoccupation, quite as slimy in their way as my
dear crabs.*

*Mr. Bell has kindly passed along to me one hundred crus-
taceans in spirits of wine, given him for identification by
Mr. Darwin after his journey around the world. Mr. Bell
has kept an equal number, and hopes by thus dividing them
to finish the task with all speed. It is a SACRED TRUST. I
am cock-a-hoop that Thomas Bell should think me capable
of the task—me, a mere collector of natural curiosities,
hardly worthy of calling myself a natural philosopher. It is
true that my cabinet contains some remarkable things—the
horn of a Narwhal, a joined pair of human fetuses, the
skeleton of a Singhalese Ape, the shriveled head of a savage,
as well as a large collection of crustaceans from the Bristol
Channel.*

*Tomorrow I shall begin decanting them for examination.
My wife has expressed a longing for the containers, as being
desirable in the kitchen. Therefore I have ordered from the
chemist a set of new glass, at considerable expense. His
Grace, my brother, who continues to hold the purse strings,
will complain, no doubt, but I say f——— the Bishop.*

*In my journal I will diligently record my study of every
specimen.*

At this point the mirror writing began, a hurried muddle of
scribbled paragraphs. Mary held the book up to the glass, but
even with its help she was often at a loss. The keeper of the
journal had been writing in some distress of mind.

*Alas, there has been an abominable misfortune. In remov-
ing the Crustaceans from their original jars, my accursed assistant neglected to label the new containers at once with
Mr. Darwin's numbers. Perhaps I should make allowance
for the fact that he is only twelve years old and a mere*

stableboy, but it was impossible for me to control my fury. Snatching up a switch, I applied it to his backside. How he howled! My youngest son appearing at that moment, I gave him a stroke for good measure, he is such a horrid little beast.

The next entry was indecipherable, except for a BLOODY GODDAMN, written forwards, and an EVERLASTING HELLFIRE, set down in the writer's sloppiest backwards hand.

The following entry was forwards again. The nineteenth-century Oliver Clare was exulting in a new acquisition to his cabinet of curiosities, a giant snail, bought from a boy in the village.

I believe it to be marine, perhaps having wandered far from shore, but I may be mistaken.

July 20, 1839. I am charmed by the gift of a very pretty young shrike, entangled in a net in the peach orchard be-longing to the parson.

At once there was more of the scribbled backwards writing:

My attempts to identify Mr. Bell's crustaceans have been hampered by the loss from my library of Rev'd Congeries' great Opus, <u>Creatures of the Atlantic Deep</u>, last seen squar-ing up a table. Without it I am in a quandary!

The ordinary hand returned in a long passage about the di-arist's health, especially concerning the corruption of his bile and the consequent fouling of his breath. *It is painful to report that my wife turns away from me in the bedchamber.* There fol-lowed an account of a consultation with his physician, who treated him with anise and fennel administered in a tot of rum. However, *Molly still WON'T,* complained Oliver Clare. *Curse the bitch, she still refuses to favour me!*

The next coded passage was in a wild, nearly indecipherable hand:

> *Bloody hell! I cannot tell one specimen from another. Crabs small and large, worms with legs, worms without legs, shrimps unlike any of my acquaintance. I curse the day I begged Mr. Bell to allow me to assist him! How shall I explain my failure? In desperation I have numbered the new jars, but in truth only <u>Almighty God</u> knows which is which. Above all, I am tortured by thoughts of <u>Mister D</u>.*

There were no more backwards passages. The next entry concerned a packet of Cantonese silkworm cocoons sent by a naturalist aboard a vessel in the harbor of Hong Kong. The last was an excited paragraph about a seagoing expedition to the Indian Ocean on which he was about to embark. *To my surprise, my brother has agreed to fund the journey. I suspect he is glad to get rid of me.*

Mary needed no more. It was obvious what had happened. In spite of his assurances to Charles Darwin that he was eager to identify all the Beagle crustaceans, Thomas Bell had been too busy to do the job. Therefore he had dumped some of them into the lap of his provincial friend Oliver Clare of Burford, who had pretended to more knowledge than he possessed.

And then Oliver had muffed it. The stableboy had decanted the precious crabs into new jars, forgetting to transfer the numbers at the same time. Finally, examining them in earnest, Oliver had been totally bewildered. His modest experience was not adequate to the task of identification. Embarrassed and at a loss, he was still too respectful of that important young man Mr. Darwin to simply flush the contents of the jars down the patent toilet at Windrush Hall. Craftily he shoved them into a high cupboard with labels straight out of Mrs. Beeton's cookbook—Jugged Hare, Potted Venison, and so on. Then he slapped his journal shut and took off on a voyage across the world.

Perhaps he hoped that a knowledgeable naturalist would come to Burford sooner or later, someone who could identify the collection and rescue his reputation. But no such person had appeared, and eventually, decided Mary, closing the book, Oliver Clare of Burford had died peacefully in Windrush Hall, with the crabs still on his conscience, hidden away in the housekeeper's kitchen along with his journal, high up in the darkness of the topmost shelf.

There were still unanswered questions. What had His Grace, the Bishop, said about his brother's failure with the borrowed crabs? Did the anise-and-fennel infusion cure his bad breath? Did his sex life improve? Above all, how did he explain his failure to Thomas Bell? Was that why his tombstone asked so pathetically for forgiveness?

And there was a last and final question. Why did the namesake of Oliver Clare of Burford—young Oliver Clare of Oxford—return the missing specimens to the Oxford University Museum like a thief in the night?

Perhaps Oliver's parents would know. Mary typed up a transcript of the journal and showed it to Homer, then badgered him into another trip to London.

CHAPTER 46

God bless you!—get well, be idle,
and always reverence a bishop.
                Charles Darwin, letter to T. H. Huxley

🦢

The house on Pont Street looked familiar. Mary and Homer had seen it for a fraction of a second when the vultures of television had caught Oliver's parents climbing into a car on the morning after his death.

Mrs. Clare threw open the door and welcomed them. Taking Mary's hands she pulled her inside. She was a brisk little round woman, given to cries of enthusiasm, horror and delight.

It had been a month since Oliver's death. The grief they had seen on her face at the funeral service was no longer visible. She did not lay its burden on her visitors. "Oh, I'm so glad you called. We've wanted to talk to someone, but except for Detective Inspector Mukerji, there hasn't been anybody."

Homer took off his coat and made polite conversation about a picture on the wall, a photograph of a young woman standing beside an old-fashioned biplane. Leaning closer, he said, "I believe that is you, Mrs. Clare."

"Oh, yes, that's me." Lucy Clare's speech was rapid and merry. "I was a stunt pilot, back in the fifties. I barnstormed all over the northern shires, doing wingovers and snap rolls at county fairs. That's how I met Bob. He'd been an RAF pilot during the war. He taught me to find my way by the stars.

He's been pointing them out ever since, even in storms of rain."

Mary admired the sturdy shape of Lucy Clare's shoulders as she led the way into the sitting room. It was apparent that the latest storm was the death of her son.

Oliver's father rose as they came in, pushing back his chair from a table covered with books and papers. He was tall, like Oliver, and he had the same yellow hair, half gray now and growing thin. The freckles spread so thickly on his cheeks were friendlier than the perfect pink and white of Oliver's fresh young face.

Lucy introduced her husband. "Bob's writing a book on the history of diplomacy since ancient times. He makes a cat's breakfast of it, I'm afraid." She flourished an arm at the litter of papers on the table, the ancient typewriter, the file box sprouting a flurry of blue and pink slips of paper. Fans of file cards lay on the floor.

Robert shook hands heartily and urged them to sit down. Lucy dumped a cat out of a chair, and in a moment the four of them were settled, facing one another in a small circle.

The visit was not a social call. Homer made a few gruff noises of sympathy, doing his damnedest to abandon his bastard British accent and talk American, and then Mary went straight to the point. "Mr. and Mrs. Clare," she began, fumbling in her bag, "have you ever seen this book before?" She undid the tissue-paper wrapping and handed Lucy Clare the journal from Windrush Hall.

"I'm afraid we took it without permission," said Homer. "We went to Burford with Professor Dubchick's daughter Freddy. My wife found it in one of the rooms that had been rented by your son. Of course it belongs to you."

Lucy Clare began to laugh. "Oh, Bob, Bob, look at this. It's Oliver of Burford again, another secret journal. And do you see?" She held the book up. "More of his mirror writing. How marvelous!" She handed the book to her husband, who turned to the first page at once and began to read.

"Mrs. Kelly, Mr. Kelly," said Mrs. Clare, standing up eagerly, "you must see this." They stood up too, and followed her to a glass-fronted bookcase against the far wall. "Bob inherited some of his curiosities."

Homer gave a snort of delighted recognition. "The shrunken head, the narwhal's horn."

"And beetles," said Mary. "Look, Homer, he didn't mention beetles."

"Oh, they all collected beetles," said Mrs. Clare. "There was a beetle craze. Every country parson collected beetles."

Homer pounced on a chance to show off. "So did Charles Darwin. He began with beetles."

"But he didn't end with beetles, did he?" said Lucy Clare. "I'm afraid Oliver Clare of Burford didn't get much farther. Not that he didn't try." She lifted the glass front of a shelf and brought out a skull with a long thick beak. "What do you think this is?"

"It looks awfully familiar," said Mary thoughtfully. "You know, Homer, it reminds me of something."

"Of course," said Homer, "the dodo. It looks an awful lot like the skull of the dodo in the museum. Could it possibly be—?"

"No, it could not." Lucy Clare laughed. "It's a flamingo from Madagascar. But old Oliver, Robert's great-great-great-grandfather—Bob, have I got it right?—did his best to pass it off as a dodo. He said he found it in a swamp on the island of Mauritius, where all the dodos were, back in the seventeenth century, before the last ones were hunted down by visiting sailors or killed by rats. He *also* claimed to have seen a living specimen flopping around in the woods." She put the skull back on the shelf. "Oh, he was impossible. After that, people began to snicker and call him Dodo Clare."

Smiling, she pointed to the painting hanging on the wall above the case of curiosities. "Here he is, Oliver of Burford."

"Oh, golly." Mary couldn't help laughing. The first Oliver had been painted as a dandy of the eighteen-forties. His crossed eyes stared in two directions. His right hand rested on the shell of a giant clam. "Oh, forgive me."

"No, no," said Lucy. "I always laugh too. Well, he was an old scamp. He wasn't above a spot of forgery, lying, theft, adultery, anything that would irritate his brother, the Bishop of Warwick. How he loathed the bishop! Of course he confessed to everything in his journals. Confessed with relish, assuming, I suppose, that his mirror writing would conceal his naughtiness, which of course it didn't."

She led them back to the circle of chairs, where her husband was still deep in the journal that had turned up in Windrush Hall. "Until a few years ago he was my favorite among Bob's ancestors. Bob's favorite too, which explains why we named our son after him." As she sat down, her face turned grave. "But that was before one of the secretaries for the Oxford Assizes cleared out an old cupboard and sent us the last of Oliver's journals, and we found out what happened later on. The last one was written in prison."

Homer's jaw dropped. "In prison!"

Lucy Clare glanced at her husband. Solemnly he closed the journal from Windrush Hall and took up the story. "On November 10, 1863, Oliver Clare of Burford was hanged for the murder of his brother."

Mary gasped. "His brother? You mean the bishop? Oh, Homer, that explains the inscription on that little tablet in the church—*Forgive.*"

"Oh, you've been in the Burford church, have you?" Robert Clare smiled grimly. "It also explains the inscription for his brother. Did you see that grand monument on the wall, the one with classical ornaments and a pediment?"

Stunned, Mary said, "Was that the bishop's?"

"Indeed it was. The poor old stone carver must have been worn out, inscribing an entire square yard of marble with praise for the achievements of Arthur Wellington Clare, Bishop of Warwick. Did you see the last words of the inscription, *Snatched by Untimely Death?*"

Homer nodded vigorously. "Indeed we did."

"You see," said Lucy, "the bishop was ten years older than his brother Oliver, but they died in the same year, 1863."

"Of course," said Mary, "because one brother killed the other, and then he was executed himself. But why? Why on earth did he murder his brother?"

"It's a long story." Robert Clare excused himself and left the room, returning in a moment with two books. "He was a great scribbler. There are eight of these journals all together, including the one you found. They make it painfully clear that the bishop was a bully. He tormented poor Oliver, disapproving of everything he cared about, especially his interest in natural history. The bishop was always pitching out Oliver's favorite mollusk or his bucket of sea worms or his prize collection of arthropods from halfway around the world. Listen to this: *His Grace my brother Arthur*—wait a minute, I have to parse it backward:

> *has refused me five shillings for the coach to Oxford to attend the meeting of the British Association for the Advancement of Science. How I long to go! Mr. Darwin is expected! Perhaps he will talk about his new theory of descent, the one that so upsets my brother. But Arthur has forbidden me to go. "You will bring shame and notoriety upon me," says he. "You will jump up and claim to have seen a camelopard." A camelopard! How absurd! Of course he plans to attend the meeting himself and deliver a discourse, which I know from experience will be mere"*—

Robert paused and ran his finger over a backwards word. "Two S's? Oh, I see:

horseshit, mere horseshit, on the Porphyritic Granite of Cornwall. My horse is lame. I will go by dungcart if all else fails. "

Robert glanced up from the book with an ironic smile. "The next part's easy enough. It's all in caps.

GOD DAMN HIS ABOMINABLE GRACE, THE LORD BISHOP, MY DETESTABLE BROTHER! OH GOD IN HEAVEN, IN THINE EVERLASTING CARE FOR RIGHTEOUSNESS AND JUSTICE, STRIKE HIM DOWN!"

"Oh, the poor wretch," murmured Homer. Mary shook her head in sympathy and looked across the room at Oliver's portrait. One eye stared back at her slyly, the other gazed out the window with an expression of astonishment, as if beholding an outlandish creature in the wilds of Pont Street. A dodo? A blue-footed booby?

Angrily Lucy rearranged the sagging pillows on her chair and beat them with her fists. "As you can see from that episode, it was the bishop who kept control of the family funds. Oliver had to beg for his share. Imagine having to bend the knee to an autocrat like that, just to buy a coach ticket!"

Robert picked up another volume and opened the cover, revealing a grubby sheaf of paper. "This is the last of his journals, the one he wrote in prison."

"Oh, it's so sad," exclaimed Lucy. "Such a passion for revenge! And no wonder. The next beastly thing that nasty bishop did was to blackball the election of his brother to the British Association for the Advancement of Science. The *bishop*, of course, was a member of the association. For him, getting in was just a matter of manipulating his lofty connections. Poor Oliver *yearned* to be a member. I mean, after all, his own scientific credentials were surely more acceptable than his brother's. But they turned him down, and afterwards he learned that his own brother had destroyed his chances. The bishop had *ridiculed* him in the presence of all the great men of British science, the very men Oliver most revered." Lucy shook her head contemptuously. "Oh, it was unforgivable."

Homer looked at her sympathetically. "You could almost call it a sufficient reason for fratricide."

"Exactly," said Lucy. "But wait till you hear the last straw. Oh, it was so wicked and frightful, but on both sides, you see, on both sides! The bishop was invited to preach in Oxford Cathedral, you know, there at the college of Christ Church. Do you know the cathedral? It's right there in the college quadrangle, but it's not just a college chapel, it's the cathedral for the entire diocese of Oxford. Anyway, they called some sort of synod or convention or something. What would you call it? A convocation of bishops? A conclave?"

"A bevy," volunteered her husband, "a bevy of bishops. A *beatitude* of bishops—"

Homer pitched in. "A *billow* of bishops, a *bellowing* of bishops, a *befuddlement* of bishops, a *bawling babble* of—"

"Stop!" cried Mary, while Lucy clapped her hands, then collected herself and carried on.

"That's right, it was a whole bellowing of bishops, all the bishops of Great Britain, along with the Archbishops of Canterbury and York, with their miters cleaving the sky and their robes afloat"—Lucy flounced her arms in the air—"and then Oliver's horrid brother stood up in the pulpit and preached against amateur naturalists who adopted the pernicious new theory of human descent. He pounded his fist and shouted that it was a sin against the sanctity of the female sex to claim that the sacred lineage of human motherhood had such a depraved ancestry. And then he thundered against his poor brother. His own *brother,* he said, might have had an ape for a mother, but if so then he was *an abominable bastard.*" Lucy lifted her hands in horror. "That is a quote, an exact quote." Exhausted, she turned to her husband. "You tell the rest. It's beyond my power."

"Well, there's nothing much to it," said Robert. "Oliver stood up in his pew, took out his pistol, and shot his brother through the heart."

CHAPTER 47

But how durst you attack a live bishop in that fashion?
I am quite ashamed of you! Have you no reverence for the fine lawn
sleeves?

Charles Darwin, letter to T. H. Huxley

"In the *cathedral?*" said Mary, aghast. "He shot the bishop right there in the cathedral?"

Homer jumped to his feet in a fury. "Well, who could blame him? Talk about bastards! His brother should have been drawn and quartered. But I suppose all the righteous indignation in England was directed at poor old Oliver. What did they do, hang him from the nearest tree?"

"Oh, no," said Robert. "They went through all the proper dismal legalities. It took six months or so, with Oliver languishing in prison, scribbling furiously in his journal, before they took him out and strung him up in the presence of a gloating priest."

For a moment Homer and Mary sat in stunned silence. Then Lucy bounced out of her chair. "We all need a drink," she said. She vanished into the next room, and came back a moment later with four glasses and a bottle on a tray.

They sipped their sherry gratefully. Then Robert picked up the journal that had come from Windrush Hall. "See here," he said, tapping the cover, "what's all this about crabs? And Thomas Bell? And Charles Darwin? Here's Darwin's name, right here on page one."

It was Homer's turn to explain. "They were Darwin's crabs,

sent home from his expedition on the Beagle. He loaned them
to his zoologist friend Thomas Bell for identification. But Bell
was too busy, and besides, he was sick, so he turned a bunch of
them over to Oliver. And then poor Oliver got them mixed
up. He didn't know which was which."

"And there was a jar," began Mary.

"A jar?" Lucy Clare leaned forward, gazing at her intently.
"What sort of jar?"

"It's another long story," said Mary, and then she took
turns with Homer telling the story of the jars of desiccated
crabs that had turned up so mysteriously in the Oxford University Museum. Homer explained his suspicion that their son
had brought them from Windrush Hall.

"What we don't understand," said Mary, "is why he didn't
bring them to the museum openly, and say, Look what I
found, the missing Darwin crabs! Why did he do it secretly, in
the dark of night?"

Lucy looked at her husband soberly. "I'm afraid we understand it very well."

Robert murmured, "Carry on."

She turned to Homer and Mary. "Did they give you a tour
of Windrush Hall when you were there? They didn't? Too
bad. If you'd seen the family portraits, you'd understand.
They make it perfectly clear. There have always been two
kinds of Clares. Sometimes the current squire stands beside a
marble column draped in fur and velvet, and then the next
one gazes at the moon through a spyglass, surrounded by his
prize chickens. They were either dreadfully stuffy and arrogant
like Oliver's brother, the bishop, or they were cranks and odd-
balls like Oliver himself. There's nothing in between."

"We kept two portraits for ourselves," said Robert, "two of
the eccentrics, Oliver and my father." Turning in his chair, he
pointed to the picture hanging over the mantel, a portrait of a
man in a bathrobe sitting outdoors on a folding chair. His feet
were bare, and a small volume lay on his lap. "He was a stu-

dent of early printed books. That one is from the Aldine Press in Venice. Alas, we had to leave it at Windrush Hall."

"Does that make him an eccentric?" asked Mary, disbelieving.

"No, but there were other things." Robert looked at her with a wry smile. "My father was a professional atheist. He smashed stained-glass windows and organized antichurch rallies. I confess it was a little difficult to be his son."

"And of course our Oliver found it difficult to be his grandson," said Lucy. She sighed. "From the very beginning he fitted into the other tradition."

"The pompous tradition, I'm afraid," murmured Robert.

"Oh, we did our best," Lucy went on. "We sent him to the local grammar school instead of to Harrow, and made sure his friends came from every part of London. But as soon as he was old enough to understand the grandeur of our connection with Windrush Hall, the whole thing went to his head. He was dazzled by the family lineage and his memory of the stately home where he was born."

"It was pitiful," said Robert, "the way he was so attached to the house. To him it was a tragedy that it had passed out of the family. He kept going there, taking the afternoon tour, gazing at the ugly rooms in which great affairs of state had taken place, bedrooms in which his splendid ancestors had died. He couldn't stay away."

"It was so pathetic," said Lucy, "his eagerness to rent a tiny part of it for himself." She shook her head in melancholy wonder. "Ludicrous."

They were talking freely, eagerly. Homer and Mary sat quietly, listening, while Robert and Lucy Clare described their son's obsession with family glory.

"It was so sad," said Robert. "I think he was ashamed of me for having given up the stately home, not hanging on somehow." His face darkened. "I think he was ashamed of his mother for being the daughter of a salesman."

"Oh, the poor dear," Lucy went on, "he was so desperate to go to Oxford or Cambridge." She stared at the rug, her round face looking old for the first time. "We knew it couldn't happen. His A-levels weren't good enough. Oh, he was good at sports, but he just couldn't get the hang of academics. Still, he couldn't *believe* they would reject him. Of course when they did, he was dreadfully disappointed."

"What did he do instead?" asked Mary softly.

"He fell back on piety," said Robert, his voice edged with sarcasm.

Lucy shrugged her shoulders. "Perhaps it was a reaction against his grandfather, the smasher of stained glass. But when he enrolled in a theological college here in London, we were glad he had something to care about. We thought it was rather a second-rate kind of place, but it was his decision, not ours."

"I confess," said Robert, "we were afraid it would lead to nothing in the end, that he wouldn't get a parish of his own. And therefore we were immensely pleased when he was ordained by the Bishop of Oxford. He spent a year as a curate in Banbury, and then he was assigned to the church at Nightingale Court. But, unhappily—" Robert paused and shook his head sorrowfully.

Lucy carried on. "Unhappily Oliver himself was mortified. You can imagine the sort of thing he had hoped for—some grand edifice with a Norman tower and a rose window and lofty pointed arches." She swooped her arms toward the ceiling. "So once again he was disappointed."

"Of course he accepted the assignment," said Robert, "but he lavished all his affection on the cathedral at Christ Church. As an outsider he couldn't participate in its rituals and services, but he cozied up to the bishop and the canons and all the other ecclesiastical dignitaries, and made himself useful, and never missed an important service, no matter how he had to juggle things in his own parish." Robert broke off with a tormented shake of his head.

"Oh, forgive us for talking about our poor dear son like this," said Lucy, "but Bob is right. I feel the same way."

For a moment they both seemed lost in sad recollection. Then Robert turned to Homer. "You asked about the jars." He glanced at his wife. "I can imagine how Oliver felt about his ancestor's wretched jars."

"You see," said Lucy, eager to explain, "he was deeply embarrassed by his atheist grandfather and all the other spotted apples on the family tree. He particularly loathed the first Oliver Clare, the man who had murdered a bishop in the sacred precincts of the Oxford Cathedral. He wanted us to pitch out the shrunken head and the sad little fetuses of the Siamese twins. He kept turning Oliver's portrait to the wall. He wanted to know why we didn't display the bishop's crozier and the sword of the admiral and the great industrialist's Order of the Garter, family relics he could be proud of. And once when he was about thirteen he smashed some of Oliver's shells."

"Oh, well," said Homer indulgently, remembering certain violent acts of his own at that age. "Children will be children."

"Of course they will," said Robert, "but it shows how strongly he felt. And now"—Robert tapped the book on his lap—"think of it, here was proof that the nineteenth-century ancestor for whom he had been named had shamefully failed no less a person than Charles Darwin." Robert shook his head. "Oh, my son, my poor son."

There was a gloomy silence. Mary studied her shoes. Homer glanced around the room, and at once the pleasant chamber with its armchairs and windows, the cross-eyed portrait of the first Oliver Clare, the horn of the narwhal and the shrunken head, all gathered themselves into a certainty. "I see," he said, boldly breaking the silence. "Your son thought the family honor would be compromised if he appeared in person with the miserable remains of Darwin's crabs and tried to explain that they had been mishandled by one of his own ancestors, a man who had been hanged for murder."

Lucy Clare nodded fervently, and Robert said, "Yes, oh, yes."

Homer went on sorting the matter out. "Think of the universal respect for the name of Charles Darwin! Even the Darwin revisionists can't do much to sully his memory. Your son Oliver must have been aware of the magnitude of the reverence. And he must have understood the historic importance of everything Darwin collected during his voyage around the world. Therefore—"

"The shame of it, that's what he would have thought," said Lucy. Tears ran down her cheeks, but she didn't bother to wipe them away. "The dishonor to the family name. Oh, it was foolish to think so, it was wrong."

Robert put his hand on her shoulder. "That's it, that's it exactly."

Mary spoke up, protesting. "Well, I think he deserves credit for returning those jars at all. He could have left them there in the cupboard, or dumped them in the river."

"That's right," said Homer, trying to leave Mr. and Mrs. Clare with a pittance of praise for their dead son. "He had a conscience about them. He just didn't want anyone to know it was his own family that had been at fault."

Lucy wasn't listening. She had been struck by a new understanding. She turned to her husband. "Oh, Robert, I see what happened. I know how he felt. It was his attachment to the cathedral. I see it now. And his reverence for the bishop, the present bishop, and his ambition to move up in the Anglican church. Oh, Robert, don't you see? The murder that happened in the cathedral back in 1863, a murder committed by someone with his *very own name,* against *a bishop, right there in the cathedral he cares so much about,* what if all that were to come up again, what if everyone knew about it? It would make him look ridiculous. He'd be a figure of scorn, a laughingstock!"

"Yes, yes, you're right," said Robert. "So if he were to return the Darwin jars to the museum publicly, then the journal would come out, and everything about the first Oliver Clare would come out, too, including the murder of his brother, the bishop, in Christ Church Cathedral." Robert turned to Homer and Mary. He winced with pain. "You see, the poor boy was so ambitious. I think he fancied himself a bishop too, one day."

Lucy dabbed at her cheeks. "Of course we worried about him all along, because he seemed to be neglecting his own congregation. He wanted something grander, far grander."

"Yes," said Mary, nodding. "Freddy told me a little about that." She glanced significantly at Homer, and they stood up to say goodbye.

Homer had a last question. "I wonder if you know about the drawing somebody scratched on Oliver's memorial in the church in Burford. I thought it was a duck of some sort, but might it not be—?"

"A dodo?" said Lucy. "Yes, of course it's a dodo. It was someone's final thrust at poor old Dodo Clare."

Mary had a last irrelevant question. "Your son was a skier, wasn't he, Mrs. Clare? Freddy Dubchick told me they went skiing together."

It drew a blank. "Skiing?" said Lucy. "I wasn't aware that Oliver ever went skiing."

"Nor was I," said Robert. "Other sports, of course. He was good at sports. But not skiing, so far as I know."

"Oh," said Mary. "I must have been mistaken. Perhaps I didn't understand her."

They shook hands with Lucy and Robert Clare. All four of them were tearful. In the past two hours, in an atmosphere of perfect truth, they had endured together a century and a half of family tragedy and trouble.

When the door closed behind them, Homer and Mary walked silently in the direction of Sloane Street to hail a cab. Homer hardly noticed the handsome townhouses arrayed on either side. Instead he saw Oliver Clare's pitiful bloodstained body as it lay on the floor of the house on St. Barnabas Street. That poor agonized young man! What did all his torments have to do with one another? His thwarted love for Fredericka Dubchick, the collapse of his belief in God, his frantic anxiety to shuck off the Darwin crabs—was there a common source, some anguished gland inside him?

At Paddington Station he found the answer as they were swept along in the crowd of hurrying men and women. "It's simple," he shouted at Mary. "It's just a question of basic drives."

Mary was jostled from behind. "Basic what?"

"Drives, basic drives. Hunger and sex, right? The urge to survive and procreate? Animals and humans too, isn't that right?"

Heads turned, bodies surged past them. Mary struggled closer and shouted back, "I suppose so, Homer. What are you getting at?"

He grabbed her arm and together they were carried along into Paddington's high open spaces. "There's a third, a third basic drive, belonging only to the very tiptop primates, namely us."

Mary laughed. "All right, Homer, I give up. What is it, this third basic drive?"

"Respectability, the urge for respectability."

"Ah, yes. Hunger, sex and respectability, Oliver Clare's obsession. Yes, of course."

C H A P T E R 4 8

Worms are destitute of eyes.
Charles Darwin, *The Formation of Vegetable Mould,*
Through the Action of Worms

M ark Soffit never told himself that he was a worm. But
in the remote center of himself, far from the surface,
the knowledge lay coiled, an organ of self-loathing. Its secre-
tion was a powerful stream that flowed all over his body, suf-
fusing it, filling him with furious resentment.

After the cocktail party at Oriel, where he had been humili-
ated by the celebrated Jeremiah Heddlestone, Mark was
irresistibly attracted to the Zoology Office in the Oxford University Museum.

It was here that Professor Dubchick was working on his
book. *A masterpiece,* Heddlestone had called it. It galled Mark
that Dubchick kept crossing him up. Mark had come to Oxford eager to work with the great man, to be able to say for the
rest of his life, *Oh, yes, we were colleagues.* But look what had
happened! On their very first encounter Dubchick had as
good as insulted him. And then he had fobbed Mark off on
Hal Shaw, who had given him degrading assignments, which
Mark had rightly refused to do. After all, a person had *some*
pride. And then when he had presented the case fairly and
truthfully to Dubchick, the man had insulted him again,
throwing his own words back in his teeth.

And now, after judging the old fraud to be senile, after

burning his bridges so that he couldn't go back, Mark had been tricked again. Dubchick was about to parade himself before the world as a central thinker, a unifier of disciplines, a sort of Albert Einstein in the field of zoology.

Mark couldn't bear it.

At quarter past twelve, a few days after the party at Oriel, he entered the museum. In the courtyard a father stood among the display cases with his two children, looking at the bones of *Megalosaurus*. A small group of schoolboys clustered around their teacher and gazed up at the giraffe. The normal humming noise that thrummed and echoed in the museum was amplified by their soprano voices. *God, a person couldn't hear himself think.* Mark climbed the stairs and walked along the gallery corridor to the Zoology Office.

The door was open. Mark walked in boldly, and found only Dr. Farfrae. She was moving busily from desk to table and back again. She looked up and said, "Oh, hello there. Mr. Soffit, isn't it? Can I help you?"

"Oh, no, I guess not." He leaned in the doorway. What was she doing? Shuffling papers into a heap, peering at one of those damned jars, going to the computer, pecking out something on the keyboard, going back to the table, leafing through the papers. "How's Dubchick's book coming along?" asked Mark.

"Almost done. I'm just checking." She gave him a gleaming look. "Lots of little details." She pulled out a chair in front of the keyboard and sat down.

"That's it? That pile of papers? You've got it all in memory?"

"Oh, yes, it's all here."

"I hope you've been backing it up?" said Mark, suddenly interested.

"Yes, of course."

"This is the printout?" Mark came forward and reached for the heap of paper beside the computer.

Helen put her hand on it. "Sorry, not yet. It goes to O.U.P.

this afternoon. They've been waiting for five years. Now, if you'll excuse me, I'll get on with it. I've got a few more hours of work before it's really ready. You know, little prettifications here and there. A few more references to check."

O.U.P. was the Oxford University Press on Walton Street, Mark knew that much. He drifted away from the Zoology Office and left the museum. At once he began running, taking the shortcut to the Banbury Road. There he took a Park and Ride bus to Summertown, where he had already discovered a computer supply store on the South Parade.

He was back in the museum, out of breath, within a couple of hours, carrying a bag. He went upstairs at once, and glanced into the office. Dr. Farfrae was still there. Mark went back downstairs and found a spot in the east arcade behind the statue of Euclid where he could be out of the porter's range of vision, yet still keep an eye on the south corridor upstairs. Euclid looked at him sternly and pointed out that *A surface is that which has length and breadth only,* but Mark was not open to reprimands from the father of geometry.

Would the goddamned woman ever leave? Mark jiggled his bag up and down. He yawned. He leaned against Euclid's pillar on one side, then the other, and shifted from foot to foot. At last his impatience was rewarded. Helen Farfrae came out of the Zoology Office, pulling on her coat. She ran down the south staircase, stopped at the porter's desk to exchange pleasantries with Edward Pound, then pushed open the outside door and disappeared.

Now the only question was, had the old biddy locked the door? Mark managed to get upstairs without being seen, and then to his intense satisfaction he found the office wide open. The woman was a damned fool! Whatever happened to Dubchick's "masterpiece" was entirely the fault of that snotty so-called *Dr.* Helen Farfrae and nobody else.

Mark's bag contained something called "utility software." It could be depended on to do the trick.

EUCLID

Extinction Info
This utility will totally obliterate single files,
entire disks, or erased data,
so that they cannot be
recovered by any means. . . .

CHAPTER 49

Off with her head!
Lewis Carroll, *Alice's Adventures in Wonderland*

Helen was beside herself. "It's gone," she said. "It's all gone. The files are gone, the manuscript is gone."

William stared at the computer, bewildered. "But it must be in there somewhere."

"No, no, it's not there. Every single chapter has been deleted. Someone went through and took them all out. See? Here's the preface, it's still here, but all the chapter files are gone. I managed to get into the hard disk, but they're missing there too. They're not in the backup directory. They've been absolutely, completely, totally wiped out." Helen threw out her arms in a wild gesture. "Oh, Professor Dubchick—"

"William."

"Oh, William, it's all my fault. I didn't lock the office door. Someone came in while I was at home checking a reference. I was only gone for an hour, but when I came back—oh, what have I done?" Helen covered her face with her hands and wept.

William's head was spinning. He couldn't comprehend the extent of the loss. "I've still got my notes. I can remember a lot of it. Of course it will take a while."

The telephone rang. Helen mopped at her face and reached for it.

There was a bright voice on the line. "Helen? This is Dora McAdoo at O.U.P., wondering where you are. We've got some champagne here. We're expecting you, are we not?"

"Oh, Dora, I'm sorry, but there's been a slight—there's been a hitch. I'll call you back."

Helen hung up and looked at William fiercely. "Listen, I know who it was. Maybe we can catch him before he destroys the manuscript. Where does that bastard live?"

But by now the bastard was out of reach. He went straight back to Wolfson, carrying Dubchick's manuscript inside his thick zippered jacket. The River Cherwell was very near. Mark went to the middle of the arched bridge over the river and dropped the pages a few at a time. Down they went, fluttering into the water, carrying with them all Dubchick's cleverness and eloquence, all his grand sweeping theories and hopes for glory. The pale rectangles drifted downriver. Mark watched as the first of them floated out of sight.

Only then did he wonder what to do next. The goddamned woman would certainly know who was responsible. She'd be after him. They'd all be after him. Mark ran back to his room, threw together a few things, and hurried outside. On the way across the quad he met the other Rhodes scholar at Wolfson, the nerd from New York City. They barely glanced at each other.

But as they passed, an odd noise filled the air. From the direction of the city center came the sound of ringing bells. Mark had never heard such a clashing and clanging. It was as though every college chapel in Oxford were celebrating his departure. The nerd from New York stared up at the sky. "Hey," he said, "will you look at that?"

Mark did not deign to look. Head down, he walked at a fast pace in the direction of the railroad station, while the bells pealed to draw attention to a miracle in the sky. Three separate and individual suns were shining through an opalescent layer of cirro-stratus cloud. The brilliant blobs on either side of the central sun were prismatic illusions, mock suns, concentrations of light refracted toward the earth by ice crystals suspended high above Oxford and Binsey and Woodstock and Blenheim Palace and Abingdon and Banbury.

The bell notes showered down upon Mark Soffit, the three suns dropped their dazzling radiance around him, but he failed to hear, he did not see.

It was a long way to the station. Mark hurried to the Banbury Road and took a cab. In the back seat he stared at his knees and invented an answer to the questions they would ask of him at home: "Hey, aren't you back early? What happened?"

Oh, Oxford's not all that great. They offered me a fellowship, but I turned it down. Their science is out of date, that's the trouble. I'm miles ahead of them. I was doing more teaching than learning, so I called it quits.

CHAPTER 50

The courtship of animals is by no means so simple and short an affair as might be thought.

Charles Darwin, *The Descent of Man*

🦢

"Freddy," said Hal, "my wife has asked for a divorce." He said it flatly, without introduction.

Freddy felt the color rush into her face. "She has?"

Once again they had met by chance in the middle of the museum courtyard. At least, it looked like chance. Freddy drifted in from the left, dreamily approaching the glass case containing the spider crab. Hal rambled toward her from the right, and stood solemnly staring up at the stone figure of Prince Albert.

The prince's whiskers were elegantly trimmed. "So I just thought I'd tell you," said Hal.

The spider crab was immense. It was at least a meter across. "I see," said Freddy. "Well, thank you."

She wanted to ask why Margo wanted a divorce. Was it because Hal was in trouble with the police? Did Hal know what Detective Inspector Mukerji was thinking? Was he about to be arrested?

The spider crab cautioned delay. Prince Albert said not now. There seemed nothing else to say. Freddy made her way by the north stairway to the Zoology Office, where she was astonished to find Hal again. He had galloped up the stairs on the other side.

"Oh, sorry," said Freddy, embarrassed. She melted away again, while her father stared after her in surprise.

Hal looked blindly at one of the crab jars, seeing nothing but blotches in a misted container. Then, to William's further surprise, he excused himself and went away.

At once Freddy and Hal nearly collided in the coffee room. At this they both burst out laughing. Destiny, decided Hal, had something to be said for it.

Mary Kelly was there before them. "Oh, Freddy," she said, putting down her coffee cup, "I want to ask you about something." Looking apologetically at Hal, she drew Freddy aside. "Didn't you say you and Oliver met on a ski trip in Switzerland? I could swear that's what you said."

Freddy looked puzzled. "A ski trip? No, it wasn't a ski trip."

"Well, what were you doing in Switzerland?"

"Rock-climbing."

"Rock-climbing!" Mary clapped her hand to her forehead. "How stupid of me! Yes, of course you were rock-climbing. With spikes and clampons and ropes, a lot of ropes?"

"Crampons. Yes, I told you. Oliver taught me the ropes."

Mary hurried away to tell the news to Homer. Freddy and Hal were left alone together in the coffee room. Now that they were no longer in the presence of the Prince Consort and the giant spider crab, they allowed destiny to take its course.

🦢

Mary was apologetic. "It was so stupid of me. I just assumed that Zermatt meant skiing. Rock climbing never occurred to me."

"We were both pretty dumb," said Homer. "We should have guessed. After all, his father said Oliver was good at sports. We just didn't think of *this* sport. Although it does seem strange to me that a pious young clergyman would risk his life on the sheer faces of cliffs, like that guy we saw on the Carfax tower."

Mary thought of Oliver's parents, bravely discussing their son with strangers, revealing his faults and vulnerabilities. "I suppose it was a way of building self-esteem. I suspect he didn't have much."

"In any case," said Homer, "we've got to tell Mukerji."

Homer hated making appointments. He set out that afternoon for St. Aldate's and plunged along Cornmarket Street. It was teeming with shoppers. At the Carfax crossing he jumped out of his skin as a truck spoke up beside him with a recorded message, *Attention! Attention! This vehicle is reversing!* In the next block he had to inch past queues of people waiting for buses. Babies abounded in strollers and prams, they were dragged along beside mums and dads. There were tourists unfolding maps, teenagers in madcap outfits, a girl with a bass viol, a boy hawking newspapers with shocking headlines, BODY PARTS FOUND IN FILE CABINET, KILLER RUNS AMOK IN GLASGOW. Homer skipped sideways as a City Link bus released its brakes with a hiss and edged out into the street. He caught fragments of conversation, aristocratic Oxford vowels, excited glottal stops, snatches of Japanese. Pigeons soared in a flock above the roof of McDonald's and fluttered down on Tom Tower, then rose again as the bell bonged twice for two o'clock.

The constable on duty at the entry desk in the St. Aldate's police station was P.C. Gilly. Homer conned him into opening the gate and letting him hurry down the corridor to the office of Detective Inspector Mukerji. But when he flung open Mukerji's door, he found the room jammed with half a dozen constables. They were crowded together on folding chairs while Mukerji lectured on the muzzle velocities of various projectiles and the resulting damage to human tissue.

Heads turned as Homer opened the door. "Whoops, sorry," he said, backing out.

"Give me ten minutes, Dr. Kelly," called Mukerji, beaming at him.

Homer cooled his heels in the reception room. He read all the notices.

WANTED

VOLUNTEERS FOR

IDENTIFICATION PARADES

£10 REWARD

FOR ALL ENQUIRIES CONCERNING
LOST/STOLEN/FOUND CYCLES,
PLEASE GO TO THE CYCLES
OFFICE IN FLOYD'S ROW.

THEIR ROYAL HIGHNESSES
THE DUKE AND DUCHESS OF KENT
VISITED THIS POLICE STATION
ON 12TH NOVEMBER 1990 TO
MARK ITS REOPENING.

The last was not a notice, it was a stone plaque. *How condescending of the duke and duchess,* thought Homer, congratulating himself on being an American.

"Homer?" Gopal Mukerji smiled at him, his glasses flashing, his black brows arching, his eyes alive with sparkling lights. "Come in. You are here to tell me that the Reverend Oliver Clare was a rock climber, is it not so?"

Homer was astonished. He admitted it humbly. "How did *you* find out?"

They went back to Mukerji's office, which was empty of constables, although a sickening chart of impact wounds was still propped on the bookcase.

"I suspected it might be so, and I telephoned the local rock-climbing club. It turned out that Oliver Clare was their best climber, with many famous ascents to his credit. Miss Fredericka Dubchick is also a member of this club, although not of the same standing."

"So Oliver knew exactly what to do with the rope that was left on the roof by Charley Firkin."

"Yes, of course. I gather that the ropes for rock climbing

are more elastic than Firkin's, but the difference would have given no trouble to an experienced climber like our young clergyman."

"He was escaping from the night watchman," said Homer slowly, staring out of Mukerji's window at the Magistrate's Court across the street. "Helen Farfrae saw him climbing up the steep side of that glass roof. I confess I hate giving up on the orangutan, but no, it was the Reverend Oliver Clare, all right." Homer turned back to Mukerji. "But Bobby Fenwick wasn't a rock climber, was he? Did you ask if he was a member of the club?"

"Of course. No, no, he was not a rock climber." Mukerji dusted a speck from the picture on his desk, a photograph of his wife, a plump pretty woman in a scarlet sari. "But he thought he could do what Oliver had done. He followed him up the rope. Tell me, Homer, what happened then?"

"Oh, hell," said Homer angrily, "I suppose Oliver sat up there on the peak of the roof waiting for Fenwick, and then, goddamn it, I suppose he just—"

They said it together: "Cut the rope."

"And then he took the rope away with him." Homer's gloom returned. "I confess I still find it hard to understand how a devout young man like Oliver Clare, a mild-mannered clergyman devoted to St. Mary the Whatchamacallit—"

"The Beneficent."

"—could have committed murder."

"I imagine it didn't feel like murder at the time. After all, he didn't lay a hand on Fenwick. He merely cut the rope with his pocketknife and let nature take its course. Gravity took over." Mukerji's beaming smile faded. "And the same was true when he tried to get rid of Dr. Farfrae and killed her husband by mistake. It was entirely passive. He didn't lift a finger in violence. It was simply a matter of moving a trestle and turning out the lights. Was that murder? Surely you wouldn't call it murder."

Homer's gloom increased. "And all because he wanted to be a bishop."

"A bishop? Surely you are joking."

"That was all the motive he had, nothing more. Well, except for protecting the honor of his family."

"The honor of his family!" Mukerji snorted bitterly. "What about the honor of Fenwick's family? That young man had a wife and child."

Homer stood up to go. "What about the suicide question? Do you still think someone actually murdered Oliver Clare?"

Mukerji tossed his hand helplessly. "We're working on it. I am deeply suspicious of Dr. Shaw and the pretty young Fredericka Dubchick. The murder weapon was his! Perhaps the murderous assault was also his, concealed by the girl's protective story that Oliver was still alive when she arrived." He shrugged. "And of course there are also some pretty rough kids at Nightingale Court who could have done it. We've been talking to the skinhead who broke Oliver's window and stole his television the week before. The boy owns a nasty-looking knife of exactly the same kind as Dr. Shaw's. Perhaps he came back to Oliver's place, hoping to pick up something else, thinking Oliver would not be there, and then Oliver surprised him, so the kid pulled out the knife and killed him. Or better still, he was wearing gloves and he picked up Shaw's knife and used it, then put it in Oliver's hand. Unfortunately this wholesome young man has an alibi. A couple of his skinhead friends claim he was with them, burgling a video store in Abingdon." Mukerji shrugged. "We are trying to break their stories. Give us a little more time."

"Thumb screws?" suggested Homer. "The rack?"

Mukerji didn't think it was funny.

CHAPTER 51

I look at the natural geological record, as a history of the world imperfectly kept, and written in a changing dialect; of this history we possess the last volume alone. . . . Of this volume, only here and there a short chapter has been preserved; and of each page, only here and there a few lines.

Charles Darwin, *The Origin of Species*

Homer's last lecture was over. His students clapped politely, a few cheered, and some hung around in the lecture hall to say goodbye to the American who had lectured them for eight weeks on the transcendentalists of Concord and told a number of funny stories. They said goodbye to Mary, too, who had taken over a couple of the lectures at Homer's urging.

Stuart Grebe was there on the last day. He was not reading for an arts degree, he was a biochemist doing crazy studies on invented life forms on his rented computer. But he often crept into Homer's lectures as part of his insane attempt to wring every drop of juice from the succulent fruit that was Oxford University.

Another part of his many-splendored plan was the long series of escapades like the Great Dodo Caper. Wherever there was an ancient ritual or a sacred cow, Stuart blasphemed it. It was as though his superabundant energy required him to climb every fence and burst every barrier, if always with a light heart. He hung a dead chicken from the ancient bronze knocker of Brasenose. He glued a pair of jockey shorts to the naked marble body of the drowned Shelley at University College. He joined in a traditional death-defying scramble up the dome of the Radcliffe Camera to crown it with a chamber pot. He dressed the heads of the Roman emperors in front of the Sheldonian in false whiskers, plastic fangs, dark glasses and women's hats.

After one of his most outrageous transgressions, Homer had chastised him. "Listen here, Stuart, it isn't so much the fact of your doing bad things, it's the childish silliness of them. One would think you were a freshman instead of a graduate student. How old are you anyway?"

"Seventeen, Dr. Kelly."

"Only seventeen!"

"I'm sorry. They kept skipping me in grade school."

"Well, then, no wonder, you poor kid. You can't help being silly. You're only a child."

Stuart rolled his eyes humbly. "Yes, sir. You won't tell on me, will you, Dr. Kelly? Rhodes scholars are supposed to be at least eighteen."

"Oh, God, Stuart." Homer sighed with resignation. "No, I won't tell."

&

"Hello, is that you, William? Jerry Heddlestone here."

"Oh, Jerry, it's good to hear from you."

"William, I can't resist calling to say how deeply impressed I am with your new book." And then Professor Heddlestone began a litany of praise.

"But Jerry, wait a minute." Puzzled, William interrupted. "How did you—? I mean, I don't understand. I haven't sent out any review copies. In fact—"

"It was one of my students, an American kid. He lent me his copy of the manuscript. Said he thought I'd be interested."

"But where did he get it?" William gripped the telephone. "Jerry, tell me, do you still have it?"

"Of course I do."

"Oh, thank God. Jerry, listen. Hang on to it, because it's all that's left. It's gone from the computer, and our only printout was stolen. Yours is all there is."

"Good Lord!"

"Tell me, Jerry, who gave it to you?"

"Well, he's a funny kid. When he appeared at his first tutorial I couldn't help wondering what the cat had dragged in. But he's turned out to be my cleverest pupil. As a matter of fact, I think he's got your entire book on disk. His name is—"

"Grebe?"

"Exactly. Stuart Grebe."

CHAPTER 52

Many kinds of monkeys . . . delight in fondling and being fondled
by each other.
> Charles Darwin,
> *The Expression of the Emotions in Man and Animals*

The Zoology Office faced south. When Homer came in to say goodbye, the room was awash with sunshine. A few dying bees from the hive on the south staircase crawled listlessly on the window.

Homer found Helen Farfrae hard at work. She was bowing over the last of the crab jars, prying off the lid, dumping the contents into a dish.

"You're not leaving for good, Homer?" she said, looking up at him brightly. "Mary promised me you'd come back someday."

"Of course we will. She wants me to say how much we enjoyed that farewell party. You shouldn't have done it, but we're both glad you did. It was a ripping party." Homer laughed. "You do say ripping, don't you?" Then he asked about the great book. "It's still all right, I hope?"

"Oh, yes. It's going to press right now. They're making a big fuss over it." Helen's smile vanished. She stood up and put a hand on Homer's arm. "Homer, what about Hal Shaw? He came in this morning with a copy of the *Oxford Mail*. There he was on the front page with his arm around Freddy Dubchick. It looked so bad! And of course that's why the paper printed it. Obviously they want people to think he's guilty of Oliver's murder. What about the police? Do you know what the inspector is up to?"

Homer looked grave. "I'm afraid Hal's not out of the woods. Mukerji thinks Hal and Freddy might have fixed up that story between them. Maybe Freddy came along and found Hal bending over the body, and then they put their heads together and concocted the story that Hal was gone when she arrived, and Oliver still in one piece. But right now Mukerji's homing in on some young tough at Nightingale Court, some dumb kid who stole Oliver's television last month and kept it with the label still on it, *Property of the Reverend Oliver Clare.* Kid with a high-class intellect. He's also a vicious mugger, according to Mukerji."

"But what about suicide? Homer, really and truly, don't you think Oliver committed suicide?"

"Damned if I know. Sometimes I think one way, sometimes another. Don't worry. I'm working on it."

"But how can you? Homer, you're leaving tomorrow!"

He waved a careless hand. "Plenty of time, plenty of time."

"Homer Kelly, don't tell me you're leaving?" William Dubchick walked into the office and clapped him on the shoulder.

Homer shook his hand. "We're off to Heathrow tomorrow. Goodbye, William. Congratulations on the great book. Goodbye, Helen dear." He kissed her. "Well, toodle-oo, you lot. You do say toodle-oo, don't you?"

It was a joke. William and Helen laughed, and William called after Homer as he strode away down the hall. "You and Mary, you'll come back someday?"

"Of course," said Homer, halfway down the stairs.

William turned and went back into the office, where Helen stood at the table, holding her dish of crabs. The slanting sunlight of early December raked across her face. It sparkled on her earrings, which were bright gold, and made reflections in the irises of her eyes. It glowed on the red crabs in the dish and glittered on the jars that covered the table.

It also picked out the individual white hairs of William's beard as he walked to the other side of the table and stood under the photograph of Charles Darwin. To Helen the picture was like a mirror. *Does he know how much he looks like him? No, he doesn't know.*

"These are the last," she said, smiling at him. "I think they must be the Porcellanidae he listed as number 357, from the coast of Patagonia."

"We're all finished then?"

"Yes, and I don't see how we can come to any other conclusion but that—"

"—they are the missing crabs. They were collected by Charles Darwin on his Beagle voyage."

"Oh, William, I'm so glad. I'm sure of it, aren't you?"

"Absolutely." William reached across the table and took her hand. "Therefore somebody's got to write a paper."

"Oh, yes, I'll help."

"*You* will write the paper. *I* will help." William reached for her other hand and leaned over the table. Helen leaned forward too. Their lips met over Jar Number 1045, a crab *admirably adapted for its habitation under the surface of round stones,* collected by Charles Darwin in the year 1834, in the waters of the Pacific Ocean off the city of Valparaíso.

CHAPTER 53

"Give your evidence," said the King.
"Shan't," said the cook.
Lewis Carroll, *Alice's Adventures in Wonderland*

🖋

Homer had been mesmerized from the beginning by the courtyard of the museum. Today, leaving it for the last time, he glanced around at the ring of stone scientists and thought how much they looked like a jury. They were all sturdy citizens, good men and true, accompanied by the solid evidence of their worth—Harvey's heart, Davy's lamp, Watt's steam engine, Euclid's triangles, Priestley's apparatus for producing oxygen. They listened and pondered and would one day deliver their verdict—*not guilty,* or *guilty as charged.*

In fact, as Homer walked out into the courtyard between Aristotle and Roger Bacon, it became in his imagination a large and sunny courtroom. The place had once housed a Mad Tea-Party, now let there be a trial scene like the last chapters of Alice in Wonderland, with a mad jury, a mad prosecuting attorney and a mad judge—*Just take off his head outside!*

After all, it was a good place for truth-telling, because nothing interfered with the fall of light. The sun bore down to show that nothing was hidden, all was visible. And the rolling murmur of voices was like a multitude of witnesses from whom nothing could be concealed.

The iguanodon was obviously the judge, with its solemn head poised high above everything else. The prosecutor was

perhaps the stork, with its sharp glass eyes and long probing beak. The defense attorney—now, who would do for a defense attorney? Prince Albert? No, he looked too fashionable, and his whiskers were too neatly brushed. How about one of the little elephants? Their massive heads were obviously full of brain. Good. Now to get on with it.

The first trial was short. The iguanodon cleared its throat—it had been a hundred million years since it had uttered a croak—and explained the matter that had been brought before it for judgment. "Was Oliver Clare murdered or did he kill himself? Who would like to address the court?"

"I would, my Lord," said Homer, speaking up loudly inside his head and trying to adopt the manners of a British courtroom.

There was an eruption in the north arcade, and the gorilla burst out of the display of stuffed primates and ran up to the iguanodon on all fours, to take the part of court hack. *The witness will please take the stand,"* roared the gorilla.

Homer looked around the courtroom at each member of the jury. They were all gazing back at him attentively. Even Linnaeus looked up from his book. Hippocrates' view was blocked by the giant brain coral, and he craned his neck.

"Members of the jury," began Homer, "I have incontrovertible proof that Oliver Clare's death was the result of suicide. What, you ask, is my proof? The moonlight. It was the moonlight on the river."

"The—moon—light," wrote the iguanodon, making a note, scratching fastidiously with a sharp claw on its left wristbone.

"You see, if you looked out the window of Oliver's room, you could see the moon reflected in the Oxford Canal and also in the river Thames. It was quite beautiful."

"Beau—ti—ful," scribbled the iguanodon.

"Oliver, you see, was a God-fearing young man. His Christian faith was everything to him. But lately he had been exposed to a different view of creation." Homer paced up and down between the stuffed ostrich and the skeleton of the giraffe, in the manner of courtroom attorneys he had seen in the movies. "Here at the end of the second millennium, the Reverend Oliver Clare was experiencing what many of Darwin's contemporaries must have felt in the nineteenth century, a horrifying sense of shock. The creation, you see, was not the

noble work of God, not even of a God with a Ph.D. in Evolutionary Studies, whose guiding hand moved through all organic form, nudging it higher and higher toward the pinnacle of humankind. That way of thinking, he was told, was poppycock. Human beings were not created in the image of God, their existence was entirely an accident, and their hope of heaven beyond the grave a myth. *Homo sapiens* was merely a cousin to the apes."

"Is that a personal remark?" snarled the court hack.

"No, no, of course not."

"Come to the point," snapped the iguanodon.

"The point is," explained Homer, "Oliver was dragged out of the great edifice of the Church of England into the godless air. He clung to the cross, the altar, the font, but at last he was outside under the cold stars. The question of God's guiding hand in history, God's benevolence, God's very existence had become overwhelming. Even Oliver's love for Fredericka Dubchick faded in significance. What good was his desire to rise in the hierarchy of the Church of England if the Church was not inhabited by the spirit of God? Was the moonlight on the river beautiful enough? Did it display the presence of God? Did it balance the harsher understanding of Hal Shaw and William Dubchick? No, it did not. *The answer was no.* There was no God, no guiding hand, no ascent to perfection, no purpose in existence but brute survival."

"So?" said the iguanodon impatiently. "What then?"

"He couldn't stand it," said Homer simply. "He killed himself."

At once the iguanodon raised its bony head and bellowed, *"Jury, how do you find? Murder or suicide?"*

The jury did not bother to deliberate. The evidence about the moonlight was totally convincing. The stone scientists turned their heads toward the judge and shouted, *"Suicide, your honor."*

The iguanodon chuckled, and said, "Well, that's that."

Homer was interested to observe that the chuckle started far down its neck and worked its way upward, clicking together the vertebrae two at a time.

"No, no, my Lord," cried Homer, his imaginary voice ringing clear in the courtroom, echoing from the glassy surfaces of the display cases and the metal sprays of pomegranates and pineapples crowning the cast-iron columns. "We're not finished. There was also a murder."

A murder! The glass cases sent the word back, and so did the pomegranates and pineapples. *A murder, a murder, a murder!* All the hard surfaces in the Oxford University Museum rang with the terrible word.

"Oh, it was murder, all right," said Homer. "In fact it was murder sublime."

The iguanodon recoiled, arching its bony neck. "Murder in the sublime degree? But that is the very worst kind!" Solemnly it bent its head and nodded at the court hack.

At once the gorilla rose to its full height and roared, *"The trial in the matter of murder in the sublime degree will now begin. All rise."*

"No, no," said the iguanodon testily, "don't be ridiculous. They can't rise if they're not sitting down." Turning to Homer it inquired courteously, "And who, may I ask, is the accused in this case?"

"If you please, my Lord," said Homer, "his name is Charles Darwin."

At this there was a stir in the court. The ichthyosaurus squirmed in its stony matrix, the tail of the quetzal rose and fell. The bison popped a vertebra, which clattered to the floor. In the upper gallery the wings of the butterflies trembled, and the beetles tossed their antennae from side to side. In the Zoology Office the Beagle crabs paddled uneasily in their jars of spirit, and the egg of the great auk fell open with a crack.

Downstairs in the courtyard a ray of sunshine settled like a spotlight on the golden statue of Darwin. There he was, the accused, the prisoner in the dock, standing awkwardly behind the coelacanth's glass case. Darwin himself seemed untroubled. He continued to gaze serenely at the display of starfish across the aisle.

The iguanodon, too, remained calm. "I see," it said, making a note. "*The accused—is—Charles—Darwin. And what is Mr. Darwin's crime?*"

"Murder, Your Honor."

"*Mur-der.*" The judge made another note. "And who, may I ask, is the victim?"

Homer stood on tiptoe, stretched his neck upward toward the head of the iguanodon, and whispered the august name.

"No!" gasped the iguanodon. "You don't say so!"

Homer nodded grimly, and the iguanodon dictated aloud another note to itself, "*The—victim—is—GOD.*"

At this there was a wild response. The dodo uttered a shriek, the bush baby twiddled its fingers and snarled at the potto, the spider monkey ran up and down its branch, the chimpanzee shuffled and hopped and chattered in a high falsetto, the starfish waggled their arms, and the crocodile opened its jaw to show all its hideous teeth.

"*Order in the court!*" bawled the gorilla. "*The prosecuting attorney will call the first witness.*"

And then, to Homer's astonishment, everyone turned to look at him—Joseph Priestley, Humphry Davy, Galileo and all the rest—along with the penguin, the ostrich, the ruffed lemur and the pigtailed macaque. To his horror he guessed that he, Homer Kelly, had become the prosecuting attorney. They were expecting him to prove that Darwin was guilty of murdering God.

"But good grief," said Homer, "I'm not accustomed to courtroom procedure. I mean, this is probably a big mistake on your part."

"*Disrespect to the court,*" thundered the gorilla. "*Off with his head.*"

"Oh, nonsense," said the iguanodon, nodding pleasantly at Homer. "Nobody's going to chop off your head. At least not yet. Please call your first witness."

His first witness? Homer looked around frantically, hoping to find a witness who could be relied on to give testimony hostile to Darwin's cause.

"I know," he said, struck with an idea. "I call as my first witness—the dodo."

At this there was a flopping sound in the corridor, as the dodo tumbled out of its gold frame, shook its feathers, and waddled into the court, gobbling like a turkey.

Promptly the court hack rattled out the oath, "Do you solemnly swear to tell the truth, the whole truth, and nothing but the truth?"

The dodo flapped its useless wings, and squawked, "I do-do." A pink feather wafted upward.

Homer smiled. He had chosen wisely. The dodo was the key. "Your extinction is at the very center of this case," he gravely informed the dodo. "Death is the operating principle, not the live-giving touch of God in the garden of Eden, don't you agree?"

Again the dodo squawked in agreement, but this time it sounded grumpy, as though not entirely sure.

Homer was in full spate. Abandoning his prosecutorial role, he began to lecture, as if the court were an enormous classroom, and the giraffe and the giant tortoise and the gray seal his earnest pupils. "All the burgeoning life observed by the accused in the jungles of Brazil, all the interconnected life forms he found in an entangled bank, they were all part of the struggle for life and the war of nature, isn't that so?"

The dodo was now distinctly annoyed, and it merely gurgled in its throat.

Homer called up from memory whole pages of *The Origin of Species*. "The extinction of forms less fit for survival permits the better-adapted to increase, isn't that right? Oh, no of-fense," added Homer, as the dodo clucked and ruffled its feathers.

And then Homer launched out on his own, inventing a crazy theory. "Gentlemen of the jury, let us think of God as a species, undergoing a normal process of evolutionary variation and change. Beginning in ancient times as an entire genus of primitive divine forms, the varieties of God were diminished by the process of extinction until only a few remained. If we consider, gentlemen, only the Judeo-Christian God, we can witness the falling away of competing species and the survival of a single variety. The nature of this variety changed over the ages, becoming more refined, more noble, compassionate and just." Homer spun around to address the encircling jury with a dramatic appeal—"Then, slowly, after a long illness culmi-nating in the year 1859, when Darwin published his great book, God began to fail. Consider, gentlemen, that the beauti-ful chapels in these Oxford colleges are merely fossilized bones like those of Darwin's giant sloth. At the turn of the third mil-lennium, God threatens to become dead as a dodo. Soon only a skull and one foot will remain."

At this there was a rattle and clatter from the skeletons hanging overhead—the beluga whale and the bottle-nosed dolphin—but whether in applause or disapproval Homer couldn't be sure. Some of the golden scientists were shifting uneasily on their pedestals, glancing out of the corners of their stone eyes at the figure of Charles Darwin, which stood so mildly among them, lost in thought.

"Oh, I don't mean," said Homer, correcting himself, "that God is altogether extinct. Here and there you can still catch a glimpse of Him, or possibly Her, because I should explain that God has recently undergone a sex change, or perhaps He's only a cross-dresser. There have been sightings, He has been seen holed up in a third-class hotel in Paris, dodging behind a pickup truck in a parking lot in Omaha, disappearing down a Roman staircase. Perhaps," said Homer, congratulating himself on his cleverness, "someone should put him in a zoo, and mate him with some old mother goddess, in order to carry on the species *Deus divinus,* or *Dea divina,* whichever it is."

The iguanodon regarded this as a frightful lapse of taste. "That's quite enough of that!" he said severely. Then he pointed a claw at Francis Bacon, the jury foreman. "The jury will now consider its verdict."

"But I'm not finished yet," protested Homer. "And what about the defense attorney? Isn't anyone going to cross-examine this witness?"

But the witness, the dodo, was waddling away, and Homer could detect a sleepy film forming over the hollow eye sockets of the iguanodon, as the court hack howled a repetition of the judge's command: *"The jury will consider its verdict! Is the defendant, Mr. Darwin, guilty or not guilty of murder in the sublime degree?"*

A hush fell over the court. For a moment the jury was silent, staring stonily into empty air. Then, abruptly, they swung around on their pedestals to face Charles Darwin. Euclid pointed a naked arm, Priestley an accusing finger. Leibnitz rolled back his heavy sleeve and thrust out a pointing hand. Even Linnaeus woke from his dream to lift his furry arm and point it at Darwin. *"Guilty,"* cried the jurors. *"Guilty, guilty, guilty."*

It was the signal for chaos. The silence gave way to a tremendous cacophony of cawing, growling, singing and roaring. There were flapping wings, rattling bones, crackling wing cases. A thousand butterflies rose in a cloud to the peak of the roof. Ten thousand insects buzzed up off their pins and took flight. In their wooden drawers the Darwin crabs scuttled sideways. In the Zoology Office an infant auk tumbled out of the petrified egg and tottered, peeping, up and down the mantel. In the courtyard the orangutan and the dark-handed gibbon

leaped to the top of a glass case, lunged at a couple of light fixtures and heaved their bodies through the air. The spider monkey romped up one of the cast-iron columns and gnawed at a wrought-iron water lily. The elephants trumpeted, the tarsier gazed at the tumult with moony golden eyes, and the bivalves clapped their shells open and shut, while the birds of the British Isles soared above everything else, uttering hoarse cries.

Homer ducked as a tern swooped over his head. Were all of these creatures celebrating the death of God, or were they objecting to the verdict? It was impossible to tell. He wanted to ask the iguanodon, but the head of the great reptile was nodding. It was falling asleep.

Homer looked anxiously at the prisoner in the dock. What sentence was to be carried out on the great man? Would he be hanged, guillotined, burned at the stake? Homer was glad to see that in spite of the verdict Darwin had not lost his melancholy dignity, although he was now engulfed in a throng of living organisms. Butterfly orchids were draped over his shoulders like a shawl, a parade of dazzling beetles crawled up his cloak, finches and mockingbirds skimmed over his head, a hundred barnacles were fastened to his trouser legs, and a slithering mass of earthworms tumbled around his feet.

No one, thought Homer, had asked how Darwin would plead to the charge of murdering God. Was he speaking up? Was he whispering, *Not guilty, my Lord?* Or muttering a confession under his breath: *Guilty as charged?*

Homer listened, but Darwin said not a word.

CHAPTER 54

"Oh, I've had such a curious dream!" said Alice.
Lewis Carroll, *Alice's Adventures in Wonderland*

🦢

The iguanodon was again only a towering heap of bones. The court hack had withdrawn behind the glass of the primate display in the north corridor, the butterflies were back in their drawers, and the newborn auk was only a fossilized shadow within its petrified egg. The jury and the accused were again merely tall blocks of stone, lost in reverie. Homer walked out of the courtyard and said goodbye to Edward Pound.

"You're leaving, are you?" said the porter, shaking his hand. "Well, I hope you and your wife have a pleasant journey home. Tell me, sir, is it true that Dr. Shaw is still under suspicion for the death of that young priest?"

"Oh, yes, I suppose so, but don't worry, Mr. Pound. I'll take care of it. Nothing to it."

And Homer did take care of it. He called Gopal Mukerji from the public phone in the basement, talking loudly and cheerfully while a school party from Bristol crowded past him to stow their lunchboxes and hang up their coats. "It was suicide, Gopal, not murder, and I can prove it. I've already persuaded a judge and jury."

"What judge and jury? Homer, my friend, are you mad?"

"Oh, never mind, it doesn't matter. Listen, Gopal."

It was probably Mukerji's Hindu background that made him susceptible to Homer's insane theory. He listened politely as Homer ranted on about the moonlight.

"And the bishop's throne," said Homer. "Did you hear about that?"

"The bishop's—Homer, what are you talking about?"

"The bishop's throne in Christ Church Cathedral. Very significant. A second crime in the sacred precincts. The first Oliver murdered a bishop in the cathedral, the second tried to destroy the bishop's throne. Proof positive of the destruction of his faith, which had once rejoiced in bishops."

After a pause Mukerji breathed a sigh into the phone. "Well, all right, Homer. I don't know what the hell you're going on about, but I'll accept the fact that Clare cut his own throat. *Why did the harp string break? I forced a note beyond its power.* As a matter of fact, I was about to arrive at the same conclusion myself. Mrs. Jarvis has produced another tidbit of information."

"Mrs. Jarvis! No kidding! She's been hugging it to her bosom all this time?"

"Mrs. Jarvis, the oracle of St. Barnabas Street! The smoke rises and she peers at the mystic auguries and makes ritual gestures." Gopal's voice faded, and Homer pictured him spreading out his arms and rolling his eyes at the ceiling. "Then she delivers her divine pronouncement. But only when its time has come."

"Well, what the hell did she say? Oh, sorry." Homer glanced apologetically at the children who were scrambling past him up the stairs.

"She never sleeps. That's what we should have realized at once. That woman does not sleep. She is a goddess, an emanation from on high, a bodhisattva. At night she floats around in the dark, observing the suffering world."

Homer laughed. "In our country we'd call her a witch. A white witch, perhaps, but still a witch. Tell me, Gopal, what did she see on the night Oliver died?"

"She saw Hal Shaw come and go. She saw Freddy Dubchick come and go. She didn't know Oliver was dead, but she guarded that house like a watchdog, all night long. She looked out the windows of her ground-floor flat and saw no one, nothing, although the moon was shining bright as day. Hal Shaw did not return. I asked her, 'Why, Mrs. Jarvis? Why didn't you go to bed?' "

"What did she say?"

"She didn't go to bed because she was waiting for the call."

"The call? What call?"

"The call of nature. The call from her intestinal tract. Mrs. Jarvis suffers from constipation. The call never came."

"I see. So she was up and about, wandering around her flat, alert for every sign, watching and waiting, is that it?"

"Exactly. Homer, my friend, it was astonishing. For once she was talkative, voluble! She told me everything about the action of the stomach and the movement of the upper and lower bowel, as exemplified in her own case. I was quite instructed."

"Am I to understand that Mrs. Jarvis's intestinal disorder has removed all suspicion of murder from Hal Shaw?"

"Entirely. Thank heaven, because I am overwhelmed with a wave of new cases. There's been a stabbing in the Covered Market, a strangling at Blenheim Palace, a shooting in a bingo parlor on the Cowley Road, and a broken body at the foot of the steeple of the church of All Saints, foul play suspected."

"It wasn't your boss at the foot of the steeple, was it, Gopal? It wasn't the realization of your dream? You didn't push him over the railing?"

"Alas, no." Mukerji laughed. "You are leaving, my friend? *Traveller, we are helpless to keep you. We have only our tears.*"

"Goodbye, Gopal. I'll miss you. I'll miss Tagore too."

Homer went back upstairs, hearing for the last time the humming reverberation in the courtyard, the spinning out of voices into a fabric of interwoven sound. He felt bereft.

It wasn't just a sentimental attachment to a fine old building. No, it was much more than that, because within these walls Homer had become a different man. The museum had picked him up and shaken him, until all the scribbled notes in his intellectual pockets had fluttered out, leaving nothing behind. His pockets were empty. He was bankrupt of mental coinage from the past.

Homer pushed open the door and stepped out into the frosty air. The lawn glittered with ice crystals. The trees, no longer shapeless clouds of leaves, displayed their rising trusses. A dog trotted along Parks Road, tugging at its leash, its master half-running behind it. Bicycles whizzed in both directions. The sky was beautiful and blue.

Oh, damn, what difference did it make that the sky was beautiful and blue? Darwin had insisted that nothing was made beautiful for our sakes. Otherwise, he said, it would demolish his whole theory. Suppose, Homer told himself bitterly, the sky just happened to be the color of mud. People would clap their hands and exclaim, *How beautiful the sky is today! How exactly it resembles mud!*

Oh, goddamn it.

Homer crossed the street and walked through the Keble gateway. Mary would still be shopping, hurrying up and down the Broad, the High, the Turl, looking for Christmas presents. On the quadrangle he looked up at the gaudy brick checkerboard walls of the chapel, and at once his head cleared.

The trouble was, the theologians claimed too much and the scientists too little. The scientists said the natural world was exalted enough, you didn't need a benevolent deity to add a lot of phony magic. Nature was complex and wonderful, but you shouldn't expect it to be good, to be kind as well as majestic. All that sort of thing was up to us. *Homo sapiens* might be an accident, but as long as we were here, we could invent our own morality.

Well, that was okay, as far as it went. The theologians went a lot further, and that was the whole trouble. They went altogether too far. They weren't satisfied with the elemental religious sense of wonder at beholding the stars, they had to attach a lot of baubles to it, until pretty soon you had kneeling stools embroidered by the Ladies' Guild, you had cathedrals and heretics burnt at the stake. Oh, it was superb, the whole tippy pile of sacred miscellany. It was drenched in human truth and life and trouble, it was choked with glorious dogmas inspiring treasures of art and music and marvelous works of charity and frightful acts of bigotry. But it went too far.

Homer climbed the stairs of his entry and found the door to their rooms wide open. Mary was back from shopping. Laughing, she showed him the things she had bought, the dodo coffee mugs, the chocolate portraits of Henry VIII and his six wives, the Oxford college scarves. "I'm told it's only tourists who buy these scarves," she said, dangling them in front of Homer, "but our nieces and nephews won't care. The stripes are beautiful, don't you think?"

"Ah, what is beauty?" said Homer, stumbling over a suitcase. "Mud-colored scarves would be just as good." He picked up the suitcase and all the clothes fell out.

"Homer dear, how would you like to go for a walk while I finish packing?"

"Well, certainly," said Homer. "If you're sure you don't need my help?"

"No, no, Homer. Just run along."

Outdoors again, he saw at once that the universe was mocking him. A blazing early sunset splashed rose-colored bars on a stretch of golden cloud. Homer crossed the street into the University Parks, where everything was flushed with glowing color. A bird skimmed from one bush to another.

It was just some ordinary bird, uttering its chirping note. It was only defining its territory. That bird and all the other birds in the world were interested only in eating, mating, and reproducing. They were not made beautiful for our sakes.

And yet—

Homer walked along the path in the direction of the river, falling back with relief on his old friend Henry Thoreau. Henry had fought the good fight, back home in Concord. He was a naturalist, and a witness to nature's mystery at the same time. *The air over these fields is a foundry full of molds for casting bluebirds' warbles. The wood thrush makes a sabbath out of a weekday.*

Henry hadn't gone too far, that was the point. He had been content with the basic religious impulse. He had exalted it. He had spent his life on his knees to the glory of woodchucks, the wonder of battling ants, the marvels of birdsong. He hadn't built a church, he hadn't invented a tormented and resurrected deity, he had stuck to his simple undergirding reverence for the world.

So the mystery remained a mystery. Thoreau didn't say what it meant, and neither would Homer. But the presence of value in the world was as real to him as the law of gravity, as solid as the rules governing the growth of the rough grass under his feet.

The bird struck up again. Philosophically Homer pinned the whole burden of his argument to this single bird in the Oxford University Parks. Oliver Clare should have listened to this bird, he should have been content with the moonlight. The answer wasn't yes and it wasn't no—it was both at the same time. Oh, it was all very well to be rational and iconoclastic, to read *The Origin* and agree to the whole thing, but every time a bird sang, something unanswerable and demanding reasserted itself.

It would never go away. A thousand years from now children would be taught the laws of biology and physics and chemistry in all their complexity, but every time a bird sang, they would be confronted with the same haunting strangeness, and the crude double nature of the world would present itself again. It was a clumsy universe, after all. It didn't make sense. Somebody had blundered.

There was a wooden bridge over the Cherwell. Homer leaned on the railing and looked at the dark water, and tried to sum things up by listing to himself the world's wonders. It was another balancing act. To every stammered rapture there was probably a riposte—

Well, come on, let's start with the seashore. Look at the way a pale translucent wave runs up a sandy beach in parabolas of foam, and then slips back. How about that?

Well, all right, that's nice, I guess, but you forget that the sand under the wave is full of little carnivores grasping at microscopic animals carried over them in the water and eating them alive.

That doesn't surprise me at all, but so what? Look, what about flowers? Take a peony, for instance, a white peony splashed with red. What about that?

Oh, I suppose peonies are all right, as far as they go. But as you know perfectly well, the only reason for color in flowers is to attract insect pollinators. I mean, you must know that. That's all it's for.

Trees! What about winter branches against the sky? The sound of the wind moving in ten thousand leaves?

Well, naturally, you idiot, the leaves are there to collect sunlight, and the wind is merely the flow of air from centers of high pressure to—

Oh, stop. You don't get it. You've got this light shining in your eyes, this giant floodlight right in front of your face, and yet you keep saying—

Light? What light?

Exactly! That's it exactly! I knew you'd say that! What light? The light of the stars, the light of Venus shining alone in a crystal sky, the light of the sun streaming through a hole in the clouds. And don't forget the fur on a dog's back, the curve of a shell, the look of falling snow, the flash of lightning and the crash of thunder, the shape of an egg, the feathers of pigeons, the spiral arms of galaxies, the beauty of women, the ripeness of blackberries in wild thorny tangles at the edge of a field, the light of the moon on the Oxford Canal—

Now, see here, I can explain all that. Why don't we start with the beauty of women? What's all that lusciousness for? You know damn well what it's for. It's for sex and reproduction. It's for another generation of bawling babies. It's as plain as the nose on your face, and listen, my friend, you've got a big nose.

Okay, okay, of course you're right, you're absolutely right, but I'm right too. Shut up and listen, because I've got more items to report. There's no end to the list, and I'm going to push it in your face if it takes all week. Quantity is something, after all, even without definitions and explanations and meanings. Take it without meanings, take it for the sake of gasping. It's gaspability I'm talking about, the gasp-arousing nature of the universe. Oh, and I forgot to mention the scales of snakes, the gills of toad-stools, the tails of swallows, the ears of bats, the smoothness of stones. Gasp, man, go ahead and gasp.

But Homer's articulate adversary had melted away. In defeat? No, probably in boredom. There was only the water moving slowly under the bridge, wintry-looking and cold, hiding a few drowsy fish. Loose sheets of soggy paper were disintegrating in the shallows, washed up against the riverbank. They were all that remained of Professor Dubchick's lost printout, dropped into the river farther up the Cherwell by the abominable Mark Soffit. They meant nothing to Homer Kelly. Turning away, he started home to Keble.

It wouldn't be home much longer. Tomorrow the word *home* would mean familiar places on the other side of the Atlantic—the rivers and woods of Concord, and winter fields the color of a lion's back.

🦢

Next morning Homer stepped out of a cab at the car-rental place on the Botley Road to pick up the Mitsubishi that was waiting for him. The salesman led him to the end of the pavement beside the frozen ditch. "Here's your key, Dr. Kelly. Would you like to see some of our hire-purchase models from last year?"

"Oh, no, thank you. We're returning to the United States today."

The salesman went away. Homer started the car and drove it cautiously out of the lot. He did not look at the ditch and the milky ovals of ice on the reed-filled water. If he had stood on the bank and looked down, he would have seen only a few stiff stalks bending in the cold wind.

But three months later, back in Concord, Massachusetts, while Homer and Mary Kelly watched the disappearance of the ice on Fairhaven Bay, and looked down their basement stairs at snowmelt from the hillside coursing through their cellar, astonishing things were happening in Oxford on the tangled bank beside the Botley Road. The roots of the weeds that had surged up last fall were once again sending up colonies of spotted stalks. Ugly as sin, they galloped up the bank and invaded the field behind the car-rental company.

The owner of the field complained to the local agricultural board, and they sent out a field botanist. "My God," said the botanist, shaking his head, "I never saw anything like it. If I didn't see it with my own eyes, I wouldn't believe it."

"It's a plague," said the farmer. "What are you doing to do about it?"

"Well, we can try one or two things." But the botanist was more interested in his scientific discovery than in the farmer's problem. Enthusiastically he took a few stalks back to his laboratory, and wrote up a paper for the Joseph Hooker Society. "I think we can say with confidence that we have a new species here, which I have named *Phragmites oxoniensis.*"

The poor farmer was thrown back on his own devices. He tried mowing the thing down, but it sprang up thicker than ever. He tried pesticides, but none of them worked. Within a couple of years *Phragmites oxoniensis* had swept its hideous stalks over the roadsides and riverbanks of Oxfordshire, and romped over market gardens and fields of hay.

It was a classic case of natural selection, the preservation of favored races in the struggle for life. The farmer wasn't happy, in fact he cursed the day he was born, but *Phragmites oxoniensis* didn't care whether the farmer lived or died. Unthinking, uncaring, it prospered and survived.

AFTERWORD

Once again, fact must be separated from fiction. The Oxford University Museum on Parks Road in Oxford is a large and splendid fact, with its courtyard, its statuary, its glass roof, its towering iguanodon and its dodo. The Darwin crabs are real too, and some of them are indeed missing. It is not true, however, that the missing ones have turned up. I was greedy to purloin the grandeur of the Hope Entomology Room for my zoologists, but in truth the entomologists have never abandoned it. The three red notebooks of Darwin's *Catalogue for Animals in Spirits of Wine* are still on loan to the library of Cambridge University and have not been returned to Down House. There is no community called Nightingale Court, although it somewhat resembles the council estate of Blackbird Leys. The stately home called Windrush Hall does not loom up on the banks of the Windrush River, and there are no memorials to members of the Clare family on the walls of the Burford church.

The warmest of thanks are due to Museum Administrator Stephen Eeley, who generously allowed this interloper to park her folding stool anywhere in the museum and draw to her heart's content. John Cooke of the Technical Support Staff took me up staircases and down ladders to see the roof with its three pyramids of glass, the storerooms for butterflies and animal skins, the racks of twisting animal horns, the shelves of bottled specimens in the Invertebrate and Vertebrate Spirit Stores, and best of all, the two small drawers of Darwin crabs. Dr. Jane Pickering, Assistant Curator of the Zoological Collections, showed me other secret places, answered my amateurish questions, and corrected mistakes in my story. (The remaining ones are my own fault.)

Other kindly readers were my magnanimous hosts on Charlbury Road, Anthony Cockshut and Gillian Avery, and my Cambridge friends Jill Paton Walsh and John Rowe Townsend.

A happy final note: that accursed new botanical species, *Phragmites oxoniensis,* does not, thank God, exist.